D0069960

CITY OF IRON AND DUST

J.P. OAKES

Fantasy
Oak

TITAN BOOKS

City of Iron and Dust
Print edition ISBN: 9781789097108
E-book edition ISBN: 9781789097115

Published by Titan Books
A division of Titan Publishing Group Ltd.
144 Southwark Street, London SE1 0UP
www.titanbooks.com

First edition: July 2021
10 9 8 7 6 5 4 3 2 1

© Jonathan Wood 2021. All rights reserved.

Jonathan Wood asserts the moral right to be identified as the author of this work.

This is a work of fiction. All of the characters, organizations, and events portrayed in this novel are either products of the author's imagination or are used fictitiously. Any resemblance to actual persons, living or dead (except for satirical purposes), is entirely coincidental.

No part of this publication may be reproduced, stored in a retrieval system, or transmitted, in any form or by any means without the prior written permission of the publisher, nor be otherwise circulated in any form of binding or cover other than that in which it is published and without a similar condition being imposed on the subsequent purchaser.

A CIP catalogue record for this title is available from the British Library.

Printed and bound in the United States.

Praise for

City of Iron and Dust:

"A fantastic book, full of wit and sharp humor, *City of Iron and Dust* careens through a modernized faerie at a breakneck pace, full of verve and unforgettable characters. Oakes spins a smart, electric, and sometimes snarky tale, showing that the beating heart of modern fantasy is alive and well."—JOHN HORNOR JACOBS, author of *A Lush and Seething Hell* and *The Incorruptibles*

"I truly wish there were more fantasies written with this verve and steel. I don't think I've loved a book this hard in quite a while." —T. FROHOCK, author of the Los Nefilim series

"A wonderful mash-up fantasy with a dash of Carl Hiaasen, a mad scramble through a burning city for the ultimate prize. Fans of Daniel Polansky's *Low Town* or Robert Jackson Bennett's *City of Stairs* will enjoy this one."—DJANGO WEXLER, author of *Ashes of the Sun*

"A hard-boiled, phantasmagoric fable of blasted myths and desiccated dreams exploding into bloody revolution. Epic, intimate and one-of-a-kind!"—DALE LUCAS, author of The Fifth Ward series

"*City of Iron and Dust* is a bloody, brutal and bold novel featuring all manner of fantastical creatures... but it's really about being human. Oakes has crafted a tale that is as entertaining as it is wonderfully original."—TIM LEBBON, author of *Eden*

"Oakes delivers wit, grit, and magic in spades, all mixed together with a heap of heart-stopping action and relentless humor. Unforgettable."—NATANIA BARRON, author of *Queen of None*

"I was sold on this 'grim for all the cynical reasons' fantasy novel by J.P. Oakes with the six words of the first chapter title. Well, two of the words weren't that important. The point is that Oakes knows we're tired of all the heroic and earnest and uplifting tropes, and that what we really want is something nasty and funny and thrilling to read."—MARK TEPPO, author of *The Cold Empty*

"The Iron City is a singular dark fantasy creation that breathes with menace and decay. J.P. Oakes' gallows humor and wit bring a sharp levity to the story that will leave you laughing, and then horrified at just what you were laughing about."—PAUL JESSUP, author of *The Silence That Binds*

CITY
OF
IRON
AND
DUST

For Tami, Charlie, and Emma

"The American Dream has run out of gas. The car has stopped."

—J.G. Ballard

Let Me Tell You a Fairy Story

(or, It's Not Epic if it Doesn't Have a Prologue)

Once upon a time there was the world that was. And you'll hear that it was golden, and that it was beautiful, and that it was everything else that everyone always says it used to be. Specific examples, however, will not be provided.

Once upon a time there was the world that was. And then it went away.

The goblins came from the North. In the world that was, this was something that happened from time to time, and this attack, like the others, was looked upon with something like pity and something like dismay. A few troops were sent to dismiss the problem, as they usually were.

But this was no longer the time that was. And the few troops were not victorious, and the goblins continued their march south.

In the wake of this defeat, the fae flung around recriminations: this was the result of poor leadership; this was the fault of some sidhe's agenda, or this brownie's ineptitude; this was all somebody else's fault. The goblins did not care, though. The goblins kept on marching. So, more troops were sent.

And still this was not the time that was. This was new. This was a hundred goblin tribes sick of being relegated and subjugated finally united under the banner of one. And that one was Mab. And Mab swept the fae troops aside like so much dust collected at her feet.

Then the war was on in earnest. And perhaps it was a war of good against evil. But perhaps it wasn't. Perhaps it depended whose side you were on.

But no matter whose side you were on, it was Mab who ended the war.

They called it Mab's Kiss. Three great fae forest cities gone so quickly their inhabitants didn't have the time to scream. Magic more powerful than any the fae had left. And right alongside those cities, the fae's willingness to fight disappeared too.

And so, the unthinkable was thought, and the fae lost the war.

The goblins built cities of cold iron then, of steel and glass. They encased those cities in great metal walls. Inside them, they cut down every tree. They herded the fae into slums and forced them into factories. They bent their heads beneath the twin burdens of labor and poverty.

The fae cried out as it happened. Enclosed within these metropolises of iron, they reached out for their magic. But they felt nothing. They could do nothing. The great iron walls kept them cut off from the earth, and the trees, and all the magic they had once known. Their magic had been amputated.

But as the fae writhed, so the goblins thrived. They innovated. They built shopping malls, and microwave ovens, and combustion engines. They invented guns, and subcultures that celebrated guns. They aired 24/7 news channels. They sold each other mortgages.

And so, the world that was went away, and the world that is

began. And in this new world, there was one city that rose far to the west. There was one city that gleamed bright across the stumps of a thousand felled trees. The Iron City.

In this city, in this new world, there are five towers, one for each of the great Goblin Houses. And everyone in this city—goblin and fae alike—looks up at them and knows in their hearts that these houses are the axle upon which all their lives spin.

Just because everybody believes a thing, though, does not mean that it is true. The end of the world that was should have proven that. Complacency, though, is such an easy sin.

Rather, there is another tower upon which all should look. This one is not so great. This one is dirty, and squalid, and nothing more than the stunted aspirations of a desperate developer who went to an early grave. Atop this tower is a penthouse, which—despite its name—is as small and filthy as the tower to which it belongs.

Inside, this penthouse is full of blood.

This is closer to the truth. This is closer to the core of it all.

Deeper into the apartment, beyond the still-cooling aftermath of violence, hidden away, still waiting to be found, is a package. It is a small thing, not even as big as a gym bag, and unassuming in the way such things often are.

It is a package bound in plastic wrap and brown tape. It is a package full of white powder, and it is the axle that the Iron City spins upon tonight. And as it turns, it ushers in not the world that was, nor the world that is, but the world that is yet to be, and tonight not everyone is destined to live happily ever after…

1

Three Assholes Walk Into a Bar

Jag

A bar. A dive. A neon sign glitching on and off above a burst of yellow light seen through a smeared windowpane. A bouncer hulking in a doorway—the type with more knuckles than IQ points. Probably half-dryad by the look of him, although his mother certainly wasn't one of the willow-tree sprites that get all the press. The smell of wet asphalt and cigarette smoke. Brownies, kobolds, and sidhe bundling past, wishing they had enough money to go in. But no one in this part of the Iron City is particularly liquid right now. They haven't been for the past fifty years. Prospects don't look great.

Inside, a mad cram of bodies. Ruddy-faced kobolds. Sidhe in imperious shades of blue. Pixies scattered across the dance floor all the colors of a shattered rainbow. A shouting, clawing mass with one thing in mind: erasing the grind of the week with bad decisions, and the possibility to one day tell a story that starts with the phrase, "Don't judge me, because I was obliterated at the time."

The fae of the Iron City are at their shift's end. They are at their wits' end. They don't appreciate the rhyme, even though the band on the stage are milking it for all they're worth. A pixie on vocals, her hair half-shaved, the other half bright as summer lilacs. She's screeching and screaming, throwing all of her adolescent energy into every word. And it's immature, and it's mostly wrong, but there's still a beauty to her passion that half the preening fae with their pints of fermented nectar can't wait to tell her about.

Behind her, a kobold has scavenged an old oak door from somewhere and is beating on it like it said something horrifying about his sister. He's broad, and wearing a shirt to prove it, muscles emerging from the shaggy mane of red hair that obscures half his features.

The slender sidhe violinist who accompanies them is perhaps hampered by her own ennui. Still, attitude counts for a lot on stage and her dead-eyed stare from above knife-blade sharp cheekbones makes up a lot of ground.

The three of them have Jag transfixed.

Jag does not belong here. Jag's neatly coiffed and perfectly trimmed hair don't belong. Her clothes with their perfect lines and elegant stitching don't belong. And Jag's race definitely does not belong.

Jag is a goblin. She is obviously and painfully a goblin. She is green-skinned and sharp-featured. She has yellow eyes with slit pupils. She is long-fingered. And while she is taller and graced with more sidhe-like elegance than most of her kind, she is still, most undeniably, a goblin.

Jag is an oppressor in a bar of the oppressed.

Jag thinks she knows all this, of course. Jag believes she is wise to the possibilities and the dangers, but Jag is the heir of House Red Cap. Her father is Osmondo Red. Consequences have been, in her experience, things that happen to other goblins.

The other reason no one in the bar is willing to cure Jag of her assumptions is Sil. Sil stands behind Jag's chair. Sil with a sword strapped to her back, and scars on her face that the sweep of her white-blonde hair cannot quite obscure. Half-goblin, half-sidhe, every angle on her body seems to have been sharpened to a point. And while her skin is too green for the tastes of the fae around her, too pale for the goblins back home, she is more than prepared to take on anyone who wants to take it up with her.

Sil

Sil hears the music. She sees the encounter with the numinous it inspires in Jag. She finds it does nothing for her. To her, the notes are simply obfuscation, hiding mutters, muting angry words.

What Sil does care about is intent. The way one gnome shifts his weight, the way another kobold stares. She cares about the purposeful movements that the fae try to dissemble. She cares about escape routes and high-priority targets.

She has the whole bar charted by now, the route of every wooden tray of spiked milk and moss-stuffed taco catalogued. She sees everything except the thing that makes Jag grin and look round at her, and say, "It's so beautiful!"

She wonders if she ever did that. Ever turned and smiled and exclaimed in wonder. She can't remember. When she looks back, her past is a mist she cannot penetrate. Only the lessons she was taught stand out. Islands of memory. Each beating distinct.

She nods, though. She has been taught to agree with her half-sister. Another lesson drummed into her ribs. Her kidneys. The back of her skull.

Jag turns back to the band, grinning. Sil checks to make sure that no one else has made a move. To make sure that Jag is safe.

In the end, that is all she does, and can, care about.

Knull

Deeper into the bar, away from the stage, and through the press of onlookers, Knull is shifting his weight from foot to foot. He is made restless by his father's pixie blood, made anxious by his mother's brownie heritage.

Every drug deal, Knull knows, is a fuck-up waiting to happen. It's not that he's a pessimist. It just that he knows the best-case scenario is that everyone goes home afterwards and makes themselves incrementally dumber.

Knull also knows that every drug deal is a chance to make serious cash. Especially when the shit he's selling has been cut three ways to Mourn's Day, and is likely to only get the purchaser about as high as a three-day-old balloon. And that's exactly what he's going to sell to the pair of dull-eyed gnomes in front of him now. They aren't regulars. They aren't locals. That means they get the tourist special.

"This?" Knull shakes his baggy of Dust at the pair. "You don't want this." He slips it back into his pocket. He points to the other baggies he's spread out on the table.

"Titania's Revenge." He picks up a bag of completely identical Dust. "It's like being kissed on your frontal lobes." He picks up another—its contents in absolutely no way different from the previous two bags. "Iron Blood. It's got a bite, but it'll be one hell of a night."

"Why," says one of the two gnomes, "don't we want the other bag?"

Knull pats his pocket. "This? Serious customers only, mate."

The gnomes exchange a look. They are big, shirtsleeves rolled up to reveal tattoos and biceps. Knull recognizes their guild brands: coal miners. No Dust, he thinks, will ever get them as high as their own sense of self-importance.

"You think," one gnome says, "that we ain't serious?"

Knull pats his pocket one more time. "Midsommar Dreams? That's dryads only, my friends. It's not personal, just biology. This would screw you up so bad you wouldn't know your own names for three days."

The gnomes exchange a look.

"I want the Midsommar Dreams," one says.

This, Knull thinks, is like taking sap from a dryad. Except it's taking money from idiots, which is potentially a whole lot easier.

"I'm telling you, guys. It ain't for sale."

One produces a fistful of coins. "You sure?"

Then comes the pantomime of indecision. "Fine," Knull says eventually, "but let me make sure you're up for it first. My conscience and all." He slips a finger into his pocket, into a baggie entirely dissimilar to the one that contains the so-called Midsommar Dreams, the one he's been holding back in case one of his regulars shows up. He dips it directly into the pure shit.

He pulls out a white-tipped finger. "Here," he says, tapping the residue off onto a tiny sheet of rolling paper. "Rub that on your gums and don't tell me I didn't warn you."

Their eyes are as big as saucers. There is some shoving to get to the Dust first. The bigger one wins. His finger goes into the Dust, and then he works it around his mouth like he's trying to unclog a drain.

His eyes balloon.

Knull has never seen the production of Dust, but he's heard about it plenty. It is a tree resin, he has been told. The resin is ground down, and can be ingested in a variety of ways. Some like to snort it, others to eat it, while others like to heat it up and inject into the vein of their choosing. You can even smoke the stuff if you like.

Users of Dust like to tell Knull that the specific method of ingestion varies the high they get, but from Knull's perspective the end result is always the same. For just a moment, for just that fae, the Iron Wall goes away. For just a moment, they touch the world that was, the world that went away. For just a moment, magic is alive within their hearts.

And then the magic goes away, and they come back, and they pay Knull so that they can do it all again.

So now, the gnome's pupils dilate, and wind sweeps his hair. Knull watches a snake weave a crown upon the gnome's forehead, and grass pushes up through the linoleum at his feet. Sunlight seems to reflect in his eyes.

And then it's over, the moment gone. The snake slithers back into nothingness. The grass wilts and all that's left beneath the gnome's feet are cracked tiles and stale puddles. He gasps, staggers, and grins.

"Shit, yes," he says.

The gnomes count out tin cogs. Knull tries to not salivate. He fishes the bag labelled "Midsommar Dreams" over. The gnomes high five each other, and then, when their backs are turned, Knull heads for the door as fast as he possibly can.

Jag

The band takes a break. Jag doesn't. She gesticulates with her cigarette. She expounds upon a theme.

"This," she says, "is *real*. Right here. Right now. That's what fae music is about. It's about the intersection of out there and in here." She taps her sternum. "That's the problem with goblin music, Bazzack. It's all externally focused. It's all indicative of a conqueror's mindset."

Bazzack—the target of this rant—is underwhelmed. He is the son of a minor colonel within House Red Cap's ranks. A rich, young, bored goblin, whose rough edges money cannot fully erase. They have known each other forever, and she is far enough out of his league within their house's hierarchy that she felt confident to bring him here without having to suffer through any painful flirtation. Still, platonic familiarity comes with its downsides.

"You do have a rough sense," Bazzack says, "of how absurdly pretentious you sound right now, don't you?"

And the thing is, Jag does. She knows what she is and where she is. She knows how both Bazzack and the fae see her sitting here. But she also knows that doesn't stop her words from being true. It doesn't stop her fellow goblins from needing to hear them. To hear them and realize that it's not just posing, or an angle, or a new look for this season's balls.

Bazzack, though, Jag is coming to see, is not the goblin who is going to make that realization.

"This," Bazzack says, just to ensure his particular brand of boorish ennui gets its moment in the spotlight, "is poor fae music, in a poor fae bar, in a poor excuse for a neighborhood. And the brooding-artiste look may get your suitors to feign a little more sensitivity, but don't pretend to be so naïve that you imagine that solicitude will last past the moment when they finally talk their way between your bedsheets."

"That—" Jag leans forward. "—is exactly what I'm talking about. You're seeing all this as a pose, as something put on for others to observe. You can't for a moment picture this as something genuine, and that's the whole—" She stabs with the cigarette. "—damn problem. Because this music isn't anything about that. It's about revealing the internal."

She glances back at Sil. At her half-fae half-sister. Her father's bastard daughter. She looks to see if any of this is getting through. To see if any of her sidhe mother's heritage is being unlocked. "What do you think, Sil?" she asks.

Sil looks at her for half a second. "The music could be a useful cover in the opening moments of a fight, for whoever wishes to initiate it."

Bazzack laughs. Jag gives Sil a pleading look.

"It may also serve to mask anyone approaching me from behind," Sil says.

Bazzack laughs harder. Sil is entirely unfazed by his amusement. The only movement in her face comes from her eyes, which go back to dispassionately scanning the bar and its occupants.

"I don't know why you bother with her," Bazzack says. "Her blood is tainted with—" He raises his voice. "—fae bullshit." The crowd studiously avoids reacting. Bazzack sneers. "You know your father doesn't want you doing this. She is a servant. Nothing more."

Jag shakes her head, reaches out, puts a hand on Sil's arm. "She is my sister." Sil doesn't react in the slightest.

"She is the accidental result of your father indulging his urges."

"How she came into this world is of no concern to me," Jag says, keen to move on from the idea of her father in the moment of conception. "She is here nonetheless, and what is happening here is part of her culture and her heritage."

It would be an easier argument to make if Sil was willing to give the impression she had any sort of emotional range beyond that of the pint glass on the table before Jag.

"You can dress this shit show and your indulgence of it," Bazzack says, stifling a belch, "in any pretty words you want. But they are literally on stage, putting on a show. It's all bullshit. Just—" another grin "—like you."

Sil

She knows how she will do it if Jag asks her. Pirouette around the chair, stab her sword directly into Bazzack's ballsack. Such a small target, she thinks, will at least make it something of a challenge.

Edwyll

The evening twists on. Deeper and darker. Glasses rise and fall. Spirits move along with them. It's easy to be despondent in the Fae Districts. It's easy to focus on the cloying air and the dirt-smeared walls, and think about what was here before the Iron Wall. It's easy to think about what could be if the fae weren't cut off from their magic.

Some, though, would rather call bullshit on such defeatist attitudes. Some think that there is still the potential for beauty left in the world, and that the sun still shines if only the fae would stop and lift their heads, and see it beyond the chimney smoke.

Edwyll is such a fae. Edwyll thinks he has a medium and a message. Edwyll is trying to channel his mentor, Lila, and create the beauty he wants to see in the world. He is trying to create something that will remind his fellow fae that life did not end fifty years ago.

He hunches over a table in the corner of the bar. He stabs and dabs with his paintbrush, trying to capture the feeling that rose within him as the band played, building counterpoints of orange and blue, shifting tones of yellow sliding into red. He tries to make the kobold-hair bristles move the way his body wanted to move as the beat bounced through him.

And yet still, despite his conviction, despite his brave face, despondency lurks.

The problem, as ever, is money. Because even if he is successful in his transformation of elation into a visual medium, who will pay for it? Who will put enough food on his table that he'll still be alive next week to create the next painting?

Edwyll isn't even meant to be in this bar. He's meant to be running home to grab some materials for his next big project. He's meant to be checking that his drug-addled parents haven't puked themselves to death. But he saw a flyer in the window about bartenders being wanted and then the proprietor needed to deal with some crisis or other, and he's been waiting for half an hour, and the band started to play, and the spirit moved within him.

But now he's hungry again, and the art isn't quite what he wanted, and the spirit is starting to get sluggish.

He sits back, looks up, surveys the bar, these fae he wants to lift up out of poverty, these fae he is too poor to uplift, and then he sees them. Brownies knocking back spiced nectar. Two green leaves sitting about the blue, brown, and red bodies of the fae… surely not.

He blinks. He tries to make sure.

Two goblins. Two goblins sitting in the crowd. Two goblins slumming it for the night.

Two potential patrons.

He looks down at what he has accomplished on the scrap of canvas he's holding. And screw it. It's good enough.

He's up and on his feet, pushing through the crowd before he has a chance to second-guess himself. He's standing in front of them before he's had a chance to figure out what he's actually going to say.

"Great music, right?"

No. Not that. That was not the thing to say.

Two pairs of startled yellow eyes turn to him. He swallows.

"It's amazing what great art can do, right?" He taps his chest. "Uplift the heart. Uplift the spirit. Change the whole world one heart and mind at a time." He flashes a smile.

Against all odds, the female goblin's face actually lights up. In defiance of logic, she smiles.

Then the male grabs the painting out of Edwyll's hand, and sneers at the paint he's just smeared.

"Peasant art," he slurs. "I thought you lot were meant to be good at this shit. I thought you were meant to be good for at least one thing."

"Hey, asshole—" are perhaps not the best words to deal with this situation, but they are the first two out of Edwyll's mouth.

The goblin stands, sending his chair flying backward.

"What did you call me?"

Edwyll knows very well what he called him. He just doesn't know if he's willing to repeat it.

Instead of repetition, though, escalation. Before Edwyll can open his mouth, a large brownie puts his hand on the goblin's shoulder. There are no butterfly wings on this fae. He is heavyset, slabs of muscle scarred with burns and painted with tattoos. An ore miner on his way to the night shift that most of his kind prefer. He has rolled up his sleeves. His wrists are the breadth of the goblin's thighs.

"This is the wrong part of town, son," the brownie says, "to say shit like that."

The goblin pushes the hand away. "I," he says, "am the only good thing to ever happen to this shitty little bar, and this shitty part of town. If I am here, then it is exactly where I am supposed to be. You, peasant, are the one out of place in my city."

Edwyll closes his eyes. Because he has always wanted his art to move people. He has always wanted it to create change in the world. But this is not what he had in mind at all.

Jag

Jag stands. Jag sees the faces around her. Jag blanches.

"I'm sorry," she says to the fae with his hand on Bazzack's chest—a brownie, or a pixie, or some mix of the two, she can't be sure. "You are entirely correct. My friend is an asshole. We're leaving."

The brownie looks at her and Bazzack with distaste. Jag puts her faith in Sil standing behind her, in the fact that there is something in Sil's eyes that normally speaks straight to every fae's brain and gives them a single warning.

Bazzack, though, has silenced enough higher cognitive functions that belligerence has become his default setting.

"We are not leaving," he spits. "We came here to have fun, Jag. And I am bored." He grins at the brownie. "Five cogs," he says. "I'll pay you five cogs if you'll fight her!" He points at Sil.

No. No. That is not why Jag brought Sil here. That is the opposite of why.

"No fae with fighting spirit left in the Iron City?" Bazzack shouts. "What if I make the pot richer? What if I pay one lead gear to anyone here who can best this half-fae in combat?"

"Shut up," Jag says.

But it's far too late for that.

"Show me the coin," the brownie gripping Bazzack's shoulder says.

"Show me something worth paying for."

The brownie leans in closer. "How about I just take all your coins."

Uncertainty rattles the bars of Bazzack's intoxication. "Jag?" he says.

Jag wants them to leave. But she also wants to see the smirk wiped off Bazzack's face. She wants to punish him a little for ruining this night. "She's not your bodyguard, Bazzack," she says.

Bazzack swallows. His confidence is starting to slip like an ill-fitting jacket. Nervous fingers fish out his coin.

"Good lad," the brownie says. He lets go of Bazzack's shoulder, claps him on the back. "Now, I'll kick this half-gobbo's ass." He nods at Sil. "Then I'll kick yours."

He looks up, levels a finger at Jag. "And then I'll kick your friend's."

Sil

The brownie's mistake is that he has made one threat too many. Two, Sil can accept. The last, though, is taboo.

So, she reaches for her sword, and then, with a flick of her wrist, she removes his hand.

2

Old Dogs. New Tricks

Granny Spregg

There is more to the Iron City than one small bar in one small corner of town. The Iron Wall encircles a microcosm. One that sprawls. That heaves. Cars clog its streets. Industry churns. Fae and goblins stumble through its avenues and boulevards. Theaters pump out morality plays performed by immoral actors. Street vendors hawk powdered dragon fangs to stockbrokers. Building styles shift like river currents. And at its septic heart, the great Houses rise.

Once they would have been fortresses. Once there would have been crenellations and monsters of yore curled in deep dark dungeons. Once upon a time, though, is a distant memory in the Iron City. These Houses are modern buildings. Their inhabitants are modern goblins. Their tastes run to neither cold stone nor dark tapestries. They prefer central heating, and high thread-count sheets, and their guards armed with something that can spit out more than one bolt every thirty seconds. This is the modern world, after all, with all its modern dangers and all its modern indulgences.

Granny Spregg would rather like it if the modern world would go fuck itself.

Granny Spregg is a creature of a world gone away. She is a gnarled fist of a goblin. She drags her leg behind her as she stomps down one of the many, many corridors that twist and turn through House Spriggan. Her cane clack-clacks on the tiles. It was a dryad's arm once. She cut it free herself.

Granny Spregg looks back on the Iron War with fondness. She remembers when her hordes broke the fae army's back. She remembers when Mab's Kiss broke their spirit. She remembers Mab…

Old goblin, she curses herself, as she bustles down the corridor. *Thinking old goblin thoughts. Getting lost in the past, when the present is so full of snares.*

No one here dares call her Granny to her face. They all use the name behind her back. There is, she supposes, some accuracy to it, even if none of the brats her children have clogged the House's lower floors with are legitimate.

She uses the name in her head. It keeps the anger fresh. Keeps her lip curled and her feet moving. They carry her along the corridor now, hobbling step after step. A victor's riches surround her. Her spoils despoiled. Fae paintings defaced. Sacred white deer, their heads mounted on plaques. A sculpture built from broken wands.

There is more modern art as well. Creations that conform to her children's tastes. *Letting them have their own opinions,* Granny Spregg thinks. *That was my first mistake.*

Thacker scurries in Granny Spregg's wake. Thacker always scurries in her wake. Granny Spregg is unsure if he is capable of any other type of movement. She moves at a pace snails would mock, and yet Thacker is always hurrying to catch up with her.

"Are you sure this is wise, Madame?" he asks, which is the most Thacker thing to say that Granny Spregg can think of. He would probably check with her about each inhalation of breath if he knew she wouldn't wear his balls as earrings if he did so.

"No," she spits at him. "Which is why I'm doing it. Certainty is the first sign of idiocy." She grimaces. "My children are always certain."

Thacker is not an idiot. He is neurotic as a brownie, and an anxious thorn in her britches, but he is not an idiot. It is why she tolerates him. She likes certainty only in her lovers, not in those she keeps around for intelligent conversation.

"Perhaps we should..." Thacker starts, but Granny Spregg is unwilling to let him get to the word "reconsider."

She wheels on him, brings the cane to bear on his throat, and he almost scuttles right into it. She advances on him, pushing him back to the wall.

"Tonight, Thacker," she says. "I have tonight. That's it. To take it all back. This house. My house. All the years of effort and this is it. Eight meager hours. The package is in the city. It is all in play. And I will not have you fuck it up for me. Do you understand, or must I sacrifice a pawn this early in the evening?"

Thacker swallows. He nods.

Granny Spregg hits him with the cane. "Yes, you understand, or yes, I must sacrifice you, you dullard?"

Thacker cowers. "I understand," he says, whimpering. "I understand."

She turns her back on him. She stomps down the corridor. She reaches the door. It has taken longer than she wanted it to. Everything does these days. The door is large, steel-mounted, and monitored. Granny Spregg raises a vein-knotted fist to knock.

"Well, then," she says to Thacker, "here we go."

Granny Spregg summons every ounce of imperious pride left

to her and shoves past the private who answers the door. Beyond this spluttering barrier, House Spriggan Military Command thrums with quiet efficiency. Goblins mutter orders into microphones with practiced monotony relaying, confirming, and processing missives. House generals lean over monitors and dispatch runners. Sergeants push figurines around a scale model of the city.

Such is the business of protecting the House's interests, of keeping a populace in check and thwarting the ambitions of their rivals. Such is the business she would reclaim.

Granny Spregg does not belong in this room. There is no efficiency left in her body. Eyes turn to look at her.

She points at one goblin in full regalia. Her knuckles are large as walnuts. "General Callart," she says through her self-loathing, "I need a moment of your time and a division of your soldiers."

General Callart, she knows, can be relied on to be professional. Her presence here is unorthodox these days, but he will always be a slave to the hierarchy of command, and even now, she still outranks him.

"Of course, Madame Spregg," he says smoothly while the bustle of the room resumes. "If you could furnish me with the details, then—"

"Perhaps before that," a voice cuts in, "you could furnish me with a 'what the fuck?'"

Another goblin steps out from behind a pillar of monitors. He is draped in unearned medals, drowning in aiguillettes. He is Privett Spregg in all his glory and absurdity.

Granny Spregg's heart sinks. Thacker lets out a sound that could generously be called a groan, or accurately called a whimper.

This, Granny Spregg knows, will now have to be done the hard way.

Skart

The Iron City, of course, is not just mansions and bars. It is also squalor and squats. It is also high-rise pillars of steel and glass. It is also shops and stalls. Indeed, the Iron City has almost as many facets as it has ways to take your money and leave you lying in a gutter.

The Iron City also has factories in abundance. They churn, and belch. These are the truest monsters of the modern world, smoke pouring from their mouths, their wealth hoarded far away from the fae they subjugate.

In such a place sits Skart. He is a kobold, skin colored as if by sunburn, red hair sprouting from him in wild abundance, his face folded and puggish. He is in his office, hunched over a desk and an ancient typewriter, the chiaroscuro of a bare lamp bulb rendering him a partially glimpsed figure of light and shadow. A clock chirps. He looks up. Finally, it is shift's end, and he is anxious to leave.

Then: a sound at his door. A creak of hinges. A scuffing of feet. He looks up, and sees a face peeking around the doorframe. One last thing left to deal with.

It is Bertyl, one of the tailors. A pixie like most of her coworkers, the bright yellow of her hair and skin are fading to cream as the years encroach. Skart smiles at her. Everyone, he believes, has a purpose they can achieve if you give them an opportunity. Bertyl has been struggling to find her purpose, but Skart believes he has an opportunity to give her.

"How can I help you, Bertyl?" he asks.

She shuffles towards him, looks back at the door. "Hello, Mr Skart, sir," she says.

Then she runs out of steam.

"You're here late," Skart prompts as amiably as he can.

"Yes, sir." Bertyl looks at her feet.

Skart knows he has to play this carefully.

"While I always appreciate company, Bertyl," he says, "is there anything specific you want?"

Skart is a fae with one of the rarest possessions in the Iron City—a sliver of authority. He is a shift leader within a garment factory. He is not even a sidhe, and his success over the old-school network of nepotism that still persists in the Iron City in and of itself suggests either profound skill or unnatural ruthlessness. Evidence supports the former. He is a kindly boss. He helps organize and coordinate the efforts of tailors and machinists. He sets schedules and hears petty woes. It is not a position of great stature, but it is one that allows Skart to make his workers' lives minimally easier. Bertyl, for some reason, seems hesitant to give him that opportunity.

"Well, Mr Skart," Bertyl says, not meeting his eye. "I mean, of late I think, perhaps, you've been pretty complimentary about some of my dresses. And it's been long hours, see. And, well, I've been here twenty years now, and so, well..." And there she seems to run out of nerve. She pants slightly.

Skart smiles. "This is about pay, isn't it, Bertyl?" he says.

She gulps. "I'm sorry, Mr Skart, sir, and I wouldn't ask... It's only that my husband, Hasp, you know? He's laid up near two months now with his leg, and things are... well they're a bit tight, Mr Skart, sir."

Things are tight. The song of the Fae Districts. Bertyl's husband was badly injured when he was buried under a half-dozen massive bolts of undyed cloth after a fraying clasp on a delivery truck gave way. Skart is well aware that Hasp has been unable to work for almost two months now. Once, Skart thinks, the story would have filled him with rage. But not tonight. Tonight he will finally do something to stop any more harm coming to the fae.

Just… not yet.

"I understand," Skart says. Bertyl sighs audibly. "And you have worked hard. And you deserve more."

She glances at his eyes, just for a moment. He smiles again.

"But for you to have more, Bertyl, someone else will have to have less. There's not more money. You know that. The goblins always give me the same amount every month. So, I have to share it out. And I have to be fair. So, I ask you, Bertyl, who should I give less to?"

Bertyl swallows. It's a question she can't answer. Others could. Others come to Skart and expound on the subject for hours. But it is a cruel question to ask Bertyl, and he knows it. He feels bad. But on the other hand, he was lying when he was complimentary about her sewing.

"I'll tell you what, Bertyl," he says, ending her agony. "You go home. I'll stay here and look at the spreadsheets. Maybe there's a corner I can cut somewhere, save a few copper teeth here and there. Maybe I can slip them your way. I know how badly Hasp was hurt."

"Oh! Mr Skart…" She almost detonates with gratitude.

"It's no worry," he says. And here he comes to the crux. "I'll be here a few more hours anyway."

She stares at him. He could ask anything of her now. Except, it turns out, to leave quickly. It takes ten more minutes of stumbling thank-yous for Bertyl to depart. But Skart's alibi is established. If anyone comes asking for him, Bertyl will swear to her grave that he is here. Hopefully it won't come to that, though. Hopefully, Skart thinks, that isn't her purpose.

He sits for a moment longer, bracing himself. He rolls up his sleeve, looks at the black marks beneath the skin. He has lived longer than most, he reminds himself. He has made it this far. He can make it just a little further.

He takes a breath. Rolls the sleeve back down. Stands up. Lets himself feel the rest of it. The excitement. The hope. His hands are trembling, he notices. Perhaps, though, he shouldn't be surprised.

After fifty years, Skart is going back to war.

Granny Spregg

"Privett," Granny Spregg says.

"Mother," he replies.

In all honesty, Granny Spregg cannot be entirely sure who Privett's father is. She knows who she said it was at the time, but given his size and disposition, there is very much a chance that there is some House Troll blood in him.

"Is there something you need, Mother?" he asks. He sounds, she thinks, like a sanctimonious asshole. Probably because that's exactly what he is. She should have hired better nannies.

"I believe General Callart has my request well in hand." This is the dance they must do. Because House Spriggan is the House she made it to be. She made the rules, and now she must live with them. She just never imagined she would get so old; that the mistakes of the past would mount so high that she wouldn't even be in charge of her own idiot son.

"I am taking a personal interest, Mother," Privett says. He exposes his teeth in something that could be called but is not a smile.

Privett. The middle child. All the insecurities so transparent in him. Hiding away with the real soldiers so he can feel like less of an irrelevance. Meanwhile, it was his eldest sister who orchestrated the coup that dethroned her.

Still, he was an accomplice, and Granny Spregg does not forgive him. Not for an instant.

"I would not wish to tax you with even a simple request," she says. "I know how overwhelmed you get."

The advantage of motherhood, she thinks, is that it lets you know exactly which pressure points are most painful.

"I am more than capable of determining the merit of your request, Mother." There is a little color in his cheeks now.

She looks to Callart, a question in her eyes. She lets Privett see exactly who she thinks is in charge here.

Callart doesn't take the bait, but Privett, she knows, is blind to any answer Callart gives. He is only capable of seeing his authority questioned. So, as she knew he would, he steps before her. He froths.

"Our operations have evolved since your day, Mother. You probably wouldn't understand the delicate tapestry. I know how the years weigh on you."

Granny Spregg needs to get her blows in while she can. She smiles thinly. "At least your sisters' barbs have some wit to them," she says.

He hulks over her. And she has become so frail, she thinks, he could probably kill her with a single blow. He might.

But, "Out!" he barks instead. "Your request is denied, Mother. I cannot have you upsetting operations you have no hope of understanding."

Operations, Granny Spregg is well aware, is a word Privett is using to make himself feel better about the day-to-day housekeeping duties that occupy most of House Spriggan's military: guarding factories and warehouses, ensuring none of the other Houses are making threatening moves, making sure that the fae are keeping their heads down.

"If Callart was capable of explaining these... *operations* to you, I'm sure he could explain them to me."

And Callart does smile at that. Just a flash, just for her. But she lets Privett see that she has seen it. A shared grin in Callart's direction. A look of quiet triumph even as she is defeated.

"Out!" Privett is purple and quaking.

And of course she must leave. No matter what barbs she plants here, her authority is gone, lost along with her youth.

She turns, hobbles. "Sorry," she says, as he fumes at her. "I don't move as fast as I once did."

Finally, the door slams behind her. Thacker, still beside her, is breathing hard. "Well," he says, "it was always a long shot. Perhaps it's better that it's over so soon."

Granny Spregg turns to look at him. "Over?" She smiles. "Oh no, Thacker. This is just the start."

3

Enter the McGuffin

Knull

In the alley behind the bar, a fox digs through garbage, and rats chitter back and forth. Among such peers, Knull checks over his shoulder. Junkies twitch, he thinks, and dealers check over their shoulders. Still, at least his paranoia isn't delusional. He needs to get out of here before the two gnomes take the Dust he sold them.

Though the sale has left him feeling flush with cash, it has almost cleaned out the final dregs of his supply. Plus, his regular clients will require more potent mixtures than the ones he's holding if they are to remain regular. It is time to restock. It is time to visit Cotter.

Cotter lives over in The Bends, which is either a cab ride or a half-hour schlepp away. In the end the math is simple: sore feet cannot stop Knull from running away from this ass-end of the Iron City, a lack of funds can. Cabs cost money.

Money. In the Iron City, it always comes back to money. Here, the days are not measured by the ticks of clocks but by the clinks of coins. Knull is glad he is not half-dryad, trying to put away coins that will last the length of a tree's slow trudge through life, because he has his eyes on riches that will buy him a more vertical sort of mobility than a cab offers.

"I'm not stopping," he'd told his younger brother when he'd left home for good. "Not even the Guild Districts, that's not good enough. Not for me."

He'd looked at the accumulated tides of shit—papers, books, dirt, and trash washed up by his parents' neglect, by the pressure of poverty, by despair, by too many days with too many missed meals, by his parents' guilt over it all, and by their desperate need to escape. He'd looked at his brother.

"You should come too."

His brother had curled his lips. "You're selling selfish bullshit as well as Dust these days?"

Knull had wanted to keep his temper, but his brother always made it hard. "It's not selfish when the only reason they're incapable of caring for themselves is that they keep shoveling Dust into their veins."

"You sell Dust!" His brother's hands were up in the air. "Do you hear yourself? Do you understand how hypocritical you sound?"

For a moment, fists were balled, for a moment this was going to go the way these conversations always went. And Knull hadn't wanted to leave like that.

"I'm going all the way, this time," he'd said. "I'm going straight to Low Spires. Musthaven maybe. I'm going as high as any fae can go in this city. There'll be me, and rich goblin kids slumming it, and there could be you too. I can bring you with me. We'll watch them blow out their sinuses on Dust, and we'll laugh at the blood. Life could be so good. Come on. We can do it. You and me. We're strong enough."

But Edwyll hadn't been. And Knull had left him behind. He'd

glimpsed Edwyll in the bar tonight, just for a moment. And they'd nodded at each other, but that was all.

Because I'm strong, he reminds himself. *Because I can make a commitment to a cause. I can take the risks and survive the odds.*

So, he goes deeper into the alley at the back of the bar, past a scrawled mural of the White Tree, half-obscured behind a red spray where a goblin patrol threw a can of paint at it, and he grabs a lead drainpipe, and he climbs up towards the rooftops and the stars.

Sil

Back in the bar, blood drips from the blade of Sil's sword. Crimson beads are stark against silvery steel. The crowd is backing away as the aura of the iron alloy—free from its scabbard—starts to sting. The blade is still, not a quiver in it.

The same is not true of the brownie who is currently at fifty percent of his usual number of hands. He quivers, alright. He flails. He screams as the iron-inflicted wound continues to burn and sizzle. Blood sprays from his stump even as he clutches the wound. It bursts between his fingers. He points it like a pistol, hoses Bazzack down, then the staring crowd.

Sil knows the kobold drummer is going to react before he does. He lurches forward and finds her blade going through his neck. With only the slightest pressure she threads the needle between his second and third vertebrae. The only noise as he drops comes from his crackling flesh.

More red on her blade.

She checks Jag. Osmondo's heir is still standing there. She is still staring. So many are still staring.

The front door is closest. She will take that path.

She grabs Jag by the arm.

"No," Jag says. But she is speaking to a moment that's already passed.

I want you to come with me to the Fae Districts, Jag had said. *I want to show you something. Something of your mother's people.* She'd been smiling as she said it, but in Sil's ear it had been a command. Had been a statement that Jag was heading into danger.

On the day Sil had first met her father, Osmondo had said, *Keep my daughter alive or I shall visit upon you a thousand plagues of pain.* He was not joking. He does not have a sense of humor.

And so Sil came. No matter that her handlers had told her to leave Jag alone that night. No matter that she had been given tasks to perform patrolling a perimeter gate. Osmondo's old directive superseded their new ones.

So now, she pulls Jag by the arm. Jag comes with her toward the staring onlookers. Sil shoves her forward then, holding onto her wrist, spinning her like they are dancing at a ball. Jag crashes into the crowd like a goblin-sized morning star. Only Sil's grip on her wrist keeps her upright.

Bazzack screams after them, but Jag was right—Sil is not his bodyguard.

She charts the progress of stools, fae, glasses. She leaps, dances over a tabletop, ducks below a beam. She slashes with her sword, drives open a bloody wedge. She grabs Jag's hand once more, heaves. Jag stumbles into the gap Sil has opened.

A bottle is thrown. Sil catches it, brings it down on the next obstacle's head, steps over his slumping form. She glances back. Jag is still alive. Osmondo is still obeyed.

Quickly and efficiently, Sil cuts an exit out of the bar.

Jag

Jag is a somnambulist in a waking nightmare. She stumbles and trips while fae are paraded before her, each one clutching a grizzlier wound than the one before. She can hear Sil grunting. She can hear the smack of a blade against meat.

Then she's outside. Pigeons billow up into the sky. A glitching neon sign advertising sparrow-nest omelets and acorn coffee to the late-shift crowd. Somehow all that has happened to her is that her shirt is untucked, and her jacket needs to be straightened, while behind her there are screams and rage.

Sil has put her signature upon the bar.

"Bazzack!" she has just enough breath to say as Sil slams her into the side of their car.

Sil shakes her head. And Jag knows. No one ever gave Sil any orders about Bazzack. And Jag's lost the opportunity to give new ones. Sil is in charge now.

Sil opens the car door. And somehow, even as the fuse on the bar's violence burns down, and the detonation of bodies that will come chasing after them thrums, she still finds the time to offer Jag her seat with a bow.

Jag dives into leather and lingering cigar smoke. She slams the door shut behind her.

Through darkened glass she tracks the shadow of the first fae exiting the bar. She sees Sil glide around it, her body twisting. Something wet splatters against the window, starts to drip.

Sil slides across the hood of the car, gets in with almost balletic grace. When she pounds her foot against the accelerator, there is a body in front of them. Jag watches as the fae rolls over the windshield, hears the thump as he hits asphalt behind them.

It is time for Jag to go home. Her quiet night on the town is most definitely over.

Knull

Halfway across town, Knull reaches Cotter's building. Even starting on a neighboring rooftop, it takes him a decent chunk of time just to climb the fire escape all the way to the penthouse. As he ascends, the Iron City splays itself below him, eager as any salesman to peddle its wares. He looks down and sees lights to mirror the stars: the spires of the five Goblin Houses punching out from the city's heart, blazing.

Around the Houses, fingers of influence are sketched out in light: great avenues bursting with theaters, museums, pleasure houses, temples of commerce, and temples to Mab built on the barrows of the sidhe who now clean their hallways and empty their trashcans. The avenues' glow withers as the city sprawls, turns septic. The white purity of the towers becomes amber, becomes guttering yellow. The outskirts of the city look jaundiced. There, factories raise their hulking heads, architectural bullies that cause the buildings around them to slouch in fear.

And then he is high enough to see beyond even that, to see the Iron Wall itself. The city's great border. Twenty yards tall, and ten yards thick. The limits of his world and his experience.

He can feel it from here. All of the fae can. All of the time. The deep bone stab of that much cold iron is always known to them. A constant stamp on their hearts and their souls: you lost, we won.

Kobolds and gnomes used to try to burrow under it, but the goblins have given it roots, salting the earth below with iron filings that send them scrambling away choking up their lungs in bloody chunks. Pixies high on Dust used to try to fly over it. Knull's grandmother died that way. The relentless metallic pulse of it stealing the strength from gossamer-thin skin, sending her crashing down. Not all who had tried to escape the city that way in the early days had died, but his grandmother had impaled herself on a spike of metal on the wall itself, and the iron had burned right through her.

Even those who don't try to defy the wall die from it. They die from it all the time. Black tumors clogging their arteries, their lungs. They cough up specks of its infection. They choke on them. And no healing magic can touch the damage that iron inflicts. Even the fae who used to live for centuries—the dryads and the sidhe—are now lucky to make it far past sixty. Now the goblins are the ones who live on into their eighties and beyond, and their most common cause of death is self-indulgence. Still, sometimes Knull thinks the fae who die of iron poisoning are the lucky ones. They at least survived long enough that time could kill them. There are many worse ways to die in the Iron City.

Iron affects fae in other ways too. It has sunk into their genes, eroded their heritage. Despite his father's pixie blood, Knull has no dragonfly wings to take him to the skies. Two ugly knubs of bone and skin on his shoulder blades are all he's got. And so he's left here, trudging up the fire escape.

He mounts the final step. Cotter's penthouse is before him. It is uncommonly quiet. Cotter enjoys the industrial beats of Trollcore and the staccato rhythms of Splatterstep. There is always a party at Cotter's place. Except, apparently, for tonight.

Knull grows cautious. He slides along the outside of the penthouse suite, peering around the edges of the blackout blinds. He sees nothing, hears only the same unnerving quiet.

He grips the knob of the door that leads in from the small

penthouse deck. The wood is cold. Goosebumps stitch his arm.

He turns the handle. Hinges sigh. The door is unlocked.

Wronger and wronger.

Knull checks over both shoulders. He's not looking for danger this time. He's searching for escape routes. There are, after all, many ways to die in the Iron City.

Money, though, he knows, is the best way to survive, and Cotter is the most direct route to coin Knull knows. He pushes the door open. He steps in.

The abattoir smell hits him immediately. His lizard brain knows what he's going to see before he uses his small pen light to illuminate the scene: bodies and blood.

Every drug deal is a fuck-up waiting to happen. Whatever happened here was deeply fucked up indeed.

Cotter is the centerpiece of the tableau. He's on the couch, two small holes drilled into his forehead, his brain making one very large mess on the wall behind him. His bare arms are mottled with bruising. His silk shirt and leather pants are crisscrossed with cuts. Someone, Knull thinks with a numb mind, was here asking questions that Cotter didn't want to answer.

There are other bodies scattered around Cotter. Two bodyguards from House Troll over by the door—a fae protected by two lumbering goblins is as ostentatious a way to protect oneself as Knull can imagine, but in the end it's done his supplier no good. Something has caved in their chests, leaving concavities of blood and gore.

There are a few dancers too—pixies and sidhe and mixes of the two trying to parlay their bodies into a few coins, a few grams of Dust. Now their nudity serves only as a canvas to highlight the damage done: bold red strokes against backdrops of blue, purple, and pink skin.

Knull wants to leave. He knows he should leave. His legs aren't listening to him, though. The part of his mind that engages the gears is stuttering in shock.

And part of him is thinking: *No one is guarding Cotter's stash.*

But of course, this was a robbery. It must have been. Cotter must have been cleaned out.

And yet… what if he was not?

Knull balances on the knife blade of risk and reward. He attempts to walk that thinnest of lines. There is a chance he knows what Cotter's assailants didn't.

He goes to the kitchen, opens the fridge. He holds his breath. Nectar beers. Half-full take-out containers leaking ivy noodles. A breadcrumb-speckled block of squirrel's butter. All where you would expect them. All undisturbed.

His heart is pounding. He moves the butter aside. The milk carton behind goes too. He fishes against the back wall. He doesn't precisely know the trick.

Flat plastic meets his fingers. No seam. No pressure plate. Nothing at all.

Which means that Knull knows exactly what the trick is.

Knull shudders. He doesn't take Dust. He's seen what it does to lives up close. And he was born after the Iron Wall went up anyway. He has no magic to miss. He has no lost past to wallow in. He is of the world that is here and now in front of him.

His finger is shaking as he dips it into the small baggy of pure Dust hidden his pocket. He rubs the ground resin against his gums.

Doors open within him. Parts of him unfurl. He hates this. He sees sights he doesn't want to see—possibilities in a world that has never held any for him—and he shouts at himself that they are lies, they have always been lies, but he is so hard to believe right now.

He turns to the fridge again. His finger trails along a countertop. Daisies and buttercups bloom from cold linoleum. Moss spreads. Grass grows, glowing with life.

He opens the fridge door, and when he lets go of the handle it is no longer plastic but a branch of living wood, leaves unfurling.

He strokes the smooth plastic at the back of the fridge, and the panel opens at once, the world springing to obey his every whim. And there isn't even a code to go deeper. There's just another handle.

The Dust high drains out of him as he heaves on the second handle, pivots the whole fridge out, taking the wall with it. He is left blinking, and hollow, and wondering where all the beauty went as he stares into Cotter's vault. On the countertop beside him, petals curl. Anemic grass withers.

He is not sure what to expect inside the vault. He has only glimpsed its opening once before. Cotter was out of his gourd, his defenses lowered.

Knull's first impression is that of a work room. He sees a wooden desk, a tool kit, knives and grinders for working with the resin. A set of scales. There are shelves holding baggies. Some are full. There is even some raw resin. A few ounces, maybe more if he scrapes all the nuggets and curls that are scattered in the desk's deep grain. Enough to make him rich in a poor world. Not enough to get him to Low Spires, maybe, but more than he could otherwise gather in a year of hustling. This is a score.

Except Knull has eyes for none of it. Because Knull now knows exactly why Cotter was killed.

Sitting on Cotter's desk is a bundle wrapped in clear plastic and masking tape. It is perhaps a foot square at the end, maybe a little more. It is perhaps two feet long, maybe a little less.

It is the largest bag of Dust Knull has ever seen.

It is a fortune even if it isn't pure, but if Cotter is lying dead and tortured on his couch then this thing, Knull knows, is pure.

He tries to do the math. Twenty, twenty-five, thirty-five pounds of pure, uncut Dust. It is everything he has ever dreamed of. It is the future he has always known he deserves. It is precisely why this apartment smells like a slaughterhouse.

Risk and reward.

Knull hesitates, but then steps forward. Because how could he not? He lifts the massive brick, grunts under its weight. It's even heavier than he anticipated. And he doesn't have to take even a single grain of it to see a world of magical possibilities opening up before him.

4
Rebels with Causes

Bee

"This is about more than your goddamn proletariat rage, Bee. This is about ensuring enduring sociopolitical equality for everyone in this city!"

"Well," Bee replies, "while I love the sort of mental masturbation that simply results in us peacefully arriving at a more equitable society, I am engaged in a more practical conversation."

These are the sorts of arguments Bee gets into.

"I," Bee goes on, "am engaged in a conversation that takes into consideration the practical necessities of actually achieving such a goal. Revolution is a necessary part of any change."

Across the room, Harretta, a blue-skinned sidhe, opens her mouth to jump in. Bee holds up a hand, forestalls disagreement. "And while not all revolutions need be violent—yes, I have read my fucking Minax, thank you—in a city so rife with stasis, I argue that such a change must by necessity be explosive."

"Bullshit," says Tharn, Bee's sparring partner in this particular disagreement. "You just want to stomp heads."

Bee considers this. "Not 'just,'" he says. "I want to do both."

They are in the building that very specifically isn't the Miners' Guild Hall. They are in a room—should any goblins ask—that is very specifically not a meeting room. The fae are not permitted the right of assembly, after all. Should a large group of fae from the Miners' Guild happen to be here at the same time twice a week then that is surely just strange coincidence, Mr Spriggan Security Officer, sir. And should money have changed hands and a verbal agreement been made so that Bee and the rest of the Fae Liberation Front can coincidentally happen to all be here at the same time so they can discuss sedition… well, yes, that would be harder to explain.

There are twenty-four of them in the room, with its low ceiling and peeling wood paneling, and unvarnished wooden floor. The youth of the fae underground. Or… one faction of the youth of the fae underground. There are always factions. There are always competing philosophies. That's part of what Bee loves about it: that the conversations are as violent intellectually as the means by which they'll achieve their goals are physically.

They sit with their chairs pulled into a circle—and there is not a pure pixie or kobold, gnome or sidhe among them. A room of half-sidhe, half-dryad, quarter-kobold, one-eighth gnome on his mother's side fae. All the old divisions of race are dissolving away. That feels symbolic to Bee, the same way the circle is symbolic. There are no leaders in the Fae Liberation Front. They are a collective. All voices are welcome. But some voices are louder than others.

"If we are to achieve a society in which fae and goblins are equal, rather than one in which we simply replace the goblins as the oppressor—" Tharn starts.

"We are in agreement about the end goal, Tharn," Bee cuts him off. "It's just about how we get there."

"But that's my exact point!" Tharn is an energetic young krowbold—a brownie on his father's side, a kobold on his mother's—who works as a runner between the goblin offices and the mine's shift leaders. He's dressed in a suit and his jacket billows around him, his arms flying as he talks, his flaming red hair wild. "Tonight's uprising," he insists, "does not have our goals in mind. It is an old-guard revolution, upholding old-guard ideals. It would lead us back to the way things were before. It would recreate the conditions that culminated in the Iron War. The cycle would perpetuate."

"Whatever stops we make later down the road," Bee makes his counterpoint, "both our journey and theirs start the same way." With a dryad mother and brownie father, he is larger, slower, and more solid than Tharn. So, he thinks, is his argument. He wears his ore-stained work shirt with the sleeves rolled up, drums his points against his thick thigh. "Better to at least travel with them," he says, "so we have a chance of arriving at an endpoint we can quibble over."

"Quibble?" Tharn is red-faced.

There's some laughter. Tharn is a very sober young man, and while Bee loves him like a brother, he has yet to realize the importance of humor to serious matters.

"It is not quibbling," Tharn says, utterly earnest. "It is the very foundation of the revolution. If we participate in tonight's activities, we are endorsing a journey to the wrong destination from the very first step."

"And if we don't participate," Bee responds, "then we miss the opportunity to even have a seat at the table when the endpoint is discussed." He looks around, catches every eye.

"Skart's uprising is happening tonight with or without us," he says. "It is broad and coordinated, and it stands a chance to result in true change. We can be a part of that change or we can be bystanders." He grins. "Plus, if we take part, we get to stomp some gobbo heads."

More laughter.

Bee looks at Tharn. "A vote?" he asks.

Tharn chews his tongue. He knows he's lost, but he's out of counterarguments.

"All in favor of participation?" Bee asks. The hands go up, Harretta's first of all. In the end, it's fifteen to nine. Bee will take that level of consensus any day of the week.

He stands, he smiles. Tharn shakes his head, then shrugs and smiles. "So be it," he says. "Let us go and kick goblins in the nuts in the name of a more equitable future."

Jag

Across the Fae Districts, Jag is not focused on the future, equitable or otherwise. She is focused on the discomforts of the present, no matter that she is nestled within the leather embrace of a limousine.

She lights another cigarette. Her hands are shaking. The Fae Districts flicker past. Dilapidated houses sag into abandoned storefronts, which slump into crumpled tenements. Litter billows as Sil drives with no heed for corners, road conditions, or pedestrians.

"Slow down," Jag says, after Sil's recklessness sends another fae mother diving for the gutter. "We're safe now. These fae aren't trying to hurt us."

The car eases to a leisurely stroll. The potholes in the road stop attempting to dislocate Jag's spine.

She sits back, tries to breathe. There's a decanter in the car door, and she pours herself a healthy shot. Afternotes of smoke and earth slow her beating heart.

I'm safe, she tells herself.

The thought causes her anger to spike again, though. That she should need to think it. That her father has created a city in which fae and goblins must flee from each other to feel safe. That old race enmities have been perpetuated for so long.

She forces herself to breathe. To unclench her fists.

"Are you OK?" she asks Sil. "Did they hurt you?" She knows it should have been the first thing she said.

Sil just makes a slight scoffing sound in response. That should be reassuring, but it's not.

"I've explained why I want us to come out here, haven't I? We've gone over this." She puffs harder on her cigarette. "You're *from* here." She gesticulates with her tumbler. "This should be as much a part of you as I am. As much as our father is. This is as much your heritage as House Red, and all its obscenities. There is still beauty to be found among the ashes. And I thought—I dared to believe—that showing you these bits of it might unlock a little piece of your heart for you."

She might as well be talking to an empty car seat.

Things have been done to Sil, Jag knows. She is not sure of the specifics. There are depths that she is unwilling to plumb. It is enough that she is aware that there is horror down there. And she is expected to not care. She is an heir to House Red, after all. Horrors are theirs to inflict as they want.

But Jag does not want. She does not want to think of Sil as an object—no matter what she has been taught—but as her half-sister. She wants Sil to think of herself that way too, but Sil stubbornly refuses. Or is incapable. Whatever the answer, Jag knows her frustration shouldn't be directed at Sil, but there aren't many targets within the limousine, no matter how luxuriously appointed it is.

"We've created an unnecessary dichotomy," she half-shouts at Sil. "Us and them. Binary thinking. We've all got to pick a side. And to even challenge that idea is insanity. To suggest that perhaps I am not so different from a fae, to suggest that perhaps your mixed heritage is an advantage, is a radical notion. I must be joking to think such a thing, mustn't I?"

Sil doesn't look back. Doesn't nod. Just keeps her eyes on the road, hands at ten and two.

Jag remembers what happened in the bar. What those hands did.

"Look," she says. "I know… some of what you were taught to do. What you've been… programmed to think you need to do. But what happened in the bar… that shouldn't— you shouldn't—"

What are the words for this, she wonders?

"I know the fae weren't blameless." Jag keeps going. "They played into the dynamic of hatred goblins have created. They helped instigate. But you escalated, Sil. And if we respond we just validate the system that subjugates them. That subjugates you."

These aren't the words.

"I just… What do you think, Sil?" she says. "What is your opinion? Do you hate what you did? Were you glad? Would you change the world? Would you tear down all the old race hatred so you could build something better? Would you shore up all the systems of control with more bodies? What would you do, Sil? What would you do if you wanted to go and listen to some music? Do you even like music? What music do you like?"

Sil doesn't turn around, doesn't say a word. Buildings thrum past them steady as a metronome.

"Answer me!" she shrieks. All the stress of the bar is crashing down on her now. "I command you to—"

Abruptly Sil pulls the car to the side of the road. Jag's seatbelt constricts around her chest. Words coagulate in her throat. Her palms are abruptly very sweaty.

Sil turns around. Jag swallows.

"There's something wrong with the engine," Sil says calmly. "This is not a good part of town. Stay inside the car."

Knull

Knull is still staggering under the weight of the brick of Dust when he hears it. It is a small sound in the scale of things. He is largely focused on trying to avoid stepping in the blood on the floor of Cotter's apartment. Broken glass from where someone's head has slammed through a mirrored coffee table crunches beneath his foot. And so, he almost misses the click of the front door latch coming undone.

In the Iron City, "almost" is the difference between having a future and being the past tense. It is the difference between "breathing" and "breathed."

Knull runs. There is no hesitation, no question. He has no qualms about his cowardice. Bravery, in his opinion, is just stupidity that happens to benefit others, and he is firmly focused on self-interest right now.

He skids through the back door, out onto the deck, still clutching the brick of Dust. He hears voices. It is not a small crowd that has come to visit Cotter's corpse.

He slows his escape, tries to be quieter as he scuttles toward the fire escape. They'll be looking for him soon, he knows. Even if they didn't hear his flight, with his hands full of Dust he didn't close the door to Cotter's workshop.

He gets to the fire escape before the newcomers start shouting. Old ironwork creaks beneath his feet, and Knull winces at more than the pain of the metal's proximity. Is it more dangerous to be slow or loud? He doesn't know. He descends in stuttering bursts of speed. The Dust makes him clumsy, sends him bouncing off railings.

Then the shout from inside. Adrenaline screams in Knull's ears that slow is no longer an option. He has to run. He has to run *now*.

The fire escape sings with the sound of his crashing footsteps, louder even than the band in the bar earlier. Then there are shadows above, the flares of flashlights. Then there are ricochets, and sparks, and the increasing danger of Knull shitting his pants.

He wants to drop the Dust. It is heavy. It is slowing him. Its plastic wrapping is slipping beneath his sweaty palms. But he cannot, of course. He is running to secure his future, after all, and this brick is his future. Dropping it would be the same as turning round and asking his pursuers to put their barrels to his temple.

He leaves the fire escape at speed, leaping, still a story up from his intended destination. He twists, lands on his back, cradling the Dust like an infant. Bullets play a staccato beat as roof tiles crack and slither away beneath him. He scrabbles to his feet, runs as fast as he can, bent over by the Dust, weaving between water towers and air-handling units. He wishes he could pray to Mab, but she's probably on the other team's side.

Shouts follow him. There are footsteps on the fire escape. Knull leaps between buildings. He has miscalculated his increased weight. Gravity reaches greedy fingers for the brick of Dust. He hits the far roof with his waist. The brick flies free from his grip, and Knull's desperation finds a higher gear. He claws for fingerholds, swings his legs up. He rolls, finding no time to stand. There are more gunshots. He doesn't know if they come close to hitting him. He doesn't care. Then he's at the Dust. And somehow the brick is still whole. He could kiss it. There's no time. He heaves it up to his chest, clutches it tight as a lover.

He runs on, legs burning, lungs heaving. The brick of Dust slaps at his thighs and slips in his grip. He runs on. A flare lights the night above him. There are more shouts. He runs on.

He is staggering when he comes to the townhouse. He has plotted this course long before. Knull collects escape routes like a gutter collects trash. He knows the townhouse is undergoing construction. He knows it is some goblin manager's weekday crashpad being upgraded for new creature comforts. Except if he's buying in this neighborhood, Knull also knows that goblin isn't impressing anyone.

Still, the socioeconomic woes of some underperforming goblin are not precisely a priority for Knull at this moment. What is absorbing far more of his attention is the chute that the fae workers are using to funnel rubble from the building's roof into the dumpster below.

He has enough presence of mind to realize that going down it head first is not necessarily a good idea. Then he is plunging feet first through yellow plastic tubing far faster than he expected. And then, he finds, that the ground is coming at him without mercy or concern.

Edwyll

Three streets away from the bloodbath in the bar, Edwyll stops to throw up for the fourth time.

Beauty, he thinks. *I went in there wanting to create beauty.*

He closes his eyes, sees the crimson-spattered scene again, hears the screams, smells the copper tang of—

Another dry heave wracks him. When it's over, he sits down hard, legs pointing heedlessly out into the street. His hands are shaking. A few crows flit by overhead. Behind him kobold digging tunes emerge out-of-key from a subterranean bar. The nighttime pedestrian traffic eddies around him.

He's seen violence before. Of course he has. This whole street has. They all grew up here. But this… this was close enough that it spattered his face.

He wipes at his cheeks, desperate to clear off any last remnant of the night that might be staining his skin. He's trying not to look at the blood-stained fabric of his shoes.

He needs to call Lila. He needs to touch base, to ground himself in who he is and what he's doing here, and he feels that most when he talks to her. He pulls himself up, stumbles to a payphone, pushes copper teeth into it with trembling fingers. Listens to it ring.

"Hello?"

Lila is a miniaturist. They met at the first gallery show Edwyll ever went to, and he almost hadn't noticed the pixie with purple skin and turquoise hair when she started talking to him because he was so lost in these ripples of color she had worked across a broken tile. That had been back at the beginning of what he now thinks of as his "awakening." When art had revealed to him that beauty was still possible in the world. That everything wasn't just shit and depredation. Back at his rediscovery of hope.

At first he'd tried to get rid of Lila, not knowing who she was, just wanting to lose himself in the art. But then he'd finally heard what she was saying, and realized she was the artist, and he'd been utterly mortified.

She lives with her partner Jallow, a gnome who is one of the few truly successful fae artists in the Iron City. In recent years the goblin youth have shown an increasingly rebellious interest in fae art, and Jallow is one of the lucky few to have found a patron—some minor noble within House Spriggan. He uses the profits to run a collective, where Edwyll finds employment and lodging whenever he can. He washes paintbrushes, runs errands, cooks food, whatever it takes to hang around them. And if the beds and couches aren't full of Lila and Jallow's artist friends then he'll crash there rather than returning to what passes for his home.

Lila has, despite the awkwardness of their first meeting, rather taken him under her wing. She'd seen him staring at the other artists as they worked and asked him about his own ambitions. She's the one who has encouraged him to always carry his art supplies with him. The oils he was using in the bar. Sticks of charcoal and graphite. And always as broad a selection of spray paint cans as he can manage. His murals are feeble still, he knows, but under her tutelage, he believes he is finding his confidence.

He needs her help finding that or something similar now.

"Lila," he says. "Lila, I need help."

"Edwyll?"

He tells her about the bar. The story pours out of him like blood from a wound.

"Breathe, Edwyll. Breathe," she tells him.

"What do I do?" he asks her, not sure if that's the question he really wants to ask but unable to think of any other way to put it.

"You poor thing." A pause. "I don't know, Edwyll. I don't think there is a thing you do when you see horror like that. I just… if it was me, I think I'd come back here, and I'd get as drunk as I could. And then, when I'd stopped waking up because of the awfulness of it all, when I could look it in the eye, I'd use it. I'd make it art. I'd turn it upon itself. I'd make it beautiful, something that cancels itself out at least as much as you can ever cancel something like that out. That's what I'd do."

Use it.

"I can't, Lila. I can't..." He can't even imagine it. The idea of turning it over. Of doing something with... that. He shakes his head, no matter that she can't see him.

"What do you want to do with your art?" she asks him.

He can't see the relevance of the question, but she asks it again, more insistently this time.

"I want..." He takes a breath, steadies himself. "I want the fae to find their hope again. I want them to know that even though our magic is gone, we can create a new kind of magic. I want them to stop looking back and look forward. I want to change the world."

"Yes," Lila says. "The world is what it is now, but it doesn't have to be. What happened in the bar happened, but you can either let it define you, or you can define it. You can change what it means. It doesn't only have to be a tragedy."

He tries to hold onto that. The idea of himself in the future. The idea of himself making the Fae Districts a place where goblins can't bring their assassins and butcher pixies or brownies or kobolds in the street. He finds some of the strength he was looking for.

"I don't want you crashing at some squat tonight," Lila says. "Come to the collective. I'll talk to Jallow, find a couch for you to sleep on or something. We've got wine."

"Yes," Edwyll says. "Yes." And then, finally, he remembers the reason he came out tonight. The object he wanted to take from his parents' house. The art he wanted to create with it. The art that could do exactly what he and Lila are talking about.

"Yes," he says again. "I just have to stop at one place along the way."

Sil

A quiet street. Streetlamps failing. The pungent smell of the weedkiller goblin patrols have used to keep all greenery in check. And limited escape routes. More of the latter than perhaps most would see, though. Sil judges she could make the leap to the fire escape in a pinch. She could go through a store window if necessary. She has options.

Next, she listens. Silence. Is there too much? She doesn't know this part of town well enough to judge. But she doesn't think she needs an escape route yet.

Yet.

She goes to the engine, pops the hood, pauses, pretends to take it in. Instead she listens again. There is still silence.

The tension in her fingers would give her away to anyone with skill. She knows it would. She's been taught to be better. But something about this is putting her on edge. She controls her breathing.

"What's happened?"

Jag is talking as she exits the car. She has not listened to Sil. This is not unexpected. Still, she has to suppress the reflex to draw her sword.

Instead, she remains examining the engine. And something about having her suspicions confirmed takes the edge off.

"Get back in the car," she says.

"What's wrong?" As if Jag hasn't heard her.

Sil pauses. She hears something now. Scuffing. A slight metallic tap. A creak.

"Somebody purposefully weakened the fan belt so it would fail," she says.

"What?"

There are no other cars on this street. Nobody else walking past.

She moves towards Jag, steers her toward the car door. "You should get inside," she tells her.

"Why?"

Did Jag have more to drink than Sil thought? Normally she needs two or three more before she becomes belligerent. It must have been Bazzack's presence, Sil thinks. She will need to take that into account next time.

Next time. Only if she plays this right.

"The tear in the belt," she says, "is only frayed along half its length."

Jag knits her brows.

"That means someone cut through the other half." She watches the shock wash over Jag's face. She seems to experience things so slowly compared to Sil. Her emotions impede her path to a plan at every turn.

"Whoever it was did not bother to hide their handiwork," she goes on. "Which means two more things. First, our saboteur does not expect us to report this sabotage."

Jag goes very still. This, Sil thinks, is good. She is becoming pliable. Though it is a little late for that. Sil is, she is sure, speaking for an audience now.

"Second," she says to the street, "they did not know exactly when the belt would break. So you must be being tailed." Jag's head whips back and forth searching the shadows.

"I do not believe I was supposed to be with you tonight," Sil says. "I was sent away. I am only here because you sought me out. I believe that someone is moving against you and your father tonight. Someone has plans.

"Still, if I am correct, and we have been observed, then our assailants must have had time to recalculate. They must have had time to bring in reinforcements. They must believe they finally have enough that they can win."

She smiles into Jag's dawning terror.

And then they come.

5

Dusted

Skart

The prospective participants in the night's rebellion meet in the basement of a factory where Skart has bought off all the security guards that he hasn't recruited. He has spent weeks clearing out goods, shipping in the equipment they will need. There are tables covered with maps and ranks of phones. Wires trail like rivers across the floor. A couple of chunky computer monitors glow with green light, their cathode rays crackling.

The crowd is large and growing larger. To the younger fae, the event has the feel of a concert—a buzz of anticipation that's not just in the air, but in their bones and blood. Its thrum takes the grinding edge off the bite of the Iron Wall. Now, they want to be told to detonate. Now, they want to explode.

The older fae are reminded of something else. Of older times. There aren't many of them now. Most who fought in the Iron Wars, and the Red Rebellion that came after, have passed away, taken by old injuries and new tumors. A few remain, some strengthened by old magic that dies hard. Some just clinging more tenaciously to life. But even for them, fighting is a young fae's game. Still, a few of the old guard retain their fighting spirit. and now they stand with Skart near the head of the room. This group remembers more than music, and the limited communion with the sublime that the goblins permit.

Skart remembers trees. He remembers skies the color of lapis. He remembers the call and cry of birds, and the bay and bark of forest life. He remembers running like a river. He remembers a world that bent to allow him to flow through it. He remembers being one with something larger than himself.

The feeling in the room now is a pale imitation of that communion in the end. It is far from unity with a whole world. It is not even the high of Dust slicing through the pain and numbness of the Iron Wall. But it is something. And unlike a Dust high, to Skart it feels real.

He looks to the other veterans. These are the ones with whom he first shared his plans.

"Ready?" Skart asks them.

Brumble grunts. She is a thickset old dryad almost a head taller than Skart, vines standing out clear in her thinning hair, skin on her arms gray and cracked. "No," she says. "I don't think we ever can be. But when no time is good for a rebellion, all are equally good." She shrugs. "We just have to do it."

A few smiles. A few chuckles. A lot of agreement. They are, Skart thinks, as nervous as virgins on their wedding night.

They have made something like a stage at the front of the hall. Wooden pallets are piled upon each other. Skart steps onto it; he raises one hand, takes the microphone in the other.

"Fae of the Iron City!" His voice through the speakers is massive. Every head turns. "Two years of planning. Two years of holding our hearts in our hands, and of fearing discovery every day. Two years of discovering setbacks. Two years of thinking tonight was not possible."

He looks at them all. He smiles.

"You proved me wrong," he says. "We're here. We're living in this moment. This night. Our night." He raises a fist. "Tonight, we take back our city. Tonight, we tear down the Iron Wall!"

It is a good speech, he knows. He has practiced it many times. He has pared it down to its essence, until it is short and sharp as a knife blade.

He sees heads nodding. He sees fists raised with his own. There are some whoops and cheers. Brumble is stamping her heavy feet.

If only it was as easy as that. But, Skart knows, the rebels are a fractious lot.

"What about tomorrow?" someone shouts.

Skart peers into the crowd. A young fae—a mix of brownie and dryad blood from the looks of him. Skart is old enough that he finds the increase in mixed blood among the youth of the day strange and slightly distasteful, but he bites back the thought. He has to treat all of them as equals if they are all to take equal part. He cocks one large ear in the young bryad's direction.

"What comes next?" his interlocutor shouts. He is standing on a chair, dressed in ore-stained work clothes. Badly scrawled tattoos cover his bare arms. His nose has been broken several times. Skart knows his type.

Skart smiles. He doesn't want to, but he knows leaders don't badger and belittle their followers.

"You don't think we have enough to be going on with for now?" he says.

"I think that if I'm going to walk a thousand miles with you," the bryad calls, still stubborn as a House Troll goblin, "then I want to know that my first step is pointed in the right direction."

Skart suppresses a sigh. The night is still young, but he already knows it will be long. He looks at the expectant faces.

"What do you want me to say?" he asks them. "You want me to tell you we'll all be living in a changed world tomorrow? That they'll be halcyon days? Do you want me to say that every goblin will be in a grave? Or that none of them will be and we'll all be sitting together eating bread and honey? What do you want?"

He looks at them all. "I don't know what tomorrow will be like. We all want different things. We all have our own visions. Tomorrow could be a thousand things. So, all I know is this: tomorrow will be different from today. And for me, after fifty years of every day being the fucking same, after fifty years of being ground into the dirt by goblin heels, yeah, different is enough."

He waits. Did he get it right? Was there enough honesty? Enough hope? Did he make sure that this fragile alliance of factions will hold?

And then the crowd starts to roar. So, Skart guesses that he did.

Knull

Knull doesn't know why the hit squad from Cotter's apartment haven't found him yet. Perhaps he put enough distance between himself and them that they lost his trail. Perhaps his escape plan was a good one and his dive into the dumpster masked his flight. Or perhaps his plan was so spectacularly stupid that no one seriously thought he would try it.

To be fair, at this point Knull isn't even sure how long he was unconscious for.

He is, however, certain that he won't be able to put any weight on his ankle for a while. His leg throbs at him with a dull kind of anger.

He sits up slowly, takes stock. The brick of Dust is still there.

The plastic wrapping is dirty and scuffed, but it has held fast. Whatever else he knew, Cotter knew how to protect his product.

Next, when he dares to look, Knull finds his ankle is swollen but the skin is unbroken. There is no white jut of bone to greet his gaze. It is just a sprain, he thinks.

Finally, there is the question of who exactly it was that was shooting at him. Surely the same group that killed Cotter. But in that case, why weren't they in Cotter's apartment when Knull arrived? Could there be two parties interested in stealing from Cotter in one night? He was in such a hurry to flee the apartment that he doesn't even know if his pursuers were fae or goblin. Hopefully they are similarly clueless about his own identity.

In the end, he decides, if he has truly shaken his pursuers, he will never have to worry about their identity again. All he needs to worry about is selling this vast brick of Dust. If he can do that, he is set.

Every journey to boundless riches, though, begins with a single step, and Knull's first step needs to be figuring out how to get out of a dumpster when he can't even stand.

He roots through the junk that surrounds him. Somehow, he expected the dumpster's contents to be softer. It is full of broken bricks and spars of wood shot through with mounds of plaster dust and snarls of electric cord. He is lucky, he realizes, that his only injury is to his ankle.

He strikes two other escape routes off his mental list.

Rummaging around, he finds two pieces of wood and secures his ankle between them, cinching the makeshift brace tight with old plastic wrapping. He adds reinforcements made from strips of discarded wooden paneling, securing the cheap pine with lengths of old electrical cord. It's clumsy and will click with every step he takes, but at least he will be able to walk.

He pulls himself to his feet, discovers fresh aches and additional cuts on his arms and legs. At first, he's unwilling to heave the Dust over the side before he gets out, scared to let it out of his sight for even that long, but in the end practicality wins out. He dumps it, then grips the side of the dumpster and, inch by inch, hauls himself out onto the street.

His footsteps are fumbling. The Dust is no easier to carry now than it was before. Here on the street, his precious cargo feels more like a liability than ever before. He wishes he'd worn a coat he could wrap around it, or that the dumpster had claimed some old discarded drop cloth. Carrying it like this feels like a form of nakedness. If he were carrying a flashing sign while screaming, "Mug me!" he wouldn't be much more obvious.

Still, this part of town is quieter than most Knull frequents. Cotter's penthouse is in The Bends, one of the better parts of the Fae Districts. Families have tucked their children into bed already. The bars will close at curfew. Knull has a chance to make it back to his pad in one piece. He just needs his luck to hold.

For twenty minutes he thinks it has. For twenty minutes the Iron City lets him think he's okay as he hobbles down empty streets and dark alleys. It plays him right up until he turns the corner onto the street that houses the tumbledown squat where he has been crashing rent-free for the past two years.

There, he sees something that makes him stop. Two figures. They pace back and forth outside the dirty piece of canvas that hides the entrance to his makeshift home. His heart stops along with his feet. He expects guns. He expects shouts. Whoever chased him from Cotter's knew who he was after all, knew where to find him, knew…

Except no. They didn't. Because as he lurks in the shadows, Knull realizes he knows this pair just as well as he knows that every drug deal is a fuck-up waiting to happen. And he knows without a shadow of a doubt that he has fucked up.

Because the tourists from the bar clearly aren't as unfamiliar with this part of town as he thought. They obviously know someone he knows. And whoever that fae is, they are also just as obviously an asshole, because they have given up Knull's home address. And now, two gnomes who bought a bag of Dust from him that was about as potent as an octogenarian's magic wand are standing outside his door, and they do not look like they want to discuss their refund politely.

Sil

Fae are coming out of doorways. They're coming down off the roofs. They are dressed in black. They are carrying hard wooden batons. Kerchiefs are pulled up to their eyes.

Sil stands before the hood of the car, feet spread, knees bent. She is a coiled spring. She is wondering exactly which ambitious lordling in House Red hired them. She wonders if she will have the opportunity to beat it out of someone.

The fae are in the streets now, a mix of half-brownies, flame-haired half-kobolds, and towering demi-dryads with bark-encrusted fists. Sil counts them quickly. Twelve in all. Behind her it sounds like Jag is having trouble breathing.

"You weren't meant to be here," says a large demi-dryad whose mother was probably related to some species of ash or oak. "But I'm glad you are. Now I get to find out if you're as good as they say."

"What do I do?" Jag squeaks.

"Get in the car," Sil says. "Lock the doors."

"Don't go anywhere," the lead fae calls to Jag. A dryad mixed with… gnome perhaps? Or maybe kobold. Sil can't tell exactly. "Be with you in a minute, princess."

Sil doesn't have time for any clever verbal ripostes, or to check and see if Jag is doing what she's told. Now is the time to engage.

One of the part-pixies tries to dart past her. Sil jabs left, drawing her sword in one clean, clear motion. The fae manages to parry the blow, her wooden baton nearly cut in half but just stopping Sil's blade from bisecting her bowels. Still, the force of the impact sends her to the floor.

The eleven other fae move only a fraction of a moment after Sil, lunging at her. She turns her movement into a roll, ducks below swinging batons, comes up low, sweeps out her leg. A sidhe falls. Sil rolls again, picking up speed; her blade comes out, comes down on the fallen sidhe's neck.

The fae make no comment on their comrade's death. The time for talk is done. This is in earnest now.

By the time she's on her feet, she's ensured that one more gnome mother will be wearing black in the morning. Her sword is between two of the gnome's ribs, poking redly from his back. But his rattling death throes are trapping her blade even as she tries to rip it free.

Two fae close in, their kobold lineage evident in powerful forearms and long sharp nails. Their batons go up. Sil twists, still hanging onto her blade. She kicks one attacker in the armpit, sends him one way, his baton the other. The second half-kobold's baton blurs past her face, her move carrying her out of range. She lets go of her blade, leg still in the air, brings the foot down on the back of the second attacker's neck. He sprawls face first into the asphalt.

Sil is without her sword now. The eight fae still standing spread out in a circle around her. The moment holds. Then she moves. She slides across the tarmac. Eight batons go up. Eight batons fall. Sil gets the fallen half-kobold's baton off the ground, parries the first.

She doesn't do such a great job with the other seven.

She makes no sound as they hit her. *Never let them know if it's working,* she has been taught. Never give an inch. Always take a yard.

The batons go up again. She moves again. She grabs the second fallen fae's baton.

Now, she comes up swinging. And her left knee doesn't want to work anymore, and she has a sharp pain in her side, and her blood is in her eyes, but she is smiling. She has been trained for this. She has been through worse.

Sil brings the first baton directly into one dryad's face, cracks her cheekbones and sees her eyes bulge with a spray of blood. Sil pivots, brings the tip of the second baton into another gnome's throat. He clacks and gasps, drops to the floor clutching his neck.

Six fae spread in a circle about her.

They close again. Life blurs. Thought leaves. Action is reaction. One move leads to another, and she flows like water. Batons crack against bone. She lets out no sound. She gives up no clue. And her batons paint the air red.

Now there are two fae spread out either side of her, a pixie and the chatty half-dryad. Sil is still smiling.

It's not joy. It never is. In truth, everything hurts. Even through the adrenaline. And these two fae still seem fresh. Rather, it is that she has been taught to smile. Opponents, she has been told, find it unnerving if she smiles as she kills.

She launches her baton at the head of the pixie. He parries it away but it doesn't matter. Sil's already used the distraction to close the distance.

She brings her remaining baton up between the pixie's legs with enough force to lift him from the ground.

That, though, gives the half-dryad enough time to get his baton around Sil's neck.

She gets her hand up in time so it's her own knuckles he's crushing against her windpipe. She's not dead yet. She gasps as best as she's able. She kicks down against the throat of the pixie whose balls are now somewhere in orbit around his spleen. She drives the heavy heel of her boot into his throat once, twice, three times.

Black is closing in on the corners of her vision as the half-dryad throttling her wrestles her away from his fallen comrade. He's yelling. He's upset. She wants to be able to use that, but she can't get enough air to taunt him. She wants to smash her skull into his nose but he's a full head taller than her, and he's crushing her against his chest. He's leaning back, putting his weight into it, making it hard for her to get enough leverage to kick his kneecaps. He knows what he's doing.

The fae has his feet set wide. She swings her legs back between them. Then she heaves herself forward, pushes off his ribs with her elbows. Her neck creaks with pain. She wants to scream but she can't get the air. She folds her legs, drives her heels as hard as she can into the dryad's knees. Does it again and again, hearing him grunt with pain. One kneecap goes, sliding away beneath her impact, and she feels her opponent's scream of pain more than she hears it. They go skidding sideways, the baton still around her neck. All the light still fading.

They hit the ground and the grip on her neck goes slack. She rolls away gasping, struggles to all fours, counting the seconds she can expend. Then she's up. Her sword is still sprouting from the chest of the gnome she skewered. She plucks it free, flicks blood from the blade.

The half-dryad is trying to get up. His leg buckles and he screams. She dips the tip of her blade into his throat. He convulses, goes still, all the fight leaking out of him and spilling over the dirty ground.

And that is the fight all done. There are four fae still breathing, but Sil knows they're broken before they do. Then they turn and run. She takes a second, just one, to inhale, to reset.

She looks up, checks the car. Jag is not in it. A quickening of the pulse. She scans. She sighs. Typical.

Jag is running. Jag is panicking. She is not looking. She has not seen the fae stepping out of the shadows, right in front of her.

Jag is tall for a goblin, with the well-toned physique that wealth, privilege, and personal trainers allow. She comes up to this fae's chest. A dryad surely, all sinew and pent-up rage—the protector of some oak tree long since turned to wood chips.

Jag steps back. Sil hears a squeak of fright.

Sil is forty yards away. She is fast, but she is not that fast. She cannot cover the distance in time.

The dryad cracks her knuckles. Sil takes aim.

She launches her sword as hard as she can. It whirls end-over-end. It whistles past Jag's ear. She squeaks again as the blade splits the massive dryad's face.

"Timber," Sil whispers to herself as the dryad falls.

It takes Jag a while to get it together, to stumble back to her. She leans heavily against the car roof. "Are you OK?" She reaches out a hand to Sil. Sil brushes it off. "Did they…?" Jag looks up and down the street. "What the fuck was that?"

Sil still can't talk. Her throat hurts too much. She shrugs. She hobbles to the car.

"You should sit down," Jag says. "You're hurt."

Sil ignores her. She looks at the engine. The fan belt is still broken. The car is still so much useless metal. Jag goes to the car door. Now she listens. Sil puts a hand on Jag's. The goblin princess looks up, and Sil shakes her head.

"What?" Jag says. "The car? It won't...?"

Sil shakes her head. She points toward the city center. The light of the Houses seems very distant from here.

"We should call someone," Jag says. "Call the House. Have someone come and pick us up. There must be a working payphone around here somewhere."

Sil looks at her. Until Jag gets it.

"But we can't," she says slowly. "Because someone made a move against us, and it could be someone in the House. We don't know who's loyal and who isn't." She looks around. "A cab...?"

Sil shakes her head.

"I know, I know. We can't trust a fae driver." Jag balls her fist. "My fucking father..." She looks around, increasingly desperate. "So how?"

Sil points to Jag's feet. To the horizon.

"We have to walk?" Jag's eyes are round circles of shock. "But... your leg. Fae just tried to assassinate us!"

Sil nods. She cannot afford to believe this will be the only attempt on them. But while the evidence suggests a plot within House Red, Sil has to assume they still have more allies there than anywhere else in the Iron City. So, she starts walking. She doesn't wait to make sure Jag follows. Sil knows she will, and there is no time to waste on coddling her now.

The night is young, after all, and there are many miles left to go.

Bee

"Now?" Tharn says to Bee as they stand among the throng in the factory where the Iron City's rebellious fae are gathering. That self-same crowd is providing full-throated support for Skart's answer to Bee's shit-stirring question. "Now, you choose to be a dick about this?"

Bee steps down from the chair he found to put his head above the crowd and throws up his hands. "If not now, when? The whole point of participating in this uprising is to help shape its future. Now is our chance to interrogate its architects."

"Now, you can posture in front of a crowd. Vain as a goddamn sidhe."

"Hey," a sidhe protests nearby, but there's not much belligerence in it.

Bee grins. "For someone who preaches unity, Tharn, you think in painfully binary ways."

Tharn rolls his eyes. Bee steps up on his box again, watches as Skart on his makeshift stage puts down another question.

"—why unity is critical. The goblins must face a united front."

Someone whoops.

Bee feels like there is something slippery about the way Skart answers questions. The down-home honesty seems like a front. For all that he hands out answers as if he is doing his best to be as clear as he can, there is something purposefully evasive in all he is saying.

"You say you can't predict the future," Bee yells. "That's fair. But you can speak to intent. You can speak to hope. So, I ask you this, can you assure me that your intent here and now is to establish a future where we coexist in peace with the goblins? Can you assure me that you don't intend a return to old ways?"

He steps down. He smiles savagely. *Deal with that one, you old bastard,* he thinks.

Up on the stage, Skart licks his lips. "What do I want?" he says. He cocks his head to one side. "Me?" Then he smiles. "I want my childhood. I want a world gone away. I want my family back. I want my mother and father not slaughtered before me. I want trees to the heavens, and birdsong in my ears. I want streams running clear. I want to run free with them. I want everything the world promised me." He looks Bee straight in the eye. "That's what *I* want. That's what you want to hear, isn't it?

"But—" And now Skart looks away from Bee towards the crowd. He spreads his arms. "This isn't about me. This is about us. That's the point of our movement. That's the point of unity. It's about the collective. It's about the whole. It's about a future we negotiate together."

And it is so close to what Bee said earlier, he knows he should dive onboard. He should raise his fist and swear to bring it down on whatever skull the rebellion asks. And yet, still he hesitates. Because Skart has answered, and answered with honesty, and yet he has also skirted around the heart of the question.

But the tide in the room is rising. Voices are lifting. Fae are cheering. The excitement boils. Skart is shouting, directing fae to speak to coordinators, to get locations that they will need to take and hold.

Bee looks to Tharn, to the rest of the Fae Liberation Front.

"What?" Tharn asks him. "What has he said that you disagree with? Tell me so I can cram your hypocrisy so far down your throat that you shit it out again."

Bee shrugs. "It's how he said it."

Beside them, Harretta laughs. She's not the only member of the Fae Liberation Front to do so.

Tharn shakes his head. "I will never do anything but love you, Bee," he says, "but you are a prideful piece of shit. Practice what you preach. Give in to the collective."

Bee chews his tongue. From someone else, he's not sure he

would take that kind of talk, but Tharn isn't trying to wound him or score cheap points. So, perhaps he's right.

Tharn turns to the others. "Do we wish to kick goblin ass tonight?" he shouts.

They cheer. Of course they do. And Bee loves them for it.

"Alright," he says. "It's on."

Skart

Skart makes sure he gives the young bryad his orders personally: a smelting factory near both the edge of the Fae Districts and the Iron Wall itself. He claps the lad on his hefty shoulder.

"I appreciate your spirit," he says. "Even if we talk at cross purposes, don't think I don't." He smiles. "The revolution is a dialog." An old adage.

The bryad looks at him, and Skart can still feel the resistance in him.

"What's your name?" He tries a different approach.

"Bee."

One of Bee's friends leans in. "And he's naturally an ornery bastard."

"Excellent." Skart laughs. "Ornery bastards are exactly what this world needs."

Bee gives a grudging smile. Skart clasps his hand hard, gives it a firm shake.

"We'll see this factory done," Bee tells Skart, and Skart nods.

Skart watches the bryad walk away. He is under no illusions that this Bee trusts him. But he trusts him enough, Skart thinks, to stick to the plan tonight. And—as long as every other plan Skart has goes well—that should be enough.

All the other assignments have been handed out. The delicately orchestrated plan of occupation, vandalism, and destruction is in place. Every rebel in the Iron City is ready to rise up and tear it all down.

Skart stands on the stage once more. A grace note, he thinks. A final word to send them on their way.

"Tonight," he tells them, "all our futures change. Tonight, we redefine everything we can be. So go. Fight. Struggle. Succeed. Make the world a better place for all of us."

That's it. The fuse is lit. They cheer and he raises his arm. He brings it down. And in the Iron City, a rebellion begins.

6

Knull and Void

Knull

"No. I'm never dealing with you again, you piece of shit."

"Yeah, I would do a deal with you, but I'm busy sticking a scorpion down my briefs."

"Are you addled as a pixie? Is this a cry for help? Are you having a breakdown? Why would you call me? Why?"

"I don't buy from you, Knull. I sell to you. You're doing this backwards."

And, also: "Go fuck yourself." Knull hears that one a lot. A track glitching over and over on the far end of the payphone. He is wedged into the narrow confines of the booth, fumbling copper teeth into a narrow slot. He tries to find a way to take the weight off his foot. He tries to not drop the Dust.

Another number tapped in. Some understanding soul has put masking tape over all the metal numbers, so his fingers aren't completely burned.

The phone rings. And rings. And rings. And then, as he's about to give up hope, a click, and a voice. "Yo."

"Hey!" Knull says, trying to get warmth into his voice, although all he can manage by this point is the output of a low-wattage space heater. "Kloffa, dude. Long time."

"Who this?"

"It's me, bro." Knull tries to pretend he has hope. "It's Knull."

"Knull? Who the fuck is Knull?"

"Knull! Your best dealer. Your number-one customer. The brixie who turns Dust into coin faster than anyone you know. Come on, Kloffa. I know you're playing with me."

A fumbling of the receiver on the far end, and muffled, "Do we know any motherfuckers named Knull?"

Knull sighs. "Knulleridge Ethelred." His goddamn parents. How long, he wonders, did it take them to come up with the most embarrassing name possible for their first-born son?

"Oh," says Kloffa on the other end of the line. "Oh."

"Yeah, dude!" Knull says, with cheer he found when rummaging down in the basement of his soul—lint-covered and tacky.

"Where you at?" Kloffa asks.

"Me, oh I'm at—" And then Knull hesitates. "Why?" he asks.

"So I can send my crew round to fuck you up!" Kloffa screams. "You owe me money, asshole! You owe me my goddamn money!"

Knull hangs up while Kloffa is still yelling. Knull regards the sack of Dust. He regards his mental list of numbers to call.

It is time for plan B.

Edwyll

Home. It's where the heart is. Edwyll knows this. Except, he also knows that that particular adage doesn't stop home from also being a half-collapsed shithole.

Still, he feels a dull glow of reassurance as he shoulders his way into the house, barging the warped wooden door through the piles of crap that always seem to accumulate in his parents' hallway. He has no idea where they come from. His parents hardly ever leave the couch. When do they find the time to collect all this junk? Who gives it to them? Why?

He has no answers, but he does find a distorted form of comfort in these familiar questions, in the familiar scenes this house contains. All its hurts and edges are blunted by the knowledge that he has survived them in the past. He can survive them again.

He has come here with purpose. He has come to claim his parents' small sculpture of the White Tree. It is the classic symbol of the fae. It is the sigil that adorned the banner they all fought beneath when they marched against Mab's swarming hordes. It is the icon of the gone-away world, rendered in three clumsy dimensions and perched upon the mantelpiece of every fae home Edwyll can think of.

He has been trying to do something with the White Tree for a year now, playing with ways to reclaim the symbol, reformat it for a new generation. He wants to make it meaningful again, dreams of using it to unite the fae once more, help them rediscover the possibilities of life instead of wallowing in what they've lost.

It's not gone well so far, but events in the bar and talking to Lila have helped the project feel urgent again, vital even. Someone has to change the trajectory the fae are on. And Edwyll is not proud enough to assume it will be him, but also feels compelled to try. Reclaiming the kitsch china sculpture from this house will be the first step in his latest attempt.

He walks down the hall, past his old bedroom and his brother's, past the fetid stench of the kitchen. The living room is at the end of the hall, and he finds his parents where he expects them to be, draped on the couch like laundry waiting to be folded. His mother is out cold. A whittled stick of a woman, all the round jollity of brownie myth leached out of her by time and poverty. His father—all his pixie brightness bleached away—rolls his eyes in his direction.

"Hey," he mumbles.

"Hey, Dad."

He tries to sit up, upsets a bowl of cold chili balanced on his chest, spilling mushrooms and beetle wings down his shirt, then collapses back. "Hey," he says again.

Edwyll sighs. He tries to keep all the anger and fear of the evening down inside him, instead of spewing it out all over his father. It's not like the old pixie is truly capable of understanding him anyway. Not in this state. After a few breaths he says, "I'll clean that up."

He does the best he can, wiping his father down, carrying the bowl through to the wreckage of the kitchen. He stares at the devastation of plates, takeout containers, and mold, sighs again, and rolls up his sleeves.

His dad's still in the same place when he re-enters the living room. "Hot water's off again."

His father blinks at him, uncomprehending. For him, Edwyll knows, this information is like a message from beyond the Iron Wall: news about a world he can barely conceive any more.

"You're a good son," his dad says eventually.

It would almost be easier, Edwyll thinks, if the manipulation was purposeful. If it was obviously designed to put barbs into his skin. Then he could tear them out with a sense of defiance. But instead, they come at him with genuine love, floundering through life to give it to him, and he is left with this sense of obligation to clear their path a little.

"When did you last eat, Dad?"

His dad is getting it together a little, starting to find a way to be defensive through the haze of the Dust in him. "Chili," he manages. "Was gonna have it. You took it away."

"You spilled it, Dad."

"Yeah." A pause, then, "Yeah."

"You need to eat, Dad."

He nods. "I know. Something in the fridge." He flaps a hand thin as a bird's wing. "Make it later."

Edwyll wonders how much mold someone will have to scrape off whatever is lurking in the fridge to make it edible. He wonders if there's any way that sucker isn't him.

His brother just left. Turned his back and walked out on it all. And on the bad days, Edwyll genuinely thinks that looks like strength: the ability to turn his back on this pair. To abandon pity. And when he was in the kitchen washing someone else's blood off the back of his hands, yes, it felt like a bad day. And he does want to just grab the cheap china tree and run.

But if he's to take Lila's message to heart, if he's to turn his fear into strength, today is a not a day when he can abandon hope. Today is a day to be better than his brother. And if he's going to try to save the fae, shouldn't he start here?

"You're a good son," his dad says again, and Edwyll can hear the breath rattling in the cage of the old pixie's chest.

"Yeah, Dad," he says as he heads back to the kitchen. "Better than you deserve."

Granny Spregg

Waiting, Granny Spregg thinks, is the worst part. She has always been bad at waiting. Back when she still loved her husband, he called her "a restless spirit." That, of course, was before she discovered his own ambitions only included her as a stepping stone, and before she'd wrestled him to the floor and throttled the life from his sinewy neck. Still... a restless spirit. She remembers that phrase fondly enough, and she has ascribed much of her life's success to it. When others look for a moment's respite, she keeps pushing, out-thinking and out-maneuvering, and by the time her enemies lift their heads, she's often already won.

Except she's never beaten age. The sand in the hourglass has kept pace with her, year after year. And waiting has become harder and harder with each grain that falls.

She sits, now, in a chair, tapping her cane angrily. Thacker picks up on her mood. He moves around her in fretful circles, straightening already straight things, wittering in a birdsong of whimpers and grunts as he attempts to fill the room with something that isn't a sense of impending disaster, too afraid to simply ask her what exactly it is that they're waiting for.

Then it comes: two light taps on the door, quiet and respectful.

Inside the room's charged atmosphere the sound might as well be gunshots. Thacker squeals, drops a jeweled hairbrush. Granny Spregg finds she has—without thinking about it—stood straight up from where she was balanced on the edge of her chair. If this is to go well, she reprimands herself, she will need to be in far better control than this.

"Well?" She looks at Thacker. "See who it is."

Thacker looks like he wants to tell her to shove that idea elbow deep into her own asshole. Still, he moves across the room, puts a shaking hand on the door handle. He pauses, looks at her again. She sets her jaw. Thacker closes his eyes, opens the door.

One of the House's goblin servants stands there, dressed in tails and a pressed white shirt. House Spriggan does employ fae servants, of course, but they are not allowed in this inner sanctum where she and her children reside. This one has the slight swagger of a senior attendant, someone who cherishes the scrap of power he's been allowed to laud over others. Tattoos are just visible peeking out from his collar. A few iron studs have been punched through his long, pointed ears. He bears a silver tray. On the tray is a single glass of port.

"From your son, Privett," the servant says. "He tells me to tell you that it is a peace offering."

Granny Spregg tries hard not to roll her eyes. Privett couldn't be more obvious if he tried.

"Come on, then," she tells the servant. "Let's get it over with."

"Madame?" The servant's brow furrows.

She sighs. "Was it 'rest in peace'?" she asks. "Or…" She thinks a moment. "'This way she'll finally know peace'?" She shakes her head. "He laughed when he said it, didn't he?"

Thacker looks like he wants to ask what it is they're talking about.

The servant looks regretful. "Ah." He looks at the glass of port. "I believe what he actually said was: 'This way, I'll finally have some peace.'"

Granny Spregg legitimately groans out loud. The fruit of her own loins. She had always thought better of them.

"Always thinking about himself," she says.

The servant shrugs. "I wouldn't know."

"Erm?" Thacker manages.

"So," Granny Spregg says again, "as I said, let's get it over with."

The servant bows. "As you wish."

Then he hurls the silver tray at her, a flashing discus of thin metal.

It's an obvious gambit: distract her, close the distance. And when Granny Spregg was younger, she would have just taken the blow, and met him head on with her teeth bared. But now she is old, and her skin is thin, and she cannot afford such bravado anymore.

She lifts her cane to parry the tray, except her old bones betray her, and her reaction times would be laughable if they weren't the only thing keeping her from taking a flying tray to the tits.

The cane only makes it half the distance it needs to travel. Then the tray slams into her, and she crashes to the floor, agony blooming from her damaged ribs.

"Shit," is about all she really manages before the assassin has burst past the shrieking Thacker and is upon her.

The cane is good for something at least. She drives its point—the dryad's old shoulder bone—into the assassin's throat. He gawks and the first slice of his dagger goes wide. It's a short, curving blade, designed for gouging and ripping, for creating wounds that won't close easily. It's more than she warrants, if she's being honest.

Still, she sees, as the assassin reels back, trying to recover, to get the blade up for a two-handed strike into her heart, he really has gone for overkill: the edge of his blade glints purple.

Stumbling into view, Thacker brings a vase down on top of the assassin's head. It shatters. The vase, unfortunately, not the assassin's head. The vase, Granny Spregg reflects, once belonged to a sidhe princess. It was considered one of the most beautiful examples of fae porcelain in existence. Granny Spregg has been pissing in it for years.

The assassin collapses in a shower of yellow fluid. He's not out—his bellowing rage is testament to that—but Granny Spregg takes the opportunity to wrestle her legs free and kick her heels into his chest, beating him back. Thacker stares wildly, searching for more improvised weaponry.

The assassin frees himself from the tangle of thrashing limbs, is up in a single smooth motion. He backhands Thacker across the face, sends the gangly goblin reeling into a writing table. Ink and pens fly.

Thacker sags. The assassin whirls back to face Granny Spregg.

"A fucking eighty-year-old," he spits. Much of his deference is gone. That, though, Granny Spregg concedes, is likely to be the case when your hair is soaked with your opponent's stale piss.

Her own ascent to standing is slower. She levers herself up on her cane. The assassin kicks it out from under her. She sprawls face first into the carpet. He delivers a hammer blow to the back of her head. Black spots swim in front of her eyes.

She's still gasping in pain when he rolls her over onto her back.

He squats over her, legs astride her chest. "I must be losing my edge," he tells her. "You really shouldn't be this much work."

He brings the knife up.

This is a familiar sensation, Granny Spregg thinks. Overpowered. Outmatched. Death waiting to strike at her.

Sometimes, though, she knows, you don't win a fight because you're stronger, or faster, or because you're more skilled. Sometimes you just win because you're willing to do things that your opponent isn't. Sometimes you win because your will to live is stronger.

The knife comes down.

Granny Spregg's hand comes up.

The blade skewers her through the palm. The assassin grunts at the unexpected impact. Granny Spregg twists with all her wizened strength, biting back on the scream billowing inside her mouth.

The assassin wrenches back on the knife. She claws at its handle with blood-slick fingers, twisting her wrist back and forth, her old bones threatening to crack and shatter.

The assassin is so much stronger than her, it's like wrestling with a statue. To even the playing field, she punches him in the balls.

He squeals, finally relinquishes the knife.

"Thacker!" Granny Spregg shrieks. "My perfumes! The purple bottle! Quickly!"

Thacker is still pulling himself from the writing desk. He stares at her dazedly.

"Now!" she screams.

The assassin is recovering, snarling.

She dives at him, the blade still buried in her palm. She waves her arm wildly, backhanding at him with the protruding blade. He skips out of range.

"Bitch."

She's never liked that word. Her husband called her that. Look what happened to him.

She comes at him again. "You're already dead," he says.

She pauses, licks the blood from her dripping hand, grins at him with stained teeth.

"Other goblins," she says, "have been telling me that for the longest time, and yet—" She spits the blood at him, and he flinches back.

She dives for his throat, then. He ducks out of the way, sweeping out his leg, slamming his calf into her ankles with savage force. She falls, a spectacular pratfall, arms pinwheeling. Yet as she falls, she feels the blade catch him. Feels it scrape down his cheek. Then the floor rises up and knocks the breath from her.

She lies there gasping. The black spots are back. There is painful pressure in her chest. It takes her four attempts to flip over onto her back.

When she manages it, though, lying there gasping and defenseless, the assassin leaves her alone. He sits on the floor, holding his face. When he takes his hands away, he stares at the blood on his hands.

"Shit," he says quietly. "Shit."

"Thacker!" Granny Spregg screams. "The purple perfume bottle! Now!"

Thacker is still staring at her. “Is this the time—” he starts.

“I will carve the lungs from your fucking chest!”

Thacker runs to her bed chamber. She hears him rattling through glass bottles.

Her throat feels raw as she waits. Her heart races. There is a fire in her lungs that keeps rising and rising. The collar on her dress feels too tight.

All the fight has gone from the assassin. He sits in the remains of her piss pot, with tears leaking down his face. “You fucking killed me,” he says.

Granny Spregg speaks through gritted teeth. “You are not the first to come at me with a poisoned blade.”

For a minute she thinks he’s going to attack again, that his faith in his poison won’t be enough to stop him from wanting to truly finish the job. But he just spits at her. “At least I’ll be the last,” he says. He leans back, props himself up on his elbow. The poison will be affecting his vision already, Granny Spregg thinks.

“I got you.” He shakes his head. “Bitch.”

Thacker arrives. He is holding twelve bottles of perfume, each a different shade of lilac, violet, indigo, and… yes, there it is. She plucks the small porcelain vial from his hands.

“I do not like that word,” Granny Spregg tells the dying assassin. “So, because of that, I’m not going to share this.”

The assassin lowers himself back onto the floor. His breath is coming shallowly now, but he still has enough air in his lungs to laugh at her. “Well, I guess I’ll be the worse-smelling corpse,” he says. His mouth twists. “The shame might kill me.”

Granny Spregg smiles her own thin smile as she unscrews the diffuser from the vial with shaking fingers. She can’t feel her legs anymore.

"No," she says, then she puts the vial to her lips, tips, and pours. She lies back. "I'm afraid you'll just be the only corpse."

Knull

Home, Knull knows, is where the heart is. Which is why, he thinks, it is very important to carve your heart from your home's ribs, and put it somewhere worthy as soon as you're able.

The house is a sagging ruin, a collapsing pile of rubble. He'd feel bad for rats if they lived here. And yet, here he is again. No matter how far he runs, or how much he makes, its gravity always reclaims him.

He stumbles across the street, his ankle throbbing wildly. The brick of Dust feels like a lead weight. He's panting hard.

He finds the front door unlocked. There's no need for a latch, he supposes. There's nothing inside worth stealing.

As a makeshift safety measure, however, it appears his parents have wedged three tons of crap behind the door, so when he pushes on it, it only opens a few inches. And with his ankle the way it is, he can't get enough leverage to push the bastard thing open any wider.

He batters at the door, smashing the gap wider inch by inch. He knows it's no use calling for help. His parents are incapable of getting off the couch.

Except then someone does come, hurrying down the hallway toward him. And then, a moment later, he is eye to eye with his brother.

"Edwyll?"

"Knull?"

Their surprise is mutual, their wide eyes almost identical.

"What are you doing here?" Edwyll asks at the same time as Knull says, "Don't you live at that artists' squat now?"

They both stand there staring at each other. Edwyll is younger than Knull, a little shorter, a little thinner, his skin a lighter purple than Knull's dark blue, his hair the yellow of a sunset, compared to Knull's teak-colored mop. Their father's pixie blood is stronger in Edwyll than Knull. Perhaps that is why they have grown so far apart. Perhaps that is why Edwyll's jaw is jutting now.

"What are you carrying?" Edwyll demands.

This is not a question Knull wants to give an answer to any more than he wants to tell Edwyll what he's doing here.

"Just help me open the door," he says. Edwyll hesitates, then grunts, and together they force it wider, and finally Knull elbows his way in.

"What happened to your ankle?" Edwyll asks.

Another unwanted topic. Knull chews his bottom lip. This time, it doesn't cut it.

"Oh, screw you," Edwyll says. "You want to pretend you're doing something so fucking important and hush-hush. You're a petty self-interested drug dealer who left me here to deal with the shit you didn't have the balls to face. So at the very least you owe me…"

Knull's fists are balling as Edwyll trails off. Knull sees his eyes come to rest on the package of Dust.

He turns, trying to put more of his body between Edwyll and the drugs, almost speaking over his shoulder. "Look," he says. "I fell. I messed up my ankle. It's fine. I just need to stash something here for… probably less than a day. Then I'm gone. I was never here."

But it's too late. Of course it is.

"Holy shit, Knull," Edwyll breathes. "You… You can't put that here!" His voice is rising.

"Eddy?" a rumble from the living room at the end of the hall. Knull sees an arm flap like a wilted reed. "Who's it?"

"Shit," he whispers. "They're awake?"

"Dad is." He turns toward the living room.

"Don't tell them I'm here." Knull can't handle them. Not on top of everything else. Not tonight.

Edwyll looks at him, and Knull sees it for a moment: the desire to wound, to cut as deeply as Knull has cut before. And it would be easier, he thinks, if he didn't understand. His heart sinks as Edwyll turns away.

"It's no one," Edwyll calls to the living room. "Just the wind blowing through."

Knull finds his own gratitude slightly pathetic.

When Edwyll turns back, though, his jaw is set. "Now get out. Blow away. You cannot stash that here." He points at him, at the Dust. "That is… Shit, that is *so* much Dust. How did you get so much?"

Knull decides to just deal with the first half of that. "I *can* stash it here," he says. "I will. They'll never even know."

But now Edwyll's looking at his ankle again. Now he's doing the math. "Oh, you asshole," he says.

"It's not—" Knull says, the denial both automatic and automatically dismissed by Edwyll.

"Who?" Edwyll demands. "Who did you screw over to get this? Who did you steal from? What trouble are you bringing down on their heads?"

And there are better ways to handle this than anger, but they have known each other too long and fought about this too often for Knull to have any other reaction.

"Why are you even defending them? You know why I left. My whole childhood was them dumping their shit on me. So, yes, I get to dump whatever shit I like here now." He points at his younger brother. "On us. They are bad parents, Eddy. They deserve all the shit they get. More than I can give them."

Edwyll's jaw works.

"You call them bad—"

"They are."

"Weak."

"They are."

"But which one of us is back here, beaten up, trying to sell the same shit that broke Mum and Dad? Which one of us isn't strong enough to take on his responsibilities? I'm not here because it's fun, Knull. I'm not here because I can't tear myself away. I'm here because you turned and ran like a goddamn coward. You are everything you accuse them of and worse."

It's an old argument. So very, very old. They've been having it for years. And at its basis, Knull knows, is Edwyll's failure to understand the fundamental lesson of the Iron City: no one else is looking out for you. You have to focus on yourself or you will drown. And Edwyll's refusal to learn that, his desperate clinging to the twin anchors that are their drugged-out, wasted wrecks of parents, means that he will drown too. Faster than most.

"Do you honestly believe," he says, "that if I went into that living room right now, they would be able to remember my name right away?"

Edwyll's hesitation is all the opening he needs to push past his brother. "They won't find it," he says as he heads down the front hall to the door that leads to his old room. "Because I won't be stupid enough to leave it within six inches of the fucking couch. And when I come back, all my troubles will be gone. All of them. Because this is it, Eddy. This is the ticket out. I've done it. I'm doing it. And all I need to do is dump this here for one night so someone doesn't roll me in the streets and ruin it all."

Edwyll trails after him down the hallway, hesitating in the doorway to the bedroom as Knull pulls piles of old magazines out from under his bed.

"You should take some of it to someone who knows how to fix that ankle," he says grudgingly.

All fae can do magic when they take Dust, but some magic is harder to perform. Healing takes training, it takes a knowledge of which arteries and veins and nerves should be knitted together, a familiarity with muscle, tendon, and bone. Bad heals can lead to tumors, to clots, to necrotic flesh where blood vessels suddenly dead-end in ugly knots of tissue.

"I'm fine," he says, balancing awkwardly. "This will make everything better." He stuffs the Dust beneath his bed, shoving the magazines back to cover it. "This will be good for both of us." He wishes he didn't feel the need to justify himself, but it's there like a thorn beneath his skin.

He straightens, turns. "You should come with me," he tells Edwyll, suddenly expansive, suddenly not quite able to stand up to the pressure of the guilt. "When it's done. There'll be enough. We can escape. You don't have to do this. You don't have to be chained to them."

"Who will take care of them then, Knull? I know you love to ignore that problem, but it still doesn't go away."

"They need to take care of themselves."

"They can't."

"That's not an excuse."

Such an old argument. They both knows its shape. It doesn't get better from here. Knull bites back the words, breathes.

"The Dust will be gone tomorrow," he says.

"Just like you."

Except he's going to be gone long before then. He has a deal to hustle. A deal to change his whole life. To save it. And it could save Edwyll too, if only he'd let it.

7

And Away We Go

Jag

"Don't run."

Jag, two rapid steps down the street, hesitates and looks at Sil. Then she looks at the street around them. At the alleyways that look like they've been gouged into its edges. At the dead bodies Sil has left on the ground.

"I'm sorry," she says. "Your leg. It's just… this feels like a running sort of situation."

"That is not why." Sil's tone is as flat as an apartment block roof. "I can run if I need to. But we are approximately 8.6 miles from House Red Cap. You cannot run that far. If you do, you will exhaust yourself and slow us down. Conserve your energy and be smart."

Jag is almost certain Sil doesn't intend this as an admonishment. It still feels like one.

They set off, walking at a steady pace. And the limp in Sil's stride is almost gone, Jag notices. She moves like something caged. But, Jag thinks, she always moves that way. It's only under circumstances like this—the slaughterhouse smell of the fight still lingering—that you really notice it. Notice that more than a fae or a goblin, she can remind you of a dire wolf from the Iron War, waiting for its moment to strike.

So many things seem so much more apparent to Jag here and now. The sour garbage stench. The greasy feel of the wet asphalt. The silence that feels like a physical presence, muffling their footsteps. This doesn't feel like the Fae Districts to her. For her, the Districts are lively, smoke-filled places where fae jostle and jockey for a position at the bar, shouting at each other free of all the inhibitions of House life. For her, they hold a golden hue that seeps into skin and bone when a band starts to play.

There is no golden hue now. Not here. Here, there is the bruised amber of streetlights. There is the splash of failing neon, like sparks floating up from a smoldering fire. There are shadows eating up the light. And none of it feels beautiful.

Someone lurches out of a side street, and Jag flinches away from them. The fae—an elderly pixie with folds around his eyes deep enough to bury bodies in—just stands and stares.

These are not, Jag thinks, the Fae Districts she fell in love with. Here, there is none of the raucous, angry pride that has always filled her heart with excitement. Here, even the plastic aspidistras perched in windowsills are wilting.

She has always known she's out of place in the Districts. She's always known that her suits, rebellious and punky in the Goblin Houses, only ever read as the uniform of privilege among the patched work shirts and stained overalls of the fae, that her soft hands don't match the rough palms of the bartenders who take her coin with a look of disdain. She's always known.

And yet, she realizes, here, on these streets, on this night, she never has. She's never come close to seeing how far from home she really is here. Her imagination has had limits. The songs she's heard have made her see poverty as something beautiful and poetic. But it's not. Now, she sees poverty in the raw. Now she understands. Poverty is a weight pressing down, constraining, confining, squeezing the breath from hope and dreams. Here, the poverty throttles her.

She wants to run again. She wants to run faster, and faster, and faster. Except all she has to run to is the father who caused this place to exist.

Or the possibility of assassins who are scheming against them both.

Sil walks five yards ahead of Jag, her head sweeping back and forth in a smooth continuous motion.

"Do you remember where you lived?" Jag asks. "Back before my father came to get you?"

Sil's mother, so the story goes, was a sidhe maid who cleaned her father's halls. Then she caught Osmondo Red's eye and he had her clean a little more than that. She lived somewhere in the Districts for a while, Jag's heard, before Osmondo Red came to collect his bastard child. After that no one knows, though all imagine a shallow grave was involved. Jag has tried to get Sil to open up about it before, has tried to make their relationship closer to something sisterly, but Sil never talks about any of it. Sil never talks about anything except the here and the now, the threats and the required course of action. Osmondo has broken her, no matter that she is his kin. And Jag has never been able to put the pieces back together.

And still now, Sil doesn't even seem to hear the question, doesn't give the vaguest suggestion that she is even thinking of responding.

They walk on. The paint is peeling all around them. The windows are broken and patched with cardboard. Grills protecting storefronts are held together by duct tape where demi-dryads are forced to work behind countertops made from the remains of their grandmothers' own trees. And it all weighs on Jag, heavier and heavier, an anchor she's dragging back to her father's house.

Noise breaks through the oppressive silence, and Jag jumps again. Sil reacts too, twitching her head. There is commotion in the streets around them. Voices, and… running feet? Jag's pulse starts to thrum.

She concentrates, tries to work out the nature of the sound. The voices aren't exactly scared, nor angry, nor joyful. But they are also a little like all those things.

Sil, Jag realizes, is moving faster.

"What is it?" she asks.

Sil holds up a hand, and Jag bites her tongue. Her adrenaline surges. The voices are getting closer.

When they emerge, they come from a side street. There are perhaps twenty of them. Fae. Jag flashes back to the previous attack, but these fae are behind them, not cutting off their route home. And rather than wearing tight-fitting black, they're dressed in loose work clothes and ragged overalls.

And yet…

All of them do have kerchiefs pulled up to their eyes. All of them are carrying chunks of wood, or bats, or Molotov cocktails. And all of them do turn. And all of them do see Jag and Sil in their incongruent finery, here on the ragged edge of the city.

Jag looks to Sil. Their eyes meet.

"Now," Sil says. "Now, we run."

Skart

Skart wants to run, to skip, to dance. It is happening. Here, now, before his eyes: the collected fae rebels are marching out to war, to reclaim this city. They are marching out with dreams of tearing down the factories and occupying the halls of power. They are fired up and ready to unleash the fury of creatures constrained for fifty years. This night will run red, and all of it will be to his design.

The old dryad, Brumble, claps him on the back. Her smile is nearly as broad as her shoulders.

"Well done," she says. Her eyes are shining in the dark of the basement. "You did it."

He turns to her, shakes his head. "This is a victory for all of us, Brumble."

"You feigning modesty," she tells him, "is as pointless as a House Bogle riddle. We all know you're the architect here."

He pushes away from her, gives her a mock frown. "The rebellion," he says, "does not celebrate the individual but the whole."

She rolls her eyes. Around them, the rest of the old guard laugh. They're all a little giddy now. And that's good, but he can't afford for them to lose focus.

"To business," Skart says.

The room comes to life. Not every rebel in the Iron City has marched to war tonight. Successful anarchy, time has taught Skart, requires a little organization. So now, fifty fae arrange tables in the heart of the cleaned-out basement. They spread out maps, and tack lists onto cork boards, and modify assignments scrawled in chalk.

From where he stands, Skart sees each piece as part of the whole. A great symphony is filling his head, every instrument playing in harmony.

However, before he's done, he needs to confirm that one tune is being played where the others can't hear it.

"Excuse me," he says to the group. "There's something I have to attend to."

Brumble arches a thorny eyebrow but doesn't say anything as he retreats to the shadows at the back of the basement. An old abandoned office sits there. A plastic barrow-marker pinned above the doorway shows that it once belonged to a sidhe—a child or grandchild of the old grave guard who fell during Mab's sacking of Avalon. The door itself has been recently oiled and it opens without complaint or sound. On a dust-mired desk sits a new rotary phone. He makes his way to it, knocking aside piles of old paper and tearing cobwebs. He dials carefully, one eye on the door, then puts the receiver to his ear.

On the fifth ring, someone picks up.

"Took your time," Skart says. His pulse is coming quicker now. "Do you have it?"

There is a hesitation. Skart does not like that hesitation.

"No." The voice on the other end of the line is missing its usual brisk efficiency. It is… embarrassed.

"What do you mean 'no'?" Skart spits.

"I mean… I do not have the package. Another party interceded."

"Another party?" Skart has become an incredulous echo.

"We gave chase," says the voice, "but they…" It breaks off. "They eluded us."

Skart's ability to repeat outrageous statements fails him. He gawps wordlessly into the phone. Everything he has done. Everything he has set into motion…

"How are you fixing this?" he says finally.

"My team is already scouring the city."

"You have an estimated time of retrieval?" Skart struggles to keep his voice low. The last thing he needs is someone walking in to check on him now.

"Everyone on my team is good at their jobs," the voice says, "but we lack leads. Whoever did this left few traces. We don't think it was a known player. Perhaps—"

"You incompetent asshole!" The words burst out of Skart. He can't control them. Because this cannot fail. Because if it does then years of planning, and years of making everything certain, are for naught.

"I might remind you of who I am," says the voice. Anger has erased its embarrassment.

"I know exactly who you are," Skart says. "I hired you because of who you are. I hired you because this job cannot have loose ends, and you assured me you could snip them cleanly. And yet, here I am listening to you try to make excuses about being unable to handle something as simple as a fucking courier run."

The silence that follows froths with fury.

"Screw it," Skart says. "I'm coming. I can no longer be certain that you and your team won't fail me."

"I assure you—" the voice says.

"You assured me you'd have the Dust by now," Skart says, "but look where we are." He slams the phone down.

He stands in the center of the room breathing heavily. He feels old. He feels the weight of the years in his bones. The black growths beneath his skin. He rubs his arms, shakes himself. He has no time for self-pity. He has to leave. He has to fix this. Everything hinges on it.

The only exit, though, is through the heart of the rebellion he is supposed to be heading up.

When he leaves the office, he has arranged his features into a paternal smile. He walks in a straight line, and heads directly for the basement exit. He does not rush. He nods at the fae he passes, the smile still fixed on his lips. He passes a table with three brownies bent over it, all of them examining a map and talking about contingencies. He passes a second where someone is wiring up phones. At a third, sidhe and pixies are laying out magazines of ammunition ready for returning troops looking to restock. He smiles at them all.

Halfway there…

"Skart?" It's Brumble's deep voice. "Skart, where are you going?"

He doesn't have an answer. He doesn't give one. He pretends he hasn't heard her deafening boom.

"Is everything OK?" She's hurrying after him.

He doesn't know what to say. He doesn't know what to do. Everything was so well planned—but this wasn't part of the plan.

She catches up, puts a hand on his shoulder. He stops and turns, feigning puzzlement or concern. Whatever he can transmute his panic into right now.

"Is everything alright?" he asks her.

She blinks. "I just asked you the same thing. Where are you going? And why do you look like you're going to be killed when you get there?"

He opens his mouth. Nothing comes out. Lies fail him.

She knits her brows, wrinkling her face until she is no prettier than a Spriggan. And how long, he wonders, will it be before her concern becomes suspicion?

But just because he can't lie, he suddenly realizes, it doesn't mean he has to tell her all of the truth.

"I'm terrified," he says in hushed tones, keeping the smile fixed on his mouth. "It's all going to fall apart, and I am too old and weak to take that."

Brumble stares at him. His whole future pivots on this moment. Then her eyes fill with sympathy and she puts her other massive hand on his other shoulder and holds him. "Oh, Skart," she whispers. "No, it's not. You're not. This is our night. This is happening."

He lets out just a sliver of his panic: a thin laugh. "I know. I know." He's hyperventilating slightly, but the lies are loosening on his tongue. "But I just… I need a minute. I need air. I can't let anyone see me like this."

Brumble nods, her eyes full of understanding. "Of course."

He nods. "Cover for me?" If he doesn't have lies, hopefully she does.

"Of course." She nods again. "We've got this, Skart. Your plan is going to work. It's rock solid."

He takes a deep quavering breath. "I'll be back. As soon as…" He reaches for something. "…when I'm steady."

Another moment, and then finally she releases him. He does his best not to scurry away. To be slow and steady. But it's hard knowing how wrong Brumble is. It's hard knowing that his plan is already in tatters.

Edwyll

Edwyll stands outside Knull's old bedroom for a long time. The poster for an old ogre metal band is still tacked up to cover the spot where, seven years ago, Knull punched the door and broke three of his fingers. Now, part of him wants to fling the door open, march in, seize the brick of Dust, and hurl the whole mess with all the danger and temptation it holds out into the street. It shouldn't be here. It wasn't fair to put it here.

And then there are the other, darker temptations too: to use it himself; to buy his own power.

He would spend the money more wisely than Knull. He's sure of that. He would use it to do better things. To get his parents out of this hovel. To help the other fae in this neighborhood. To empower them, enable them. He could help lift a whole street out of poverty, help the other fae see what they could achieve if they banded together. He could…

He couldn't sell it. He doesn't know the fae Knull does. And even if he could they'd be more likely to steal from him, the same way Knull had stolen the Dust to begin with. And even if he were to succeed, the foundations of the whole enterprise would be septic, would be based on theft, and addiction, and sucking more and more fae down into the mire of trying to recapture the past, one snort at a time.

He shakes himself. A tremor that runs through his whole body. He chose to be different from Knull a long time ago. He's not going to revisit that decision now. He has picked his own path out of the Fae Districts. A harder path, perhaps, than Knull's, but a cleaner one.

Art. Art will save him. And if he does it right, it will save other fae without leaving a stain on his conscience.

He turns his back on the bedroom, heads back down the hall to the living room. He came here to get something. It's sitting on the soot-stained mantelpiece, no more than six inches tall, its clumsy branches pointing to the ceiling. The porcelain White Tree. He picks it up, slips it into his messenger bag among the paint tubes and spray cans.

"Eddy?" his dad calls from the couch. His mother has started to snore.

"I'll be back in a few days, Dad. OK?"

"You're a good son," his dad says, and closes his eyes again.

If I do it right, Edwyll thinks, *I can save them.*

He heads out into the Iron City, and the night. He feels skittish and high-strung out on the streets, eyes searching for white-haired half-fae killers. The presence of the brick of Dust back at the house doesn't help either. There's too much danger on all sides.

His heightened nerves let him sense the change in the city's atmosphere more quickly than he might otherwise. He hesitates outside the local printing press, head up like a fox scenting for fresh garbage. It seems to him that the Fae District's typical slow slump into sleep is inverted tonight. Instead of a few staggering drunks mumbling to themselves, he can see fae scurrying back and forth, yelling and calling to each other.

He thinks that perhaps some party somewhere got out of hand. A crowd high on Dust charging through the streets, remaking the world in small stupid ways, inviting eventual reprisals when the goblins find out.

The revelers are coming closer now, he realizes, and he shrinks back into shadows, adrenaline still sparking, images of the bloodbath in the bar still playing in front of his eyes. The crowd's calls come clearer. A brash jumble of excitement and anger. Above him, the building's façade peers down grimly.

He should have brought some of Knull's Dust, he thinks. Just a pinch. Just for protection. Lila is always telling him to be more practical.

The group comes running down the street whooping. Hooded jackets and kerchiefs mask their features. Guns and clubs are brandished. He braces himself, grabs in his bag for something to use in defense, finds that he is—absurdly—holding a fountain pen like a sword. These are not the circumstances, he is sure, under which it is mightier.

But the group doesn't surround or menace him. Instead, someone tries to high five him.

"Brother!" one fae shouts, a shyad—a dryad-sidhe mix—from the look of her, skin a pale gray, whorls on her cheeks lending her an unworldly beauty. "Tonight you are liberated! Tonight you are a free fae in a free city. Tomorrow you will be king!"

She bows and somehow it doesn't feel like mockery. Edwyll half-bows back. The mob cheers.

"Now," the shyad says, "if I could ask you to step aside. You are on the very threshold of the building we desire to visit."

"Fuck yeah!" shouts a gnome from the back of the crowd, and a few others laugh.

Edwyll doesn't know what is going on, and he is still very aware of their weapons, but he doesn't feel any sense of threat from this group.

"All yours," he says, and steps away. He pauses a few yards back, curious as to what such a group could want with the local printing press. He sees four of the fae up at the door, holding something heavy. He peers, then gasps as they throw a small steel battering ram into the door lock.

"But this—" he starts to say, but then they do it again. The lock cracks loudly. The door flies open.

But this is our *factory*, he had been about to say. Because he does feel a sense of ownership over it. This is the printing press where half of his friends work, where most of their parents have worked, where his own parents pick up odd jobs when they're together enough or desperate enough to leave the house. Where he has helped move the massive reams of paper when the collective hasn't had enough work for him, and when the bars don't need someone extra on the taps or washing dishes in the kitchen. He has grown up breathing this factory's fumes, and watching its ink stain skin and streets. The dull iron ache of its heavy machinery in his gums is as familiar as the rumble of hunger in his belly.

Of course, the factory is not really *theirs*—it belongs to some Goblin House, and green-skinned bosses occasionally come to visit and berate everyone, and cut pay—but it has defined the rhythms of the neighborhood that he has thought of as home for so long. When it is busy, they all are. When it suffers through hard times, they all do. And now this gang of fae is violating it.

The fae seem to care nothing for his feelings, though. They pour through the ragged doorway, still whooping. Two hold out cans of red spray paint as they go, staining the frame like a wound. He stares after them. The whole incident has probably taken less than a minute. He is not sure what to do about it. What he can do about it.

Use it, Lila would tell him. He tries to heed the lesson.

He is about to step away, about to decidedly not get involved and keep himself clean of whatever chaos is about to happen, when a sound erupts from within the confines of the factory: a sharp, barking retort. He jumps at the suddenness of it, but can make no sense of it.

It comes again—an angry, violent sound. Then again. A rising cacophony of small explosions, each one cracking through the night.

He was curious too long, he thinks. As soon as he saw these fae coming he should have started to move away.

The shyad appears in the doorway, her back to him, swaying wildly. Still Edwyll can't put it together. Is she drunk?

Then she collapses, and Edwyll sees that her whole chest is sheeted with blood. It pools around her in a slow ebbing tide.

Someone else appears in the shadowy room beyond the doorway and the body. Edwyll hears more small explosions, sees sharp flares of light. The figure twists and spasms. Chips of brick fly from the frame, stinging his skin.

Gunshots, he realizes. *I am hearing gunshots.*

Bullets spatter against the doorframe. They whine through the air around him.

Then he is running, hands over his head, bellowing in shock and alarm. Then he is searching desperately for cover.

Granny Spregg

Granny Spregg clatters through the halls of House Spriggan. Her cane taps and clacks. Thacker scurries after her. Everything feels very familiar. Everything, she knows, has changed.

"Knock," she commands when she and Thacker arrive at the door to House Spriggan Central Command. "Beat on it like your daddy beat on you."

Thacker grimaces. But in Granny Spregg's opinion, if he doesn't want her to use his personal information against him, then he should learn to hold his drink better.

Thacker knocks—loud and long. After a moment, a uniformed goblin answers.

"Madame Spregg?"

"Could you tell me," she asks, sweet as a saccharine-coated dagger, "is my son still here?" She beams. "I have a gift for him."

The goblin nods. "Major General Privett is still—"

She pushes past this minor nuisance in a uniform and surveys the bustling room. Privett stands at its center, gesticulating like a Dust-addled semaphore messenger. General Callart nods and smiles along, waiting to get back to doing his job properly.

It is Callart who sees Granny Spregg first. He clears his throat. Finally, Privett turns.

This is the moment she has been waiting for. The expression on his face. The widening of his eyes and the contracting of his pupils. The slight tremor in his jaw. This makes the throbbing pain in her punctured hand worthwhile. This sends shivers running through her old body.

"Mother," he manages.

"I brought," she tells him with a growing smile, "a peace offering." She gestures for Thacker to step forward. Her attendant bows his head and proffers a silver tray. On it is a single glass of port.

He stares, transfixed by the glass.

"I feel that we left on bad terms. I wanted to make it up to you." She pushes the tray closer to him. "Please, drink."

He hesitates. The whole room is staring.

"Mother—" he starts.

"Shhh," she hushes him. "No need to say a word."

She has them all in the palm of her hand. Privett takes the glass. The tremble in his jaw has reached his hand.

General Callart clears his throat. He, she has to remind herself, has gained his position through merit rather than through the station his parents held when they fucked. "I hate to ask this, Madame Spregg," he says, "but are you entirely sure this port is still good? It looks remarkably… purple."

Granny Spregg smiles at him. At her son. "An unusual grape," she says, "but I believe Privett is familiar with it." She holds Privett's gaze. "Please," she tells him, "drink up."

Privett gets the glass halfway to his lips but doesn't seem to have the strength to lift it any higher.

And the whole room stares. And they all know that she has won.

All the aches in her old body seem to fade.

"Madame Spregg," General Callart cuts in again, "when you were here earlier, weren't you requesting the assistance of a division of soldiers?"

She pauses before she answers. Because why shouldn't she luxuriate in this?

"Oh yes," she says finally. "I believe I was."

"Major General Privett," says General Callart, "given the recent change in circumstances we were just discussing, perhaps we could spare your mother a few troops?"

Privett is still staring at the glass of port. "What?" he says.

"Your mother," says Callart. "We could spare her some troops now, couldn't we?"

Privett's eyes stay on the glass for another beat. Then finally he looks up. "Erm," he manages. He looks at his mother. She adopts her best withering look, the one that always reduced him to tears when he was a child. Which, of course, he still is.

"Yes," Privett says. "Yes, whatever you say."

Everyone is still staring, and the little shit knows it.

"If you'll excuse me," he manages. And then he sweeps from the room, as imperious as a school child all dressed up in Daddy's clothes. He's still carrying the untouched glass of port with him.

The door swings shut. General Callart smiles. He bows slightly. "Madame Spregg," he says, "I believe the room is yours."

8

Fight Night

Bee

The ache of the Iron Wall grows stronger as Bee approaches the smelting factory. It growls in his gut and creaks in his bones. The ringing in his ears is intensifying by the minute, and he knows it will last for days after this.

Next to him, Tharn rubs his jaw. "Always gets me in my back teeth."

"This is a shit assignment," someone says.

"Because Bee couldn't keep his mouth shut," Tharn agrees.

Next to Bee, Harretta rolls her eyes. "Because the Fae Liberation Front is all about following orders without question now, is it?"

No one picks the fight, though. They're all feeling the Wall. They're all feeling the rising tension of their goal as it comes closer.

It's a simple enough assignment, of course. Occupy the factory. Deny access. And rig the place so that if they are forced to retreat, the means of production are blown to kingdom come.

What's more, they've been given a good, defensible position. In fact, Bee is forced to concede, it's a good, defensible plan: hold the city hostage; stop the machinery from turning; dam the flow of gold in and out of goblin pockets.

But he, the Fae Liberation Front, and the other front-line assault forces are only part of this plan. While they hold the factories, provocateurs will slip into the streets and ensure that the goblins don't keep their cool or set up drawn-out sieges. Instead, these agents will drive spurs into the goblins' flanks and send them hurtling heedless towards these good, defensible factories. And from them, Bee and others like him will defend for as long as it takes. Because although they know that they will suffer countless casualties, they also know that their losses will be nothing compared to the damage they are going to inflict on the attacking goblins. And that, of course, is the breaking point: that slaughter. Because it is seeing the goblins fall that will break the shackles of fear holding the city's masses placid. And liberated from their terror, the fae will rise up with their brothers and sisters, and the Iron City will fall, and this jewel in Mab's crown will be shattered to pieces forever.

At least, that's the plan.

So for now, Bee sees, it will be days spent close to the Iron Wall, its rusty saw blade cutting into all that is natural and magical within him, polluting him.

And all because he couldn't keep his mouth shut.

But it's not a fight worth picking. It's not a fight that matters. It's the *cause* that matters. It's the liberation of the fae. And that is what they are doing here in the end. Fractious goals or no, all of the Iron City's rebels are united by that cause. They are finally doing something. So they hold their bickering, and they creep ever closer to the factory.

They cover the last thirty yards at a flat run. They pile up on either side of the big wooden gates. Green paint peels from them in long curls.

Another of the Liberation Front, Jerrell, has been given the bolt cutters. The chain holding the gates shut snaps with one bite of their heavy jaws. They push the gates open—each one large enough to admit even House Troll's tallest members—and brandish their weapons, but the courtyard beyond is unlit and silent. Shadowy mountains of ore loom. A flatbed truck, parked on a diagonal, bisects the space. Wheelbarrows are lined up like impatient workers waiting for their shift to begin.

Tharn signals and they spread out wide. Bee has been given a pistol and a length of aluminum chain to defend himself. He shouldn't need any of it. The factory should be dead and cold tonight. But they have to be prepared. He has been told to be ready to use the pistol only as a weapon of last resort. They cannot afford its noise tonight. The fewer who know of their presence inside the factory at this point, the better. He wraps the chain tight around his fist now, and lets a length of it trail beside his thigh.

The courtyard is clear. Bee points at a door leading into the main body of the factory. They swarm toward it.

Inside, everything is shadow. Everything smells of rock, and dust, and metal. The furnaces lie dead and cold. Massive machinery crowds in on them. The surrounding steel deepens the ache in Bee's bones.

They move at a crawl. Almost no light makes it into the factory's monolithic interior, and Bee is virtually blind. Nearby, Harretta smacks her knee against something, then curses, mostly because she's a sidhe, and of all of them, except perhaps the half-kobolds, she should be the best in the dark. Still, she is faring better than many. The whole group clank off obstacles as they go. Muttering and disagreements flicker in and out of existence. Adrenaline is going cold and fear is edging in.

"Can we risk some light?" Tharn whispers.

"Yes," Bee replies quietly. At this point, he honestly thinks it would be the less obtrusive option. He pulls out a lighter, flicks it on. The flame is paltry, though. If anything, it makes the darkness seem bigger.

Someone else pulls out a flashlight. It's Jerrell again, Bee sees, he of bolt-cutting fame.

"Well," Bee says as the beam of light slices through the darkness, "that's the element of surprise gone and fucked, isn't it?"

Jerrell gives him the finger. The shadows retreat. Everyone laughs in a space become suddenly mundane.

And then the first shots ring out, and Jerrell's head explodes like an overripe melon.

Skart

Across the Fae Districts, now far from the factory that recently birthed his rebellion, Skart is rising through the air. The elevator surrounding him rattles and shakes like a grandfather gyrating to the songs of his youth. Skart curses it at length, but the oblivious machinery moves no faster. He looks at his watch. Despite the threats and money he hurled at his cab driver, he has already been gone from the rebellion's headquarters for almost half an hour. That is too long.

Finally, the elevator shudders to a halt. Skart heaves the folding steel door open, not bothering to wrap his fingers in his sleeves to protect them from the metal's bite—his skin is already scarred, his body already riddled with small black tumors; caution is a long way behind him now. A dryad—spirit to some cedar tree stump somewhere, all burls and brawn—blocks his exit. A machine gun is slung idly across her chest.

"I'm here to see Merrick," Skart snaps, trying to push past the broad fae.

The dryad's massive hand holds him steady.

"Merrick!" Skart shouts.

"Let him go." Merrick speaks from beyond the dryad's bulk. The mercenary has regained much of her confidence since her phone call with Skart. Here, surrounded by her team, she feels safe.

Released, Skart straightens his shirt as he crosses to the open penthouse apartment door. Merrick stands at the center of the slaughterhouse scene beyond. She sneers at him, the perfect stereotype of smug sidhe superiority. A massive goblin bodyguard lies at her feet, one of House Troll's lesser sons, his chest caved in by a shotgun blast. The apartment's gnome owner, Cotter, is slumped on the couch, mutilated, his brains upon the wall.

Skart balls his fists.

"What?" Merrick asks. "You didn't hire me for my subtlety."

"I hired you," Skart says, "for results, but I don't see any evidence of those either."

Merrick's swagger sours. "And they'll come even slower with you here, getting in my way."

"Tell me what happened." Skart is eager to take the most direct route from Merrick talking shit to eating it.

Merrick doesn't even have the decency to appear abashed as she tells the tale. "Cotter wouldn't give up where he keeps his stash," she says. "I got bored asking, figured we could get the answers quicker on our own. We didn't find anything in the apartment, so I expanded the search area. While we were out of the apartment, someone snuck up the fire escape. They knew right where to go."

"Show me."

Merrick's expression doesn't get any friendlier. "Gerretta," she calls to the dryad in the hallway. "Show Mr Skart—"

"No," Skart interrupts. "You."

Merrick arches an eyebrow. "You really sure you want to piss me off?"

Skart keeps his voice under control. "Are you sure you want to get paid? Because if I'm either disappointed in you or a corpse that doesn't happen."

He meets Merrick's gaze head on and doesn't blink. As much as it would shock Merrick to hear it, he has seen far worse than she has to offer.

Finally, Merrick grunts. "The kitchen," she says, and leads the way.

Skart sees how it was done right away. A magical lock in the back of the fridge. Dust required to get Dust. It makes him wish he'd had the funds to deal with Cotter directly rather than through Merrick. He thinks he might have preferred the drug dealer to this self-important thug.

He pushes through the narrow opening in the back of the fridge, views the hidden room where the Dust was prepared. He picks up a small baggie, weighs it in his hand.

"And you have no leads," he says. It is not a question.

Merrick lurks back in the entranceway, casting shade. "We'll have them soon."

"No." Skart shakes his head. "You won't. You are a blunt instrument and now this needs a scalpel."

Merrick puffs up like a bullfrog, but Skart holds up a hand. "You will still be paid. I'll see to that. But your work is done."

Merrick works her jaw. She doesn't like the insult, but the cash will take the sting out of it. She slouches away, grumbling.

Skart waits until the apartment is quiet. He opens the baggie, regards the pure white powder within. A hunger wakes in him.

He tips the baggie and pours its contents into his mouth.

The power burns in him. It tears a hole. It shatters the shackles the Iron Wall has put on his soul and suddenly all the majesty, all the beauty, all the magic of the world comes bursting back to him. It breaks him down, and it makes him something primal. His skin splits, and power steams from the rips. It scalds the flesh around his eyes, his nostrils, his ears. When he exhales, it boils on his breath.

And it is so beautiful to be this way. It is so very good to burn. He would take more, and more, and more of the Dust if he could. He would open up his heart and give birth once again to the world gone away. A light—golden and green—is glowing inside him. He can hear birdsong. He can hear the river's chuckle. He can smell the flowers in bloom.

But then he pulls himself back from that brink. He wrestles with the power and its siren song of pyrrhic immolation. He brings it to heel.

Skart grabs ahold of his senses, hauls them roughly to the fore. Abruptly, the stink of blood and bowel is almost overpowering. The glare of the kitchen's single bulb makes him shield his eyes.

But suddenly so much more is apparent to him as well. Not just the moment he lives in, but the lingering remains of what has happened before. He learned this long ago, back before Mab's army marched, back when the kobolds' underground cities were a wonder to behold, lit by bioluminescence and torchlight, halls full of songs and joy. He learned this as a hunter with brothers now long dead. He learned this when he could only imagine innocent uses for it. Not many know such hunting magic now. Merrick certainly doesn't. Skart still remembers, though. He has made sure to hold onto the old ways.

Now, he sniffs the air with senses magically enhanced. He can track the scent trails of Merrick's team as they came in and out, stained with blood and gun oil. Then, as he heads back into Cotter's hidden room, he picks out one more scent. One that's younger, cleaner, more loaded with fear.

This, he knows, is the trail of whoever took the brick of Dust. The weapon with which he plans to remake this city.

Skart follows it into the living room, out onto the balcony, towards the fire escape, down. After a few floors, he sees where the thief jumped onto the roofs beyond.

And Skart knows, standing out in the cold night air, all is not lost. Not yet.

Sil

Sil's speed is failing her. Too much stamina has been beaten out of her tonight. The exhaustion is going to kill her.

Not directly, of course. That will be the yelling rabble of fae chasing her and Jag down the street.

She does the math. If she cannot outpace this mob before she runs out of energy, how much energy will it take to stop them? And, knowing that, can she find optimal fighting ground before she no longer has that energy?

But then, of course, all her planning, all of her training blows up beneath her feet.

Jag trips, sprawls to the ground. She lifts her head up, panting hard. She's drawn a bloody scrape along her chin. She doesn't get up. Sil doesn't even bother to tell her to do so. This is Sil's battleground now.

She spins. There's a low row of shops on one side of the street—a mix of cheap restaurants and delis. On the other side is the source of those shops' income: a paper mill, its windows shuttered and dark. She scans for a fire escape, spots one.

Then the mob arrive.

"Well, well." One pixie steps forward. "What we got here?"

He's playing for time, trying to get his breath back. Sil doesn't mind. She is too.

"Couple of gobbos come to play tourist, is it?" the fae asks his friends.

With her hair obscuring her features, and so many young goblins dying their green locks less natural shades, and with the chartreuse tint to her skin, Sil often reads as goblin. There is nothing to be gained from correcting anyone now. Being only half-goblin doesn't make fae any friendlier, and they lose a lot of their deference.

"Having a nice night out, are you?" the talkative pixie asks. A circlet of white ash swings around his neck. "Want to send a postcard home? Maybe we can help you. Wish you weren't here." He laughs at his own joke. A couple of others in the mob do too.

Sil nods. "Comedian," she says. She starts to walk forward. "I know a joke."

"Cocky little fucker, aren't you?"

"What's ten inches shorter than you and red all over?"

"Why don't you go—" the pixie starts, but never finishes. Sil's blade comes out, sends his head toppling to the floor.

Everything is very quiet as the corpse pumps blood into the street.

Then it begins.

The mob roars its outrage and fear. And they're too amped up, too committed to this path to back away. They can't give in to the urge to flee. Not with all their friends there. So, they come at her as one, fists raised, clubs held high, lengths of aluminum chain swinging.

They are not warriors but there are twenty of them. The fight smothers her. Bodies smash into her with dead weight, driving her back, driving her down.

This is not the first time she has been here, though. These were always the worst of her lessons. They would bring prisoners to her by the busload—demi-dryads, old kobold miners, prisoners from House Troll—put them in a courtyard, and tell those big, bruised inmates that they could walk free if only they could take this small half-fae down. Those were ugly days, spent under a screaming, clawing pile of frantic fae, proving that she could be more animal than them, biting and gouging, blood filling her mouth until she retched.

But it was necessary. It was what she had to do to obey. And failing to obey would have been so much worse than fighting forty desperate fae with hands and teeth. That had been drilled into her. You learn a lot about what can be worse than other terrible things, she knows now, when you're tied to a chair in a room with a tutor armed with a drill and no conscience.

Here, now—she breaks free of the mob, tears out of their grasp, goes for the fire escape, for higher ground. She leaps, catches the bottom rung of the ladder, hauls herself up hand over hand while the mob bays at this retreat, leaping and grabbing for her. Someone scrabbles at her foot, trying to pry off her heavy combat boot, but their grip gives up before her laces do. Then she's up, still climbing rung over rung onto the old iron structure. It's awkward with the sword, but awkward is infinitely preferable to dead, and the iron will hurt her pursuers more than it stings her, her father's goblin heritage offering a buffer, reducing the iron's stab to a barely noticeable throb.

She catches her breath on the first landing. Below her, the mob is jumping like hungry fish. Fingers scrape the bottom rung. Then finally, someone climbs on someone else's back. Then they're all doing it—transformed from fish to ants—piling up on each other, swarming upward.

The fire escape shudders under this assault. Sil retreats another flight higher. More and more of the fae are crowding onto the stairs, clinging to the metal cage that contains them. A few are on the underside of the steps, trying to pull themselves up bodily despite the iron that must be burning their fingertips.

The metal shivers again. There is a cracking, popping noise from above.

Sil realizes what is happening.

She dives for one of the windows as the whole fire escape gives way beneath the weight of the mob. Ancient metal scrapes against one arm, stinging like fire, skewing her flight, but then she collides with the rotten wood of one pair of shutters and they crash around her, slamming into the ancient window beneath. Wood and glass burst. Outside metal and brick are screaming. Fae are screaming.

Sil lands in a ragged pile on the dirt-spattered floor of the factory. She lies there panting, listening to the sounds of destruction echoing from outside. Clouds of dust billow up. Shakily she gets to her feet.

It is only when she's at the window, gazing down at the chaos and ruin, that she realizes she has left Jag down in the heart of it.

Bee

In another factory not so far away, a furnace rings like a gong as a bullet smashes into it. Bee flinches as sparks fly, only three inches from his head.

"Shit!"

Tharn crouches next to Bee, sweating, swearing, holding a heavy machine gun with two shaking hands. "Where did they come from?"

Bee doesn't know. He doesn't have time to point out that he doesn't know; that he's just as ambushed as everybody else here; that, yes, the question does need to be answered, but not right now. Right now, all he has time to do is move.

He bursts from the furnace's questionable cover and fires his pistol—his weapon of last resort—twice in the enemy's general direction, feeling the gun wrenching at his wrist. He dumps the chain—useless at range, and making his aim even worse—then grabs Tharn by the collar, and heaves them both towards a crucible, one of the massive, ceramic-lined steel buckets that hang from chains set into tracks in the warehouse's ceiling that the workers use to transport molten metal around the factory.

More shots dance and spark on the floor around them. They crash into the crucible's far side, setting it to swaying.

"Shit!"

Already three of the Fae Liberation Front are dead, their number cut from twenty-four to twenty-one. Jerrell was the first victim of the ambush. Then another—Colvin—had been shot in the neck. Colvin and Jerrell had always been friends and it seemed almost as if seeing Jerrell go, Colvin had leapt into the next great adventure to stay beside him.

Then there had been a mad scramble for cover, and for even the slightest sense of what was happening. "Red Caps!" someone had yelled. Bee still doesn't know who, but they must have decided to risk taking another look to confirm the presence of the distinctive red berets because there had been a scream a moment later, and Bee had seen the body fall, so that was the third down.

Tharn still isn't firing the machine gun, is still not doing anything but clutching it like a child with his blankie.

"Shoot something!" Bee yells at him. He swings round the edge of the crucible and squeezes off a shot with his pistol. He ducks back into cover. Tharn stares at him uncomprehending.

"Give me that." Bee wrestles the machine gun from Tharn's numb fingers. He presses his pistol into Tharn's hands. "That still has twelve shots left," he tells him.

Bullets are still pinging against the crucible. Bee is terribly aware that it hangs a clear six inches off the floor. One bad ricochet and he'll be hobbled for life.

Tharn is still staring, still hyperventilating, still not fighting.

"Just get in the crucible," Bee tells him.

"What?" Tharn stares at it wildly. The bucket is massive, eight or nine feet tall, more than half that across. At five-foot eight, Tharn isn't going to make it in there on his own.

"I'll give you a boost," Bee tries to explain.

Tharn still doesn't move.

"Fight or get in the bucket!" Bee yells at him.

A round sparks less than a foot from his boots. Bee grabs Tharn around the waist, hoists him up toward the crucible's lip. Bullets spatter against its thick side. Tharn tumbles over, legs kicking. Bee doesn't know how long the crucible's walls will hold. He doesn't know how painful it will be inside a bucket of cold steel. He doesn't have time to think about it. He doesn't have time to think about anything.

He definitely doesn't have time to think about how the thing he's about to do is profoundly stupid.

He steps out from behind the cover of the crucible.

The goblins from House Red Cap don't see him at first. They are too focused on the massive swinging target he just abandoned. They are lined up on the galleries overlooking the main factory floor where they have the fae pinned, are perched on walkways and steel gantries, while the fae try to find whatever cover they can, regardless of how much iron it contains. The goblins have rifles and pistols. They are raining down fire.

Bee's mind starts to catch up. In the moment's pause, it threatens to have time to think.

He braces the machine gun against his shoulder as best he can and squeezes the trigger.

The gun kicks like a mule. His barrel flies upwards, bullets smashing into the factory ceiling. The noise is deafening in his ears—a steady chug-chug as the mechanism spews ammunition.

He wrestles with the gun, heaves its bouncing barrel back down, and sweeps it back and forth across the upper walkways. He can't see anything beyond the flare of the muzzle. He doesn't know if anyone is shooting at him. He's sure he's as bright as the sun down here in the darkness. But this is all the plan he has. All he can do is wave the weapon back and forth and pray it buys someone else the time they need to figure out a better one.

Adrenaline distorts time. Moments expand and contract. Life passes by in a stutter of near static images. Then finally the gun's mechanism clicks—small and tinny after the monstrous roar of its barrel—and Bee is standing there, panting as if he just ran a mile, stupid as an ogre. Then he slams himself back behind the crucible's cover.

Silence. Or maybe he's blown out his hearing. There's a ringing in his right ear that won't stop. His shoulder feels bruised and his legs are shaking in a way he can't control. He thinks perhaps he's going to throw up.

"Tharn!" he bellows. "Tharn! I need more ammo! Give me a magazine! Come on! Come on!"

He's still shouting and clawing at the lip of the crucible when someone grabs him by the shoulder. He swings round, ready to smash the butt of the magazine into their face.

Harretta flinches back. "It's over," she tells him when she seems sure he won't strike her. "It's all over. They're on the run. You gunned down half of them. We won."

And with that Bee feels all the strength go from his legs, and he slumps to the floor.

Jag

In a street outside a different factory, silence has fallen. Metal has thundered and crashed around Jag. Dust has billowed. But now there is silence.

Slowly, she picks herself up. The paper mill's fire escape is a twisted ruin in the street. Bodies are a twisted ruin around it. Not all, though. And as the survivors begin to stir, sounds come back to the world. Some pick themselves up, coughing and spluttering. Others examine ragged cuts and broken ankles. Some just lie there and start to scream.

Jag backs away. She doesn't run. She doesn't think she can. Maybe it's for the best. She doesn't draw attention to herself moving like this. Dust has painted her gray and brown so her skin and hair can't give her away either. Her sharp features still can, however, so she keeps walking, one slow step after another.

She waits for Sil to appear. She saw her dive into the factory, but she knows Sil is OK. Jag cannot truly consider otherwise. The idea that Sil will be there to catch her when she falls is one of the inviolable rules of her universe.

"Get that bitch," she hears one of the still-standing fae say. She almost flinches back, almost gives herself away, then realizes that the fae is pointing toward the ruined factory.

"Where's that other one?" someone replies.

Jag presses into the shadows.

All told, there are still fifteen or so fae on their feet. They pick up spilled weapons. Some grab jagged spars of wood broken free from the factory's interior.

Jag retreats further and further. She watches from a distance as the fae disappear into the darkness of the paper mill. Then she counts the seconds. She waits for Sil to emerge, dripping with their viscera. She knows this will happen.

The street falls quiet. The whimpers of the injured fae seem oddly muffled in the slow-settling dust. Gradually, Jag feels her breath come under control. She's OK. She has survived. Sil has saved her. Sil will be here in a moment.

Then there's a shout from the factory. Distant, but clear. "Oh shit, it's—" and then the words are cut off sharply.

Immediately, the street shudders beneath Jag's feet. A bass rumble that rolls through the asphalt and shakes her knees. She looks around, trying to pinpoint the source. Then another boom comes, and then a third sharper cough of sound.

Smoke suddenly billows from the paper mill's windows. Glass and splintered shutters are blown from their frames. Then another coughing, cracking series of explosions. Flame follows the smoke.

All of a sudden, the whole front of the paper mill seems to slump. Bricks spill into the street. Steel beams slide free from hidden moorings, and doorways blink shut. And then Jag stares in horror as the whole paper mill—all its contents, and all those still within it—is transformed into nothing more than a smoking pile of broken rubble.

9

Making Plans Like They Matter

Bee

"This is fucked. It's all so fucking fucked."

Tharn is still shaking. He's pacing, staring wildly about the shadowed factory. "We've got to get out of here."

"Leave?" Harretta stares at Tharn. "We just took this place. We can't abandon it now."

The surviving members of the Fae Liberation Front are gathered about the pair. They all stand, stark as silhouettes in the middle of the factory floor. Their dead are still scattered around them.

Bee is sitting with his back to the crucible. He is watching them all. He is smelling blood and oil. He is trying to figure out what he thinks.

"This was an ambush!" Tharn shouts. "They knew we were going to be here!" He waves his arms wildly. "They know everything. The revolution is *over*. We have to go to ground."

Harretta stalks toward Tharn. "Fae died for this, you coward! They paid for this with their lives while you hid in a bucket!" Bee isn't sure if Harretta knows that she's crying or not. He doesn't know if she knows she's still holding her gun as she screams into Tharn's face. "And now you want to say that sacrifice is worth nothing?"

Tharn doesn't back down, although Bee isn't sure it's courage that's propping his friend up. "We'll all die," Tharn says, "if we stick to the plan."

"You—!" Harretta shouts at the same time that Tharn goes to say, "They—"

Bee thinks he's figured out what he thinks, though.

"Shut up, both of you."

Eyes flick to him as he uses the machine gun to lever himself up off the ground. The gun is now a prop with power, he knows. He has bought himself some authority with it.

"Tharn's right," he says into the space between Tharn and Harretta's rage. "This was an ambush. The goblins do know what we're doing. Staying here is foolish."

Harretta opens her mouth. He holds up a hand to forestall her. "Harretta's right too. We can't slink away," he says. "We can't let Jerrell's life mean nothing. Or Colvin's. Or Tabbat's." In the thirty seconds of respite since the last bullet rang out, Bee has had time to stare at the third body splayed out on the factory floor, has had time to think about all the times he and the brixie clashed, and collaborated, and laughed, and drank, and sang, and hoped, and feared. Has had time to feel nausea crawling up his esophagus like a beast trying to escape.

"We know the goblins knew we'd be here," he says, "but we don't know what else they know. We don't know how they know it. We don't know who else is in danger. But we can find out. The Red Caps are running right now. They're maybe a block away. We can follow. We can warn the rest of the rebellion."

The others stare at him.

"Follow them?" Tharn says. Bee still can't hear the courage in his voice.

"We were told to stay here," Harretta says.

Bee looks to Harretta. *"Told to?"* he asks her. "And here I was thinking we were rebels."

She looks at him for a moment, chews her tongue. Then she shakes her head. Bee grins.

"To the vote?" she says.

It's only one against, and even Tharn comes with them as they start to hunt.

Jag

Jag stares. And Jag stares. And Jag stares.

Sil is inside the paper mill. The paper mill that is not a paper mill anymore. Because now, the paper mill is a pile of rubble. It is clouds of dust and bursts of flame. Now, it is a ruin and it has ruined all the lives that were inside it.

Just now, it has ruined Jag's life.

Jag doesn't remember when she first met Sil. She doesn't remember what they told her when they first introduced her to this older child with her white hair and strange pale green skin, and whether she was excited or afraid. She cannot remember a time before Sil at all. And they are not exactly close despite all her efforts. It's impossible to get close to Sil, after what has been done to her. Sil cannot think of herself, Jag suspects, as someone, or even something, that others can approach. And yet she is always there. She has always been there, ever since Jag can remember. Sil is like a limb. The idea that she can be lost makes no sense to Jag.

And yet, also, the idea that Sil has survived this disaster. This detonation. This ruin…

She was the one who asked Sil to come along tonight. She was the one who sought Sil out. And perhaps that decision saved Jag's own life, but, for Sil…

Jag takes two steps towards the paper mill—towards what's left of it. She stops. She can't get any closer to the consequences of her own decisions.

She has to be alive, Jag thinks. Thinking anything else has been unthinkable for so long. But what else can she think staring at this mess?

The back half of the paper mill is still standing. Pieces of it keep collapsing, tumbling down into the fires below.

Jag takes another step forward. She stops again.

What can she do?

And of course, the answer is nothing. Because that is the answer to her whole life. What does her father trust her with? Nothing. What does her mother care for beside staring obliviously into an alcohol-hazed future? Nothing. And so, Jag has rejected their lives, and their values, and has tried to embrace what the fae have brought to the Iron City. And here she is now, surrounded by the fae's poverty, and their hatred of the goblins, and what have all her efforts bought her? Nothing. These fae don't care that she has argued to her wealthy friends that they are overlooking a cultural goldmine. They don't care that she has sabotaged the social standing of some debutante who was rude to a fae servant. Because what has that done for any of the fae living here in these slums? Nothing. It is all nothing. She amounts to nothing.

And now, here, the final culmination of all her attempts to help. Her plan to get Sil back in touch with her fae roots, to unlock her awareness of the potential of her mother's heritage… it all ends in this, in Sil's ending.

So, she stands, and she stares. And she stares. And she stares.

Sil does not emerge. She does not stand, shaking rubble and brick dust from her hair. She does not come to save Jag—neither from the fae nor from herself.

As the dust starts to settle, Jag does see shapes moving—silhouettes emerging from doorways; the locals come to see what has happened to their street, and their source of income. They have come to see what has been destroyed, and who has destroyed it. And they will find her, another goblin standing in the center of it all.

She cannot stay here. She can see, in her mind's eye, Sil standing there and shouting at her to move.

It hurts, turning around. She is not just abandoning the safety and security of Sil, she is walking away from her hopes for what their relationship could have become, of the ally she had hoped to cultivate. She is leaving her half-sister behind.

She tries to keep Sil's advice alive in her mind. *Walk*, she'd said. *Don't run*. So, Jag walks. She keeps her head ducked, trying to hide her features. She is filthy as a kobold's fingernails, and the dust and dirt mean she's not obviously a goblin from a distance, but she's not sure she can stand close scrutiny. Some fae stare at her from their shop doorways. A dryad calls out, asks if she's alright. She keeps walking.

Others call too. "What happened?" asks a stout gnome wearing a wife-beater and boxer shorts. "What happened?" asks a sidhe wrapped tight in a lime-green robe, her hair in curlers. Jag keeps walking. She keeps on doing what Sil told her to do.

There's a crowd at the end of the street. "What happened?" they ask as she tries to push past. She shrugs, mumbles. Someone grabs her shoulder. She shakes them off. Her heart is pounding. They are too close.

But then they let her pass. Perhaps they know somehow that she has already been through enough. Perhaps they worry she carries trouble with her. Perhaps they just don't care about her when there is a whole disaster to care about just over her shoulder.

So, she stumbles down the street. She walks away. Leaves Sil behind. Her sister's body twisted and broken beneath a ton of bricks.

Skart

Blocks away, the last of the Dust is burning through Skart's system. He can feel the Iron Wall closing like a vise around him, slicing off his connection to the magic and beauty of the world. The last tenuous strands of the trail leading him to the thief stretch out before him, leading down the street. And there, at the end of it, is a small hobbling figure. At the end of it is Knull.

Skart knows exactly who Knull is. Everybody from Knife Bend to the Wallows who values their wallet knows who Knull is. A hustler, a con man, a dealer, a Dust-peddler, a waste of good oxygen, and a bloodstain waiting to happen. In many ways, Skart is surprised that the goblins haven't swatted Knull yet. He supposes that for all his efforts, Knull has not yet flown close enough to those flames to get burned.

Not until tonight.

Knull, though, does not have the Dust with him. He is hobbling along, a makeshift splint strapped to one ankle—all indicators of a night of misadventure—but the large plastic-wrapped package is clearly absent. That means he has stashed it somewhere, or given it to someone, or sold it, or ingested half of it, or given it one of a thousand other fates. So Skart cannot simply flay him alive and take it back. He needs information.

Of course, he could flay Knull alive and take the information… And that, Skart thinks, is tempting.

Still, Skart has been tortured before. He knows getting the right information takes time. Time he doesn't have. Even now he can see signs of the revolution leaking through the normality of the night. Too many fae are on the streets. There is too much energy buzzing among them. He can hear scuffles like thunderstorms on the horizon. There is the sound of everything slipping out of his carefully constructed control. It eats at him. It gnaws. But he needs the Dust.

"Knull!" he calls, hurrying to catch up, trying to think clearly through the last haze of the drug.

Knull spins, fists up. What he plans to do with them is beyond Skart.

"Hey!" Skart holds up his hands, palms out. No threat. "Hey." He smiles.

"What you want?" Knull keeps his distance.

Skart knows Knull, but the problem is Knull knows Skart too. Skart has been a vocal antagonist of Knull's supplier, Cotter, for years. That was what had given tonight's plans much of their symmetry, what had made them so satisfying. Many a time Skart has mounted a soapbox and declared Dust an important weapon for social liberation, and decried those who see it only as a means of personal advancement. He has told fae not to buy from Cotter's dealers. He has told fae not to buy from Knull.

Which all makes it feel a little awkward when he says, "I'm looking to buy some Dust."

"From me?" Suspicion burns in Knull's eyes like a fever.

Is there any way, Skart wonders, to make this sound believable?

Inspiration strikes. “Ironically,” he says, “from Cotter. I need bulk and I need it fast, and my usual supply has dried up.”

Knull, Skart knows, knows Cotter is dead. Knull knows that Skart knows that Cotter is dead. But for all this knowledge, Skart doesn’t have a clue what Knull is going to do next.

Knull hesitates. “You hate Cotter,” he says.

“I’m desperate,” Skart says. “The city is desperate. Tonight is desperate.” He’s warming to his theme. “I need to make a deal, and I need to make it now. I will make it with anyone.”

Too much? he wonders.

“How much?” Knull asks.

Maybe not.

“Thirty-eight pounds,” Skart says and immediately regrets it. It is too specific. He tries to shrug. “Give or take.”

“Yeah,” Knull says, blithe as a lamb. “I know a guy who can do that. Not Cotter, though. Someone else.”

Skart actually claps his hands. This is genuinely too easy. “Perfect,” he says. “You can bring it to me. I’ll give you the—”

“Half up front,” Knull says.

“What?” Skart stares at him.

Knull blinks. “The money,” he says, as if not sure something so painfully obvious can possibly be the source of confusion. “Half up front.”

And Skart genuinely hadn’t thought of that. He was never going to pay Cotter the back half of the Dust’s cost. He has Merrick’s fee to be sure, but the whole point of Merrick was that she was the vastly cheaper option. But he’s been so caught up in the night’s calamity the thought of Knull wanting to be paid has not entered his head once.

“But…” The pause is too long, too awkward. “But I’m not buying it from you,” he manages, which given the time, he thinks, is pretty good cover.

Knull blinks again. “Erm…” he says. “Finder’s fee.”

Improv, it seems, is not one of Knull’s skills.

Skart tries to decide how desperate he is. “How much up front?” he says.

Knull cocks his head to one side. He is practically salivating. His pupils are as wide as a Dust-head’s just as they OD.

“Street value…” he mutters. “Pure… Half up front…” He looks at Skart. He looks like he’s about to start laughing. “Million and a half golden gears.”

Skart almost punches him right there.

“Fuck you.” It’s out of Skart before he can get himself under control.

Knull shrugs. “You told me you were desperate.”

The little shit. How much can he pull together? “I’ll give you…” Skart does quick mental math. “Fifty thousand up front.”

Knull blinks again. There is low-balling, after all, and there is figuratively punching someone in the balls.

Then, abruptly, Knull’s demeanor changes. His swagger abandons him. He glances up and down the street, skittish.

“Nah,” he says. “Nah. I’m not here if you’re not serious.” He takes steps away, each one escalating the sense of panic rising in Skart’s chest. “I’m having you on, anyway,” he says. “I don’t know anyone.”

Shit. Shit. Shit. Knull is spooked. Skart’s number wasn’t just insultingly low, it was scarily low. Suddenly, Knull thinks it’s a setup. He thinks Skart is just here trying to figure out how to roll him for the Dust. Which, in the end, is exactly what he’s doing.

Skart scrambles for lies. For a second time tonight, he washes up on the shore of the truth.

“I don’t have the money,” he says desperately. “Not up front. But I can get it.” He almost says *You can trust me*, but if there are any words more likely to set off Knull’s bullshit-meter then Skart doesn't know what they are. "It's for a cause," he says instead. "It's for the Fae Districts. It's to liberate us. Once I have that Dust, I can make sure you get as many golden gears as you want."

Which with the sort of power the Dust would fuel, he could actually do.

He won't. But he could.

Knull looks at him, weighing him. He shakes his head. "Fuck off," he says.

"There's nothing?" Skart says. "Not an ounce of feeling in your heart for your fellow fae? There's no one here you want to save?"

"Yeah there is," Knull says. "That's why I want three million golden gears."

"You think too small." Skart's frustration can't help but leak out between his gritted teeth.

"What?" Knull says. "You think I should ask for five?"

Skart is on the verge of resorting to violence when suddenly he pauses. He stares. Because just as suddenly, a group has appeared in the street. And they should not be here.

Knull sees Skart's look, hesitates, then glances over his shoulder. His body goes rigid. "Oh shit," he says. "Gobbos."

A group of ten, hooded, dressed in black, armed. A commando group.

"Spriggans," Skart says.

"What?" Knull is slowly stepping away.

"Yellow ribbons," Skart says. He can see the insignia on their arms. "House Spriggan. They shouldn't be here."

Why are they here? And Skart knows it for a certainty now: he's been away from the rebellion too long.

The pack of Spriggans turns, sees them. Skart grabs Knull's arms.

"Let us," he says, "continue negotiations elsewhere. Right now, we need to run."

Knull looks down at his ankle. Skart gives him a sour smile. "Try."

Jag

Jag is still trying not to run. She's getting worse at it.

Even as midnight approaches, the Fae Districts are buzzing. Fae stand around in small groups outside homes and stores chatting animatedly or drinking and staring, transistor radios playing dense rhythmic music. Pigeons and bats whirl in the sky. From time to time, armed groups bundle through intersections. The crowds watch them like foxes frozen by headlights. Occasionally sounds that may or may not be gunshots punctuate the night.

The temptation to find a payphone and call House Red is growing, but Jag remembers Sil's warning. Sil plotted out a way home. A way to stay safe.

But did Sil plot out all the variables? Something, it is becoming clear, is happening. Jag doesn't think anybody knows exactly what it is. She's too scared to stop and ask. The moment, though, is building. The sense is pervading the city that events will be clear soon. And every fae in the Iron City seems to be desperate that no one else figures it out before they do.

"What happened?" they call to Jag. "What happened?" Over and over. "What happened?"

She wants to wipe the dust and dirt away. It draws every eye. But if she does… the green of her skin will be obvious. Then when an eye reaches her, it will be so much worse.

"Hey!" someone shouts to her. A gaggle of sidhe youth preening outside a corner store. "What happened?"

Jag tries not to run.

"Hey! Hey!" Shouts follow her. "Why you so unfriendly?"

She risks a look back. A few sidhe are wandering down the street after her.

Don't run. Don't run.

"What you do?" one says. "You do something? You bring trouble here?"

Don't run. Don't.

"You rude."

"Think we should teach her some manners."

Jag looks back again. The whole knot of youth has pulled away from the corner store, is following her.

Don't run. Don't. Don't. Don't. Don't.

Jag tries not to run.

She fails.

Bee

Bee presses himself tightly against the roof tiles. Scents of soot, stale rainwater, and mold fill his nostrils. His chest pistons up and down as he tries to regain his breath. His heart thunders, machine-gun loud.

They've been chasing the Red Cap goblins for ten blocks now—first racing to keep them in view, then furtively ducking behind chimneys, A/C units, and water towers, desperate to avoid another gun battle, desperate to not pick up more casualties.

Now, Bee has only a gutter to hide behind.

Tharn lies next to him. Bee wants to check that his friend's head is back in the game. To make sure he's mastered his fear, that he's not a danger to everyone here. But Bee doesn't dare. He can't be overheard. The Red Caps are standing in the street almost directly below them.

One of the goblins talks into a radio handset. Bee can't hear the words, just the tone. It doesn't seem like anyone involved in the conversation is happy.

The Red Caps start running again. Bee and the others peel themselves off the rooftop and start running too. They try to keep the distance constant, try to stay quiet.

Tonight, the city below has a strange energy. Too many fae are out on the streets. Smoke is rising from factories that should lie quiet. Shouting echoes from faraway avenues and alleyways, distant and hollow. More gunshots than usual reverberate between the buildings. Bee thinks about the other groups sent out to claim the city in the name of revolution.

Twenty-one members of the Fae Liberation Front run across the rooftops of the Iron City now. There were twenty-four at the evening's start. And Bee knows that revolution is a violent act. He's read his theory. But what if, he wonders, Tharn was right? What if the revolution is over already? What if they're already defeated?

The machine gun bounces and clatters against his hip. He both does and doesn't want to have to use it again.

The goblins turn abruptly left, disappearing through a gap in a tall chain-link and green tarpaulin-covered fence into an empty lot and out of sight. Bee can see a fire escape ahead of them descending down into the space. He holds up a hand. The Fae Liberation Front stumbles to a halt.

"Why'd they go in there?" Harretta is panting hard.

"Am I a mind reader now?" Bee approaches the fire escape with a sense of trepidation, grinds to a halt five yards away.

Harretta knots her brows. "You OK?"

He doesn't want to say he's scared. Especially after his big-man act back at the factory. Tharn puts a hand on his shoulder. Perhaps, of all of them, he understands.

Together, they lower themselves, crawl forward. The smell of filthy roof tiles is becoming familiar.

Bee looks down on an undeveloped lot. Tall fences topped with razor wire isolate it. Security cameras peer into adjoining streets. It is an unfriendly space.

Tonight, it has become a little more so.

A series of blood-colored tents obscure the dirt and weeds. Goblins scurry between them, clad in back, eponymous berets clamped in place. There are tables full of guns and ammunition. Some goblins strip weapons, reassemble them; others examine clipboards and point with purpose.

Bee would love to pretend that this is some rich goblin camping expedition. He would love to pretend that it is innocent. He would love to pretend that he stayed back in the smelting factory where he was ordered to stay, or anything else that would mean he's not perched precariously on the edge of a rooftop peering down on a House Red Cap mobile military command center.

He would love to pretend that Tharn isn't right, and that the revolution isn't utterly fucked.

10

Iron Fists and Lead Feet

Granny Spregg

Granny Spregg paces. Her palm throbs. Her hip aches. She wants to stop and rub it with her uninjured hand, but she can't afford for the command center's soldiers to see her infirmity. Not tonight.

"Any word?" she says instead.

"None yet." General Callart answers her as smoothly as if it's the first time she's asked.

She sent a tactical unit into the Fae Districts an hour ago. She gave them a very specific address to visit, and very clear directions about what to do when they got there. She had them repeat it all back to her.

Then it was out of her hands. They were out running through the Iron City, and all she could do was stay behind, pacing and aching.

She curls a lip at Callart. It is an unreasonable response to his polite answer. She doesn't care. She has been too powerful for too long to be reasonable.

She paces. She aches. Then, finally, the door to the command center flies open. A slender sidhe runner sags against the frame, breathing heavily, stared at by everyone.

"A scout," he manages, still sucking on the air like a vacuum cleaner going through its death throes. "Returned. He's down—"

"I'll see him alone." Granny Spregg cuts the runner off, and cuts the legs out from under the anticipation filling the room. She hobbles away through the deflating atmosphere. Thacker scuttles after her.

The runner leads her down corridors that transition from grandeur to functional to downright shitty. Grunt humor graffitis the walls. *"What's black and white and red all over? I don't know, but if it's got tits, I'll fuck it."* Such, she thinks, is the quality of the soldiers employed by House Spriggan. But if this scout has good news, then she may finally have a chance to improve that quality.

The debriefing room is small and functional, and smells like an abandoned gymnasium. The goblin scout stands beside an orange plastic chair. He hasn't sat down while waiting. He is one of the good ones. It's why she picked him for this mission. Just because she hasn't been in charge, doesn't mean she hasn't been paying attention.

"Stand outside," she tells the sidhe runner. Then when the lackey is gone, she says, "Report."

"We entered the target location at 2330 hours," the scout reports. As he does so, Thacker gently drums his fingers against the door. It's a cheap trick as countermeasures go, but it will at least defeat the runner's ear, which is certainly pressed to the door's far side right now.

"Cotter was dead when we got there," the scout goes on. "There were signs of a violent altercation. We did reconnaissance and found a mercenary group in a bar nearby. After brief observation, their conversation led us to believe they were involved in the Cotter incident. We… cleared the bar, and interrogated them.

Their leader—a sidhe called Merrick—took the credit when pressed."

"Shit." Granny Spregg is pacing again. Her hand throbs. She takes the goddamn chair herself, easing creaking bones into its meager comforts. "What about the package?"

It has not escaped her notice that the scout is empty-handed.

"Missing. The mercenaries didn't have it either. Someone took it before they arrived, they claim. Another player. They didn't know who. Neither do we."

"Fuck!" Granny Spregg wants a table to flip. "Fuck." She says it again, trying to think. "OK… OK… So, Cotter orders the Dust from beyond the Iron Wall. It comes in. We hear about it. But someone else does too. They send mercenaries to steal it. I send you. But one more player gets there first. Before the mercenaries. Before you." She looks up at the scout. "And I don't have my Dust."

"No, ma'am." The scout meets her gaze. This, he knows, is not his fault.

"You're attempting to track down the thief." It's not a question.

He nods anyway.

"Fuck." Spoken a third time, like an incantation. "Do you know who sent the mercenaries?"

"A kobold. A local civic leader—" But she's already waving off the answer. If this kobold doesn't have her Dust, he doesn't matter. She needs the Dust. It is the sun around which her plans orbit. It is the match with which she will light a fuse.

She cannot march to war on the strength of empty hands.

She must fill them with something.

She looks around the room. *What is to hand?*

Thacker meets her gaze. She smiles at him. "Call the runner back in," she tells him.

Thacker blinks.

"Did I stutter?"

The runner has a politely curious expression on his face as Thacker ushers him in. He is burning to know what is happening, she knows, burning to have gossip to share with his peers, or to sell to a tabloid, or to some other House.

"Close the door, Thacker," she says.

She can feel the sidhe's anticipation building. Granny Spregg turns her back on him.

"I need you," she says, speaking to the scout instead, "to carve out his heart."

"Ma'am?"

She meets his gaze. This will be thin grounds for her plans, but desperate times…

She nods. The scout's hesitation is only momentary. "Ma'am."

"What?" the runner manages.

Then the scout is on him. An elbow to his face, snapping the cheekbone, the eyeball sagging. The runner clutches at the wound, screaming. He's not trained for this. He's left his belly exposed.

Thacker glances anxiously at the door. Still, such sounds are not entirely out of place down here. Interrogations often go awry in House Spriggan. So much of success, Granny Spregg has found, depends on a refusal to lose one's nerve.

The scout unsheathes his sword and disembowels the sidhe in a single stroke. The smells of blood, bile, and shit fill the room, as the runner collapses. The scout slits the runner's throat just to make sure. Thacker scuttles into a corner trying to keep the gore from washing onto his shoes, a look of violent distaste on his prissy features.

The scout goes about his work. There's an efficiency to his butchery. Quick strokes in and out. Nothing misplaced. When he presents Granny Spregg with the heart, his arms are red to the elbow.

It is funny, Granny Spregg thinks, how similar fae and goblins are once you get inside them. All the differences that they fight over, and yet so many are only skin deep.

"Thacker," she says, not taking the proffered item yet. "Go find us an ice box."

She smokes a cigarette while they wait, and feels a crawling nausea in her stomach as she does so. She examines the stab wound in her hand. Thacker washed and bound it, but still… is that a small purple line snaking away from the bandage and toward her wrist? It's hard to tell amongst the mess that her veins have become. She thinks she took the antidote in time. But did it smother the chemical's fire completely? Only time will tell, and she has less and less of it.

Thacker returns. The heart is placed in a nest of ice. Thacker closes the box with a little click, holds it like it's about to detonate.

"You," Granny Spregg says to the scout. "Let me tell you the new truth of this heart. It is a goblin heart. You brought it back with you. The fae cut it from one of your fellows." She nods. Yes, this is what she'll do.

"Now," she says, "for the next step: take this to General Callart, and as you do, think about which of your fellow soldiers you like the least. Tell Callart that this heart belongs to that soldier. That done, get back out there and hunt. Find me my Dust."

"But if you do not—" She leans in close. "—and the sun rises before this plan is finished, then I will need to cover our tracks. That means, if we plan to live to see another nightfall, you will need to kill whichever of your compatriots you have told Callart this heart belongs to. So pick the name carefully. We have tonight and tonight alone."

She turns to Thacker, ignoring the scout's salute. "Seal this room. Get someone we trust to clean it up." She looks at the ice box. "Tell them that, if this works, they will be richly rewarded."

A glance back at the scout. "Everyone will be."

Thacker and the scout nod. But they know, and Granny Spregg knows, that everything hinges on that one statement: *if this works.* And without the Dust, and with only an ice box and a sidhe heart to her name, that *if* is thin hope indeed.

Edwyll

Edwyll thinks his hands have stopped shaking.

Again, he thinks. Again in front of his eyes. The violence of the Iron City erupting right in front of him like a skull hit by a bullet.

Is it bad luck? Is it an omen? Is it just the way life is—the poverty, the oppression, the constant hatred of the goblins pressing down? Is this the obvious and natural reaction, as predictable as the ticking of a clock? Should any of this surprise him?

He doesn't know. All he knows is that it horrifies him. Sickens him. Terrifies him. Leaves him sitting here with shaking hands and a slideshow of grindhouse gore ready to play every time his eyes close.

Use it.

Lila's advice sounds heartless now. Sitting here in the wake of yet more death. A cold, calculating way to look at the world.

But if I want to do something to change it, he thinks, *maybe I need to be cold. Or if not cold, just… harder to hurt. Thicker skinned.*

Or is thick-skinned just what cold fae call themselves to justify their callousness?

And yet he would change this. Sitting there, fighting through the aftershocks of adrenaline, that certainty takes hold of Edwyll with a sudden fierceness. Fear sublimating to anger like steam to snow in the sky above, ready to plunge down and transform the landscape utterly.

Another blink of his eyes. Another glimpse of blood and bone detonating, everything coming undone.

He would change this. And he has one way to do so. His weapon of choice.

He reaches into his messenger bag for a spray can of paint. And finds something else. A reclaimed treasure.

He pulls out his parents' White Tree. The symbol of the fae become useless, become self-defeating.

Use it. Change it.

He wants to put this city back together. He wants to reassemble it as something new and beautiful. He wants all the fae to feel the way he feels when he sees the beauty that still lives within them. Not the same as it was. Transformed. Sublimated like steam to snow.

He looks at the cheap china tree, its inelegant branches clumsy and blunt. He looks at the walls of the building he's hiding in. A squat currently abandoned. Filth on the floor. Empty cardboard cartoons of old rice and moldering moss patties. The scent of urine. A few lazily scrawled tags in among obscenities. Such a typical space for the Fae Districts. Such a predictable space.

Change it.

He reaches into the messenger bag again. His fingers on a spray can feel like touching hope. Feel like the filling of his chest when he's at Lila and Jallow's, and the collective there is talking about seeing more than the Iron City immediately before their eyes. A way of still seeing beauty.

He pulls the paint can out, feels the weight of it. He shakes it back and forth and the clack of metal pea against aluminum walls settles him.

Green. He's taken the green can. He can do something with green.

The first strokes are broad, sour-neon splashes that mean nothing more than his hand is still shaking. He works with that, though. He thinks of the music he heard earlier, the angry buzz-saw rattle of its basslines, the violent thunder of its drums, and the pixie's vocals floating over that chaos. Beauty emerging from darkness. Yes, he can work with that.

He finds browns, bloody reds, bruised purples. A nest of vines and thorns appears. He thinks of the sound of gunfire. He thinks of bodies falling. The thorns grow higher.

He is, he thinks, creating something monstrous.

Or is something monstrous creating him, he wonders? Is the Iron City—polluted, perverted, corrupted—reaching out? He sketches bodies caught in the briars, limbs pushing through from shadow. His hands are still shaking.

Yellow streetlight splashes through his hideout's broken windows. His artwork looms through shadow, towers over him.

This is so much darker than anything he has made before. Even as he shifts to a paint brush, every stroke seems brutal. But he looks at the White Tree again and thinks, *There has to be contrast; there has to be darkness.* In the end, he feels, you need that for a glimmer of hope to shine.

Sil

At first, it is so dark, Sil cannot know for sure if her eyes are open or not. Perhaps, she thinks, her eyes no longer work. So much of her feels broken right now.

A great weight is pressing down on her, like the thumb of some ineluctable god. She can hardly move her arms or legs. She has been buried alive.

She does not panic at this revelation. Weapons do not panic, after all. Rather, she simply slows her breathing, presses her shoulders back and down, clenches and unclenches the muscles in her thighs and calves, going through the exercises without thought.

When done, she unfurls her fingers, and tries to get a sense for what entombs her. Knowledge is power after all, albeit not much power down here in the dark.

She feels a cold surface, rough, interrupted by sharp fractured angles. She cannot place it. She pushes harder, then harder still.

Something grinds, gives way. Light and dust drift into her limited world. She chokes and squints.

She cannot remember exactly what happened. She was with Jag… She was climbing… Memory billows around her, elusive as smoke.

She begins to move in whatever small ways she can. She bends a swollen knee, rolls a bruised wrist. Every motion hurts, but her prison starts to buckle. Air brushes against a bloody graze. She works her whole arm free.

She picks and pulls now at the things crushing her. Then she recognizes them in a sudden rush. Bricks. Layers of them covering her entire body. She is not buried deep, though. She works her other hand free, pulls blocks of baked clay away from her face.

She sits up in the ruin of the paper mill, stares into a world of drifting smoke. She coughs and tries to put her memories back together piece by piece.

The fae, she recalls. The attack. The fire escape. She remembers steel shrieking, and then diving through the mill's rotting shutters. Then prowling, getting ready for an attack, hearing the mob come in through the door downstairs, hearing them approaching. Then…

Then a shout, an explosion. A detonation. She doesn't know

what set it off. She was flung through the air, skidded beneath old machinery. Bricks rained down like bullets, clanging and clattering off the old iron. Then something had collapsed. Something fundamental. She had felt the whole world tilt beneath her. She had been poured down into oblivion, rolling out of her hiding place, bricks grinding against her like millstones.

And then… nothing. And then… now.

Jag. The thought is like a lightning strike. She left Jag outside.

Keep my daughter alive or I shall visit upon you a thousand plagues of pain. She sees Osmondo Red once more, sitting on his throne, his whole body hunched around his distended stomach, snarling, a goblet of wine in his hand like some parody of a golden age king.

She must find Jag. This is the imperative tattooed into her psyche. *I think therefore I must find Jag*.

She stands. Her whole body screams at her. Her left knee almost gives way. She grunts, casts around, grabs a spar of broken wood to use as a crutch. Two paces later, she goes back to collect her sword. It lies on the base of her abandoned brick coffin. The cloth wrapping on the hilt that protects her from the iron's dull throb is torn, but still serviceable. The blade is dusty but not bent. At least that makes one of them.

Hands full, she hobbles through drifting brown clouds, searching for the street, and for a sense of the city she has temporarily misplaced.

When she finds it, it lunges back into clarity. Figures mill about: fae staring at the collapsed factory. Too many. Jag, she thinks, is not safe.

The fae register her emergence from the ruin. They point. Their attention matters little to Sil, though. They are civilians, after all—collateral damage waiting to happen.

"Jag!" she tries to shout, but dust and pain clog her bruised throat. "Jag!" she calls again, a dry bark of a sound, but Jag doesn't come forward.

Rather, someone else approaches from the crowd, a hand outstretched—whether in kindness or aggression, she doesn't have time to judge. She whips out the scabbarded sword, cracks the length of its blade across their forehead and sends them reeling away.

The crowd shrieks, scatters like startled birds. Twenty seconds later she is alone in the street. Jag is still not there.

"Jag!" she barks again, waiting for her to come crawling out of whatever hiding spot she's found.

She does not come.

"Jag!"

Sil's pulse comes quicker now. When she calls Jag's name, she feels a tightness in her throat.

"Jag!"

And Jag is not there. And she is not. And she is not. The absence of her draws out, becomes undeniable. And Sil cannot think it, but now she must.

She has lost Jag.

And now, here, standing alone in an empty street, Sil starts to panic.

Granny Spregg

"What are the fae?"

Granny Spregg stands in House Spriggan's library. Her family has joined her. Privett is there, still smarting from their earlier encounter, hunched on a small leather pouf, sending sullen looks at the fireplace that crackles and smokes behind his mother. He is, no doubt, thinking about the possibilities of shoving her into it.

Her daughters are there as well: Nattle and Brethelda. Nattle sprawls on a chaise longue, mountainous dresses dribbling onto the floor, cigarette smoke billowing above her. Brethelda sits straight-backed in a leather chair, wearing a gentleman's morning suit, the rod still clearly rammed irretrievably up her ass.

These three are the children Spregg: the de facto rulers of House Spriggan, one of the five great houses to rule the Iron City. Her offspring. The despots she has deposited into the world.

General Callart has joined them as well. And Thacker too, of course, fidgeting and shuffling.

Now, Granny Spregg waits for their answers. *What are the fae indeed?*

"Nothing," Privett mutters.

"Peasants," Nattle says, fishing in her petticoats for a fresh smoke. She is always smoking. Even through the pregnancies that gave Granny Spregg her unwanted moniker.

Brethelda stays silent. Because she is the smartest of all Granny Spregg's children.

"Fuel," says Granny Spregg. "The fae are fuel. Without them, the engine of our wealth runs dry. Their labor drives us forward. We need them."

"I am overwhelmed with gratitude," Privett mutters.

"That," Granny Spregg snaps at him, "is because you will forever be a petulant child. They do not deserve gratitude. They lost the Iron War. We won. It is the privilege of victory for us to do with them as we please, to revisit upon them the ignominies they visited upon us for so many generations. It is our pleasure to throw their children on the fire and watch them burn."

"Do you have a point, Mother?" Brethelda looks bored. And she, in the end, is the one Granny Spregg must sway. She is the one the others will follow. Scoring cheap points off Privett will only get Granny Spregg so far with her.

"Remember this," she says to her eldest daughter. "When you were born, we had no fae healers kneeling at our feet. We were still in the North, and a midwife had to stitch my cunny back together with thread. So, at least do me the service of listening from time to time."

Granny Spregg knows she has never been very good at pandering to her audience.

But Brethelda quirks her lips, and Nattle guffaws out loud. Privett, though, still looks like someone who's just got done fellating a lemon.

"Fuel." Granny Spregg heads back to her main point. "Fuel spilled—" She pauses for a significant look. Brethelda, she knows, likes pomp and high-handedness. "—can burn a house down."

She lets it sink in.

"Do you remember that literature teacher Mummy got us?" Nattle says suddenly. "He loved metaphors like that. What was his name again?"

Granny Spregg has seen Nattle throttle a brownie to death with a violin string. The air-headed heiress act does not deceive her for a moment.

Granny Spregg signals to Thacker, and he scuttles forward, puts the ice box down on a small coffee table.

"The fae," Granny Spregg says as he opens the ice box, "have forgotten their place."

They all look at the heart. And all Granny Spregg can hope is that the anatomy teachers she hired did not do such a good job that the infinitesimal differences between a goblin heart and a fae heart are visible here. Because this, right here, is her moment of drama.

"One of ours?" Brethelda asks.

Granny Spregg notes with satisfaction that it is hard for Nattle to look so sanguine now.

"No," she spits at Brethelda. "I cut it from a calf in the kitchens and brought it here to waste your time."

She is glad Thacker is standing behind the rest of them. His poker face is shit.

Brethelda turns to General Callart and arches an eyebrow.

"We sent a scouting troop into the Fae Districts tonight," Callart says. "A scout brought back this. He told me it belonged to a private third class called Jibberts."

The scout has done his work well. Callart has bought the story. His conviction adds strength to her deceit.

"Well hopefully he died before he passed that awful name onto any children," Nattle says.

"And why did we send a scouting troop into the Fae Districts?" Brethelda asks. Even as a child, neither candies nor casual violence would ever tempt her away from her obsessions. Granny Spregg wonders if she would be proud of Brethelda if her daughter wasn't such a bitch.

"Are you concerned that the fae might be justified?" Granny Spregg drips with disdain. Hopefully it doesn't look as rehearsed as it really is.

"I am concerned that poor management may have provoked the fae and led to house assets becoming endangered." Brethelda looks her dead in the eye.

"Don't you manage the troops, Privett?" Nattle says, staring at the ceiling.

"I didn't fucking send them," Privett snaps, because he's still an idiot.

"So, you don't manage the troops?" Nattle feigns confusion. "Are you dressed up like that just for playing toy soldier?"

Brethelda's dry smirk is back.

"She..." Privett froths, and gesticulates at his mother. "... interfered."

Brethelda's transition from impolite amusement to polite curiosity is smooth as a well-oiled mechanism.

Granny Spregg wants to roll her sleeves up for this one, but it is General Callart who speaks next.

"Our venture was minimal in scope," he says. "Madame Spregg knows what she is doing. This is an act of unwarranted aggression by fae who have forgotten their place."

Granny Spregg tries to judge Callart's motives. Why defend her? She has amused him tonight, she knows, but his loyalty is not so easily bought. She doesn't hold it against him. He did what was necessary to hold onto his position after her children deposed her.

Rather, she realizes, there is a shivering note of anger to his voice. *His* soldier has been killed. He is outraged.

She has an ally.

At least, she does as long as her lies hold.

"The fuel," she says, capitalizing on the moment, "threatens to burn. We need to remind the fae who they work for."

"A show of force, then?" Brethelda asks. And she is not just asking about the troops. Brethelda always speaks in layers.

"I'm here asking, aren't I?" Granny Spregg says, more petulant than she would like. She forgives herself, though. Because she doesn't have the Dust yet—just an ice box and a heart of questionable provenance. Because she cannot challenge Brethelda yet. Because no matter what the House troops do in the streets, her show of force here and now, in this room, is minimal.

Brethelda finally lets her smile spread over her whole face. "You are, aren't you?"

Nattle giggles. Even Privett smirks, though Granny Spregg cannot say for certain that he knows what he's laughing at.

She doesn't say anything, though, just waits, back as unbowed as age and osteoporosis will allow.

Brethelda looks away, takes a breath, makes sure everybody knows this is her decision.

It is all posturing.

"No matter how we provoked them, and I'm sure you two did screw this up somehow," she says, looking from Granny Spregg to an outraged Privett, "Mother is correct. We cannot let this stand. We must show decisive action."

She steps over to Callart, places a hand on his shoulder. "A battalion, you think?" she says to him.

She angles her back just a little toward her mother. Cuts her out of the conversation in little ways. But, Granny Spregg simply waits while the details are hashed out. And Brethelda tries to spoil it, and take the joy from it all, but in the end, the truth is that Granny Spregg has gotten her way. The moment may have ugly wrapping paper, but it is still a beautiful gift. And when they all have left, she looks to Thacker, and she smiles.

Edwyll

Edwyll steps back, looks at what he has created. The mural towers over the room, massive, foreboding, reaching for something better, desperate. And looking at it, there is a moment of pleasure before the doubts set in, before the flaws start to stand out brighter than the splashes of neon paint he's sprayed. For a moment he thinks he might be close to saying something meaningful.

Then he shakes his head, steps away. Close, but… it's still not right. Not quite. It's still lesser than the idea in his head.

He goes to the window, looks out at the Iron City just visible through the smears and stains on the cracked glass. The city he would save one painting at a time if he could. Is it safe out there now? Or… safe enough, because it cannot ever be wholly free of threat. He wants desperately to get back to Lila and Jallow's. But he doesn't want to become part of the night's body count trying to get there.

The street outside is a long one, running several hundred yards in either direction, only cut off to the east by the crest of a slight hill, the slope running down in a long decline to where he can just make out a distant T-junction to the west. It's hard to see much of it. And there is smoke rising behind the buildings opposite, but the glow of the fire is on the horizon, not here, not now and in his face. And sometimes that is as safe as the city can seem.

Slowly, carefully, Edwyll opens the squat's door, peers out onto the street. It's quiet its whole length. He licks his lips. This is about as good as it's going to get.

And then a figure appears at the crest of the distant hill, and he freezes, staring, trying to assess the peril. The figure, he realizes, is running. But is it pursuer or pursued? He can see no quarry for the figure to be hunting, so the question becomes what is chasing after it? Edwyll shrinks back into the doorway's shadows, ready to dart away into relative safety.

The figure has made it almost halfway to Edwyll before its pursuers appear. Edwyll is almost on the verge of writing the runner off as a lone lunatic, running from phantoms. It's not as if mental illness is uncommon here in the Fae Districts. But then the pack of silhouettes comes jostling and jogging over the rise. They're too far away for Edwyll to really make them out but from the fearful glances the runner casts over their shoulder, the relationship is clear.

What did the runner do? Edwyll wonders. How much innocence can they claim?

He looks at them more closely, trying to see what clues their appearance can give, how much he can ascertain about his own state of danger from their arrival.

And then, the shock like plunging his face into ice water, he realizes he knows them. Knows *her*.

The goblin from the bar. The goblin with the bodyguard who turned a night out into a bloodbath. The goblin whose appearance seemed to herald the night's descent into horror and shit.

Edwyll flinches away just from the sight of her. His eyes are desperate, searching for the swordswoman, searching for the danger. He does not want to die.

Then, slowly, logic catches up. If the goblin is running then her bodyguard cannot be here. If the goblin is running, then her sins have caught up with her.

He shouldn't care, he thinks. He should be full up with images of the bodies in the bar. She is the oppressor, and he is the oppressed.

But that has never been the world Edwyll wants to create. And as the goblin draws closer, the panic is too raw in her eyes for him to be heartless. Her breathing too ragged. The pack of fae pursuing her are shouting and catcalling. He does not want them to do whatever it is they intend to do.

He can imagine Knull screaming at him. Because what sort of weak, pitiably soft-hearted fool would save one of the oppressors when the chance to exact revenge—to see revenge exacted—is so close?

She has a good lead on her pursuers, over two hundred yards at least, but she can't shake them, not on this long, faceless street. There is no one here to save her.

Except him.

He stays there, watching her draw inexorably closer, dragging her fate behind her as surely as if it was tied to her ankle.

"Yo, bitch!" he hears from the crowd behind her.

"Gonna fuck you up!"

Why would I save her?

A patron. The thought rises out of the churn of his mind. That was what he thought when he first saw her. That's why he approached her back at the bar. Because a patron would give his art a platform, would give his voice and his message a loudspeaker. Would give him a chance to change things.

From a few streets away there is the sound of gunfire, a low whoomph. The pursuing fae cheer. The goblin lets out a terrified shriek. Several raccoons burst from the cover of nearby garbage cans and go running for cover.

Edwyll looks at the gaggle of fae. How far away are they? How clearly can they make him out? How big of a risk would it be to…

"Over here!" he hisses. He hasn't thought it through, and the goblin is almost past him, but he can't watch this. He can't. Not again. He doesn't want the Iron City to be this way. He doesn't want the fae to be this way. He wants to change things. Maybe this is something he can change.

The goblin looks at him wildly. She is caked in dust, almost white with it, except for where tears and sweat have left little rivers of green down her cheeks.

"Come on!" he says, risking a little more volume. "I'll hide you."

She hesitates a moment longer, the fae drawing closer, and closer, then suddenly darts towards him, and the doorway, shoving past him with a desperation that precludes gratitude. Edwyll shuts it behind her but can still hear the calls of the fae.

"You can hide, little rabbit," one yells, "but we'll still find you."

How close are they? Edwyll wonders, heart still pounding.

Surely still too far away to pick out a precise door. Surely.

"In the shadows," he says urgently, glancing back at the goblin. She is standing in the middle of the room, staring around. No wonder she ended up being chased by some mob. He wonders if she is touched in the head.

He goes back to the doorway, holding the rough door closed, trying to plan out what he can say. To these fae. To the goblin. When it's over. How he can make her see that she owes him.

He hears a hand hammering against a door a few buildings away. His heart hammers right back.

"Come out, little gobbo!" another fae yells from the street outside. Rats scuttle in the far corners of the squat.

"Hide," Edwyll hisses, all his attention on the door, focused on the inevitable—

Thump. Thump. Thump. A hand thundering against the wood. The door rattling in the frame. Only Edwyll's foot keeping it closed.

An inarticulate shout of excitement from the fae outside. Someone shoves on the door harder, unbalances Edwyll, and he only just manages to catch it in time, so it only opens a sliver, doesn't fly open, doesn't reveal everything.

A sidhe face leers through the gap, eyes wide with victory, and then almost immediately on its heels is confusion. Edwyll is decidedly not their prey. Edwyll and the sidhe stare at each other.

"Where is she?" The sidhe is perhaps twenty years old, wearing a heavy wooden chain and with flint studs in his ears. Tattoos crawl over his neck, and Edwyll can smell the whiskey on his breath.

"Who?" is all Edwyll can manage.

"My little rabbit."

"What?" Edwyll's throat is constricting. This is stupidity. He is risking too much for too small a hope. Who is to say that this is even a rich goblin he's hiding?

More fae are jockeying behind the one who banged on the door, trying to peer in.

"We saw her go in this door," the lead sidhe says.

"It's just me in here," Edwyll says, and he tries to make it sound confident, but it emerges as a whisper. It would be so easy for them to push him aside.

He sees anger curdle in the sidhe's face. His nerve fails, and he opens his mouth to blurt out that she is here, right here, but then the sidhe turns away, throws up his arms. "Must have been another house," he says. "Keep looking. We'll find her."

Edwyll's breath rattles out of him as the pack spills back out into the street. He needs to close the door, but the glare of danger's headlights has not faded from his retinas. He stands, still watching, still recovering, as the fae move down the street, kicking and knocking on other doors. Then one bursts open and suddenly there are three angry demi-dryads—half kobold judging by their wild red manes of hair—in the street, wild-eyed and tangle-bearded. They wave broken bottles at the pack, and shriek, and fall over each other, and then the pack of fae are all laughing and running away. And still Edwyll clings to the door like it's a raft in the night.

And then they're gone—the pack. But the goblin is not. She is still right here with him.

One more breath. One moment to close his eyes and compose himself. To remind himself that he did this for a reason, that his future hinges on this.

He opens his eyes. He turns around.

The goblin is standing just where he left her, only three paces from the door. If it had been pushed open just an inch more, the fae would have seen her. As if she never really cared about his survival at all.

"I—" he starts.

"What is that?" The goblin cuts him off. She is pointing at the back wall of the house.

Edwyll's mural is vast and sprawling, lit only by the spill of streetlamps and moonlight coming in through the still open doorway and dirty windows. The dark thorn bushes sprawl about the ruins of the room in angry streaks of neon green and crimson, curling darkly over bodies and limbs. Desperate eyes stare out from stark shadows. And then, in the center of it all, arching up over everything—dominating, defiant, renewed—is the White Tree. Its bark is silver in the moonlight. Its leaves are gold. And to Edwyll, even in his own rendering of it, it is beautiful. It is shelter. It is the promise of a world that has shed the shackles of its past and embraced what is here, and now, and precious in a living world. It's what the fae of the Iron City could see if only they would raise their heads. If only they would hope.

At least, that is what it is to him, or was meant to be.

"Just a mural," he says.

"Who painted it?" the goblin asks.

"I did."

Finally, the goblin turns and looks at him. She stares, those yellow eyes gleaming bright as torches in her skull.

"You?"

"It's rough," he says automatically. "More an idea than—"

"It's beautiful." She cuts him off. She turns back to it again, as if drawn to it. "Your painting. You've made something beautiful."

11

Making It Worse

Knull

"Shut up," Skart says.

Knull—who hasn't said a word for a while now—closes his mouth.

Knull isn't entirely sure how he got into this situation. He had been on the move, making plans, setting things in motion. And then, when Skart appeared, it had felt as if—after years of struggle, after years of choosing short-term pain for the distant hope of a long-term payoff—life was finally doing the right thing by him. Sure, Skart was a stuck-up hippie gone moldy around the edges, but he had gold and he wanted to spend it. What's more, he wanted to spend it on Knull's Dust.

But then it had all soured. Then there had been House Spriggan goblins in the street. And then there had been running, and scurrying, and hiding. And now Knull is here, pressed up against a wall in a dark alley, and Skart is telling him to shut up.

"We should split up," Knull whispers. Better to cut his losses now, he thinks. Because there is no way a deal can be done if they're both chained up in a House Spriggan cell.

Skart seizes his arm with a strength surprising for his scrawny limbs. "We stick together." And then, because Knull's face must be telegraphing his alarm, he adds, "I can keep you safe."

Skart, Knull thinks, must be seriously jonesing for some Dust. Which is decreasingly convenient as he hears sounds at the end of the alleyway.

"Down," Skart hisses, and forces Knull behind a pile of rotting garbage.

Knull is about to open his mouth to bitch about this bullshit treatment, when a beam of light stabs into the space above his head. He watches as it works its way methodically back and forth across the alleyway's walls.

"One... two..." Skart counts steady as a metronome while the flashlight beam oscillates.

He reaches fifteen and the beam clicks off. Knull looks at him, sighs in relief, and goes to stand. Skart's grip on his arm tightens. The kobold is still counting.

When he gets to twenty the flashlight beam comes back on, sweeps back and forth one more time. Then it clicks off again.

This time, Knull stays right where he is.

When Skart reaches forty, he lets go of Knull's arm and stands up. He looks down at Knull. "How," he asks, "have you lived this long?"

And that is some serious bullshit as far as Knull is concerned, but he's still waiting to see if someone caps Skart in the back of the head so he stays quiet.

Skart moves to the far end of the alley. "If we are to take control of the Iron City," he says to Knull, "we have to know it. We have to make it ours in our minds." He reaches up to a small, wire-reinforced window, half-obscured by paint and mold. There are iron strands in the glass, but the old kobold doesn't even flinch.

Perhaps, Knull thinks, he is tougher than he looks. "Knowing it that way also helps when you need an escape route," he says. He slips out a knife and ten seconds later, he swings the window open. "Come on."

Knull still hesitates. He's been shot at enough tonight.

Skart sighs. "A twenty-five-second examination is the basic search pattern for goblin special forces. Any longer and they risk having their prey get too far ahead of them. They've moved on for now. When they can't find us, though, they'll come back and search more thoroughly, and then it will take more than a few garbage bags to save us."

And how exactly, Knull wonders, does Skart know the basic search patterns for goblin special forces? But, on the other hand, Knull doesn't want to be sitting here trying to figure that out when another goblin with a gun comes poking down the alleyway.

Knull is beginning to think that tonight might not be his lucky night after all.

Sil

Sil's fear is a rat inside her skull, clawing and raging against the walls of her self-control. Her handlers took time and care to build those walls, but they can't last forever. Not when it feels like her lungs have been torn from her body, not when she must find them before they're gone forever.

Keep my daughter alive or I shall visit upon you a thousand plagues of pain. Osmondo Red was not joking. He has no sense of humor.

Streets flash past her. Fires cast the smoke clouds in shades of malevolent orange. Some fae try to drag a stiff coil of woven hawthorn strands across a road, its barbs reflecting the streetlights dully. Even in that paltry light her skin is green enough for them to pull weapons as she approaches, and when she's done their task is left half-finished, the barricade ending in a pool of blood and hewn body parts.

Jag is not there, though. Sil does not rescue her. She does not save herself. She runs on.

Keep my daughter alive. There will be nowhere Sil can hide.

And yet somehow, there is a hiding place for Jag. As much as Sil runs, as much as she searches, Jag eludes her—a rich goblin's gemstone, lost in the gutter. And no matter how much Sil cuts at the fae who get in her way, they do not tell her where to find Jag. And with every drop of blood that spills, Sil's panic rises.

Bee

Bee's breathing is sharp and shallow. His heart trips and taps against his ribcage. Below him, a once-empty lot has been filled with foreboding. House Red Cap commandos mill and organize. They arm themselves.

"We have to take them out." Harretta is at Bee's elbow, peering down.

Crouched at the roof's edge, fingers white-knuckled on the gutter, Bee glances at her face. He's not sure what he expects. Something bloodthirsty, he thinks. Her expression, though, is studious, as if she's working on a particularly difficult math problem.

"Are you crazy?" Tharn—crouched behind them both—gives voice to Bee's inner monologue. "They're *commandos*. We have to get back to the rebellion's leadership, tell them what's going on."

Bee would really like it if Tharn were right.

"By then," Harretta says, "these goblins will have left. And they're not going out there to hand out chocolates and roses. The blood they spill will be on our hands."

Bee really wants Harretta to be wrong.

"We're outgunned, outnumbered, and outmatched." Tharn doesn't back down. "If we attack now, we'll be killed. Then everyone else you're worrying about will be too. This is our chance to get out a warning, to organize. A thoughtful retreat saves more lives than blindly rushing in."

"We split up," Bee says. It's the obvious middle path. "We send some back to report."

"They already have four soldiers to every one of us," Tharn whispers. "You want to make those odds worse? We have to get out of here."

"Oh," Harretta says, nodding, "the coward wants to retreat."

Which is exactly what Bee was hoping she wouldn't say. Because it's unfair. Because it's not true. And because it's precisely what everyone else is thinking.

Tharn opens his mouth, says nothing. What can he say?

Bee wants to agree with Tharn. But is that because of his own cowardice? And does he want to wear his fear as a badge? Does he want everyone in the Fae Liberation Front to see that every time they look at him?

Tharn turns to him, a question in his eyes. Does Bee have his back?

Bee does not want to lead the Fae Liberation Front. He does not believe in leaders. But he does want his voice to be heard among the chorus.

"Well," Bee says slowly, "I mean they have literally put themselves in a kill box."

Tharn looks away. "You don't even know what a kill box is."

Bee shrugs helplessly. "It's square… We'll kill them in it…"

Harretta pushes the advantage. "To the vote?"

Tharn shakes his head, gives in to it. "To attack?" he asks the assembled rebels.

Twenty voices whisper back, "Aye."

So be it.

Bee unslings the machine gun. Its metal feels cold and sharp in his hands. It is designed to do one thing. To make him one thing.

Tharn is next to him, the revolver out. His jaw is set. Above them, the moon peers between two clouds, paints one of Tharn's cheeks white, leaves the other untouched. He doesn't look at Bee.

"You want the machine gun?" Bee whispers. He wants Tharn to know that they are still friends. He wants the others to see Tharn with the instrument that saved them in his hands, to know Bee still believes in Tharn. He also doesn't want to fire that thing ever again.

Tharn hesitates. Bee pushes the gun at him. When Tharn takes it there's a slight tremble in his hands that Bee pretends he doesn't see. Tharn hands Bee the pistol.

Below them, the goblins are splitting into two groups, one near each open edge of the lot, connected by a narrow stream of runners swapping messages and flitting into blood-red tents.

These goblins are preparing to murder fae, Bee tells himself. They are going to murder innocents.

Except, Bee is not exactly innocent, is he?

He puts his crosshairs on a goblin's torso. Does he have a wife? Children? Does a mother complain to him that he forgets to send cards on her birthday?

Revolution is a violent act. It is an upheaval of norms. It shakes the world and forces it to settle in a new pattern. Bee knows his theory. He has read his books.

And yet, as the other fae open fire, he thinks that Tharn is not the only coward. He thinks that he is here, hiding his fear behind this gun. He thinks he is going to throw up.

Then he fires. He watches the goblin buck and go down.

Next to him, Tharn opens up with the machine gun. Its blazing stream of bullets walks between bodies, chews up tent fabric. A box of ammunition explodes. Tharn leans over the roof's edge, lips pulled back in a rictus leer.

The goblins return fire. Bullets patter the concrete below Bee. The gutter cracks, splinters, falls down like a great clunky streamer thrown in celebration of this destruction and mayhem. Something whines past Bee's ear. Another round passes so close to his scalp that his hair blows in its breeze.

Then one of the goblins' shots clips Tharn's shoulder, throws him up and back. The machine gun releases its primal scream towards the heavens, then goes quiet. Someone's head detonates next to Harretta. Bee feels blood and bone spatter against his cheek.

He keeps on firing, though. There is nothing left to do. They are committed. Perhaps, Bee thinks, the more he fires, the sooner it will be over.

His gun locks, his magazine empty. He rolls away from the building edge, reloads. His hands are shaking. His clothes are wet with sweat.

He goes to swing back to the fray, finds he can't. His body won't respond. Rational parts of his brain are screaming at him that this is suicide by goblin commando. He screams back at it that his friends are dying out here, because he didn't have Tharn's back, because he is too much of a coward to risk being labeled a coward.

He swings back, fires once, stares down on a slaughterhouse scene. Below him, the only movement is twitching.

The Fae Liberation Front lie on a rooftop beneath a smoking sky. They stare down at the massacre they have enacted. They wait. Some of them bleed. Below them, bodies fall still.

Slowly, they realize their work is done.

Bee isn't the first to stand up. Neither is Harretta. But when they both do, she claps him on the shoulder.

"Kill box," she says to him. "Fuck yeah."

Bee still thinks he's going to throw up.

Knull

Skart helps Knull up through the window at the back of the alleyway. Knull tumbles headfirst, scared to flip and risk his injured ankle. He lands on his shoulders in a pile of old sacks that stink of mushrooms and dung. Skart follows after him, showing surprising agility for an old man. But the craggy kobold still massages his back as he stands.

"Not what I once was."

"What?" Knull asks. "Relevant?" He feels bitter about all this. He also can't help but feel it's all Skart's fault.

Skart shrugs and fails to rise to the bait. Knull looks around the room. A little light from the street filters into it from another narrow window in the opposite wall. He can make out shelves and cans, little else.

"What is this place?"

"A storeroom," Skart says. "A safe space. No one but friends come here."

To Knull, though, the place looks like a rat trap. If the Spriggans come in here, they're both boned.

"Anyway," Skart says, "back to business."

It takes Knull time to realize what Skart's actually saying. "You want to iron out a Dust deal in *here*? With them outside?" What, Knull would like to know, is wrong with this fae?

"It'll be twenty minutes before we can be sure the Spriggans are gone," Skart says, pulling deeper, Knull supposes, from his well of esoteric goblin military knowledge. "We have the time."

Knull just shakes his head.

"What's more," Skart plows on, "I think that considering I just saved your neck, we might be able to negotiate a bit on price."

Knull thinks this might actually be the most absurd thing he's heard so far. "Why?" he asks.

It's Skart's turn to stare. "I just *saved your life*."

"Yeah," Knull nods. "Which is great for you because now I can still connect you to the fae with Dust to sell."

Skart pushes both hands through his bushy red hair. "Can we please dispense with the fiction that the seller isn't you? It would make things so much easier."

Knull couldn't agree more. Still he's surprised it's taken the old kobold this long to figure it out.

"All right," he says. "So, you buy the Dust off me. Same as I said before, half up front."

Skart scoffs. "You want over a million gears before you even prove you have this Dust?"

Which, in the end, Knull had been hoping for. Because one and a half million gears would get him so far away from Skart that he'd never *have* to follow through on the deal, and it would let him find a new seller, and make even more off that schmuck.

Still, it is perhaps reassuring that Skart is demonstrating the most basic of street smarts, even if it will mean more work on Knull's part. "I'll take a photo of the stash," he says. "Bring that to you." There will, of course, be nothing in the background to identify the Dust's location. Skart might know about special forces search patterns, but Knull knows Dust deals.

"I need to do this deal tonight," Skart says. "Now."

Knull almost laughs. How many rookie mistakes can the old kobold make in one night? *Never let the mark know how much you need what they have.*

"I told you, I'll be able to get you the money," Skart says. "More than you're asking for. If I get the Dust tonight, then you can have riches beyond your wildest dreams."

Knull knows a bullshit deal when he hears one. Because it sounds exactly like what he'd tell someone he was trying to rip off. There is enough earnestness in Skart's voice, though, that he thinks the kobold might genuinely believe what he's saying. This sort of passion is so foreign to Knull that he can't help but pull on the thread to see where it might lead.

"What are you going to do with the Dust?" he asks.

"Change everything." In the thin light Skart's expression is impossible to read.

Knull thinks he's meant to be impressed. He's not.

Skart shakes his head. "Don't you feel it? It's already happening out there."

The only thing Knull feels is the junkie energy that's coming off the old kobold in waves. He half expects Skart to start with the flashbacks next.

"The city is rising up," Skart says. "Fae are in the streets. The goblins have refused to relinquish power so now the fae are seizing it."

And Knull has been through a lot, but finally, he thinks, he might be about to lose his shit.

"What?" He throws his hands up. "You idiots are doing this again? *Again?* And you want me to sell you Dust on the promise of an IOU? Tomorrow, you'll be in a goblin jail being tortured, and at best I'll be sitting with my dick in my hands. *Screw you.*"

He thinks his vehemence has caught Skart off guard, but the

old kobold recovers fast. "You want to live like this?" Skart asks. "You want to be under the goblins' thumb?"

And Skart really doesn't get it, Knull realizes.

"Of course not!" he shouts before he remembers he's meant to be hiding from goblin special forces. "That's why I'm trying to get three million gears," he hisses. "Because *that's* the answer, you dumb shit. *Not* kicking the goblins in the nuts. That just means reprisals. It always means reprisals. It always makes things worse. Always."

And in the face of his unexpected fury, Skart just grins. Like an asshole.

"Not tonight," Skart says. "Tonight is different."

"No it's not!" Knull really cannot get over this crap. It's like his parents are telling him that *this time* he really can trust them with the baggy of Dust. "It's always the same fight, over and over and over, with you idiots." He finds he's poking Skart in the temple. "We lost it. We always lose it. You're fighting for something that's already been decided. Just let it fucking go already."

And finally it seems like he might have shaken Skart's sense of smug superiority.

"Let it go?" the old kobold asks. "Let go of the deaths of my family? My friends? Let go of a world of green, and good, and light, and hope? You are an ignorant fucking child. You don't even know what's been lost."

And that's it. Knull's out. He's done.

"Screw you," he says. "Keep your money. I'll find someone who's…" But he can't keep on track. It's gnawing away at him, this constant stream of horse dung that Skart is spouting. His anger slips its leash. "You're fighting for a gone-away world!" he spits. "It's not even out there beyond the Iron Wall anymore. Even if you could win, you're fighting an old, irrelevant war."

Skart's fists are balled. "Do you have no feeling in your heart for anyone but yourself? Does it not even cross your mind to lift your fellow fae up to the sun?"

"There is no sun in this world," Knull snaps. "There's smoke, and smog, and rain, and I know you can't believe it, but I like it that way. It's my sky. It's the one I was born under."

Skart shakes his head. "You are selfish, and you are lost. And you don't even recognize when someone is trying to save you."

"I don't want to be saved by you. I want to save myself. You should too. Make the most of *now*. This is the world we live in. This is our home. All you old-timers go on about what we lost. You're lost. You're in the past and you can't get out."

"With that brick of Dust," Skart says, "the old world is a click of my fingers away."

Which is, of course, insane. Because Knull knows that while you could pretty much do whatever you wanted with that much Dust in your system, you'd be too busy detonating, with each and every one of your blood vessels tearing its way out of your body. And if that's really the extent of Skart's plan, then Knull knows he has definitely been here too long.

"Fuck this." He heads back to the window.

"Where are you—" Skart starts, but Knull has already grabbed the sill. It hurts to haul himself up with his busted ankle but it's worth it as he glances back and sees the expression on Skart's face.

He's still grinning about that when he reaches the end of the alleyway and finds himself staring directly into the barrel of a Spriggan's gun.

12

When the Bodies Hit the Floor

Skart

Skart should have known. Of course he should. It should have been obvious that of all the idiotic choices Knull could make, he would make the most idiotic one available. It was so obvious, Skart almost feels—as he stares at the window Knull just disappeared through—that he might be the stupid one here.

There is, of course, only one thing he can do now. Skart is beginning to realize that there are no choices left on this path, just ugly necessities. So, no matter how much he'd rather avoid this, he grabs the windowsill and follows in Knull's wake.

By the time he has his head out the window, the Spriggans have Knull up against a wall. One goblin has a gun in the young fae's mouth, and another is rhythmically tenderizing his balls. For his part, Knull is simply crying.

The first Spriggan pulls his weapon from Knull's jaws. "Where is it?" he spits.

Knull is gagging and sobbing. The second Spriggan punches Knull in the gut while the first repeats his question.

"Where's what?" Knull asks, which means he's either more resilient than Skart thought or even dumber.

The first Spriggan grabs Knull by the throat. "You think we pulled you off the street at random? You think we're idiots? You left a trail, you schmuck. We've got dogs. Your fae rebels may think they're clever bastards, but they haven't broken all the CCTV cameras. We tracked you here. So, we know you're our fae. Now give it up."

They don't wait for an answer, though, just punch Knull in the gut again. He goes to the ground mewling.

They will, Skart thinks, probably work Knull for another minute or two before they get serious about wanting answers. He considers letting them extract the information he wants, then using it to get the Dust himself. But there's no guarantee he could get to the Dust ahead of the goblins. He's not as young as he used to be.

He thinks of the black growths in his arms. Thinks of a ticking clock.

The pair go back to their work. They're so intent on it, they don't even look up as Skart wrestles his way through the old window frame.

The third goblin positioned directly below the window does, however. He puts his gun to Skart's skull.

"You're going to watch this," says Skart's new friend. "And then you're going to tell us everything you know."

"Yes, yes," Skart says. "I know."

He is fairly sure that this isn't what the Spriggan expected. In fact, he's staking his life on it.

The Spriggan's moment of confusion is just that—a moment—but it's all Skart has. He ducks, hurls himself back into the commando's body. He brings his arm up, locks the Spriggan's wrist, wrenches. There's an audible snap.

Skart plucks the gun from the air as it flies free. Behind him, the goblin is grabbing at Skart's throat with his uninjured hand. Skart reaches around his own body and jams the gun barrel against the commando's ribs.

He pulls the trigger twice and the pressure on his neck lessens.

For the other two Spriggans, Knull is rapidly becoming less interesting.

Skart grabs the toppling commando, spins his body round, uses it as a shield. Rounds strike the goblin's body armor, drive Skart back. He's hunched up against the wall. But being pinned down isn't going to work. It's only seconds before they find his ankles or an exposed elbow.

He pushes up off the wall, taking the dead weight of the commando with him. He's roaring.

There is not much magic left in the Iron City, but not all its works have been undone. Some things that were done before the Iron Wall went up are written in flesh and bone. There was a time when he was young, and a warrior. A time when he was sent into the frontlines of battle with magic carved into his skin. Magic to make him stronger, faster, *better*. And he is old now. He is broken now. But the magic left a mark. He has made it further through life than many fae. He has seventy years to call his own, even if he can feel the final curtain calling him. And the magic left him still capable of something more than his age would suggest.

He just isn't sure if it's enough.

He staggers forward. He can feel bullets hitting the back plate of the commando's Kevlar vest already. An arm has almost come off. He's only halfway down the alley. It's not far enough.

This is so much harder than it used to be. This is so much worse than when he was young and shirtless, marked with runes, Dust burning in his veins, fighting for his homeland, fighting with a vigor lost somewhere in the grind of the countless years.

He fires the pistol under what's left of the commando's armpit. The shots are astonishingly loud between the alleyway's walls. He misses with all of them, but it's enough to buy him eight more yards.

He flings the ragged corpse forward, charges after it. But he's misjudged the distance. He needed about five more yards.

The commando's gun comes up in his face. He skids to a halt.

"Nice try, motherfucker," the Spriggan says. Skart doesn't really think he appreciates the effort all this has taken, though.

Still, it's an opening, and Skart will take it. He swings his legs up into the Spriggan's crotch.

Then they're down on the ground wrestling. The last Spriggan stands over them, trying to line up a clear shot, but Skart is grappling for all he's worth, pulling on almost seventy years of tricks and cheats, fighting as dirty as he can. He gouges at an eye, a mouth. He knees the commando in the balls for good measure. He hears a shoulder joint pop and for a moment he isn't sure if it's his or his opponent's.

Then he's underneath the commando, a gun barrel pressed into his opponent's kidneys. His other arm is around the commando's windpipe. The commando's fingers dig into the ropey sinews of his arm. It hurts, but at least Skart knows where the goblin's hands are.

He's panting so hard, it takes him a moment before he can tell the last goblin, "Let my friend go."

"Fuck you," the commando he's holding onto tells him. "Fuck you both."

The Spriggan he's actually talking to hesitates, however.

If the goblin goes for a shoulder shot, Skart knows he's fucked. His captive has no body armor there; the bullet will go straight through and take out Skart's gun arm. It will force him to let go. The goblin will be injured too, but he will recover. Skart will never be allowed to do so.

It takes a certain amount of willpower to shoot your friend, though. Skart is banking on the idea that this goblin doesn't have it.

"Let my friend go," Skart says again. "You do that, and everyone walks away."

"Cap that fae shit now," Skart's captive says. Apparently, he is far more suicidal than Skart had hoped. Skart digs the barrel of the gun deeper into the commando's kidneys, but all he earns himself is another, "Fuck you."

Behind all this, Knull is slowly clambering to his feet, inching his way up the alley wall. His eyes are wide. Skart can't be sure how much of all this he's taking in. This pair really put the panic in him.

"It's OK, Knull," he says. "I've got this."

He needs Knull to understand what's happening. He needs him to know Skart is saving his life.

Knull makes some non-committal grunts.

"You shut your hole," the free commando says, although it's unclear which of them he's talking to.

Then, finally the goblin does the obvious thing and puts his gun to Knull's head.

It's not the smart thing to do, but it is obvious.

"Put the gun down," the standing Spriggan says, "or your friend dies."

"Sure," Skart says as reasonably as he can. "But he's the only one who knows where the Dust actually is."

And that gets the goblin's attention.

"Let me get up," Skart tells them.

This is perhaps the hardest part. Because the commando whose kidney he's violating wants to kill him so very badly, he will take the smallest opening. So Skart keeps the gun pressed deep, keeps it far from prying hands, keeps his own free arm pressed to the commando's neck. And he keeps on praying.

Skart wasn't afraid of death for a long time. For a long time, he didn't care if he lived or died. Not once the first set of uprisings after the Iron War—the so-called Red Rebellion—went south. After so many of his friends died. For a long time, it didn't seem like there was much left to live for.

Now, though, now he feels each of these seconds ticking past.

"OK," he says once they're up. "Now we can talk in a civilized way."

"I'm going to find your family and put them in the ground," his captive tells him, although he is very late to that particular party.

"Well," Skart says, "not all of us are civilized."

"You're a dead fae talking."

Honestly, Skart would like to indulge in a little more banter, and get his breath back a little more, but tonight time is of the essence.

He shoots his captive. He feels the body jerk, the spasm of it pulling him off balance. He goes with it, shoving straight toward the last, stunned Spriggan.

It's all just shock in the end. Nothing more than that. It's all just doing what your enemy won't expect you to do. Hitting them in their blindspots.

And for all this, he gets at most half a second to save Knull's life.

He throws the dying commando into the living one's gun arm. The shot rings out, as the commando fires reflexively. The bullet ricochets off the wall behind Knull's head. Knull screams. Skart yanks the flopping goblin's body back and slams it into his opponent again. He uses the body like a battering ram. The shot goblin is bleeding out, but he struggles weakly, makes everything a little bit harder. Skart's muscles scream as loudly as Knull. He can't keep this up.

Skart slams the goblin forward one more time, lets him go, because he has to. The full weight of the goblin tumbles into the last commando. The living and the dying goblin both collapse to the ground.

This, of course, is the moment when Skart should press his advantage. He should end it here.

He glances back at Knull. And Skart doesn't just need the drug dealer alive. He needs him *grateful*. And he really doesn't know, with someone as self-interested as Knull, if he's there yet.

This, he thinks, *is going to suck.* But there are no choices anymore.

The goblin commando kicks his now-dead partner off himself, stands up.

"You fucking—" he manages before the rage just takes over and he levels his gun at Skart's head.

Skart backs up fast and hard. Knull is right there under his feet. They fall, limbs tangling.

The commando looks down at Skart and Knull lying in the dirt.

"Get up," he tells Skart. He's still pointing the gun.

Skart gets up. Knull doesn't move at all.

"Drop the pistol."

Skart drops it.

The Spriggan pushes the barrel of his gun into Skart's face. Then, after a moment, he moves it right, moves it down. He points it at Knull. He keeps his eyes on Skart, though. "I don't think I believe your friend is the only one who knows where this Dust is," he says. "I think you're a liar, just like all the fae. I think I'm going to kill your friend and then beat the truth out of you."

There is no question. This is going to suck.

"No!" Skart flings himself forward. He puts himself right in front of the barrel. Right as the gun goes off.

It is like being at the center of an explosion. Like coming apart. The pain is massive. He lies there gasping. There is a hole in his guts, and it is full of fire. He's trying to scream but the pain is too big to get out through something as small as his throat.

The goblin looms over him.

"I only need one of you alive," he says. "And I am going to enjoy this."

It costs Skart a lot to get the words out, but it's worth it.

"You talk too much," he says.

And then Knull fires the gun. He fires the gun that Skart dropped right into his lap. He points it directly at the Spriggan's skull, and he blows the bastard's brains across the wall.

Skart smiles. Just for a moment. And that done, he closes his eyes, and decides to simply bleed for a bit.

Granny Spregg

The waiting, Granny Spregg thinks, is going to kill her. There is some irony to that considering that from some angles most of her life looks like just passing the time in between assassination attempts. Still, she's never considered before that passing the time itself might actually be what finally finishes her.

She perches on her chaise-longue, flanked by black leather armchairs posed like bodyguards. Thacker approaches with a silver tray. "Would you like some tea?"

"I'd like you to go screw yourself."

Her breath is coming fast. The night is cool but she feels hot and the air is close. Maybe Privett has tried to kill her by breaking her room's thermostat. It's stupid enough for him, although probably too imaginative.

In the end, she can't take it anymore. She stands. "We are going to the command center."

"But—" Thacker still struggles with his tray. "—they said they'd send a runner. They said that as soon as a scout reports back from the Fae Districts they'd—"

"Do you need me to clean your ears with a poker, Thacker?"

"Let me get the door for you."

Thacker is about to put hand to handle when the knock comes. Granny Spregg's heart gives a spasm. She and Thacker exchange a look.

"Well?"

Thacker swallows, hesitates. "Right," he says. He opens the door.

Thacker does not then welcome in a runner, though. He does not surreptitiously usher in a commando scout. Thacker simply stops and gawps.

"Brethelda," Granny Spregg says, as if her daughter is the only possible creature who could ever come to her chamber door. "Do come in."

Brethelda stalks forward slowly. "Mother," she says as she looks around the room.

"Let me guess," Granny Spregg says, settling back down on her chaise. "You need advice on dealing with the opposite sex?"

Brethelda cocks her head for a moment, then nods. "Of a sort."

The problem with teaching your children to hide their motives, Granny Spregg thinks, is that then they can hide them from you.

"Well—" Granny Spregg beckons Brethelda to a chair. "—tell Mother everything."

Brethelda comes forward but does not sit. She stands stiffly. She has always done things stiffly. Granny Spregg had a doctor look into it once. Apparently, it's caused by Brethelda being a tight-assholed bitch from birth.

"Now, who's bothering you?" Granny Spregg asks.

"Osmondo Red," Brethelda says.

"He's a little old for you, isn't he?"

Osmondo Red is of Granny Spregg's vintage—a relic of the world gone away; a veteran of the Iron War. He is also a goblin bent almost as much by his hatred of everyone and everything as he is by age. And what's more—what's so much worse—he has held onto power. Granny Spregg would rather like to throttle him with his own intestines.

"It's not just Osmondo, Mother. The heads of House Bogle, Hobgob, and Troll would also all like to know why I just marched to war on the Fae Districts. They are worried about their factories, their supply chains, their investments. They are worried, Mother, that you are not just declaring war on the fae, but on them. And given your past actions, we can perhaps both understand their perspective."

Granny Spregg permits herself a smile. "Do I worry you, Brethelda? Have I put a shiver in your shins?"

Brethelda walks to her mother's writing desk, grabs the chair, pulls it over to sit opposite her. She perches on its edge. Granny Spregg has a greasy, uneasy feeling in her gut.

"Do not mistake me, Mother," Brethelda says, "for someone other than who I am. I tolerate you because you are my mother, and because from time to time you amuse me, and because sometimes I find it pleasant to look upon you and know how far I have caused you to fall."

Her tongue appears between her teeth for just a second—an almost lizard-like licking of the air.

"I know the fae forgot nothing," she continues. "I know they were provoked. And I know that you provoked them. The fact that I have not asked how or why you did this is not because you have somehow tricked me. It is not because you are my tragic blindspot. It is simply because you are now so far beneath me that I do not give a fuck what you do. It is meaningless.

"Now, though, the other Houses are riled, and someone needs to go and eat shit. And I find, Mother, that I have no appetite for shit. I am all full up after listening to you and your petty machinations in the library. So now, I am telling you to go and make nice. See how well you can lie to them.

"Now, do you understand me, Mother, or should I have Thacker write it down for you?"

Granny Spregg chews through several ripostes. "I should have douched," is where she settles.

Brethelda smiles. "I'm glad we understand each other." She stands. Thacker twitches. "Don't worry," Brethelda tells him. "I'll see myself out."

Granny Spregg waits a full ten seconds before she meets Thacker's eye. "And you thought I'd have to beg to be allowed to go."

Thacker swallows. "I stand corrected."

"You slouch-like-a-winded-boar corrected, Thacker."

"As you say."

Granny Spregg stands, checks the clock on the wall. The wait was shorter than she thought. She still feels sweaty and short of breath, but she has purpose again. She starts to move across the room. She'll need her necklace if she's to see Osmondo Red. The one of dried fae ears strung tog—

The room suddenly lurches sideways. Granny Spregg staggers a step. Then she finds that the room has tilted around her, has reached up and smashed her in one ancient cheek.

She lies, breath hitching in and out. Her vision spirals, contracts, and Thacker is only a blur as he comes rushing towards her.

Edwyll

In the filth-strewn main room of a squat many miles away, Edwyll stands very still.

"They've gone," he says.

The goblin staring at his mural flinches, spins around. She looks at him, as if trying to remember where she is. Then she steps forward, holding out her hands as if to take his. "Thank you," she says. "Thank you. You saved my life."

Edwyll finds himself nodding.

"I'm Edwyll," he says.

"Jag."

"From the bar." He is not sure why he says it. He's not sure what to say. How does one turn the topic of conversation to payment in the form of lifetime sponsorship?

Not this way. Jag's face fills with shock, then fear. She shies away from him. "No," she gasps. "You were there? I didn't—" Then she recognizes him, he sees. She shakes her head violently. "That wasn't." Her eyes are large, imploring. "Please," she says.

For a minute he doesn't understand. And when he does it's with a sense of shock. *Forgiveness,* he thinks. *She's asking for forgiveness. From me.*

That is not the sort of thing a goblin asks for from a fae. The butcher doesn't ask forgiveness from a cow. And yet here they both are.

He tries to see it from her eyes. Does he seem like a threat? He doesn't feel like a threat. He just saved her life. He doesn't think she can be telling him this to try and fend him off. It feels… genuine.

"I didn't want what happened in the bar," she says. She's not looking at him. She's looking at his mural again, he realizes. "I came here because…" She looks down at the floor for a moment, then up again, and her eyes glance off him and go back to the painting. "Because there's still so much beauty here. There's so much good. And so many goblins either refuse to see it, or pretend they can't see it. But I just wanted… I wanted to try… Sil… with the sword, she's my sister. My half-sister. And terrible things have been done to her. She's been made into something so cold. So, I wanted her to see everything that I see here. I wanted her to feel what I feel when I come here. But everything I wanted was the opposite of what happened. And I was stupid, and naïve, I see that… But I didn't want what happened. I swear."

She reaches up, brushes at an eye.

He believes her. It's almost against his will but he does. Her earnestness convinces him.

"Thank you," she says again. "If you saw what happened in there… I didn't deserve kindness from you."

He shrugs, awkward now. All his thoughts of demanding patronage as payment feel clumsy and demeaning now.

"I just want to get out of the Fae Districts and stop causing trouble," Jag says. "I just… I need a way home."

"A cab," Edwyll says.

She looks at him. "Do you know a driver you can trust to take me home safely? To House Red?"

No, he does not. He looks out at the burning, shouting city. "Not tonight," he says.

They stand there in awkward silence. Could she hide here, he wonders? Just sit in the shadows and hope no one else comes here with the same idea? Hope those sidhe don't come back to make sure they didn't miss something?

She's turned away from him, is looking at the mural again. "This," she says. "This is why I came here. Because things like this exist here."

"Thank you," he says.

She looks at him. "You really did this?"

He shrugs again. Nods. "Yeah."

"It's..." she trails off for long seconds. "Wow."

He opens his mouth. *Clumsy, and awkward, and mercenary.* But she is a House goblin. When else will he get this opportunity?

"With patronage," he says carefully, "I could create more." It feels crass as soon as it's out of his mouth. It feels as if he is trying to buy himself success for the price of a dozen bloody bodies left in a bar.

She blinks at him. He opens his mouth to take it back. And then she says:

"Yes."

"What?"

"Well..." She looks around them. "I am miles from home, and everyone in between here and there seems to want to kill me. And the Fae Districts are on fire. And I don't know what's happening. But I do love your art. And if you can get me home, if you can keep me safe, then yes."

And in among all of that, the only word that was really clear to Edwyll was *Yes.*

He wants to laugh. Because there is a path forward. A way to change things, to make things better.

"Come with me," he says. "I know what we can do."

Knull

Skart is bleeding all over Knull's shoes. He is, in fact, bleeding over quite a lot of the alleyway. Although, Knull supposes, it is quite hard to tell where Skart's blood ends and the Spriggans' begins.

Knull gets up. It takes longer than usual. His body pulses with agony. His ankle screams. One of his eyes won't open. Tears leak down his cheeks.

They were going to kill him.

The dangers of the Iron City have, of course, always been known to Knull. No fae grows up here without knowing how close they walk to the precipice of a goblin's displeasure each day. But, for Knull, that danger has always been something that happens to others. The careless and the foolish.

Except then he was up against a wall with a gun in his mouth and a fist in his crotch. Then, the danger was all around him, inside him. He was sodden with terror. And then, it left him here, gasping and trembling, like someone half-drowned in his own fear.

Now, he looks down at Skart. It went worse for the old kobold. Stupid bastard, getting himself killed.

There's nothing Knull can do about that, though. He cannot make anything better. So, slowly Knull starts to drag himself towards the alley's exit.

Behind him, Skart groans.

Knull stops. Skart groans again.

So, not dead yet.

But… soon.

Surely.

Knull takes another step. Skart coughs—wet and followed by a mewl of pain.

Knull tells himself he doesn't owe Skart anything.

Except the old kobold did drop the pistol into Knull's lap. He did throw himself in front of the Spriggan's gun. He did beat the commandos to the floor.

Knull didn't ask him to, though.

But…

Knull hobbles back to Skart. There is a small black hole in the kobold's stomach. It wells with blood. Skart's ruddy face is knotted in pain.

He'll be dead soon. There's nothing Knull can do. Knull's too beaten and too bruised to help. It's too much to ask. It's… It's…

"Factory," Skart gasps. "On Steel and Main… fae there… heal me…" He takes a long, shuddering breath.

Fuck.

Fuck.

Knull wants to howl it. He wants to run from here screaming the word into the night. He wants to curl up, and hurt, and heal, and forget that Skart ever existed. He wants to find someone who will pay him for his Dust, so he can live somewhere beautiful and wonderful, and so very far away from all this shit.

He doesn't owe Skart anything. He repeats the words over and over and over in his head.

Cursing all the way, Knull bends down. Cursing all the way, he heaves Skart up onto his shoulder. His ankle screams, and he whispers obscenities back at it. Then, staggering, spitting, and still cursing as he goes, he carries the kobold out of the alley and away towards a factory on Steel and Main.

Bee

Bee and the Fae Liberation Front descend into the gun-smoke haze of the abandoned lot. The goblins lie splayed on the floor, some looking peaceful, eyes closed, only a single black hole telling the truth of their slumber. Others dissemble less and have been disassembled more. They end abruptly. Limbs lie severed from torsos. Fist-sized holes mark meaty exit wounds.

The whole place stinks of gunpowder and copper.

Bee takes tentative steps. He doesn't want to step in the blood or tangle his feet in a loop of intestine.

Behind him, Tharn descends one-handed, cussing a storm. They've bandaged his shoulder as best they can, but the wrappings are already the same color as the goblins' hats.

"You OK?" Tharn asks when he stands beside Bee.

Bee thinks about that. He'd wanted to come out and knock some heads. That's what he'd said. Now, he still feels sick.

"No," he says.

"We should look for papers," Harretta is telling the others. "Anything that shows why the goblins are here."

Some eyes flick to Bee. "Aye," he says, as if it's a vote. "*You* OK?" he asks Tharn as they start splitting off into groups.

"Well, it feels like there's a fire brand in my shoulder," Tharn says. "So…"

"So, someone finally pulled it out of your ass then?"

Laughing makes it a little better.

"Should you go back?" Bee asks him more seriously. "You wanted to warn people about what's going on. Maybe this is the time. You can have that shoulder seen to properly there."

Tharn shakes his head. "We made a decision. As a collective. To stick together. To not weaken the group."

"Like you're adding strength," Bee says, and Tharn makes an obscene gesture with his hand.

Finding a little more laughter in the night, they push back a tent flap and enter a small dark space, lit only by the holes their barrage tore through the fabric ceiling. There's a table in the center. Papers are scattered over it. A goblin is scattered over them.

They can't read anything in the dark, gore-splattered tent. They take the papers out into the lot, try to make typewritten text out through the crimson smears.

"Shit," Bee says.

"What?" Tharn is holding a sheet of paper up to the glow of a streetlight.

"What do you have?" Bee asks instead.

"Requisition form," Tharn says, squinting. "Ammunition, and… shit, they brought a lot of grenades."

"Hmm," Bee says. "Well, I have radio codes for thirty-five groups of House Red Cap commandos sent to the Fae Districts tonight," Bee says.

Tharn lowers his sheet of paper. "How many?"

Bee can see from Tharn's expression that his own must be suitably grim.

They call the others to them. Soon, grim becomes a unifying look for the Fae Liberation Front.

"OK," Tharn says when they're all appraised. "Now, we *have* to let the others know."

Harretta shakes her head. "*Now,*" she says, "speed is more important than ever before. We must press our advantage before they know we've found them out."

Bee looks up to the roof edge above. "We left three more friends up there."

"To the vote?" Harretta asks, speaking as if he hadn't.

"No debate?" Tharn asks sharply.

"There's no time," she replies.

Bee looks at Harretta. There still isn't anything bloodthirsty on her face.

Tharn, apparently, isn't going to let this go, though. "Do you seek leadership?" he asks.

And those, in the Fae Liberation Front, are what pass for fighting words.

"What did you just ask me?" Harretta's pale blue skin mottles purple—her sidhe regality mixed with punkish anger.

"You know we have to discuss a motion," Bee tries to say.

"Did I not ask for a vote?" Harretta's fists are balled.

"You attempted to bully a result," Tharn insists.

Their voices rise. Everything around Bee smells of blood. He has been swallowed by the glory and the horror of the fight.

"—coward—" Harretta says.

"—demagogue—" Tharn spits back.

Glory and horror. Aggression and caution. The whole world split into dichotomies. Fae and goblin.

Old arguments. New arguments all around him. But Bee finally thinks he knows whose side he's on. He remembers why he was excited for this fight.

"Quiet!" he snaps.

They both stop, stare at him. At his audacity.

"This," he tells them, "is not what we do. This," he tells all the gathered fae, "is not what *I* do. I don't command. I don't lead. None of us do. We are a collective. We debate. And that does not mean screaming hate into each other's faces. It doesn't mean accusing. Because we don't do that. We're the Fae Liberation Front. We're about fucking liberation. From a mindset. From an outlook. We fight for a future unshackled from artificial binaries. We knock heads so we can heal minds. So what—" He stares at both Tharn and Harretta. "—the fuck is all this?"

And he doesn't expect shame. They're all too angry for that. But he does want them to listen. That's all he's ever wanted. A voice. And that's what he's here to fight for in the Iron City tonight.

"Now," he says, "a position has been put forward: to pursue these goblins and value speed over reinforcements. Tharn offers a counterargument: to tell the uprising's leadership. I have a third path: we split the group, sending one back as a messenger, while the rest of us pursue. Who else has something to add?"

Silence. For a moment it's all silence, and just the sullen stares of Tharn and Harretta in the middle of it all, and he thinks it was for nothing. But then Chow, a stout pixie with a blood-soaked bandana on her forehead, the red stark against her orange skin, says, "What's changed since the factory? How can we afford to thin our numbers now by sending messengers back if we couldn't then?"

"And we can't send only one back," says Ashette, a coal-black kobold-pixie with hair the color of a sunset. "It's too dangerous. It would have to be three at least."

And that's it. There. Voices expanding on an idea. Riffing on it. Evolving it. Imperfect, inelegant, perhaps impossible. But seeking for something better. And that idea is what binds the Fae Liberation Front together. That is why they fight.

Two minutes later, and Bee says, "To the vote."

They vote again to go on together, as one. They are in this together. They are scared to send back a small group, finding safety in numbers. They all have their own different reasons, and they don't all agree, but when the vote is cast none of them question the result.

Harretta smiles. Tharn fingers his gun nervously. But neither won or lost as far as Bee is concerned. It's the process that matters to him, not the result. And, to him, this finally feels like a victory.

Sil

Sil is spinning. Every battle feels like it ends in disaster. Jag is nowhere she looks for her. The Iron City is a labyrinth, and she simply cannot walk any further.

She knows she should know what to do. Questions were removed from her life a long time ago. *If this, then this* is the truth of her existence. Except losing Jag was never a variable she was allowed to contemplate.

After a while, she walks forward again. She has to. It's the only course of action she can think to take. She's lost her sense of direction, though. Her gaze bounces off street names, reads letters that never coalesce into words.

She wanders. She stops. She spins.

This part of the city is quieter, she thinks. The violence that possesses the other parts of the Fae Districts hasn't infected these streets yet.

If the streets are quiet, then… what?

She walks forward again. Or is she going backwards? Has she been here before?

The crackle of a radio interrupts her. It comes from a doorway, an apartment complex service entrance. She stops. Could it be Jag?

But Jag has no radio.

"—sit rep. Oscar-crimson-five reporting—"

And somewhere in her scrambling mind, she finds a tiny pane of clarity through which she can stare. Oscar-crimson-five is a House Red Cap call sign. It's one of their commando groups.

Osmondo has found her.

For a moment, the urge to flee flares in her, almost overpowering. The only thing that holds her still is her shock at its existence. It is as if she has wandered into a familiar garden to find a weed towering over her, something massive and terrifying.

She backs away from her own urges and into the commandos' arms. She has stopped knowing herself.

They are crouched in the corridor-like space between two buildings—twelve of them in a tight oval. Their commander has a flashlight pointed at a map. They all look up.

"Asset Sil reporting in," she says. The words are automatic. There is comfort in that. She knows what to say.

The commander's eyes widen. He looks from her to his troops. "Asset Sil," he repeats.

She nods. She is well-known in House Red. There is no point dissembling.

He licks his lips. "And what is Princess Jaggered's status?"

"Princess Jaggered..." She hesitates over the words. All calm departs. Again, she feels the urge to flee along with it. "She's in the wind," she manages.

The commander blinks. "She's not secure?"

Sil's breath is tight in her lungs. She wants to punch someone. "I confirm this." It feels like asking for the gun to be placed against her temple.

The commander nods slowly. He lifts the radio to his lips, lowers it, then raises it again. "Oscar-crimson-five," he says, "Operation Winnow update. Asset Sil has reported in. Jaggered is in the wind. Repeat, asset Sil and Jaggered are separated and Jaggered is in the wind."

The static that follows fills Sil's skull. It echoes.

"Red base confirms Oscar-crimson-five." The radio spits out the hissing words. "Asset Sil in your possession. Operation Winnow proceeding as planned. Bring her home."

Signal and noise. And there is so much noise in Sil's head. And yet, there is something in that message. Something that snags at the ragged edges of her mind.

A cut fan belt. A plot within House Red...

The commander stands. He extends a hand. "Time to come in, asset Sil."

He smiles.

That, Sil thinks, is his mistake. Because none of this—*proceeding as planned; Operation Winnow*—is the reaction of a house thrown into chaos by the loss of its daughter and heir.

And so…

If they're not worried by Jag's loss…

If this is what they anticipated…

…then *these* goblins are a threat to Jag.

Finally, Sil knows exactly what to do.

The commander is a good soldier. He's been slowly signaling his team to surround her. She sees him realize what's going to happen in the moment before she moves.

He goes for his gun. She drops to the floor as he snaps off the shot. The bullet that would have caught her in the gut sears a path through the air above her head, slams into the knee of the commando directly behind her, sends him spinning away like a bowling pin.

Sil rolls, comes up and draws her sword in the same motion. She brings it up into the crotch of one of the other commandos. He howls, collapsing around his collapsed anatomy. She stretches out her smile. She brings the shock and awe.

The second shot is fired past her right hip. She pirouettes left, snaps out the blade. Her target catches the blow on his armored shoulder rather than in his neck. She keeps on moving, though, her stride not faltering as she lets the blade scrape up towards the goblin's cheek. He stumbles back, she extends a leg, sends him sprawling.

The building walls press close; it is a small, tight space. It's not good for gun play. She smiles wider.

One of the commandos figures it out faster than the others. The butt of his gun catches her in the side of her abdomen. Her body snaps around the blow, trying to flow with it as much as she can. Her sword swings wildly, and she feels a tug on the tip. She hears a scream. Good.

Another commando kicks out. She catches his foot, drags him toward her, sword at his throat.

A moment of pause. She has a hostage. But still the gun barrels start to come up.

She flicks the sword tip against her captive's artery. Blood makes a monochromatic rainbow, flies everywhere. She drops, as around her commandos blink and splutter. Guns go off. Something catches her in the shoulder. She grunts, keeps hold of her sword, keeps pushing.

Crouched low, she stabs out again, again, again, again. She aims for gaps between armored plates, skewers guts and punctures organs.

Another rifle butt, this one to the back of the head. There's no riding it out, as it sends her to the floor. A foot crunches down against her ankle, grinds against the bone.

"They said you'd make it difficult." She recognizes the commander's voice. It makes her think less of him. He should know better than to gloat. He should know better than to let her know exactly where his foot is. She flicks the blade back. There is a meaty thwack; the commander howls.

He flails away. Her ankle released, she flips forward, comes clear off the ground. Bullets chase her arc through the air, but they're already too late. She skewers the commander through his open mouth.

Two are left. One on either side of her. They stare. Her sword is stuck somewhere between their commander's upper vertebrae. He has a pistol in a hip holster, though. She snatches it out, snaps off a shot to the left, brings it over to the right.

She's gotten cocky. She's taken too much pleasure in knowing precisely what she has to do. She hasn't shifted her weight enough. She has presented too much of a target.

The final commando's rifle goes off. One shot in the shin. The second into the meat of her thigh. The rest of the burst goes past her hip.

She fires as she falls, catches her last opponent below the jaw, takes off the top his skull like she's opening a can.

Then she hits the floor. And then she and the fight are all done.

13

That's Another Fine Mess You've Gotten Me Into

Granny Spregg

There are many things Granny Spregg would like to see upon waking. Her children in chains and begging forgiveness. The eviscerated corpse of Osmondo Red. Several swarthy members of House Troll with a serious aversion to clothing. Thacker, however, is not one of these things.

Thacker hovers over her, hands fluttering like spasming butterflies.

She turns from him, hawks and coughs. Her phlegm is pink as it hits the pillow.

"Get me up," she growls.

He has carried her to her bed. He props her up now, plumps pillows at her back.

Granny Spregg examines her hands. Between the knotted knuckles and thick twists of veins a purple stain is spreading up her forearm.

"It seems," she says, "that our antidote has only delayed the inevitable."

Thacker almost shits himself. "I'll… I'll…" he stutters.

"You'll not forget what is on the line," she tells him. "There is a quantity of Dust in this city capable of turning me into an all-singing, all-dancing gymnast who floats through the air farting golden fae skulls. Poison is nothing. Time is everything. How long was I out?"

Thacker swallows. "I wasn't… I didn't… I wasn't sure if you'd wake up. I didn't look."

She grabs him by the lapel with one poison-stained hand. "Guess."

"Ten… ten minutes?"

"Then, Thacker, we are on the verge of being late for our appointment with the other Houses."

Thacker's eyes almost fall out of his skull. "But…"

"The plan, Thacker," she tells him. "The plan solves everything."

"…you're dying." Thacker seems to think this is new information.

"So are you," she snaps back. "I'm just doing it faster. Now get my ballgown out and fetch the car. Quickly."

Knull

What, in the name of every hell there is, Knull would like to know, does Skart eat?

He staggers. He stumbles. He aches. And Skart's body lies slumped over his shoulder like a sack of skin and leaden bones.

How has one old kobold gotten so heavy?

Every part of Knull hurts. His ankle pulses fire up to his knee. Life-debt or no, Knull is about to dump the bastard and run when finally Steel Avenue comes into sight. The factory's smokestacks puncture the skyline a few hundred yards away.

Just a little further…

He doesn't make it.

"Hold still, friend."

The voice sidles out of an alleyway. A lithe-looking pixie follows. He looks about as friendly as he sounds.

"Street's off limits." The pixie is all tattoos and lazy confidence. "And my friend on the roof over there has iron sights set on your skull if you want to argue the point."

Knull is too tired, and too hurt, and too covered in someone else's blood to take much offence.

"Just returning lost property." He dumps Skart onto the street.

A little of the pixie's laconic cool escapes him. "Is that…?" he asks.

"Probably." Knull turns away. He's done with this bullshit.

Behind him, a pistol is cocked. When Knull turns back around, the pixie holds something small, snub-nosed, and aggressive. "Oh no," the pixie says. "No, you're coming with me. Now, pick him up."

Knull doesn't even have the energy to object. He hauls Skart up and starts hobbling down the street to the factory. Another unfriendly pixie lets them all inside without a word. He eyes Skart draped bloodily over Knull's shoulder.

The stairs down to the basement nearly break Knull. He almost loses his footing three times. Ahead of him, the pixie bustles self-importantly. "We've got Skart!" he announces as they emerge from the stairwell. "Make way! He's hurt."

No one makes way. No one looks up. The scene is pure chaos. Fae hurtle back and forth, shouting as they go. Bleeding fae nurse injuries everywhere. Old schoolroom blackboards fill the spaces between them. Maps half-obscured by red marker scrawl peel from the boards and pile in drifts. A huge dryad stands at the center of this scrum, gesticulating wildly. No one seems to be paying her any attention.

"Werzel, get me a report on Thoroughgood Avenue! Where are the supply runners now? What the fuck is happening in the Slacks?"

A thin sidhe bundles down the stairs past them, her long hair flapping in her wake. "More reports of goblin activity in the Iron Elbow," she shouts to no one in particular. "We've lost five. Wounded incoming."

It's more babble thrown into the maelstrom of sound. The pixie keeps pushing Knull towards the massive dryad. He keeps calling out, "We've got Skart!"

The dryad almost tramples them, stumbling to a stop barely a foot from Knull. She stares at the group, puzzled. The pixie repeats his message again. "We've got Skart."

The dryad looks electrified.

Knull drops the body. He almost drops down right beside it, just manages to turn his collapse into the act of sitting down. He's just going to watch the rest of this play out from the floor. He's too tired to be anything but a spectator.

The dryad screams for healers and two more pixies come running. Their eyes are glazed, pupils dilated. The sound of birdsong seems to echo from somewhere behind their heads. Their aprons are stained red and brown.

"I think he's been shot," the dryad says. She looks at Knull. "Has he been shot?"

"Uh," is about as articulate as Knull can make himself.

The healers kneel. One reaches into a pocket, pulls out a pinch of Dust, snorts it. The sound of birdsong intensifies in Knull's ears. He sees grass sprout through the concrete beneath her feet. Her hands pulse with yellow light. She sets them on Skart's abdomen.

Skart's eyes fly open. He writhes. The second healer has

positioned herself at his shoulders. She holds on tight. There is a wet sucking noise. A small leaden ball flies up and out of Skart's guts. The dryad catches it in one gnarled fist.

Beneath her, Skart collapses. Dried blood flakes off his body. The damp stuff runs thickly back into the slowly closing hole in his abdomen.

The healer lets out a long breath. Butterflies flutter from her mouth, evaporate into nothingness. Beneath Skart, the grass wilts, curls up, drifts back into the ether, leaving untarnished concrete behind. These side effects of Dust use are usually temporary, and no one here looks likely to take the life-threatening volumes of the drug that lead to more permanent forms of this spill-over magic.

The healer stands. "Give him a minute." She and her assistant head back into the crowd. Knull notices a small trickle of blood running from her ear. How much Dust has she taken tonight? he wonders. How much more can she take before she's lying on the floor next to the fae she's trying to heal?

And for what, he wants to know. What is being achieved out there? Because from the state of this factory basement, Skart's uprising is in a bloody shambles.

And now the old kobold is waking up just in time for Knull to tell him, *I told you so*.

Skart stirs, opens his eyes. Slowly, he sits up.

"Praise be." The big dryad reaches down to help him. Skart stands, but as he does so, his eyes settle on Knull. He nods. There's gratitude in it.

Knull shrugs. He doesn't know how he feels about any of this. Except tired.

"Skart," the dryad is carrying on. "What happened?"

Skart's eyes leave Knull, flick up to the dryad, to the chaos in the room.

"No," he says. "You tell me. What happened here?"

The dryad seems to deflate, her courage collapsing beneath her skin. "They knew," she said. "Everywhere we went, there were goblins. They were waiting in the factories. They waylaid our fae in the streets. They ambushed our propaganda teams."

She puts her head close to Skart's, speaks so Knull can only just catch the words. "I wasn't prepared for this."

Skart puts a red hand on her gray cheek. "It's OK," he says. "I'm here now."

About them, fae have started to notice Skart. They're starting to stare. A hush falls. Knull watches as Skart plays it for everything it's worth.

"So," he finally says, when all eyes are on him. "So, it's a fight we're in. Well—" He looks around. "—that's what we wanted, isn't it? We didn't come here to throw the goblins a fucking tea party."

The room is surly, though. They've gotten more than their knuckles bloody tonight. Skart keeps pushing.

"It's hard. I know that. It hurts. I get it. We had a plan. It failed. Someone sold us out. Now, you want to turn tail, to run and hide, and hope they don't find us when the purges come. I get it. I do. I do."

He pauses again, but this time he looks at Knull. "Because that's a familiar story, right? It's the same story we've told so many times before. We rise up, we fail, the reprises come. History repeats over and over again." He looks up once more. "Well, I don't know about you, but I'm sick of that story."

There's a stirring in the crowd now. They're interested. They want to be convinced that they haven't just made everything worse.

"We hoped for the element of surprise," Skart says. "The goblins stole it from us. Perhaps we should be used to that. It's hardly the first thing they've taken from us." He gets a dry chuckle from some parts of his audience. "But surprise isn't the end of the fight," Skart says. "That's the opening three seconds. Momentum can change. I was in the Iron War. I know."

"They have us outgunned!" someone shouts from the safety of the crowd.

"Outgunned." Skart nods again. "With bullets and steel, right? Well, those help, yes, but they're not what wins a fight. Hearts and minds. Will and courage. That's what wins. And that's what we have. The goblins think they have broken us, but we are here—in this room, out in those streets—because we refuse to be broken. We have been forged, hardened, and baptized by oppression. We have a will they cannot match and we will fight on long after their spirit is spent.

"We," he says, "have magic in our hearts. You say they outgun us. I say they never could in a thousand years." And then he pauses, and he looks down, and he stares Knull right in the eye. "We have Dust. We can change the very world."

Then he looks away. Looks back to the crowd. His voice rises to a shout. "They tried to take our magic, our spirit, and our soul from us, but we are the fae. We hold on. We will not be denied. And our magic will rend the flesh from their bones!"

Now, the room cheers. Now, the room loses it for this deranged old kobold, with his deranged old dreams. Knull, though, isn't cheering. He's not on his feet and stamping. He's sitting there and he's breathing hard. Because the bastard is putting this on him. A whole revolution that he doesn't want. Every injured fae in this room.

Skart just told everyone that this revolution depends on him giving up his brick of Dust.

Jag

The Iron City, Jag thinks, has gone septic. All the tainted wonder and dirty beauty of the Fae Districts has fled, just like its citizens have fled from their beds out into the streets in their threadbare robes and cheap polyester pajamas. Some clutch small plastic radios. Others have chosen handguns. They all know something is happening. They all know it's bad. There's thunder on the horizon after all. Except it's not thunder, it's bomb blasts and gunfire.

Edwyll has led Jag from the squat, out onto these crowded, confused streets. Now they veer away from these clusters of concerned citizens, aim for emptier streets where Jag's sharp features are less likely to give her away. Then they realize that the only others using the emptier streets are armed gangs.

They're halfway down one street when shots ring out overhead, two groups, one on either side of the rooftops, gunning each other down, cursing and screaming. Jag and Edwyll hurtle around a corner, crash into another crowd.

Some call out the old refrain—"What's happening?"—but more scream and burst into a miniature stampede. Jag and Edwyll are bustled and bundled along.

An old brownie catches Jag by the arm, holds her against the battering tide of bodies. "What's going on?" he demands, while Jag desperately ducks her head. "What's causing this?" He sounds furious.

Edwyll wrenches Jag free. They run on.

They take refuge in a small alleyway between a bakery and a grocer's. It smells of bleach and rotting cabbage.

The crowd rumbles and grumbles past them, drifting in search of news and safety.

"Come on." Edwyll pushes away and she follows. Increasingly,

Edwyll seems almost mythical to her—some creature stepped out of a story, or a painting. She goes back again in her mind to the mural he painted. He had spoken about it so dismissively, as if it was nothing, and yet to her… that vision of the White Tree rising up and out of the misery and the violence, the vision of something beautiful emerging from the chaos, reaching up, aspiring, uplifting, hopeful… It was what the city could be if it just tried. Or… it was the city she had always wanted to see. And Edwyll had put it right there in front of her.

Now, Edwyll leads her through that city's streets. Leads her to safety.

Or…

"We're heading away from the Houses," she says, an ember of suspicion flaring in her.

"I can't get you there tonight," he says. "But I can keep you safe until this chaos dies down."

She smothers the ember. She has to trust him. There's no one else left.

He takes her further and further away from the burning lights of the Houses at the city's heart. Occasionally a car burrs past them, travelling too fast for the street's tight confines. They pass a crowd of fae who seem to be having a street party. The Iron Wall looms a little larger. It is the circumference of her whole world. She's never been permitted to see what lies beyond it, and it has gained a sense of mystery and wonder for her. She came out here to a fae poetry reading once, and the pixie on stage called it "the world that was", and that is how she has thought of it ever since.

Then, finally, Edwyll comes to a stop. He's in front of a wooden door that's been painted red, blue, and green, fractured shards of color defying the eye's attempt to find a pattern.

"I have friends here," he tells her.

She nods, and it strikes her suddenly that she is behaving with him just as she would with Sil. Old patterns are taking over. She is letting him take charge because there is danger about. But she hardly knows him. She has no guarantee that he is not leading her to greater danger.

She needs, she thinks, to stop thinking like the privileged heir of Osmondo Red and start thinking more like Sil. She needs to take charge of her destiny. She just needs to work out how.

Before she can, though, Edwyll has knocked and a female voice has answered from the far side of the door. "Who is it?"

"It's me." Edwyll puts his lips to the edge of the doorframe, calls as quietly as he can. "Edwyll."

The door swings open, revealing a matronly-looking pixie in dirty overalls wielding a bat with three nails driven through it. Jag steps back, alarmed.

The pixie looks at the bat, seems surprised to find it there. "Sorry," she says, lowering it. "Talluck made it for me. He's calling it 'the last recourse of discourse' and telling everyone that he wants to use it in a performance piece."

This is all unintelligible to Jag, but Edwyll laughs. There has been a change in him, Jag can see, in the few seconds since he knocked at the door. He seems suddenly lighter on his feet, the tension on his face gone. "Is Talluck here?" he asks.

The pixie nods. "We all are. Me, Talluck, Threm, Jallow. Keeping our heads down." She nods in Jag's direction. "You brought a friend, I—"

And then she really sees Jag and her mouth falls open a little. Jag turtles into her dress shirt's collar.

"Oh," the pixie says.

"We need to get off the streets," Edwyll tells her. "We need somewhere safe."

The pixie keeps on staring at Jag. "We?"

"She's OK," Edwyll says, and the tension has stepped back into his throat. "She's not a threat, I promise. I wouldn't do that to you."

The pixie finally wrenches her eyes from Jag. "OK," she says, a little breathless. "Well, then. You better come in."

Granny Spregg

Finally, Granny Spregg allows herself to relax. The ballgown she has changed into only permits the slightest slackening in her spine, but it is not the least comfortable armor she's worn. And it is better suited for the fight she's heading into than a steel breastplate or a Kevlar flak jacket. But for now, she tells herself, things are in hand. Nothing, she reiterates, can be done from within the plush confines of the limousine. Anxiety will only speed up the poison working in her veins.

Up in the driver's seat, Thacker is faking confidence and slowly navigating their departure through House Spriggan's many and complex defenses. They pass through iron gates and over drawbridges. Snipers aim guns at their vehicle as they go by. Dour goblin soldiers inspect their identities.

This level of security is standard for all the Houses. The peace between them is uneasy, after all. In her day, Granny Spregg always preferred something more ostentatiously offensive. Now, though, Brethelda has ensured everything at House Spriggan is sleek and modern. Uniformed guards stand to attention, devoid of nuance and humor. A mile away, House Troll's brutish barricades far outshine them when it comes to unsubtle savagery.

You can tell a lot about the Houses, Granny Spregg thinks, by looking at their defenses. House Hobgob has hidden itself behind a maze of machines, each one devious and sharp-bladed. House Bogle has its labyrinth. And, of course, there is House Red Cap, its face utterly inscrutable, a blank cube of concrete and steel, devoid of windows and doors. Its method of entrance is one of the Iron City's most closely guarded secrets. Despite the efforts of Granny Spregg's best torturers.

Now, as the gates of House Spriggan finally close behind her, Granny Spregg can see these other Houses gathered about her, raised like the fingers of a clawing hand, each one desperate to tighten its grip on the city's heart. Tonight, she thinks, House Spriggan will finally achieve that goal. Thanks to her. As soon as she has secured her prize.

The drive to their destination takes all of five minutes. The Opera House sits equidistant from all the Houses, a place made neutral because every partisan pull on it cancels the other out. It sits at the true heart of the city, a central hub, and the Iron City's entire political and social scene revolves around this axle—in its ballrooms, and its quiet speak-easy bars slipped like blades between corridors and conference rooms, and in its vaulted chambers where societies meet to scream slogans and drink themselves into a stupor. Any singing done here is almost an afterthought—an aping of sidhe customs designed more to rub the fae's noses in their defeat than to entertain the ear.

It is also as safe a place as the Iron City has to offer. The Houses have not agreed to abstain from assassination attempts here, exactly. It is merely obvious to everyone involved that—given how unavoidable this location is—six months after the first trigger is squeezed, they will all be dead.

Outside, Thacker pulls the car to a velvet-smooth stop. He opens Granny Spregg's door with exaggerated elegance. He has always been good at the pomp and circumstance. It's a shame,

Granny Spregg thinks, about everything else.

The splay of cars already parked indicates that Granny Spregg is the last House head to arrive. The others, she is sure, wanted to array themselves in aesthetically overwhelming displeasure, in order to maximize how much Brethelda would have to crawl.

"Alright, Thacker," she says. "Showtime." She grips the door handle.

"But, Madame Spregg," Thacker whines, "having the Dust at this juncture was somewhat vital—"

She hauls herself up and out of the car and he finally deflates into silence.

Granny Spregg will never crawl, but neither can she sweep into the Opera House's entrance hall. Rather, she stalks in as best as she is able, stabbing the ground with her cane.

The Opera House's architecture looms around them: massive, ostentatious, overwhelming. They walk beneath arches three stories tall, painted gold and draped with velvet and oil paintings. String quartets ooze soft melodies from hidden annexes. Red carpets lead everywhere. If you are visiting here, you must be a VIP, after all.

Their destination: The Hall of Horns—a circular room lined with the heads of seven white harts, reserved for the rare times the heads of the Houses meet. It is buried deep within the Opera House. Anyone eager to attack so much concentrated power will have to steer a course along a route rife with ambush spots.

Which is what allows Osmondo Red to ambush Granny Spregg.

He launches himself out of an alcove, hissing as he comes. Once, when they fought side by side in the Iron War, he was tall and proud, roped with muscle, with blood on his teeth and fire in his eyes. Age and power, though, have soured him. He has collapsed in on himself. His belly is vast, his arms and legs gnarled and withered. His head is a sunken portrait of savagery, wobbling atop his swollen torso. And yet despite the depravities of age and excess, he has lost none of his bitter energy. He still retains the angry purpose that bore him across battlefields, and this is how he comes at her now—ready for war.

Thacker squeals, and almost breaks into a full retreat. Granny Spregg stands her ground.

"Bedlack," Osmondo spits when he stands before her.

It is so long since Granny Spregg has heard her own first name, she almost doesn't recognize it. "Osmondo," she manages to sneer back.

"The bitch has sent you to crawl for her, I see." Osmondo's breath is sour, and his eyes red.

"Brethelda sends her warmest greetings," Granny Spregg says in her coldest voice.

Osmondo leans in. "I know you, Bedlack." His teeth are flecked with spots of black and red. "I know you like to consider yourself a player of games, so much smarter than the rest of us. You have come here to pluck at us like a harpist on her instrument, isn't that right?"

None of this is a compliment. Granny Spregg smiles all the same. "You do know that the phrase 'throwing your weight around' isn't meant to be taken literally, don't you, Osmondo?" she says. "Tell your chef to go easy on the butter."

Osmondo forms a gnarled fist. Thacker cowers on Granny Spregg's behalf. Osmondo doesn't strike, though.

"Words," hc hisses between pointed teeth. "Always words with you. Do you think the others will feel more sympathy for you if you go in there with a blackened eye and a bleeding lip? Do you *want* me to beat you, Bedlack?" His face is inches from hers.

"Yes, Osmondo," she says. "Words. They're quite harmless, I assure you. You only find them frightening because you don't understand them."

Osmondo, she knows, is monolingual in his methods of persuasion. He understands only aggression. He bullies and he butchers until he gets his way. There is no subtlety to him, and the only way to tame him is to refuse to be intimidated.

Osmondo, though, isn't rising to her bait. "Words won't save you," he hisses. "Not tonight. I know where your troops are, Bedlack. You've sent them to rile up the fae, and I know that now you stand at the head of a House exposed. So, I don't give a fuck what you have to say tonight. I will find an excuse, and I will march into your House, and I will find your children, and I will wear their corpses as my cloak. That will be the legacy of your words, Bedlack. A House of blood and woe."

He leans back, self-satisfied.

It takes some effort, but Granny Spregg summons a small huffing laugh. "You still can't tell if I want you to hit me or not, can you?"

Osmondo grimaces, and then faster than she would have imagined given his age, he slams a fist into her eye, and sends her spilling to the floor.

He stands over her. "I don't care what you want, Bedlack," he says. "I want to hit you. And I get what I want. Tonight, I want to watch your House bleed."

Bee

"We should have taken that last left."

"That would take us straight into their line of fire."

"We should circle round."

"But these are all straight roads."

"Oh, shut up, you ass."

The Fae Liberation Front—however much they do not want to admit it—are lost. An address on Canal between Bridge and Arch Streets is attached to the call sign "Oscar-crimson-five" from Bee's sheet of discovered goblin commando groups. However, out here in Smog's Bend the streets are unfamiliar, and determining the best route is proving as divisive as any other argument they've had this night.

Chow, the pixie, has a map out and is examining it with her brow deeply furrowed. "I think it's an apartment block," she says. "But we wouldn't want to occupy an apartment block, would we?"

Bee shrugs. He doesn't really care *why* the goblins are anywhere. He just cares about making sure they aren't there anymore.

"This is Arch Street," someone else says, pointing to a street sign.

They stop, stare at the sign warily. Harretta approaches Bee and Tharn with similar caution. "We should," she says hesitantly, "have a plan of attack."

Bee's eyes flick to Tharn, but he—thankfully—does not scream at her that she's dictating what the group should do, and simply nods. And for her part, Harretta doesn't add to the conversation, even though she is clearly yearning to tell them more.

Bee, however, has no plan in mind, and apparently Tharn doesn't either. Finally, Bee says, "Well, if you have a suggestion, Harretta…"

"Two groups," she says immediately, "one small and fast to scout a way into the apartment building. Then, once they report back, the main group goes in big and loud. Meanwhile, the scouts head to the back of the building, looking for an alternate means of ingress so they can flank anyone else we come across."

Bee looks at Tharn, shrugs. "Sounds good to me."

Tharn nods.

And that's all well and good, except, of course, it doesn't sound good to Bee in the slightest. Rather, it sounds like charging death down and daring death to make its move.

But he doesn't say that. He doesn't say anything. Instead he listens as the group whispers the plan back and forth—tweaking, refining, negotiating—and by the time they're done, there are two groups of scouts moving forward, one high and one low, while another group of four will watch their back trail. Meanwhile, the remainder will wait for the scouts to give the all clear.

As a group, Bee thinks, they have approximated military know-how. Maybe there should be some comfort in that.

He goes with the scouting group that's sticking to street level. There are three of them: Bee; Garfaux, a purple-skinned sidhe; and Gange, a ginger-haired kobold. They all move at a light jog. Bee holds the machine gun—reclaimed from Tharn once more—tight to his hip, trying to reduce its clatter. He suspects the gun is the reason the other scouts were so happy to have him along.

It is better, he thinks, to be out in front, to meet whatever the world has to offer head on.

The apartment block looms before them, a cheap modern construction without a single straight line to call its own. Aluminum struts twist between buckling plasterboard panels. There is a service entrance to the side of the building. A wooden gate flaps open.

As they approach, Bee holds up a hand, holds the group still. An awkward game of charades plays out, then Garfaux and Gange finally understand, and flit to the far side of the gateway, pressing themselves to the wall.

A smell fills Bee's nostrils, newly familiar to him. It is metallic and meaty and causes his stomach to clench.

He lets the gun barrel lead him around the gateway, already knowing what he's going to see. He blanches anyway. Bodies are scattered across the floor—goblins skewered and in pieces, their red caps askew atop their lolling heads. Shell casings have been scattered through the coagulating pool of blood.

A goblin is propped up against one wall of the narrow space, panting shallowly, her hair dyed white and flecked with red. There's a hole in her thigh and a sword in her hand.

"Shit on a stick," Garfaux breathes beside him. "What happened?"

"I did."

It's the goblin on the floor. Bee meets her gaze and almost takes a step back. Even with her eyes half-lidded, her stare speaks to something in the back of his skull and tells it to run. It's an absurd thought, though. She's on the floor… She's bleeding out…

And yet… is she responsible for this slaughter? Bee looks more closely, and realizes he's made a mistake. Not a goblin. Or… not completely. There is fae in her ancestry too—maybe sidhe or pixie, something fine-boned enough that the sharpness of her goblin heritage still dominates, but also something that has paled the green of her skin, rounded her pupils.

Not that any of this makes her potentially less deadly. Her sword could well be responsible for the wounds he sees. And so… is she on his side? Her goblin-sharp features don't suggest she is. There again, her pale skin is far from a bright goblin green.

Then he understands. Some goblin's unwanted bastard trapped between two worlds, neither of which wanted her.

He steps toward her, a toe-tip touching the pool of spilled blood. "What's your name?" he asks.

The half-goblin spits in response. And given everything she's likely gone through in life, Bee isn't sure he can blame her.

"You killed these goblins?" he asks.

Nothing. The same dead-eyed stare. It's like looking into a lizard's eyes.

A radio crackles on the floor. Bee jumps.

"Oscar-crimson-five," the radio blares. "Report in. What is the status of asset Sil? Repeat, what is the status of asset Sil?"

Bee looks from the radio to the half-goblin. "Asset Sil," he repeats. "Is that you?"

Nothing.

"Asset," Garfaux mutters next to him. "That means she's working with the goblin bastards."

Bee looks at the bodies. "So," he asks the half-goblin, "why would you kill goblins if you work for them?"

Nothing.

"She's lying," Garfaux says.

"She's not saying anything."

Garfaux shrugs. "Lie of omission."

Another examination of the half-goblin. Still nothing.

"Let go of the sword," he tells her, "and I'll bind your leg."

She looks at him for a moment longer, and then finally closes her eyes. Then she opens her hand and the sword falls away.

Bee lets out a breath he hadn't realized he was holding. "OK," he tells Garfaux, "you go and get the others up here. I'll see to her."

Garfaux licks his lips. Bee can sense his uncertainty, his fear. But what else is there to do? If they're to get any more information about what's happening tonight, then it seems they'll need asset Sil's cooperation.

As Garfaux starts waving the others down, Bee crosses to Sil. He kneels and starts ripping a makeshift bandage from a nearby dead goblin's shirt.

"You know," she says, just loud enough for him to hear, "I don't need my sword to kill you."

His blood goes cold. He turns sharply to her, but she's just lying there, eyes still closed.

"Well, I'm glad you haven't," he manages, playing it all much cooler than he feels.

But she doesn't give him anything else, not a single sound even as he binds her leg tightly.

Edwyll

Elsewhere in the Iron City, Edwyll ducks gratefully through a rainbow-painted doorway and follows Lila inside an old townhouse. Behind him, Jag hesitates on the doorstep. He goes back, gives a little half-bow and ushers her in with a sweep of his arm.

"I promised you safety," he says. "You'll be safe here. This is not a hotbed of sedition." He points. "This is Lila. She's an artist."

"Mostly I'm just a waitress," Lila says, stepping deeper into the hallway. "But if Edwyll vouches for you, then you're welcome here."

Jag nods, steps inside. As they follow Lila he leans over. "She does the most beautiful miniatures," he tells her.

Jag nods again, but it's not clear to Edwyll how much she takes in. She is staring at the walls. Edwyll finds himself grinning despite the night's events. He loves Lila's house. Jallow, Lila's on-again, off-again-partner, is a muralist whose work is as expansive as Lila's is tight and controlled. His great washes of color spill across the walls. He and Lila started a collective whose members come and go through the house like the tide, paying rent in creativity, adding to the decorations. There are artifacts from Talluck's performance pieces strung from the ceilings. Lila's miniatures are dotted in amongst the chaos alongside Threm's photographs of working-class fae in factories, and out on the Iron City's streets.

"This is..." But Jag doesn't have the words.

Edwyll nods. "Yes. Yes, it is."

The house has been busy of late, rooms packed with artists. It's made it difficult for Edwyll to crash here. He sleeps on the couch when he can, but Jallow doesn't like it. Lila has told him that Jallow thinks it sets the wrong creative tone. And to be fair, Edwyll's room at his parents' house is always available, but he's slept out on the streets more than once to avoid that particular destination.

Lila waits for them in the living room. Most of the furniture in here has been scavenged, repurposed, and reinvented. Couches have been sutured together, patched wildly. Chimera writing desks teeter-totter on mismatched legs. Lanterns and lampshades metastasize, casting light in strange patterns, leaving oases of shadow at random intervals around the room.

It is, to Edwyll, the most perfect room in all the world. It is imagination come to life, unfettered and pure. Lila and the others of the collective have made a world they want to live in. They have aspired for better than this falling-down, ramshackle house should ever allow, and to Edwyll's eye, they have succeeded wildly.

Talluck—a massive demi-dryad, a drome to be precise, child of a dryad mother and gnome father, and as broad as he is tall—is hunched over a diorama of a stage, manipulating tiny figures of plastic and wood. He half looks up as they enter, lets out a grunt that Edwyll takes as a greeting. Over by a coffee table, Jallow is leafing through a folio of black-and-white photographs. The table, Edwyll knows, has at its heart a small chunk of iron that Jallow has buried beneath layers and layers of imported maple wood, until its sting is reduced to a near negligible itch for all but the most sensitive fae. Jallow—from hardy kobold stock—has burned his hands to shit making them, despite thick protective gloves of ivy banding and spider silk. Still, Edwyll has listened to him tell other artists that it is worth it. "The metaphor of reclamation," he says. "The idea that we can still come back from this. That we can bury the past and find a better place once again." He calls them "rehabilitated objects" and they enjoy a small but lucrative market among House Spriggan nobles. It is this money that funds the collective.

"Hello! Hello! Edwyll!" Threm, the fourth member of the collective, lurches up off the couch grinning. A gnome, in his early fifties, he carefully cultivates a careworn appearance. The battered camera around his neck is something of an affectation, but he is a photographer for *The Grind*, one of the Fae District's local newspapers. He is bringing the camera up, just about to capture Edwyll in the viewfinder, when his eye falls on Jag.

Of all of the collective, it is Threm whose reaction worries Edwyll the most. He is the one whose art is most political. Who has been arrested the most times. Who has needed to go into hiding in the collective's basement more than once.

Lila catches Threm's expression. "She's a friend of Edwyll's," she says quickly. Something in her tone makes the others look up. Talluck drops a diminutive wooden figure.

"She's a patron," Edwyll says. "My patron."

He feels the shockwaves ripple out across the room. This is, he knows, possibly even more startling than walking in here with a goblin on his heels. More in violation of everything these artists hold to be normal.

Talluck has been making his miniatures for two decades, Lila her miniatures for almost two-thirds of that time. Both of them have made small sales to goblins before, but nothing of any real note. Jallow had to hustle for the best part of a decade before his star began to ascend. For Edwyll to waltz in here, still shy of his twentieth year, and casually announce that he has a patron… it's a grenade thrown right into the established order of things.

"A patron?" Lila is the first of them to recover. She is looking at Jag quizzically.

Edwyll turns to look at Jag too, his breath catching. Because she doesn't have to follow through. She doesn't have to do anything. She is a goblin. She doesn't truly owe him anything. She can call him a liar and no one will do anything.

But as Lila looks at her, Jag's face brightens. She beams at the room. "Oh, I just… It's hard to say. I just saw his work and…" She trails off, but her eyes are bright.

And Edwyll knows that she is leaving things out, weaving an alternate narrative that does not place her at the bar, in among the bodies. And he knows that if he says anything then this patronage will be forever tainted in the others' eyes. Will always be bloodstained and mercenary, and he doesn't want them to see it that way.

The group are staring at Jag, waiting for her to go on. The silence drags. Jag looks uncertain.

Then Lila claps. She grabs Edwyll in a hug. "Oh my goodness! Tonight of all nights you find a patron!"

The moment in the room breaks. "I say!" Jallow shouts. "A drink!"

Talluck sits back down at his diorama, grinning as he unfolds a figure's bent arms, and Threm finally takes his appraising eyes off Jag, and pushes a hand through his hair, and says, "Well, at least there's some good news in the Iron City tonight."

And it actually feels honest, here and now in this moment. And Edwyll knows that the jealousy will set in, but it hasn't yet, and Edwyll finds himself smiling. Because maybe it doesn't matter *how* he got a patron. Maybe all that matters is that he *did*.

"What was it about his work that first struck you?"

Edwyll spins round. Somehow Lila has separated him from Jag, has the goblin by the arm and is leaning in conspiratorially. He senses danger, tries to get closer.

Jag smiles at Lila. "The message," she says, not missing a beat. "It was just so clear. This vision of the future. So bold and bright, and so in defiance of the status quo. It was inspiring." Another smile. "I was inspired."

Edwyll edges closer to them. Talluck is shouting at Jallow to get them drinks now, damn it. Threm is staring at them through his viewfinder. Jag links her arm with his, pulls him close. Threm puts the camera down, chews his lip.

"I want him to do something political," she says. "Something big, and disruptive."

"Something that will make fae stop and pay attention," Edwyll says. There's a sense of wonder in his voice, he hears. But everything in the room has stopped feeling expected. Because what she's suddenly talking about, this work she is fucking commissioning in front of everyone, is exactly what he wanted to create. It is as if they have somehow tuned into the same channel, are repeating lines from the same script.

"Here you go." Jallow has brought the drinks. They clink glasses.

Talluck says, "To Edwyll!" and for just a moment all the horror outside is forgotten and Edwyll feels like the center of the world.

And then Lila sighs, and asks, "How is it out there?"

The good feeling drains away. The splatter splash of guts and gun blasts plays out across the theater of Edwyll's mind.

"Bad and getting worse." Jag speaks before Edwyll can recover. He is struck by how unfazed she seems talking to these artists. How here, in a tight room, with the city shut away behind doors and walls, her nervousness is gone. He wonders exactly what sort of fish he has landed here.

"Well—" Threm sits back on the couch, massages his camera. "—it'll be worse tomorrow. When your..." He stares at Jag and trails off.

But Jag nods. "It's OK," she says. "You're right. And it will be exactly as wrong as you believe it to be. This uprising is a natural consequence of..." She hesitates. "...how the Houses—my House—treats you," she says finally.

Threm's eyebrows go up. Jag looks slightly shocked at her own words.

"We want to make a statement." Edwyll can't help himself. And it is not quite a lie, he thinks. Because she said she wanted him to create something political. And he feels convinced suddenly that they do want to create the same thing. He feels confident bringing her into the vision that is forming in his eye of the piece he will create. Something like his mural, but bigger, grander, more refined. The metaphor clearer... "We want to create something," he says, "that can help disrupt the cycles of violence."

"Now *that,*" Lila says, "is something I can drink to."

They sit around Jallow's coffee table. Drinks are raised, and blessings bestowed. The bottle's golden contents burn pleasantly all the way from Edwyll's tongue to his toes. The others demand details of the first time Jag saw his graffiti, how she tracked him down. And with each lie they tell, Edwyll's heart calms a little. They are natural collaborators, he finds, feeding off each other, creating a myth of their past.

"And what was it about the piece that spoke to you?" Lila asks as they bring the story to the night's mural.

Jag blinks, looks to Edwyll. "I just..." She shakes her head. "All my life I have been told what the Iron City is. Who I am in it. Who the fae are. They've told me all this history, and how this is the only logical conclusion. And it's never felt right to me. It's never felt true. And when I looked at Edwyll's art, I just... I finally saw someone who could take that feeling out of my heart and put it on a canvas."

Edwyll thinks he is going to explode.

"We need more goblins who think like you," Talluck—still sitting and toying with one of his figures—rumbles to life.

Threm, tugging on the camera around his neck, looks sour. "Goblins like Jag here are as rare as unicorns. All the rest are still caught in old enmities."

Edwyll feels unexpectedly defensive. "Well," he says, "the same can be said for many fae as well."

Talluck and Jallow both nod.

Threm snorts. "I don't see any goblin artists begging and scraping for fae patronage," he says. "Given the power differentials in the Iron City, I find it easier to understand why the fae hold onto their grudges."

All eyes shift to Jag. The silence is an awkward one.

"No," she says. "No, Threm's right. The goblins have no reason to oppress any more, but they—we—persist."

The whole room's attention is fixed on her.

"Look," she says, "I've been outside. I've seen what's happening. It's a riot. It's the unheard of this city shouting. Some of the fae have been pushed over the edge by the goblins. And tomorrow—brutally, unfairly—we know there will be reprisals, and more fae will suffer. Not just those out there pushed to the brink, but all fae, normal fae.

"It's a cycle. It repeats. The goblins push, the fae break, the goblin use it as an excuse to push harder. It needs to stop. But every time it's the minority speaking the loudest. On both sides, the extremists break first. Everyone else out there—all those like Edwyll, and me, and you—who aspire to a better world through non-violent means are being drowned out. Because they're given no vehicle to speak. They're given no banner to unite behind. So, it all just repeats. It becomes its own self-fulfilling reason to oppress. History caught in a loop. No one ever moving on, just staring back at a war most of us never even lived through. Caught within the Iron Walls."

She's spilled her drink. She realizes everybody is looking at her. Edwyll is staring at her.

"Well," Talluck says, finally standing. "Hear fucking hear." He laughs.

Jallow raises his glass, and Lila and Talluck join in. Jag is blushing, and rubbing the back of her neck. Threm still worries at his camera.

Edwyll is still staring. He sees Jag in the room, sees all of them, sees all the art and inspiration and love they have made in this place, this space—but he sees beyond it too. He sees a tree blooming over them all. Protecting. Guiding their eyes to the skies.

"No banner," he says slowly and to himself. "No banner to unite behind."

"What?" Lila leans forward from her seat on the couch.

"Jag said it," Edwyll says. "She said there's no banner for the fae to unite behind. They're all out there, in the streets right now, running for cover, none of them knowing where they can go. It's chaos. Because no one's bringing them together. No one is giving them a banner to unite behind."

"Oh…" Jag looks embarrassed. "It's… just an expression."

"But it doesn't have to be." He puts a hand on her arm. "We could give them a banner. A sign. Something so they know they're not alone." He's babbling a little, the words rushing out of him in a flood. "Something to show them where they can be safe. Where they can come together. Where they can unite." He feels the sense of wonder again. "A symbol to ignite a movement. To break free."

She's staring at him, eyes wide.

"Yes," Talluck rumbles again. The big drome picks himself up, starts pacing back and forth, nodding to himself. "Yes," he says again. "Art as political movement. Political movement as art. A marriage of the two. The movement as the symbol, the symbol as a voice."

"Here he goes," Threm mutters, "as if House-unsanctioned art gets any play." But Lila just laughs as Jallow rolls his eyes at both of them.

But Edwyll is caught by Talluck's enthusiasm. By his words. "A symbol," he repeats.

Jag is still staring at him. "A tree," she says.

And then Edwyll sees. He sees how everything he's been trying to accomplish with his art, his symbology, his politics can be achieved.

"A white tree," he says. "The symbol of the fae redefined as a banner of unity."

Jag nods. "Breaking free of the past."

Granny Spregg

The Hall of Horns has never been a welcoming space. It is, after all, an architectural testament to slaughter, and the tearing away of all that is precious; a marker of a victory devoid of joy or glory. It is what it was designed to be: the true heart of the Iron City.

The heads of seven white harts hang upon its oak-paneled walls. At the consecration of this city, the masters of the five Houses slaughtered a stag apiece and hung their prizes here. Mab cut the other two heads free herself—two because she is better than all of them, and because she wanted to make sure they never forgot. Now, the harts' glass eyes reflect the low chandeliers' light and stare down at the assembled crowd that stares in turn at Granny Spregg.

Osmondo Red is there, of course, smiling cruelly to himself. Guntra Trog of House Troll too, dressed in a ballgown that probably plays host to a small circus when she doesn't need it. Ethrek Hobgob, small and sour as a lemon, looks almost as shriveled as Granny Spregg despite the fact that she is half her age. And Jeremark Bogle lurks around the edges, fingers steepled, feet always moving, head weaving sinuously from side to side.

"Ah," Granny Spregg breathes as she enters. "My *daughter's* peers."

Ethrek Hobgob's sour face crumples even further. Granny Spregg isn't entirely sure how she manages it. "Brethelda doesn't even deign to meet with us herself?" she asks. "Instead, she sends her elderly and—" She touches her eye. "—*clumsy* mother?"

Granny Spregg just smiles. There is never any pleasing Ethrek so she normally finds it easier to just keep pissing her off. "My daughter," she says, "is as inscrutable as ever. All I can tell you is that I am here." She winks with the eye that is already swelling from Osmondo's punch.

"Go fuck yourself." Guntra Trog is direct at least. Granny Spregg has always liked her the most of this new brood of city leaders.

"Maybe later," she replies, and Guntra tries to suppress a smile.

"So," Ethrek presses, "you offer no explanation for Brethelda's refusal to obey our summons?"

Granny Spregg merely shrugs. "I could offer many explanations, Ethrek. I could tell you that her latest partner has lost the keys to the chains she used to tie Brethelda to the bed last night. I could tell you that she is as likely to answer your summons as she is to shit a live turtle. I could tell you—"

"So many words." Osmondo Red leans forward, mouth twisted. "And yet so little to say."

Granny Spregg resents that. She'd just been getting into her stride. Still, she smiles beatifically at him. "So much meaning to go over your head, Osmondo."

"You are here," Osmondo goes on, "to answer for House Spriggan, to defend it and its actions."

"Does House Spriggan answer to you?"

Osmondo Red smiles a wide smile. "It may."

Granny Spregg looks to the others. "And what about House Hobgob? House Troll? Are we all accountable to each other now? Must we ask each other's permission to do our business? Must Jeremark ask permission to buy, and sell, and charge commission in his counting houses? Must Guntra submit a form before she drills another mine? What about you, Ethrek? Do you want to kowtow to all others before you put your next building up? Is that the freedom we won in the Iron War?"

Osmondo Red growls, but Guntra Trog speaks over him. "None answers to another. Not in this chamber. Not in this city. Not except to Mab."

But Mab is far to the North, too preoccupied with her own apotheosis to worry what happens down here amongst the mortals she has left behind. And they all know it.

"However," Ethrek Hobgob says, "we must all live together. The Iron Wall encircles us all, after all. When one House endangers the others, we must look to our own interests. We must question if House Spriggan's independence is to our best interests."

"*Endangers?*" Granny Spregg arranges her features in an incredulous expression. "And what is it exactly that House Hobgob fears?" She leans just a little on the last word, looks at the others, sees if anyone else will swallow the bait she's flinging indiscriminately around the room.

Ethrek sighs like the schoolmarm she was always meant to be.

"You attempt to equate precaution with weakness, Bedlack. I will not rise to your jibes."

Others, it seems, are willing to swallow the bait whole.

"She attempts," Osmondo says, taking another step toward her, "to weasel her way out of the shit her daughter has pulled. And I won't stand for it."

"Brethelda?" Granny Spregg arches an eyebrow. "What has my daughter done?"

That throws them. Just a little. Enough to make them hesitate in their eagerness to cram their own power down her throat.

In the silence, Jeremark Bogle finally sidles forward. "Really?" he asks. "*Really*? You pretend to not know your own House has marched troops into the Fae Districts, that it stirs them into an uprising? Are you that far removed from power now?"

And now Granny Spregg is fighting to hold the smile back, because it really is all going so well. "Oh no," she says, "I know all about that. I'm just not sure what you think Brethelda had to do with it."

And the pause in the room is longer this time and accompanied by an exchange of glances. Granny Spregg plays it out as long as she dares. "Let me be clear," she says, finally. "Brethelda had nothing to do with it."

If Ethrek Hobgob purses her lips any harder, Granny Spregg thinks, she is likely to turn her face inside out.

Osmondo recovers first. He always could spot an opening. And Granny Spregg has, in the end, just split her House's defenses wide apart.

"So," he says, leaning in, "you are telling us Brethelda has lost control? You are telling us that House Spriggan is steered by the winds of whatever upstart seizes control? You are telling us that someone needs to step in and take control?"

He is smiling. The poor bastard really thinks he has her.

"No, Osmondo," she says quite calmly. "As ever, you misunderstand. I am telling you that *I* am here. I am telling you that you are dealing with *me*. I sent in those troops. And if you assume that this was all some overreach on my part, some foolish error, then I shall relish the opportunity to chop your dick off."

And now, the fist of House Spriggan starts to close. And there Osmondo Red stands, right in its palm.

"You think my House exposed," she tells him. "You think our troops scattered. You think you have an excuse to step in. You think this is all in error. But it is to my design, Osmondo. This meeting here. Your attendance. Understand that, Osmondo, and get ready to bend your ancient fucking knees."

Her breath is coming a little hard. Her pulse is racing, and she can almost feel the purple stain crawling up her arm, polluting her veins, scratching away at her mortality. And yet she has not felt this alive in years.

Osmondo Red stares at her, bares his teeth. Guntra cocks her head to one side, her smile gone now. Ethrek Hobgob licks her tight lips with a dagger of a tongue, and Jeremark Bogle worries his slender hands.

"You ask me to explain my actions?" she says to them. "If any of you were worthy of your titles, you would have already asked yourself, why might House Spriggan expose itself this way? Why might it take this risk?" She looks into their dumb cow faces one by one.

"Why?" Guntra rumbles slowly.

"I have recovered from the Fae Districts a weapon they intended to use against us," she tells them.

"A weapon?" Jeremark darts his head forward at the word.

"Dust," she says. "So much Dust that a fae willing to take it could wipe the Iron City from the face of the world. So much Dust that they could scrape the goblins from existence like scraping mud from their shoe. Enough Dust to end us all. And I have saved you from it. You are welcome."

She pushes on, doesn't give them a chance to process what she's saying.

"But now it is mine. This Dust. This weapon. This power that could wipe out all the Houses of the Iron City. Or…" She pauses. She has to pause. This is what it has all been for. This moment. "Or," she says again, "just four of them."

It has been months in the planning. And she has had to crawl, and bow, and scrape, and she has feared that it would not work, that it could never work, but now the looks on their faces make it all worthwhile.

All she needs now is the actual Dust.

"It'd kill you to take that much," Guntra says.

But it's all just posturing now. Granny Spregg can smell their fear. Jeremark Bogle looks even more manic than usual, his whole body swaying. Ethrek is gnawing at her lower lip. Guntra's knuckles are white as she clenches her fists.

Osmondo, though… Osmondo… she can't tell.

"You have this Dust?" he asks. He speaks slowly.

And this is the knife blade she must walk along without slipping.

"Would I have come here if I didn't?"

Then she waits, trying to prepare her next parry, the next veil of diffusion and confusion. But then Osmondo just nods curtly back, turns away, and stalks toward the door.

She stares as he goes. They all do.

"Osmondo!" Ethrek calls out, but he doesn't turn back, just lets the door slam behind him. "Osmondo!" Ethrek calls again pointlessly.

It takes Granny Spregg a moment, but then it hits her. This is a retreat. This is Osmondo yielding the field of battle.

She looks around the room. She can see it in all their eyes.

She's won.

14

Of Romance and Rage

Knull

"You OK?"

Knull looks up, blinks, feeling heavy-lidded. One of the pixie healers from earlier is standing over him, the one who held Skart's head, twisting chunky wooden rings around slender fingers. She's young for a healer, he thinks. Not much older than him, somewhere in her early twenties. That magic is complicated, and it's hard to learn when you're dependent on a drug to perform your craft. Right now, she looks as tired as he feels.

"I'm fine." He shrugs. "You?"

The words seem to bounce off her. "Let me know what you need." She fishes in a pocket and pulls out a baggie of Dust. "I can fix you up."

"No." Knull's reflex is immediate and absolute. The pain from his ankle is radiating up to his knee, and the rest of his body doesn't feel much better, but he doesn't want anything to do with Dust unless it involves a profit margin.

The healer shrugs. "Suit yourself."

He expects her to leave, but she leans against the wall next to him, pulls out a cigarette. It strikes him as funny—this goblin affectation in a fae rebel's mouth. He doesn't laugh, though. He's a long way from laughter right now.

Some order has been restored to the factory basement where the fae are attempting to salvage what's left of their rebellion. Most of the wounded—those not in need of urgent care, and those who have already delivered the news of how they sustained their injuries—have been shunted upstairs, to bleed and grumble somewhere where they won't get under everyone else's feet. Skart flits between the remaining groups, pointing at maps and gesticulating at charts. Fae nod and point in ways that look meaningful. The runners they send out seem to move with more purpose than before.

And yet it all still feels pointless to Knull—useless writhing beneath the goblins' fists.

Skart hasn't come and asked Knull for his Dust since his little speech to rally the troops, either. After all his significant looks, he's barely spared Knull a second glance since then. And there's something about that that bugs Knull. They saved each other's lives. And now… Is he important or not? Is his Dust worth something or not? Not, he reminds himself, that he'd sell it to fae so doomed to failure.

Although, if Skart did succeed, the goblin coffers would be as easy to rifle through as any corpse's pockets…

Knull shakes his head. It's all bullshit. It's all another con. Just because he doesn't see Skart's angle doesn't mean it's not there. He has to remember that the Iron City won't ever change. Money is the only thing that will set him free.

He becomes aware that the pixie healer beside him is making an odd sound. He looks up. She's sobbing.

"Oh. Shit." He tries to get up, grunts from the pain, wobbles, and then is finally standing beside the healer with no idea of what to do. He hovers a hand over her shoulder, unsure if physical contact is helpful or not. "Look," he says. And then, "Erm."

"Shit." The pixie wipes her eyes with the back of her hand furiously, smears blue mascara over orange skin. "I'm—" She looks away.

"It's OK," Knull says. "It's shit here. I get it."

The healer still doesn't look at him. "There's just… There's so many of them," she says. "It wasn't supposed to be this way."

"It's always this way," he tells her. "Every uprising is the same." And that, Knull thinks as soon as he's said it, probably wasn't tactful.

When she turns to him, the ferocity in her face makes him duck back, but her anger, it seems, is aimed elsewhere. "Maybe so," she says. "But if this is how change is achieved then this is what we have to do. Because everything *has* to change."

There's no point trying to get her to see sense. No one in this room, Knull knows, is going to see sense.

Still, he tries to make her see sense.

"What if this doesn't change anything, though?" he says. "It's never made things better before."

"Because before this," she says, hammering her words, "we've always broken before we go the distance. That isn't going to happen. Not tonight. Tonight, we stay strong."

It's zealotry, pure and simple. And yet, she seems to draw strength from it. The light is coming back into her eyes.

"But you're going to die," he tells her, despite knowing better than to do so. "If you don't stop attacking then the goblins won't either. Half the fae in the Iron City will be dead by morning."

"But the other half will get to live free."

"Yeah, but you'll be dead. You won't get to enjoy any of it." Knull has trouble getting past that bit.

The healer smiles, pushes herself off the wall. "What is death?" she says. "You ask me, my da working fourteen-hour shifts with iron ore, the tumors crawling up his arm, the ones my magic can't touch—he's dead. My ma trying to polish enough goblin shoes to afford groceries—she's dead. Me, watching them, knowing I can't help, and that I'll never be able to help—that's when I'm dead. But not tonight. Tonight, none of us are."

She takes a final puff from her cigarette, tosses it, grinds it beneath her heel. "But of course, *you* know better." She sweeps a hand at the whole floor. "You're so much smarter than the rest of us. Only you've got it figured out."

She nods her head—a sardonic smile on her face, although not a wholly unkind one—and she heads back into the scrum.

She's intercepted on her way by a group of fae bundling down the stairs, shouting and yelling as they come. There's three of them, and they're carrying a fourth, blood pouring from his body. The others all have deep cuts of their own—in their arms, and legs, and chests. One of them has a face that—unless the pixie has a lot more skill remolding flesh than Knull credits her with—will always scare kids from now on. If he makes it. If any of them make it.

And yet, once they've laid their friend down, some of them have to be called back to be stitched and tended to. They're so eager to get back to the fight, they chafe at the wait.

Because they're idiots.

Because they've been conned.

Except Knull still can't see the angle. He can't see how just one fae benefits. He can see only how they all benefit.

Or none of us. Because we're all dead.

It's just history repeating.

Unless it isn't.

He thinks about the block of Dust. He thinks about a penthouse. He thinks about dryad dancers, and wine.

And he thinks about all these fae lying dead. He thinks about what his block of Dust could achieve. About what it would take to buy victory.

What would he be in that world? Happy? Or dead?

He doesn't know, and the more he watches, the more he doesn't know what to think anymore.

Sil

"Want anything?"

It's the bryad who bound her leg. He's young, with tousled hair, and the sort of body that comes from long hours of labor. He also has the sort of face that comes from being punched a lot.

The other fae who found her in the alley—among the scattered remains of the Red Caps who tried to kill her—have brought her inside the apartment building's lobby. An artificial fruity scent is in the air, a fae's desperate attempt to recapture the scent of a home they never knew. Most of the building's inhabitants are doing the smart thing, hunkering in their rooms, hiding until this storm blows past them. But these fae—who should know better—they now just sit or stand about, laughing, lounging, and relaxing.

She says nothing because, in the end, that's the rule. Give nothing. Take everything. And she will obey the rules.

Want anything? What could she want that this fae possibly has to offer? What do her wants have to do with anything?

A half-kobold with a bandaged shoulder comes over, stands beside the bryad. "Fraternizing with the enemy, Bee?"

He holds his injured arm gingerly, and she senses weakness.

She could punch this new fae in the groin, tear out his throat with her teeth as he collapses, snare the feet of Bee as he backs away, get her legs around his throat and choke him out…

And then what? Then there would be all the rest to go through. And while she can stand on this leg, it would slow her down. She would take more punishment taking them down. It would be unavoidable. And none of it would bring her closer to Jag.

"We don't know she's an enemy, Tharn," Bee says.

"Just exploring new depths of unfriendliness then, is she?"

"Look," Bee says, "I just want to know what it is she wants."

Bee looks down at her again. She glowers.

Except…

"Have you seen a goblin tonight?" she asks abruptly.

"Yeah," Bee says with a huffing laugh, "I've seen a few. The ones you left alive weren't very friendly."

She shakes her head. It's as if he is willfully stupid. "No. Not a commando. A civilian. She's young. Your age. She's wearing a suit. Probably looking very scared."

Bee and Tharn exchange a look.

"Dude," Tharn says, "I've been with you all night, where would I have seen her?"

Bee shakes his head. "Sorry."

Sil closes her eyes again. She was right. They have nothing that can help her. After a minute, they go back to their blather. They laugh. The fae are laughing. Despite everything around them…

So clueless. So close to death.

Except…

Happy?

Sil has never come across anyone like these fae before. Even when Jag is interacting with her peers, she can sense that she's always on alert, always trying to manage her defenses. With these fae, everything is open. Everything is there to be read and used against them.

Want anything? She turns the absurd question over in her mind. Why would anyone ask her that? What *does* she want?

She wants Jag.

But no. As she thinks about it, she finds that that is not quite a want. It is a *need,* and there is a difference. She has to find Jag, but she has no idea whether she wants to or not.

More fae are laughing. But what use is happiness? Happiness does not keep you alive. It does not put food on the table. It does not keep the wolves from the door. It is a useless emotion.

What does she want?

Sitting there, divorced from Jag, from purpose, Sil realizes that the *idea* of wanting something has not occurred to her for a very long time. And then it strikes her very suddenly, as she watches these fae, and their useless, happy laughter, that perhaps the idea of wanting something was taken from her. It's something that the Red Caps took. And then she thinks about the fact that they just tried to kill her. And about the fact that she just killed some of them. And she doesn't know if she wanted to kill the commandos or not. But she thinks that maybe even though she doesn't know what she wants, she does also know, definitely and clearly, that she does not want to be dead.

Edwyll

Edwyll shakes the paint can. Inside the metal ball clacks and rolls. A blue bed sheet is stretched across the wall before him. He aims the can, breathes, hesitates.

He holds the can out toward Jallow. "You do it."

The gnome laughs. "Oh no. This is your idea. You have to say it with your own voice."

Jag leans forward. "Do it." A slight twitch of her lips. "This is what I'm paying you for."

He takes a breath, manages a single white streak across the blue cotton fabric, then stops, hands shaking. "No. No, I can't." He turns to Jallow, to Threm, to Lila and Talluck. "You're all…" *You're all so much better than me,* he wants to say.

"No." Talluck strides forward from the back of the group, the floorboards shaking beneath his feet. "Art is not this way." He plucks the can from Edwyll's hand. He leans in close. Edwyll can smell his breath, sweet and loamy. "Art is not tentative," he says. "Art does not hesitate. Art *is*. It must be. It tears out of the heart. It brings blood and muscle. It hurts."

He shoves the paint can back into Edwyll's hand. "Paint it like you mean it."

Jag claps. Lila nods.

Come on, Edwyll tells himself. *You've got this. You're an artist. You have a patron. And she's watching you.*

Then, he paints in earnest.

"Yes!" Talluck says next to him, and Jag is his echo.

"I'm going to get more drinks," Lila tells the room, but no one is focused on anything but the painting now. Edwyll sinks into the pattern of it, losing everything to the movement of the paint, to wrestling with shade, and pulling the form out of the blank canvas.

He's not sure how much time has passed when he steps back. He's breathing a little bit faster, but he feels like maybe he's starting to get closer to the place he's aiming for.

"Yes!" Talluck claps him on the back so hard he stumbles.

Jallow is nodding. "There is something to it, yes. Something raw…"

"Perfect," Jag breathes, barely audible.

He's starting to glow, starting to think that maybe it is as good as it felt when he was making it. Then he catches Threm's expression. The gnome with the camera looks sour as day-old milk.

"What?" he asks the photographer.

"Threm..." There's a warning edge to Jallow's voice. Lila pokes her head out of the kitchen to see what's going on.

"Oh, the art's fine." Threm waves a hand. "A bit neo-primitive for my tastes but he's a brixie who knows his way around a paint can, no doubt." He shakes his head. "But the message. The message is..."

"You don't want to unite the fae?" Jag speaks before Edwyll can find the words, shows no hesitation in the face of these greater artists.

"A message is more than its intent," Threm snaps. "It's tone. It's nuance. Here, you're somehow managing to be both insipid and unrealistic at once."

"Oh, come on, Threm," Lila says.

"You think there will be critics as kind as me?"

"This is kind?" It's not quite anger in Jag's voice, but it's heading in that direction. An imperial goblin tone that sits poorly in the room. Edwyll shifts uncomfortably, trying to put himself between the pair. He has been deferent to the full members of the collective for so long he cannot feel fully comfortable with this new, antagonistic direction Jag is heading in, regardless of whether she is his patron or not.

"I could be less so," Threm spits.

"Threm!" Jallow snaps.

Threm looks at him. Jallow looks at Jag.

"Oh!" Threm throws up his hands. "Oh, I'm sorry. Should I be bowing and scraping before my goblin better? Is that the problem? Might she go back and talk to your Spriggan masters, Jallow? Might she cut you off from the teat? Can art only exist if it's compromised?"

Jallow takes a step toward Threm, and Threm sneers. Suddenly, the massive bulk of Talluck is between them.

"She," Jallow hisses, "is our guest."

The pair stare at each other. Jag is shaking her head. Edwyll is trying to wring his paint can like it's Threm's neck. Then Threm throws his hands up.

"Yes, yes," he says. "I'm the asshole." He rubs his hair with one hand, leaves it in spikes. "I'm the one oppressing the voice of a fae." He grabs one of the half-empty drinks, takes a swig, seems to see that he hasn't carried the room.

Lila fetches a smile from somewhere, flashes it at Threm from the kitchen doorway. "Come in here and help me," she says to him.

Threm nods, a little bob that is caught somewhere between being curt and contrite. He disappears after her into the kitchen.

"Don't mind him," Jallow says into the tight little absence the gnome leaves in the room. "Someone like him, struggling to find hope—he's exactly the sort of fae we're trying to help."

Talluck nods, but Jag's fists are still clenched. "I'm sorry," she says. "I just need—"

She turns abruptly, stalks toward the hall.

Edwyll looks at the others. And he doesn't know what to think. He wants Threm to be full of shit, to be a bitter old gnome whose art has achieved little, and whose heart has shriveled up. But he heard the edge in Jag's voice. He saw the goblin trying to silence the fae. And they've all seen too many House security guards take that attitude to its extremes for the moment to seem innocent.

Jallow just shrugs at Edwyll. "She's your patron."

Talluck won't give him anything else. Lila, who might try to help him more, isn't even in the room. He curses under his breath, turns, pursues.

He finds her in the hallway, pacing. She looks up, sees him coming.

"That—" She takes a breath. "Asshole."

And she's right and she's wrong. And he doesn't know how to tell her that. Doesn't know how to keep her happy and keep true to the artist he wants to be. The one who pushes back on goblin oppression just as much as he pushes back on fae despair.

"Look," he says. "It's always easy for fae to see the worst in a goblin—"

"Oh." Jag shakes her head. "He was right about all that. I was an asshole too. I should have known better." She turns back and forth, trying to find more room to pace in the narrow space. "It's the art. That he would criticize the fucking art, Edwyll. The message. I can't stand that."

And for a second time he is left staring at her.

"Who are you?" he asks.

"Me?" She doesn't understand. "I'm Jag."

"But *who* are you?"

She stares at him for a moment, seems on the cusp of saying something. She shrugs. "I'm just a goblin. Just someone sick of the bullshit, and looking in the mirror and seeing an oppressor. I'm just someone who wants to make a difference for once in their life." Another sort of helpless shrug. "And I think in what you paint… maybe I've found a way I can do that? Or at least help. Maybe I can find other artists like you. Help them be heard."

He thinks back to the bar. The slaughter. The dead fae everywhere. And he thinks to now. And maybe it's her guilt. Or maybe she really never did intend it. And maybe, just maybe in the Iron City, magic is still real, and they found each other, and they're going to make a difference.

Granny Spregg

"It's working. It's actually fucking working."

Granny Spregg knows it shows weakness to say it out loud, that it betrays how fingernail-thin her grip on her plans has been, but she has to do it. In the confines of the limousine, with only Thacker to hear (and really, when does Thacker count?), surely she can say it. Surely then she can release the pressure that has been building within her for months in one final ecstatic shout.

She punches the air with a knotted fist.

"Congratulations, ma'am." Thacker, once more in the driver's seat, once more navigating the short drive between the Opera House and House Spriggan, seems to believe his input will add to the moment.

Granny Spregg ignores him. Her fist is throbbing angrily after that punch. She pulls back the sleeve of the long glove she's been wearing, examines it. Her hand is almost entirely purple. The veins no longer stand out from the palm. Tendrils the color of port wine have crawled up to her elbow.

Excitement threatens to curdle to nausea. She tries to keep on believing that her rapid breathing is because of adrenaline.

"However, ma'am—" Thacker is for some reason still talking. "—we do still need to secure the Dust…"

"You need to secure your mouth." It's a weak return. Largely because he's right.

One step at a time, she tells herself. *You have troops in the Fae Districts. You have bought them more time. Everything is coming together.*

Her eyes linger on the purple stain, though, as she rolls her glove back up.

Still, she is not dead as House Spriggan opens up its gates to welcome her home. She is not dead as guards question Thacker, and scan his retina, and take his blood. She is not dead as dogs sniff at the trunk. And she is not dead as she steps out of the car and into the courtyard. She is still victorious. She is still the one who cowed all the other Houses in fear.

She does, however, come a little closer to mortality when Brethelda bursts out of House Spriggan, storming into the courtyard with her jackboots clacking on the cobbles, her mouth set so straight architects could use it to draw their plans.

"Mother!" Rage bubbles on Brethelda's lips. "Mother, what did you do?"

Granny Spregg bows her head. So, the wires are already coming in. The first ripples of her actions. It won't be enough for Brethelda to know the precise details yet, though. Hopefully, even when those specifics start coming into focus, she will take her time seeing their full ramifications. Audacity has always been hard for Brethelda to grasp.

"Don't frown, dear," she says. "You're never pretty when you frown."

Brethelda blows through this opening gambit with a face set like a bulldozer. "Was I not entirely clear, Mother? Are you too infirm to understand direct orders?"

Inside, Granny Spregg smiles. This fight will be a good one. "Sometimes having your head up your ass can muffle you a little, my darling."

Brethelda balls her fists. Granny Spregg wonders if she's about to be hit in the face again. What a night.

"I told you to go and eat shit, Mother," Brethelda hisses, "and yet you return to me with your breath mint-fresh. You return to me, and all I hear is news of House leaders caught between fear and rage. So, answer me, Mother, why shouldn't I calm them all down by flying your flayed skin from the flagpole?"

Granny Spregg knows deep down that she has not done a wonderful job raising all her children. Still, at times like this, she is a little proud of the job she did with Brethelda.

"Well, dear, because—" Granny Spregg says, and takes a breath.

And then she takes a breath.

And takes a breath.

Each one feels smaller than the last. Each one feels sucked through a straw, and someone is gripping that straw tighter, and tighter, and tighter, and tighter.

The world narrows to a point. Darkness closes in. It frames Brethelda's rising confusion and rage. Her face, in fact, is so comical Granny Spregg would laugh if only she could catch her breath.

If only she—

If—

Skart

It has all come so horribly close to falling apart. The rebels' spirit almost fled at the first signs of resistance; the rebels themselves almost fled along with it, almost slipped away into the shadows again, to lick their wounds again, to hope they survived the reprisals again. It was almost every other rebellion. *Again.*

Skart won't let it happen. He runs from table to table now, snuffing fires as quickly as he can. And half the time he doesn't need anything except an opinion and an air of certainty, but without leadership—without someone grabbing them all by the scruff of the neck and dragging them forward—it all threatens to collapse into paralysis.

And still, for every small fire he puts out here, the larger conflagrations are burning out there in the Iron City, eating up the streets, threatening to eat up all his plans. And the more he stands here and is told about the chaos, the worse it gets, and the more everyone else obsesses over the minutiae and fails to see what's really happening.

"Goblins were seen where?" he asks a gnome barely out of his teens. The gnome points at a map again, again, again.

"Red Caps?"

"Not all." The gnome is sweating. "Some wore yellow."

"House Spriggan," Skart breathes quickly. He leans in closer to the map. "Where? Where precisely?"

The gnome's eyes go wide. "I… erm…" he splutters. "Not everyone…"

"The ones you know," Skart says with as much patience as he can muster. It's not much.

The gnome points, and points again, and again, and again.

"You're sure?"

The gnome shrugs helplessly. Brumble lays a gray-barked hand on Skart's shoulder. "The reports aren't organized, Skart," she says. "He's doing the best he can. Better than most could."

Skart takes a breath. None of them see.

But then he smiles, and bows, and says, "I'm sorry. It's just… they're all over."

And they are. House Spriggan and House Red Cap goblins are scattered over the map like a rash.

"I need…" Skart glances towards the offices at the back of the basement. He glances at Knull. He glances at all the other little fires. So much to do… Still, there's one thing he can't put off any longer.

"I need time to think," he says, and then he holds up a hand to forestall Brumble as her jaw hinges open. "Five minutes. That's it."

"Last time…"

"I'm not leaving the building, Brumble. And I'm not asking permission. I am explaining."

She works her jaw, but in the end he hasn't left her with anywhere to go, and by the time she nods, he's already stalking back to the office with the well-oiled door and the new rotary phone. Once there he checks no one has followed him, then crosses to the phone and dials a number that only one or two other fae in the whole Iron City know.

The phone is picked up on the second ring. "Speak." The voice on the line's far end is full of caustic command.

"There are Spriggans here." Skart keeps his voice level, keeps the inflection neutral, but it is in the end an accusation. "There are Spriggans everywhere."

There is a pause on the phone. When the voice replies, it is a hiss of barely contained rage: "Bedlack Spregg has the Dust."

That stops Skart. He stands in the dusty old office staring off in silence.

"Did you hear me?" Osmondo Red says from the other end of the phone. "You have failed. The whole plan is fucked. Wrap it up."

Wrap it up. The death knell. Everything he has worked to create. Everything he is fighting to achieve, all dismissed with three words. But Osmondo Red is not someone you defy easily, or without consequence.

And yet…

"No," he says.

"What did you say to me?"

"She's lying. She doesn't have it. She—"

"Then how does she fucking know about it?" Osmondo is

shouting. Skart almost wants to check his cheek for the goblin's phlegm.

"I don't know." He is working hard to keep his voice level. "I don't know how she found out, that's why I'm calling you. But she doesn't have the Dust. I swear."

A pause. "Do *you* have it?"

Skart delays as long as he can. He has to work out exactly how to say this. "I will. It was… intercepted…"

"Intercepted?" Osmondo's shout is so loud it makes the phone bark static.

"It's a nobody. A low-level dealer." Skart is speaking quickly now. "I have him. He's here with me. He stashed it, but I am… persuading him to share its location with me. It won't take long. I swear."

More silence. Skart feels compelled to speak.

"Don't end this," he says. "I will retrieve the Dust. The presence of House Spriggan troops will work to our advantage. The whole purpose of this rebellion is to flush the dissidents into the open. Whatever else they're here to do, the Spriggans will help do that."

A long, slow inhalation on the other end.

"Osmondo," Skart says. "Please." He's not above begging. He's not above anything anymore. Those days are dead, long buried and rotting. Like he will be soon. "This is my last chance."

"Fine," Osmondo snaps. "Call me when you have the Dust. If it isn't within the next two hours, I pull the plug."

Skart nods into the dark. "It won't be a problem."

There's a pause, a throaty breath on the line. Skart is breathing hard, anxious to return to the scrum, anxious to make this work. *Say it,* he wants to scream down the phone.

"My daughter," Osmondo says finally. He is being careful, Skart thinks, to keep his tone neutral. "She's out there in all this.

You…" He pauses. "You haven't heard anything?"

Skart licks his lips, unsure what he's expected to say, unsure if this will return the plans to fresh jeopardy. "No."

Another hesitation and then a snort from the end of the phone. Skart waits to hear what Osmondo has to say next but the line dies. The conversation, it appears, is done.

Skart stands there, calming himself, calculating. *It's OK,* he tells himself. *I can make this work.*

He turns back to the door, resolute once more. And then he stops cold.

Standing behind him, eyes wide, is a young pixie, perhaps in her early twenties. Her mouth is working but she makes no sound.

Skart's heart hammers at his ribs like it wants to be let out. Sweat leaps from every pore. Then Skart smiles just as wide as he can and he takes a step toward her. "I know you," he says. And he does. She is one of the pixies who healed him earlier. "How can I help you?"

"I…" she says. And she takes a breath. "I…" she says again. "I saw you come back here." Her voice is rising in pitch. "I thought you looked… a little in pain. Maybe? I thought maybe… maybe I could help?" Her question, though, isn't really about his health.

"And how much of the conversation I just had did you hear?" Skart asks her. He's still smiling.

"I…"

But he already knows.

"I imagine it all sounded quite confusing."

She doesn't quite nod. She doesn't quite shake her head. He steps closer. He puts one hand on her shoulder.

"That's OK," he tells her.

"It is?" she asks.

"Not really."

Then he drives a stiletto up into her stomach, punching towards her lungs, nicking her heart. She gasps, a sliver of sound. He moves his hand from her shoulder to her throat. He twists the knife, and air and blood rush out of her, and he steps out of the way of the widening spill.

The pixie's legs go out from under her. Only his hand on her throat keeps her upright. Her eyes roll back. He keeps ahold of her, keeps the wound open.

After a minute he lets go. She falls to the floor in a heap, just meat and bones now. He pushes her out of view of the door, then cleans his hands on her apron. After a moment's debate, he leaves the knife still stuck in her.

Then, with a sigh, he opens the office door and slips back out into the basement. There is, after all, still a lot of work to be done.

15

Realizations and Repercussions

Sil

There is, Sil is sure, something deeply wrong with these fae.

They are in an apartment building lobby—which is itself, she would like to remind them, in the middle of a riot that is almost a warzone—and do they check their armaments? Do they order scouts placed? Do they prepare to move to higher ground with good lines of sight to get recon for the battle to come? Or do they, for some unfathomable reason, casually stand about discussing what to do next? Do they raise their fucking hands when they want to take a turn to talk?

They do. They genuinely do. Maybe, Sil thinks, they genuinely want to die.

None of this should be a concern for her, of course. Their deaths are of no consequence. They know nothing of Jag and so, unless they choose to become an obstacle or a threat, they can be dismissed.

But why, a small voice in her mind says, *is Jag of consequence to you? Why beyond the reasons House Red Cap has given you? The House that tried to kill you. That left you here with a hole in your leg watching dumbass fae raise their dumbass hands as they discuss matters of war.*

These fae, that voice says, *who have done more for you in thirty minutes than House Red Cap has done for you your whole life.*

How long, she wonders, has that voice been there? How long has it been talking, while she has refused to listen?

Why is she listening now?

If House Red Cap wants to kill her, then that, she has been taught, is its prerogative. She is but a cog in its machine. Sometimes cogs wear down. Sometimes machines are updated. Her life—she has been instructed again, and again, and again—is forfeit to Osmondo Red's will. If he raises a sword and asks her to bow her head, then it is her unquestioning duty to stare at the floor.

These lessons were hard learned. Why should she disobey them now? Why should she consider struggling to her feet and screaming at these fae that the clock started ticking the moment the commandos she killed stopped reporting in?

She doesn't know. In the end, she is no more effective at answering her own questions than the absurd circle of fae is at preparing for war.

And so, all her decisions are robbed from her one by one, and time marches on, until she has none left.

The fae are coming to the end of their discussion. They are starting to move with the urgency they should have possessed fifteen minutes ago. This is when the first shot rings out.

The goblins come at the fae exactly as she knew they would. Two shots through the door—both kill shots—then the flashbang. She squeezes her eyes shut, opens her mouth. It doesn't render the concussive blast fun, but at least her abused senses don't shut down. She's still aware enough to see the goblins start to come in through the door, to see them cut down three fae within the first three seconds of the fight.

Other fae—smarter, quicker, luckier—throw themselves free of the immediate onslaught. One of them, for no reason she can tell, flings himself forward, tangling with one of the oncoming goblins. They both spill to the floor in a flailing bundle of arms and legs, spoiling the textbook entry.

Another fae—a brixie or a bridhe, she can't tell in the chaos—levels a pistol at the mess of goblins trying to barge past their fallen colleague. He only gets off three shots before he's gunned down, but it's enough to amplify the chaos.

And still, through the gun smoke, and screaming, and diving bodies, the outcome is obvious to Sil. A disorganized rabble versus trained commandos. One side with body armor, the other with workshirts and patched pants.

She should leave now, as fast as her injured leg will allow. She should take advantage of the chaos. She has no doubt that she is at least one of the intended targets of the attack. But for just a moment the commandos are preoccupied with the fae.

She should use their deaths as cover. She owes them nothing.

She shouldn't want to save them from themselves. Nothing she *wants* should affect anything in her life at all.

And yet now, she finds… it does.

She tries to get up. She bends her leg, screaming as she does it, no matter how much she tries to bite down on the pain. She feels the wound tear open a second time, warmth spilling down her pants leg. She keeps on going, refusing to give in, but her leg is disobedient, collapsing beneath her weight. She falls back, howling.

From the floor, she sees order start to emerge from the chaos. The goblins dictate its nature. There are six of them in the lobby now, fanning out wider and wider, establishing firing positions, closing down the fae's angles of attack. The fae are pressing back towards a hallway and a bank of elevators, knotting up, trying to find cover, ceding control. They need, Sil knows, to run into this fight's teeth, to refuse to give the goblins room to exercise their superior fire power. But they don't know that. They're just civilians. Just fools. Just expendable waste. No good to her or anyone.

Then, a machine gun starts up, old and chunky, clattering through its cycle. She sees Bee standing in the mouth of the hallway, wrestling with the gun as bullets fly wildly about, puncturing the ceiling and floor in equal measure.

She sees him asking to get shot. The fool. The expendable waste.

The one who bound your leg and asked you what you wanted.

She kicks toward him as best she can, slithering across the floor, leaving a red trail from the freshly opened wound in her leg.

She barely makes it two yards before the inevitable happens.

The bullet clips Bee in the hip, sends him to the floor. Fae dive for cover as he spins, finger still on the trigger. When he loses his grip, the silence is almost as alarming as the cacophony that came before.

"Throw down your weapons." A goblin voice rings out, syllables short and clipped. No bargaining chip is proffered, but these fae might just be stupid enough to comply. Or to vote on complying.

Bee lies still on the cold linoleum tiles. His eyes are squeezed tightly shut from the pain.

"Open your eyes," Sil whispers. She wants, right here, right now, for him to open his eyes.

The world of course does not care what Sil wants. It never has. And yet… Perhaps it is a miracle. Perhaps Bee hears her. Perhaps it is nothing more than coincidence. But Bee opens his eyes.

"The gun," she mouths at him, desperate now. "Give me the gun."

He blinks at her, but she can't tell if he sees anything beyond the confines of his own pain.

"I'm going to count to ten," a goblin shouts at the huddled fae. Meanwhile she knows he is signaling desperately to his men, setting up a crossfire, ensuring victory no matter what the fae do.

"The gun," she mouths to Bee again. She *wants* the gun. And she doesn't know why. But, she's starting to realize, she doesn't care why or why not. Right now, it's enough to know what she wants.

"Give me the gun."

Bee closes his eyes again.

Behind him, someone stands, throws a gun into the center of the lobby.

It lands too far away from her. She can't do anything.

Another gun follows. Another gun that lands just yards out of reach.

And they're actually doing it, she realizes. It's not a ruse or a ploy. They're just giving in to the command to be slaughtered. They're doing, she realizes, just what she was taught to do.

She thinks she wants to scream.

And then Bee shoves out his arm, and the machine gun starts to slide across the floor. It spins, barrel and grip whirling end over end as it hisses and skitters across the chipped linoleum. And everyone watches as it skids past the other two weapons. Everyone watches as it lands in Sil's outstretched hand.

"Asset Sil?" It's the same as before. A different goblin, but that same question, that same moment of hesitation. That tiny window opening to give her the slimmest of chances to cling to life. And at least, she thinks, her loyalty to the House has bought her that.

Then she opens fire.

And she wants it, she finds. She wants to see the goblins buck and writhe. She wants to see their blood in messy spatters on the walls. She wants to see their guns come to bear and she wants to deny them their victory. She wants this, this rage, or revenge, or anger, or hatred, or fear, or whatever it is. She wants it even though she doesn't understand it. She wants it because it is hers. Because she made it herself. She wants it because House Red Cap did not cram it down the throat of a child and make her believe it was the only way to be. This thing is a thing of her own design. This massacre. This murder.

This victory.

Knull

Knull is nursing a water bottle someone just gave him. He looks up as more footsteps approach, hopeful of food to accompany the drink. This time, though, it's Skart. And the kobold is smiling.

"I think," Skart says, "that it's time we talked."

Knull doesn't think that it's time they talked. He thinks he'd rather find a way to put this whole revolution on pause while he gets his head clear, and has some stronger drinks, and maybe even fixes his damn ankle.

Except, he knows, deep down, that's not what he wants. Because if he could press pause, he'd think about none of this. Rather, he'd work incredibly hard to ensure that when the world resumed he could say, *Sorry, Skart, but I found another buyer. I don't even have the Dust anymore…*

Sorry, Skart, that all these fae are dying for nothing…

He realizes Skart is still waiting for an answer.

"Um, yeah," he says. "Sure."

"Maybe we can find somewhere quieter to talk?" Skart says. "There are some offices at the back. Maybe we can use one of them."

Knull was hoping to not move again for approximately the rest of his life, but he sighs, and grunts, and gets to his feet. Then his ankle almost buckles as he tries to put weight on it. Skart reaches out, steadies him.

"Didn't one of our healers see you?" His face is full of paternal concern.

"No Dust," Knull mutters. "Not having that."

Skart furrows his brow, but he doesn't say anything. He just offers up an arm and lets Knull lean on it as they hobble toward the back offices. Knull tries to not feel grateful.

"Skart!" The big dryad calls from the center of the floor. There's a slightly frantic air to her.

Skart glances in her direction. "I'll be with you in a moment, Brumble. Mr Knull and I have important matters to discuss."

Knull looks at Brumble as a drowning creature looks to a distant spar of wood while Skart directs him to a dusty door. Its glass pane is so filthy as to be impenetrable.

"Just through here." Skart opens the door, which screeches on ancient hinges.

Knull steps through into a room bare but for two rusting filing cabinets and a substantial smattering of rat droppings. Behind him, Skart scrapes the door closed.

Knull licks his lips. Despite the mostly empty water bottle in his hand, his mouth feels dry all over again.

"I think you know why I asked you here," Skart says. He ducks his head. "But before we get into that, I have to ask... Dust. Why do you hate it so much?"

Knull studies Skart's ruddy face. The old kobold is impenetrable, his angle impossible to judge. Not that it matters, Knull tells himself. He doesn't have to tell him anything. He owes him nothing.

Except his life.

"Dust," he says finally, "is for idiots."

He expects Skart to scoff, or to roll his eyes, or to tell him that he's the idiot, but Skart does none of these things. He just looks thoughtful. "But Dust," he says finally, speaking slowly, "is our connection to our past, to who we really are. It's the one way back to the magic that was severed from our souls."

"Magic?" Now Knull is the one scoffing. "Let me tell you how fucking magical it is to watch your parents rot from the inside out. Let me tell you how magical it is to find out your mom decided there were better things to spend money on than food this week. Let me tell you how magical it is to watch a father spin around in a field of daisies just before he goes off to blow a few more goblins to get the coins to do it again. Yeah, it's a source of fucking wonder, alright."

"Ah." Skart bows his head. "You poor child."

"I don't want your sympathy."

Skart nods. "I imagine not. But you don't get to control how others feel, Knull. Most of us hardly get to control anything in our lives. That's the lot of the fae in the Iron City, really. No choices. Just walking the paths the goblins have dictated for us."

"And how exactly does addiction give fae more choices?" Knull has been holding onto these arguments for a long time.

Skart nods. "It doesn't. But Dust is hardly the only addictive substance in the Iron City. There are medicines that can heal in the correct doses, and harm when taken to excess."

Knull gets to scoff before Skart does. "Yeah, well, nobody is saying cough medicine is what defines us as fae. No one says, 'Choke this shit down, even if it kills you. Even if it kills your kids.'"

He's trying to get a rise out of the old kobold. He doesn't know why, but he wants to make him angry. But Skart just keeps on nodding.

"But you don't sell cough medicine, do you, Knull? You sell the very thing you profess to hate. The very thing that keeps us oppressed."

"Yeah. Yeah, I do." Knull isn't going to apologize for his life choices. He's lived with them longer than Skart has. "I do it because the only way out of the Fae Districts is money. And if you're dumb enough to think it's anything but that, then I'll happily take your coin and leave you behind."

"Money." Skart nods again. He just keeps on nodding. "Yes, that makes sense. But Dust isn't the only way to make money. So, why not start a store? Why not get a job in a factory? Why not—"

"Because it's bullshit." Knull can only stomach so much of this horse dung. "No one gets out with what they make from those jobs. They're dead ends. Rat traps. There's only one way to make enough and that—"

"Is to condemn more fae to the same addiction that robbed your parents of their will and you of your childhood?" This time, it's Skart who cuts Knull off. This time, it's Skart with the fire in his eyes and on his tongue. "How much do you hate yourself?" Skart asks him. "How deep have you buried that? Do you even acknowledge it to yourself anymore?"

It's like a knife blade. It's like all his defense being ripped away with one fine, precise slice. "Fuck you," he gasps.

Skart shakes his head, keeps talking. "But I didn't do this to you, Knull. Dust didn't do this to you. The goblins did. They set the trap, and you walked in. They rigged the game so that the only way out is to become complicit. Push the addiction that keeps hundreds of fae trapped in the hopes that maybe just you—and you alone—can get out. And that's the joke, Knull. That's what sends them laughing to their beds: there is no way out. The Iron Wall is a perfect circle. The goblins control all the ways in and all the ways out. And if you get big enough to hit their radar, they'll crush you. Do you really think the goblins will let you keep anything you get from selling that Dust? Do you really think you'll be wealthy enough to challenge a House if you piss them off? We both know the answers to those questions."

Knull wants to leave this room. He hates this room. And still Skart won't stop talking.

"You want a choice, Knull. You want to be free. But you're as addicted as anyone else. The idea of freedom has been shoved down your throat, and you can't get the taste from your mouth. And the goblins drip-feed you that dream to keep you in line, to keep you doing their bidding. They've given you no choice at all."

And it's every doubt that's haunted every night. It's every time he's questioned his ambitions and every time his decisions have felt shallow and selfish. It's every time he's turned his back on his brother amplified and reverberating without mercy. It's every time he's felt no better than his parents.

"The only way to choose," Skart keeps on, not taking a moment to break, not acknowledging the rasping of his breath, the dampness in his eyes, "is to tear the whole system down. That is what the Dust is for, Knull. That is who we are. That is why I arranged to have so much brought into the city at once. Because every system has its limits. And I am going to overload them. I am going to make sure there isn't any more horror, Knull. I am going to make sure no more children have to watch their parents waste away in a toxic dream.

"All I need to achieve that," Skart says, "is for you to choose to help me. Because if you don't, then you're right: we're all trapped, the reprisals come, and history repeats.

"So, Knull," he says, "what will you choose?"

Granny Spregg

Granny Spregg opens her eyes. She closes them again. She had thought it couldn't get worse than seeing Thacker upon waking. She was wrong.

"I know you're awake, Mother," Brethelda says to her. "In fact, I think it's time for all of your charades to come to an end."

This time, Granny Spregg keeps her eyes open. She is, yet again, in her bed. Thacker has, yet again, plumped the pillows behind her head.

"How bad is it?" Brethelda says.

"Oh, don't pretend you care, dear." Granny Spregg is too tired to dissemble. Thacker has even taken her ballgown off her, left her in her undershirt. She feels more vulnerable than if she were just naked.

"You are my mother!" The force of Brethelda's shout catches Granny Spregg off guard. Brethelda, who has been sitting on the edge of the bed, is now standing. She even takes a few moments to visibly calm herself.

"I am," she says, still breathing hard, "as often as I wish that I was not, very much your daughter, Mother. Now answer me—are you dying?"

Granny Spregg licks her lips. "I am trying very hard not to."

Brethelda shakes her head. "Games. Always games with you." She turns to Thacker. He wilts in the corner. "How bad is she?"

Thacker looks wretchedly at Granny Spregg.

"Look to me, Thacker," Brethelda demands. "I am the head of your House. I am the one you owe your fealty to. If you are to pay obeisance, you pay it at my feet. So, tell me now."

Thacker sobs.

Granny Spregg sighs. "At least do me the decency of holding onto your composure while you betray me, Thacker."

Thacker gulps. "Her arm," he manages.

Thacker has at least done her the decency of leaving her gloves on. But Granny Spregg is too old to waste time dragging this out any longer. She peels one off. "He means this."

Her arm is lurid purple to the elbow now. As she rolls up the sleeve of her undershirt, she sees the violet tendrils reaching up to her shoulder and out of sight.

"Ah," Brethelda says. "Poison then. Will you tell me who? Or—" She turns to Thacker. "—must I get the answers from your servant again."

Granny Spregg knows her expression is sour. "I was perhaps a little too enthusiastic in my belittling of Privett earlier."

Brethelda's face is made of stone. "I see," she says. "It appears I have been lax." She pushes her hand through her short cropped hair. "It is time to clean house." She looks to Thacker. "Come here."

He approaches hesitantly, still sniveling, ashamed eyes on Granny Spregg. "I'm sorry," he mouths to her.

"Now," Brethelda says, as he stands before her. "I need you—" And then with a sudden violence she kicks out his knees. She seizes his head as his body collapses one way and wrenches it in the other direction. There is a crack loud enough to bounce off the walls. Thacker goes limp.

Granny Spregg stares.

Brethelda drops the body. She takes a long calming breath.

"Thacker," Granny Spregg says. She commands him. But he just lies there and doesn't say a word.

"Now, Mother," Brethelda says while Thacker still just lies there, "you have been up to mischief, and you have come to mischief."

Thacker's eyes are wide and staring.

"But you are old, infirm in body, and now I suspect in mind as well. You are not wholly to blame."

Thacker's pigeon chest is still.

"You have clearly been enabled. And it takes little imagination to figure out who your accomplice was."

Brethelda finally looks down at the floor. At the little, scurrying goblin, so pathetic, and so desperate to please.

No more.

Brethelda looks back at Granny Spregg. "You are my mother. I love you. I do this for your own good." She smiles. "I hope the time remaining to you is peaceful. Now, I would stay, but you have left me with much to do."

Granny Spregg is barely paying attention. She is still staring. Thacker is still just lying there. And it takes her a moment to realize what is happening, but then Granny Spregg finally feels the tears running down her cheeks.

Sil

In an apartment building on Canal between Bridge and Arch Streets, a lobby is full of gun smoke. Cracked plaster crumbles, patters down on a linoleum floor. A framed photograph slips from its hook, falls. Someone's breathing is very labored.

Sil, still lying prone, sees a figure stumble out from the rear of the building, groping through the haze. She swings the machine-gun barrel up, works the mechanism loudly.

"Woah! Woah!" The figure flings his hands in the air.

It's one of the fae. She lets the gun barrel fall.

I already shot all the Red Caps…

Others start to stumble out into the lobby, dazed, bewildered. Some clutch wounds. Someone calls out, "Who's hit?"

Many, it turns out. Six fatally. The fae lay them out in a row.

They take the plastic leaves from a fake potted plant, and cover the eyes of the fallen.

The number of wounded is comparatively low. Only four have been clipped by bullets. The goblin commandos shot to kill, and they knew their business well. Bee, still lying on the floor, grunting in pain, is—from some perspectives—one of the lucky ones.

A brixie with long blue hair kneels beside Bee and pulls a small plastic bag from her pocket. She examines its contents. "They only gave me enough for one high," she says, "but now seems like the time to use it."

She sticks her nose in the bag, inhales. Sil sees her suddenly haloed by sunlight. The floor ripples at her feet, and fish leap and splash from the quivering tiles. The brixie reaches down and Bee's hip glows. There is a wet sucking noise. Bee sits up with a gasp.

The brixie walks to each of the wounded in turn, lays on hands. Soon they're all up, standing, staring. They don't celebrate, though. Rather the gravity of the bodies claims them, and they drift to stand beside the dead.

Tharn breaks the mood. "You mean you've been able to do this all night," he says, "and I've been wandering around with my arm in a sling?"

"I was trying to save it to get the most from it!" the brixie protests. "Good thing I did."

Bee puts a hand on Tharn's freshly healed arm. "Not the time."

"Anyway." The healer stares around, slightly glassy-eyed. "I think that's everyone." A snake weaves in and out of her hair.

Bee glances up again; his eyes fall on Sil. She's not paying attention. She's focused on the goblin corpses. The ones that she didn't have to kill. The ones that she killed anyway.

"Quick!" Bee says. He points at Sil. "Before the high's gone! Get her leg."

Sil looks up, realizes she's the subject of discussion. Bee's words register, and she expects objections from the others, but instead there is a rush of activity, and suddenly she is surrounded. And then the brixie is placing hands of white light against her leg, and Sil can hear birdsong and feel the sun on her face, and a breeze blowing through her hair, and the air is sweet, and—

—then it's over. Then she's in an apartment building lobby surrounded by fifteen fae all staring at her, and she's feeling as if she's lost something, although she couldn't say exactly what.

Bee offers her a hand up, but she ignores it, rising smoothly. She tests the limit of her leg. It is as good as new. No tightness. The same range of movement. She nods at the healer. She thinks she should probably say something.

"Good work."

They are all still looking at her. She can't tell why. Then the one called Tharn says, "Well, you kick ass."

There are smiles at that, and someone else says, "I vote she gets to keep the machine gun now."

And then there's even a little laughter. And then there's a pause because there are still six fae bodies lined up in the room.

"What are we…?" someone starts, but she can't finish.

Bee shrugs. "My vote? Payback."

There's a pause. Then: "Aye." It's Tharn again. All eyes go to him. He smiles at them all, a little helpless. "I'm terrified," he said. "But screw these gobbos. If they want a fight, I'll give it to them. So, yeah. I vote aye."

"Aye," another says then. And then another. And then the rest in a rush, a whole chorus of them all around Sil. Then they look at her, and she's not sure what to say. What they're planning is suicide.

"Well," Bee says, covering the moment as best he can. "Now we know what we're going to do, we'll have to work out how to do it. So, I say we pour a drink for the dead, and get talking."

Another chorus of ayes. Not defiant, exactly, but far from defeated. Solemn, perhaps, and with rising solemnity as they step towards their fallen brethren. Bee looks back at Sil from where they stand lined up.

"You can join us," he says. "If you want."

She almost smiles at that—those words—but she catches herself in time. She doesn't think the fae would see that smile quite the way she means it. Then the idea of their reaction strikes her as funny, and she has to fight even harder to keep her smile pushed down. She feels as if she is not quite herself, as if she is watching herself from inside her own skull.

She doesn't know where the fae found the bottle of whiskey, but Bee holds it and recites lines from an old poem that she doesn't know.

"The circle continues," he finishes. "We return to feed new growth." He upends the whiskey. A golden trickle baptizes the dead.

Then he's done, and they're just standing there. The atmosphere edges from solemn to sullen.

"How do you all feel," Bee says then, "about getting the fuck out of this place and talking on the move?"

Another chorus of ayes, and in an eager flurry of activity they head to the streets. Sil collects goblin guns as she goes, stuffing spare magazines into her pockets. A few other fae copy her.

Out on the street, Bee puts the whiskey bottle to his lips, takes a heavy slug. Then he passes the bottle to Tharn, who drinks and passes it to the next fae. One by one they upend the bottle. And then it's pressed into Sil's hands.

"You killed those goblins," Bee says. "You're one of us now."

She regards the bottle—its label of a spreading oak tree. "I…"

she says. "I've never…" Alcohol, she knows, slows your reaction times. It impairs judgment. It gets in the way, she has been told again—and again, and again—of serving Osmondo.

"Well," Bee shrugs. "If you don't want to…"

He reaches for the bottle, but then with a desperation that takes her by surprise she jams it to her lips and pulls on it.

And oh, oh, oh. It burns. It burns like fire. And she takes it as long as she can, which is so much longer than most, but then she pulls it away, braying, and choking, spraying the liquid fire over the rest of the fae, who are smiling and chuckling.

"Why?" she says, her eyes streaming. "Why would you…?"

Bee plucks the bottle from her hands, takes another swig. "Pyrrhic inclinations?"

A sinewy dryad is shaking her head. "I can't believe I just laughed. I didn't think I'd…" She looks back at the apartment building.

"They want us to laugh." Bee presses the bottle into the dryad's hand. "They want us to laugh, and love, and shout, and screw, and be alive. They want us to live a liberated life. All of us."

They keep on walking. The bottle ends up in Sil's hands again. She regards it balefully.

"Let me—" Bee starts, and then she takes another slug. She will not be mastered by a mere beverage. She doesn't spit any out this time, but her eyes are still streaming when she stops.

The bottle goes round and round again. And then several more times. When it's empty, Sil sets it down reverentially on the curb. She feels loose and wild. Every movement feels dream-like. *You are half sidhe,* a voice says in her mind. And of course, she has always been that; it has always been a reason for her to know her place, but this is the first time she has ever felt it. Half of her is tearing free, coming to the fore.

"I want to take Dust," she tells Bee suddenly. "I've never taken Dust."

He laughs. "Taking the liberated life seriously." He has kind eyes, she thinks. She can't remember anyone else with kind eyes. "Well, Dust is precious, and we have precious little. I'm sorry. I think we've used most of it. We need—"

"Do you have any more whiskey?" She also likes whiskey. She feels warm from head to toe.

Bee smiles again and shakes his head. "Who are you?"

"Told you already," she says. "Sil."

He nods. "Asset Sil."

She flips him the finger. "Fuck asset. Fuck House Red." She stares around, some part of her brain screaming at her that there will be consequences, that this is madness, but… there aren't. She has escaped House Red Cap's reach.

"You worked for House Red?"

She looks at him again. There was a time when she wasn't going to tell him a word. When he was the enemy. But, no, he is House Red Cap's enemy, and she is their asset no longer. She's tearing free. She's coming to the fore.

"I did," she tells him. She leans a little on him for support. "A bodyguard. A servant." And then she reconsiders. "A slave," she says.

"But now you're free." Bee wraps an arm around her shoulders. "Now you fight back."

"Yes." And she likes how that sounds. "Now I find Osmondo Red and I make him red." She likes that even more. "I smear his red across the walls. I smear his whole House across the walls."

"Well," Bee says, "points for enthusiasm."

"I hate him." Sil is realizing that she has a name for it, the feeling she has when she sees him. "I hate him. I hate him. I hate him." She can't stop saying it. They made her own mind a prison and every time she says those words, she breaks free a little more, comes apart a little more, and she doesn't know what will be left at the end, but she wants to find out.

"Did you…" Bee is staring at her quizzically. "Did you meet him?"

Sil nods. She licks her lips. Her tongue feels thick. "My father," she says.

Bee blinks, so she says it again. He stares. "He's your…"

"Father," she says for a third time to make it fairy-tale true.

"Shit."

"I hate him."

"He sent goblins to kill you." Bee's eyes are not so kind anymore.

"I killed them instead." Sil likes that as well. She pulls out her sword. She stares at it in the streetlight. "I wonder…" she says.

Something is tearing free. Thoughts liberated, rising in her mind like dust motes caught in a beam of sunlight. She reaches for them, then hesitates, unsure.

What does she want? At her most basic, her most fundamental? What does she *want*?

"I want to kill Osmondo Red," she tells Bee. She stops, and turns, and looks him right in the eye. And she's knows it's true. It's her heart's unspoken desire finally uttered aloud.

"I want to kill Osmondo Red. And I know how to do it."

Granny Spregg

"Mistress Brethelda! I bring urgent word! Mistress Brethelda!"

The runner bursts into the bed chambers. The mistress of House Spriggan has just turned her back on Granny Spregg. The tears have just begun to paint Granny Spregg's cheeks.

"Mistress Brethelda! I—"

The runner takes in the scene.

"Speak," Brethelda says, her voice as empty of emotion as Thacker's body lying dead on the floor.

"I…" the runner tries. "I… I am sent… I have urgent…" His eyes flick to the body, back to Brethelda. He tries again. "Osmondo Red is at our gates. He demands to see the…" His eyes go to Granny Spregg this time. "He demands to see the Dust that Madame Spregg spoke of."

A moment as still as Thacker's chest.

Then Brethelda turns. "Oh," she says, and her mouth is full of teeth and rage. "Oh, Mother…"

Their eyes meet. And she could stop now, Granny Spregg knows. She could stop struggling against the pain. She could give into the clawing hands of age, and history. She could rest. She could let the world move on without her hand scrabbling for its turn on the tiller.

Except, Granny Spregg knows, she is as incapable of doing that as she is of breathing fresh life into Thacker.

"All the Dust in the house," she says to Brethelda, sitting up straight in the bed. "Every ounce we have. Get it. Gather it. Compile it."

Brethelda opens an indignant mouth, but Granny Spregg doesn't have time. She rounds on the runner. "Go to the kitchens. Get thirty-eight pounds of powdered sugar. If we do not have that much, supplement with flour. Put it in a clear plastic bag. Use the Dust Mistress Brethelda gives you to make a layer on the top. As thick as you can. Then bind it airtight with packing tape. Be careful, but do not be neat. Dirty it. If there is pig or beef blood nearby splash that on it. Then bring it to me in the Room of Hours. All of it."

Brethelda is staring at her. "You—" she starts.

"Meanwhile," Granny Spregg says, "I will stall Osmondo for as long as I am able."

Brethelda is grinding her teeth. She is getting ready to dig in her heels. Granny Spregg meets her eye.

"I will save *your* House."

Your. The word tastes bitter. It tastes like Thacker's death. But Osmondo is poised to sweep them all over the edge and Granny Spregg has to give a little here. It is all too close, and all too precarious.

"Fine," Brethelda snaps.

And like that, the runner is gone, and Brethelda too with a shake of her head, and Granny Spregg is hauling herself from her bed. She heaves on a pair of tapered pants and an old military jacket, the relic of a lover whose wardrobe has outlived any other fond memories she has of him. It is not much, but it is good enough for Osmondo.

She hobbles down House Spriggan's hallways, travelling as fast as she can. Osmondo is not a patient man. The pain in her arm has reached above her elbow now.

It takes her old bones almost ten minutes to make it through the sprawling corridors of the House to the Room of Hours—as deep into the House as any outsider will ever be permitted. The journey is startlingly quiet without Thacker's constant harrying. She tells herself she enjoys it. She thinks she is going to have to be considerably more convincing when she talks to Osmondo.

Before the doors to the room, she pauses, straightens her jacket. Thacker does not tell her that her hair is well coiffed. She takes a breath. She feels faint and brittle. Brethelda has surely been using the pretense of security procedures to delay Osmondo's entry into the room. He is likely almost rabid with irritation.

It would be delightful if everything wasn't so dire.

She opens the door. She steps inside.

Osmondo Red is just entering the room from a door opposite hers. His back is to her and he's screaming back at whatever hapless guard Brethelda sent to delay him.

"Utter bullshit!" he's shouting. "I'll raze this place to the—"

"Osmondo," Granny Spregg says, desperately trying to hold her voice steady. "I had thought my feminine charms faded, but it seems you cannot stay away from me."

He spins on his heel, glares. "You," he hisses.

"Yes." She inclines her head. "I told you, in all of this, I am the one who speaks for House Spriggan. This is my design, Osmondo. You are here at your appointed hour."

Which, of course, he damn well isn't, but she will keep this fiction of control spinning for as long as she can. There is still a chance to make it all come true. And there is still a chance that if it all goes to shit, then she can ensure that it will all go to shit for Brethelda along with her.

"I think," Osmondo says, "that if I stabbed you now, bullshit would actually flow from your veins."

Which given the workings of the poison in her system, isn't too far from the truth.

"You doubt me," Granny Spregg acknowledges. "You are a goblin of little faith."

"I have about as much faith in you as I have in a wet fart's ability to knock over one of Ethrek's tower blocks." Osmondo starts to stalk toward her. "You have been stuffed full of lies as long as I have known you, Bedlack, and now I think you have forgotten where they end and the truth begins. I think you are an addled old fool who has come up with a scheme she thinks will give her back her House. I think you forget how you fell from grace in the first place."

He is inches from her now, lips pulled back from his teeth.

"This is not the first time you have overextended, Bedlack," he says. "This is not the first time you left your House exposed. Last time, Brethelda saved this House. And no matter what you tell yourself in the dark, it was not because she was ambitious, or because she had always wanted to depose you, or because you are an ugly whore of a mother who has always treated her own children like shit. She took over because you were no longer fit to lead. And that is still true.

"But she cannot save you this time. All your feeble machinations and designs have achieved is to expose Brethelda as another incompetent. All they mean is that when I scour you from the face of the city, I will do it with impunity."

Osmondo is so close his lips almost brush hers. "All I came here to do," he whispers, "was to thank you for the opportunity."

Granny Spregg's heart is trembling in her chest. And in so much, of course, Osmondo is right.

It was an uprising fifteen years ago. For the first time in a long time, the Houses' grip on the city had felt precarious. The fighting in the streets had gone on for days, bodies piling up against store windows and in the Houses' courtyards. But finally, the tide was turning in the goblins' favor. And in the bloody chaos of it all, Granny Spregg had seen an opportunity. She had organized a counterstrike not against the fae, but against the other Houses. Commando squads running counter-ops, taking out tactically placed teams from Houses Red, Hobgob, Bogle, and Troll; creating opportunities for the fae to pummel House Spriggan's opponents.

And it had worked like a dream, just as she had foreseen. It was her masterstroke.

And then it was not.

She had underestimated the fae. She had overestimated her commandos. She had lost too many in the fights with the other Houses. Suddenly she too was struggling to hold the city secure.

And then one morning she had gone to the operations center, and all her generals had been there, and Brethelda too, and Osmondo Red, and Guntra Trog, and Ethrek Hobgob, and strange, squirming Jeremark Bogle. All her enemies, all lined up, all in her seat of power. Even Privett and Nattle had been there—her two idiot children dressed for war. And Brethelda had explained in quiet, simple words that Granny Spregg's time was done. Her war was done. Brethelda had brokered new peace, new trust, so the fae threat could be met with a united front. And Granny Spregg had raged, and spat, and clawed, and armed guards had dragged her back to her chambers, as she frothed all the way.

She has been clawing her way out of them for fifteen years. Fingerhold by fingerhold she has crawled back toward power. And she has lost so much along the way. In the end, she had only Thacker left. Now, even he has been taken from her.

Osmondo turns his back on her, starts to move towards the door. She gathers her breath.

"The only insulting thing that you have managed to suggest," she tells him, "is that I don't learn from my mistakes."

He turns, looks back. And she couldn't have timed it better if she wanted to. The door behind her swings open and a servant staggers in, struggling under the weight of a package wrapped in clear plastic.

The servant slaps the brick down on the table between them, bows, departs. Osmondo stares. Granny Spregg can tell he wants to look away, to read her expression, but he can't. His jaw works slowly.

"We've known each other a long time, Osmondo," Granny Spregg says. "So, for old times' sake, I'll let you try a little if you like." She reaches into a pocket, pulls out a penknife, proffers it to him. She tries to keep her hand very steady.

Finally, he looks away from the massive, plastic-wrapped bundle. He looks at her. He looks at the knife. And she is acutely aware of exactly how much harm he could do with it.

She prays he is as overwhelmed as she needs him to be. She prays that he is so much on the back foot that he cannot take even a half-step forward.

Each of the Houses has a small amount of Dust. It is a good tool for war if your soldiers are suicidal enough. If they don't mind injuring themselves almost as much as they injure their opponents. But times have been peaceful for so long that the Houses mostly use their supplies for recreational purposes.

Dust can get a goblin high if she's feeling masochistic enough. They aren't creatures built for magic, though, and the power of it can tear flesh, can warp muscle and wither organs. There is some stockpiled too for emergencies, for the bodyguards of a House's head to use in a last desperate attempt to fend off attackers. But goblins can build nothing lasting with magic, and so none of them hold much. Certainly, none of them hold anything close to this vast bulk of Dust. Most of the city's supply is in the hands of dealers, but none of them have held this much before. Not until Cotter smuggled this in.

"No," Osmondo says finally. "No. I won't take whatever bullshit poison you are trying to get in my veins, Bedlack. You do it. You show me this is real and not more of your bullshit dramatics."

She tries to not scream in victory. Because only she knows how solid the straws he thinks he's grasping at really are. And only she knows that he's just handed her the opportunity to yank them away from his grasping fingers.

She slices open the sack, skims just a thin layer from the top of it with the blunt little blade. She raises it to her nostrils, and inhales.

She can taste the sweetness of the sugar at the back of her

throat even with this thin scraping. But then the Dust hits and all sweetness is forgotten.

—vines rising like chains—thorns thrashing through her mind—an eclipse, the sun in full retreat—night stretching fingers across the world, raking the earth with jagged fingernails—buildings falling—bodies splayed in the limbs of trees—the screaming of birds wheeling in the sky—a hawk with its beak in the entrails of a stoat—an animal's head twisted in pain—a great black tree rising—

She emerges from the visions gasping. Her skin feels tight and brittle. Power is bulging within her, threatening to spill out. She can feel it splitting the skin around her mouth, her nose, her eyes. Dust is not meant for goblins. She grits her teeth, and it feels like the lightning is on her tongue.

She extends one gnarled finger toward Osmondo Red's wide-eyed face, and as she does so, the years drop from the digit. Her finger is suddenly slender, and elegant, and straight for the first time in over a decade. And as she points, a black-leafed vine unfurls from beneath her fingernail, extends out to brush Osmondo's cheek and circle his skull, and curl around his throat.

"Do you believe me now, Osmondo?" she asks him, and her words are a red mist between them. "Or am I still a liar?"

He opens his mouth. She doesn't know if he has the words to answer. She doesn't care. The vine tightens, crushing, constricting. His eyes bulge. He gurgles.

She tries to push back on the poison in her veins as he stares at her. Tries to use the spare power sparking and juddering through her system to buy just a little more life, a few more hours to do what she must. She doesn't have healing knowledge, though, and the Dust is burning away, fizzing off her incompatible physiology, scouring her veins as much as she pushes back at the pollution in her blood.

And then it's gone. The dizzying power rushing out of her. The ecstatic sense that she can do anything. To anyone. And all she's left with is the desperate trembling pain, and the feel of the blood oozing out all over her.

She takes a shuddering breath. She feels the poison rushing into the spaces that the magic has left. She feels her heart skipping, trying to keep up with her ambition, staggering. And through it all she still meets Osmondo's eyes, and she bares her teeth, and she says, her voice rasping, "So tell me, Osmondo. Who the fuck is going to raze who from the earth tonight?"

She manages to stay upright just long enough to see him turn tail and run from the room.

Bee

"I'm sorry," Bee says to Sil, "but you know how to kill *who*?"

The strange, drunk, deadly half-fae is weaving back and forth in the street. She's tapping the side of her head.

"Osmondo Red," she says. "I can get to him. I can get in and out of House Red Cap. I can slide up right beside him."

Except, of course, no one can do that. House Red Cap is the most impenetrable House in the Iron City. While others rely on armed guards, traps, and labyrinths, House Red Cap is simply a blank box of concrete and steel with no way in or out. The location of its door is the most heavily guarded secret in all of the Iron City. Bee knows that from time to time resistance forces have captured House Red Cap members. Some have been tortured. None have ever given up the location of that door.

Could she really be Osmondo Red's bastard? He doubts it. The story is almost certainly a myth told to warm some poor half-fae child in the dark. But... what if? What if everything she's saying is true?

He turns to ask the others, to start the debate, to give them some purpose, but as he does so they round a corner, and everything stops.

The parts of the city they have been walking through have been relatively untouched by the night's upheaval. Until now, the Fae Liberation Front's troubles have felt confined to empty lots and lobbies. That ends here.

The street before them is full of fire and rubble. A factory has collapsed, spilling into the road in a great slouching mass of bricks and steel struts. Flames gutter from the blackened windows of the houses stacked up around it. There are bodies half obscured by wreckage and smoke.

They step into the street silently. All thoughts of purpose have fled from Bee's head. There is only shocked reaction. A stumbling forward into the moment, horrified and appalled. They check the bodies, searching for signs of life. An old brownie stirs, and they haul him free from a pile of snapped wooden beams. They prop him up at the side of the street, and blood oozes from a gash in his forehead. No one else seems to know what to do after that. They leave him there, half-conscious.

They go on. They have to go on, don't they? They don't debate it, just seem to fall into it. A shocked probing of the wound they have found in their city. A wordless, horrified desire to understand the extent of the damage.

In the next street, all the ground-floor windows have been smashed. Bullet holes riddle the stonework, and the doors have all been perforated by the violence. A pair of female sidhe lie in the center of the road, their torsos almost cut in two.

The next street is a charnel scene. Bodies piled haphazardly, set on fire.

The next street is quiet. They all walk down it, waiting for a horror that doesn't come.

The street after that is covered with broken bottles, bricks, and shell casings. Blood spatters the walls and the floor, but all the bodies are gone.

From the next junction, they can see goblin security vehicles. Flashing lights blink malevolently through the drifting smoke. Hulking APCs trudge back and forth between smaller vehicles, machine gunners poised at their summits.

The next street is strewn with more wreckage. It looks like grenades have been fired into the upper stories and onto the roofs. Rooms stare blindly up onto the night sky.

"What the fuck?" Tharn breathes. He's the first one of them to speak in minutes.

No one has an answer.

There have been uprisings before, of course. There have been reprisals before. There was one fifteen years ago that went on for days. But Bee was four years old then and barely remembers the few days he spent in his aunt's basement complaining about how bored he was, while his parents huddled together and prayed. He has read of what happened—they all have—but those are words on a page. They are not the red horror of it before his eyes. They are not the scent of it in his nose. None of them have ever felt it quite like this. The anger they know, but the fear is new.

Motion draws Bee's eyes. Harretta has collapsed to her knees. Tears stream down her face. Others bury their faces in their hands. Of them all, it's Tharn who rushes to Harretta's side and puts an arm around her.

"The bodies…" she manages between sobs. "All… All those fae…"

Bee swallows. Would it have been better if he sided with Tharn back when they first found the goblins? Could he have changed this?

More movement. This time it's to his left. He spins around, drawing his gun. Sil has her sword pointed in the same direction.

A small fae face appears from a doorway—a pixie, her face pale in the blackened brickwork.

"Are they gone?" the pixie asks.

Bee looks back. He can still see splashes of light from the security vehicles a few streets away. He shakes his head. The pixie darts back into cover.

One question reminds him of another. He was talking to Sil before they entered this hell of smoke and ruin. She was telling him something miraculous. *Is it true?*

He turns to her now. "How?" he asks. "How do we get to Osmondo Red?"

She turns to him. She doesn't seem as drunk as she was, but she doesn't seem shocked by the horror they have just walked into either. She surveys it clinically. He remembers again that first impression he had of her, of something deadly, of something antagonistic to his existence at a primal level.

"When you want to enter House Red," she says, "you must go to a certain building. The exact one changes every day. It may be an apartment above a bakery. It may be a penthouse suite." There is an odd affectless tone to the way she speaks now, as if she is reciting a lesson well learned. "There a goblin will greet you. You will only ever see him in one of these rooms. He is blind, deaf, and has had his tongue cut out. You must tap on his arm in a certain sequence or he will attack you. He is very skilled.

"Once you have won his trust, this goblin will show you to a chair. You will sit, and he will put cotton in your ears. He will blindfold you. He will take you down to the basement and into a car. Someone will drive you to another location. That location will also change every day. There you will be led downstairs into a tunnel. When the blindfold and cotton are removed, you will be inside House Red."

This is already more than Bee has ever heard, but he still doesn't see how it helps.

"The secret," Sil says, "is that there is no door. House Red is as featureless as it looks. The second room you are taken to, the room you never see—not Osmondo's wife, not his daughter, not even his own troops—is full of fae. They are chained, their wrists fastened to their ankles, behind their backs. They spend their lives on their knees. Their tongues have also been removed. Iron bands blindfold them and will never be removed. When you wish to enter or leave House Red, they are given Dust. They open the walls. They close them behind you. This is all they will know for the rest of their lives."

Bee stares at her. "No," he says. Around him, fires burn, and revolutionaries sob. He shakes his head. "No," he says again. Because that is not a door. It is too pointlessly cruel. Too cartoonishly monstrous. "You said everyone who goes there is blindfolded," he says. "How could you know that?" He needs to poke holes in her story.

"I was taken there as part of my education. I was taken there so I would understand my place." She is starting to shudder, Bee sees, something violent that seems to originate in her spine. "Osmondo Red has a fae who works for him. He would take me there and tell me that I should never forget that my mother was fae, that I was no better than these 'hinges.' If I failed, if I did not obey, that is where they would put me."

She swallows several times. "The lucky ones," she says, "die of starvation."

She does not meet his eye for a while. Then she says, "There are twelve rooms that the fae hinges can be taken to. I know all of them. I know their pattern. I am the bodyguard of Princess Jaggered, the heir of House Red. I was told these things in case the first line of defense falls. I was told these things because I have been made to be perfectly loyal. I was told these things because I have had disobedience and rebellion torn from my head."

She looks back at him and her smile is utterly mirthless. "I am interested in educating my tutors on the errors they have made in this process."

She makes a little curtsy, smooth and perfect, her sweep of white hair bobbing. Behind her, a building collapses just a little more. Smoke drifts from a window. "Would you like to join me?" she asks him.

Bee feels a little breathless. Everyone else, he realizes, is listening too. All the survivors. All of them who are not lying dead in the lobby of an anonymous apartment building, or on a dirty rooftop or cold factory floor. All of his friends who haven't been killed yet.

Someone touches his arm. Bee jumps, but it's Tharn. "I know," Tharn says. "I know how repetitive this is going to sound, but we have to tell everyone else what she's telling us." He grabs Bee's arm. "This really could change everything."

Bee doesn't disagree. When he looks to Harretta, she doesn't either. All the heads he can see are nodding.

"OK," Bee says. "All those in favor of taking this knowledge to the leaders of the rebellion?"

"Aye," Tharn says.

"Aye," Harretta says.

"Aye," Bee and Sil say in unison.

Edwyll

Edwyll leads Jag back to the living room in the collective's well-decorated home. They enter side by side, and for the first time their partnership feels not like a lie he has made up and forced upon this goblin, but like something true. They enter the room united by common purpose and vision.

He sees the banner still taped to the wall, the ragged violence of the White Tree that he crafted. The twisted snarl of its roots tangled in blacks and purples. And it is *something*, he thinks. It could be something. Together he and Jag could make it a message that lasts.

As they step back into the room, he sees that Threm and Lila are back, sitting on the couch. The drinks are poured. The tension is still there. Talluck is staring daggers at Threm. Threm studies his drink.

Jallow grins at them despite the obvious tension. "A manifesto!" he booms. "That's what we really need. To get the principles and aims down on paper. Something we can put on flyers to make the idea concrete in fae's—"

Threm is already rolling his eyes when a sharp crack from the hallway interrupts Jallow. All eyes turn. Edwyll tries to place the noise. Then there's another, a flat, harsh noise. There's the sound of something cracking.

"What—" Threm starts.

And then the cracks come in a sharp stutter-shout. Glass shatters. The doorframe to the hallway splinters and shreds. The sheet with the tree painted on it jerks and flaps. A hole appears in the wall. A glass shatters where it sits on top of one of Jallow's rehabilitated coffee tables.

"The floor!" Jallow shouts. "Get on the floor!"

And it's only as the musty scent of a rug hits Edwyll's nose, and its wiry threads hit his chin, that he realizes that the riots have reached the street outside, that someone is firing indiscriminately, the bullets ripping through the house's cheap fabrication materials.

Stuffing erupts from the couch in short white bursts and then everything goes still.

Edwyll lies there, heart smashing against his ribs, trying to punch through his chest and the floor in one desperate attempt to bury itself in the dirt below.

A soft, heavy "whump" of sound from out on the street. Threm lets out a whimper.

They lie there waiting. After a minute Edwyll picks up his head. The others are there too, prone on the floor, trying to look around.

"Is it..." he starts. "Is it safe?"

"I think maybe..." Jallow starts.

"No!" Threm erupts. He jerks up from the floor, is there on all fours, stabs a finger out at Jallow. "No, it's not safe! This city is tearing itself inside out."

"This is why we need the sign. The manifesto." Talluck rolls back onto his haunches. "This is why a signal of hope is more important than ever."

"A *manifesto*?" Threm is virtually spitting. "You think a *manifesto* is going to save us? Do you understand what's happening out there? What's always happening out there?" His stabbing finger lances out at Jag. "Do you even know who that is? Do you know what will happen if goblins come in here and find us with her?"

Edwyll blinks. He tries to understand. "That's Jag," he says. He looks at her. And then from her face he sees that she is not just Jag.

"That," Threm says, "is Princess Jaggered Red, daughter of Osmondo Red, and heir to House Red Cap. That is the favored child of the House of Oppression and Hate."

"Jag?" He stares at her, but she won't meet his eyes.

"Ask Lila," Threm says. "She knows. She actually pays attention to what happens out there in the city. She's had her eyes open enough to see her photo in the goblin broadsheets."

Edwyll looks to Lila. The pixie smiles apologetically. "I thought you must know."

"Jag?" Edwyll says again.

"Everything I told you about my intentions is true," Jag says. She doesn't look at any of them as she talks. She speaks to the floor. "I am not my father."

"Maybe," Threm says. "Maybe not. But the ransom your father would pay for you might still be our only safe passage out of this firestorm tonight."

Edwyll blinks, tries to process. Suddenly everything is happening too fast.

"What?" Talluck rumbles, so at least Edwyll doesn't feel like he's the only one left behind.

"You think this is as bad as it's going to get?" Threm is almost shouting. "You think a few rogue shots through the door is the apex of the horror we're all plunging into? This city is a barrel of dry leaves and oil cans and tonight someone lit a match. Reprisals are coming like Mab's Kiss and I for one have never had any interest in martyrdom."

"Be quiet," Talluck growls. "You're scared and you don't know what you're saying."

"Has the wood rot set in already then?" Threm sneers. "First you think a painting of a tree can save the city. Now you think hoping the goblins go away can get us through the night. You need to wake up to reality. You need to wake up to the fact that that goblin is our only ticket to tomorrow."

Jag is shaking her head, watching Threm, watching the fear in his eyes. Edwyll feels something rising in him, feels his own fear curdling, coagulating, becoming something brutal and ragged.

"You fucking coward." He hears himself say it, but he can't quite believe it. He is saying this to Threm. The gnome whose work inspired a whole generation of photojournalists, whose monographs he has pored over at night. But he can't not say it. Not now. "You turncoat, selfish piece of shit." The profanity is burning out of him. He wants to grab his paint cans. He wants to spray them into Threm's face.

"She wants better for this city," he shouts. "She's here with us, doing something about it. And all you care about... all you can do..." He is up off the floor. He is marching on the alarmed-looking little gnome, and he doesn't know what he'll do when he gets to him—he feels out of control, freefalling—but he is half-excited, half-terrified to find out when he gets there.

But before he does, there is the unmistakable sound of someone kicking down the front door.

16

And Then It All Goes to Shit

Granny Spregg

Granny Spregg is trying to not slump out of her chair and onto the floor when Brethelda finally comes to find her. Her lungs feel as though they are full of thorns. Her breath comes in sharp, shallow bursts.

Brethelda looks down at her. "It seems," she says, "that Osmondo Red left here in a state of distress."

Granny Spregg isn't up to doing much more than exhaling. It has been years since she took Dust. She didn't expect the toll to be this great.

Brethelda crosses to the sack of powdered sugar still on the table in the center of the room. "Let me see how much of this I have figured out." She taps the bag with one finger. "You smuggled a mother lode of Dust into the city. You lost it. You sent commandos into the Fae Districts to recover it. You were found out, but tonight's fae rebellions saved you. You sent in more troops, but you still didn't find the Dust. The other Houses found out. I sent you to talk peace, but you told them you have the Dust. Osmondo Red called bullshit. You pulled this stunt to deceive him."

She turns back to Granny Spregg, considers. "No," she says. "That's not quite it, is it?" She leans in, examines Granny Spregg's face. "But I'm close."

Granny Spregg takes a few breaths. She never did enjoy being clever when there was no one around to appreciate it.

"I would have Thacker bring tea to Callart in the operations center," she manages. "He would smuggle out as much intelligence as he could glean. Bring it to me. I picked up on a report that—" A ragged breath. "That Privett missed."

"Osmondo Red." She smiles. "He's the one. Our agents picked up the chatter months ago. He'd arranged for an agent to smuggle it in. That's why I needed the troops, why I needed to usurp Privett. I needed a division of soldiers to steal it from Osmondo. But someone else got there first." She permits herself a blood-stained smile, as much to take a break from talking as anything else. "That was my only mistake. Everything else—" She locks eyes with Brethelda. "—was to my design. I wanted to be found out. I wanted you to send in more troops. I wanted to be sent to talk to the other House heads. I just…" She takes a long breath. "I was just meant to have the Dust when I went. Make those fuckers kneel."

Brethelda isn't focusing on the important parts. She isn't applauding her mother's brilliance. "Osmondo Red smuggled thirty-eight pounds of Dust into this city. What was he planning?"

Granny Spregg doesn't have the energy to shrug. "Don't know. Don't care."

Brethelda's frown deepens. "And what about you, Mother? What did you hope to gain? Because… well." Another shake of the head. "Look at you."

"This," Granny Spregg says through gritted teeth. "Is. My. House." She spits a wad of blood onto the floor.

Brethelda closes her eyes. "Oh, Mother." And for a moment

her sadness looks genuine. "You are the past, Mother. You are history. You have to let the world move on without you."

"Never."

And she won't. Not while there is breath left in her body. She tries to get to her feet. Her cane scratches against the floor. Her knees tremble. She doesn't rise, but she keeps on fighting anyway.

"Please, Mother. Stop." But Granny Spregg doesn't. She never will. "You're bleeding again."

Granny Spregg puts her hands on the table, tries to stand. Her wrists buckle. She sprawls down, finally losing her fight with gravity, spilling onto the floor in a puddle of stick limbs and stiff cotton.

Brethelda turns away, opens the door. Two large House Spriggan guards are waiting outside. "My mother is infirm in body and mind," she tells them. "Carry her back to her room and put her to her bed. Remove all the sharp objects you find. Lock the door when you leave and stand guard. I will attend to her as soon as I can consult a doctor. However, for now she has lit fires that I need to put out."

"Fuck you," Granny Spregg says from the floor.

The two guards pay her insults no heed. They hoist her up by her shoulders and her ankles and carry her across the room.

"Give up, Mother," Brethelda says. "For your own sake. You have no allies and no power left. It is time to rest. I shall ensure that House Spriggan recovers the Dust. I shall ensure that House Spriggan reaps all its benefits. But also know that you will never see a single grain of it."

She comes close. She places a hand against her mother's bloody cheek.

"This," she says, "is defeat."

Edwyll

Everyone in the collective's rowhouse has gone still. Edwyll is still standing over Threm, fists balled. Threm and Talluck are still sitting back on the floor. Jag is still on all fours. Jallow and Lila are still pressed to the musty carpet.

Every eye has gone to the door. Every ear is tuned to the sound of cracking wood. Then come the tramping footsteps, numerous, coming at speed. Talluck rises, massive, lip curled. Jag starts to scramble toward Edwyll, Threm curls into a ball.

Goblins hurtle through the doorway. Four goblins with guns and yellow bands around arms and scalps—House Spriggan, Edwyll thinks. But that doesn't make sense, because didn't Threm say Jag was House Red's heir? But there is no time to figure out the inconsistency because four goblins are shouting and screaming at them all to get down, to get back, to get on the floor, to show them their hands. Goblins who hit Talluck in the gut with the butt of a gun and double him over.

Edwyll wants to scream. Wants to scream and scream. He is trying to stand in front of Jag so they can't see her. So they don't do whatever it is Threm was suggesting they'd do.

"What did you do?" Talluck bellows at Threm. "What did you do?" He repeats it over and over until a goblin hits him with a gun butt once more—this time in the side of the head, sending him to the floor.

Jag stays on all fours, head bowed.

"What did you do?" Talluck shouts again, even though his mouth is muffled with blood.

"Nothing," Threm yells back, even as the goblins keep yelling at them all to shut up, to lie still. "I did nothing!" he screams.

"Liar!" Talluck is still struggling. Gets hit again. There's an ugly cracking sound, and Talluck goes limp.

Edwyll howls with rage. A gun barrel is thrust into his face. He goes very quiet.

In the silence that follows, one of the goblins stalks forward. "Where is she?" he asks the room.

"Hiding behind the brixie."

Edwyll's eyes go wide. Lila is pointing at him. Is pointing at Jag behind him.

She smiles sadly at Edwyll. "Threm's right," she says. "I just realized it before he did. I called them here."

Edwyll keeps looking and looking and looking and still it is Lila there, saying these things to him. Lila who encouraged him; Lila who told him of spots to paint on the streets; Lila who pushed him to be better than he is; Lila who is his friend, his confidant, his mentor. It is Lila who is pointing at him. At Jag.

The Spriggans start to close. "No," he says. "No. Why?"

"Because we exist at their whim," Lila says. "Because this house, this life—it doesn't just exist because the world loves art. Grow up, Eddy. You're smart. Be smart. We exist because House Spriggan pays coin for Jallow's art. They are the ones who allow Jallow's art to put food on our table. And I do not bite the hand that feeds. But then you come here with Jaggered Red. With the heir of House Red. And you say you want to save this city, Edwyll, but you don't understand it at all. Not its rivalries. Not its players. Not its risks. So don't look at me with horror because you don't understand the consequences of your actions. Because you don't understand the danger that you've put us all in. Look at me with gratitude as I save you from yourself, and be thankful that all it will cost is one goblin's skin."

And Edwyll keeps looking and looking, and still all he sees is a thing in Lila's form. This thing that looks at him with pity and anger, and no regret at all.

And then he snaps. And he is lunging at Lila, hands outstretched, and she is reeling back, and Spriggans have him by the arms and are hauling him away, shouting, shouting. There is so much sound. And Jag is behind him, coming up swinging, screaming at them to get off him, and a Spriggan is leveling a gun.

Then there is a roar, and suddenly Talluck is not limp on the floor, is not dead or unconscious. Instead, the huge demi-dryad is coming up, bringing both fists into a Spriggan's guts, lifting the creature off the floor with a great two-handed blow and sending him flying away.

A gun goes off, deafening in the small space, but no one seems to fall back, and Talluck is still going, grabbing another Spriggan around the neck and swinging him in an arc.

Then there is more gunfire, and Talluck's body seems to ripple under the onslaught, and the goblin he has by the neck drops to the floor, and smoke starts to fill the room.

Edwyll is on the floor again, is clawing forward, is screaming Talluck's name.

More gunfire. Edwyll freezes, waiting for the pain. But this time the goblins are falling, and he looks, and Threm has a gun, has somehow seized it from someone, and is spraying bullets wildly, barely hanging onto the end of the weapon as he tries to wrestle it into an arc around the room.

Artwork splinters, cracks, sprays shrapnel. Wood pulp flies off rehabilitated objects. Murals are defaced. Holes are punched into the faces of photographs, and periods like fists are smashed into lines of poetry.

The goblins are firing. He is rolling, desperately trying to find cover. Threm goes down. Lila is screaming. And this is her, Edwyll thinks. This is the horror Lila has put in the world.

Silence then—longer than the chaos it has replaced, gun

smoke drifting through the room. Then grunting, sobbing, an ugly gurgling sound. Edwyll looks up. Threm is just feet from him, sputtering as blood leaks from a hole in his neck. A noise Edwyll cannot control or identify wrenches out of him. He crawls toward Threm, but by the time he gets to the gnome, Threm has gone still.

Everything seems still now. Edwyll sits up. He stares. The goblins are lying on the floor, bodies shredded. Talluck's massive body is splayed and punctured like a felled tree.

The tree Edwyll painted is still tacked to the wall. The sheet of cloth is tattered and ragged, stitched with bullet holes, their edges seared black. The symbol of hope is obscured by destruction.

Lila is curled at its base. The pixie is rocking back and forth. She has Jallow's head in her lap. His blood spreads around them both like the train of a great crimson gown.

Edwyll wants to say something, wants to spit into Lila's face. He wants to scream that the pixie brought this on herself. He wants to put his hands around Lila's throat and demand why, why, why she did this, knowing that no explanation can ever be enough. He wants to laugh in Lila's face and tell her that this is the beauty she created.

He can't do any of it. He looks down at Threm. His heart feels like it's dying. All the hope and blood in him congealing into something dark and bitter. Because Threm was right.

Just like Lila said he was.

Movement to Edwyll's right. He flinches around, bringing his fists up, not knowing what he'll do with them.

Jag is there, staring at him, shell-shocked. She looks at the bodies. She shakes her head. She reaches out to him, but Edwyll steps back. He feels cold and lonely.

"We should..." she says.

Lila's head snaps up, her eyes two coals burning white. "You..." she hisses.

And there are things Edwyll wants to say. There are things he wants to scream in her face. There is Threm's blood and Talluck's that he wants to dip his fingers into and run down her cheeks while telling her that she is the one responsible.

But he can't. He just can't. He is too fixed on the image of her telling him that the collective is just House Spriggan's plaything. That her artistic principles mean nothing when push comes to shove. That the heart of the collective is, and always has been, a lie.

So Edwyll turns his back on her. He has nothing left for the pixie. For her broken promises.

He looks toward the door, toward the Iron City beyond. Toward the chaos and insanity that is the night, the riots, the uprising. There is only one other safe space he can think of. One other place where—no matter how sad, and small, and pathetic it is—he survives.

"I want to go home," he says to Jag. "I'm going to take you there."

Jag nods. "OK."

Lila stirs, but they keep on ignoring her. Keep on walking away.

"He's dead," Lila shouts at them. "He's dead because you brought that goblin here."

And Edwyll knows that's not true. But he knows that it is too.

They walk down the broken hallway. And they are still together, they are still united by purpose. But in the Iron City, Edwyll is no longer wholly sure what that's worth.

Sil

Sil is sweating. She is trying to hide the tremor in her hands. Desire has broken free inside her mind, but it has brought friends with it. Doubt and fear swill in her skull.

You will obey. She was broken down and rebuilt around this phrase. *You will serve.* This was the limit placed on her will. They beat it into her. They broke her bones to teach it to her. Then, when she was healed, they would just break them again. And when that pain stopped being a sufficient motivator, they showed her that pain could always get worse. Some tutors seemed to enjoy that lesson especially. One—a fae in Osmondo's employ—most of all. And so, she has screamed her throat bloody before. She has begged, and groveled, and offered up her body to escape. Those tutors simply watched. They did not laugh, or sneer. They did not show pity. They just watched and waited until the lesson was learned.

Now, she knows her lessons are lies. Now, she is free, and there is joy in that—there is leaping ecstasy at the thought of all that she could do—and there is rage too in the recognition of what she has lived through—but there is also so much fear that she thinks she might buckle under its weight.

Am I going to do this? The closer they get to the fae leadership, the louder and more frequently the question rings through her head.

Would it just be easier to kill these fae?

The answer, of course, is yes. She doesn't want to, though. And that matters. And she does, truly and deeply, want to erase Osmondo Red from the face of this city. She wants it a thousand times over. She wants to drive the blade into his heart again and again and again.

But she is so very scared of wanting it.

"Almost there," Bee says.

Her stomach lurches. She has been so lost in her own head she has lost track of where they are. If she doesn't get her head on straight, she'll be dead within thirty seconds of entering House Red Cap.

Or maybe I can send others in instead. Or maybe we can ambush him. Or...

The factory that the Fae Liberation Front is leading her toward is well guarded. Armed fae watch them from rooftops and alleyways. They communicate with well-rehearsed hand signals. No one in the Fae Liberation Front seems to notice them.

Sil hesitates on the factory threshold, fear rising up her spine like a tide. She wrestles to make her own desire the master she serves.

"Down here." Bee points towards a door and stairs that lead to the basement.

It's a good defensible position, she thinks. The guards outside are set up well, with long lines of sight and good coverage to ensure that they're hard to sneak up on. One fae can take down many before they're likely to be injured. Within the factory, the path to the basement door is winding, difficult to navigate. The steps down set up a natural chokepoint. It's how she would have set it up. How she was taught to do it.

"It's a kobold in charge," Bee tells her as they head down the stairs. "He's old school, lot of goblin hatred in him, but I think when it comes to the chance to take Osmondo Red's head, that's going to be in our favor." He smiles, a jagged slash of teeth in the darkness. She nods, feeling once more like a spectator, watching herself go through these motions, not quite believing in them.

Am I going to do this?

There is a surprising familiarity to the scene at the bottom of the stairs. Someone has approximated a goblin war room.

She sees stations set up for operations, supply management, reconnaissance, and intelligence. Instead of the clipped efficiency of a goblin operation, though, these fae move with frantic excess. Pixies run and sidhe shout. Dryads blunder back and forth. It all is so very fae, she almost sneers. Some things, she supposes, are hard to unlearn.

"Hey," Bee calls to a tall dryad near the center of things. "Where's Skart?"

The dryad looks at them, slightly wild-eyed. "An office," she says, "at the back. But—"

The Fae Liberation Front ignore the rest, marching Sil with them to the back rooms. There are five offices there, but voices emerge from only one. Bee knocks, then opens the door without waiting for an answer.

There are two fae within. One, a disheveled youth, wearing dirty clothes and a stunned expression. The other…

The other…

The other…

All around Sil, the world fades away. The chaos of shouting is muffled. The scuff of bodies pressing in evaporates. The faces of the expectant Fae Liberation Front drift off into shadow.

Now, here, it all comes down to this: to him, and her, and memory.

Skart

One more minute and he would have had the Dust. Just one more.

"What will you choose?" he had asked Knull, and it had been as if he were playing the brixie like an instrument, as if he were strumming a beautiful tune.

"I…" Knull had opened his mouth, and the silence had been like the orchestra breathing, taking a moment before the great crescendo.

"I'm not going to force you," Skart had said. "I'm not the goblins, Knull. I'm everything they are not. This is a real choice."

"I don't..." Knull had shaken his head. "I..."

"If you help me end the oppression," Skart had said, "then you no longer need to escape it."

And that had done it. He'd seen it in Knull's eyes. Something between surrender and enlightenment. The seed from which resolve would grow. And in a minute, he would have had the location of the Dust. In a minute, everything would have been over.

But then the door had swung open, and there were fae there.

And her.

And her.

She has always been beautiful to him, although he has never told her this. She has always been a source of wonder. And although they have been more intimate than many lovers, he supposes he never will.

"Imposter," she says. Her hands fumble at the sword in her belt.

She shouldn't be here. That was never part of the plan. Jag was meant to come into the Iron City alone tonight. Sil's presence, even without Jag, means that the missing Dust is far from the only thing to have gone wrong tonight.

"Betrayer," she says, and her voice is shaking. She has her sword out. Around her, fae are falling back, are shouting, are fumbling for weapons, but none of them can stop her. Of that Skart is very, very sure.

He has seconds to decide what to do, he knows, seconds to decide what he can still recover from these ashes. But he supposes, in the end, there is no choice for him. Ever since he found the bodies in Cotter's apartment, he has suspected that everything has been narrowing down to this moment.

"He is Osmondo Red's fae!" she yells.

Skart looks Sil in the eye. And there is regret in this moment. She must have achieved so much to get this far. But she, he knows, has no choices either anymore.

Quietly he says to her, "Mnemosyne."

Sil

Sil doesn't remember her mother. She used to know her name, her face, the sound of her voice as she invoked the barrow rites that all sidhe children learn, but these things were taken from her. She cannot remember exactly how or when, but she knows that it was her tutors who were responsible.

She remembers her tutors. Those that Osmondo sent to train her to be the perfect bodyguard for his daughter. She remembers that they were all cruel. That they all hurt her. That they all taught her things she did not want to know.

One of them, though, stands out the sharpest in her memory. A mental image with edges sharp enough to cut.

He had dead eyes. That was the first thing she noticed about him. Some of her tutors had eyes that would sparkle when she did well. Some had eyes that sparkled when they hurt her. Some eyes were as thin as sheets of glass—the only things between her and unfathomable rage. But his eyes were always dead. There was nothing behind them to see. No joy. No cruelty. No desire at all.

He was not a goblin. That too was different. All her other tutors were like her father: sharp-featured, short, with mouths full of teeth like knives. But this one was soft, and tall, not quite like the sidhe, but more like her mother than anyone she'd seen in a long time. At first, she thought that would make him kinder, would mean that he would sympathize with her, and resent the cruelty of all the goblins who said they were trying to beat the fae out of her. That mistake was one of the very first lessons he taught her.

There are things he did to her that she still cannot think about. Things with knives, and drills, and saws. Things with dogs, and beetles, and worms. Things with his hands.

"It is important to know," he said to her once, "just how much damage can be done to you. That way you will always know whether or not you are broken. On this journey, you will think you are broken many times, but know now there is always so much worse I can do to you."

She has run on broken ankles. And every time she fell, he did worse to her.

She has served tea while holding her guts in with one hand. And for every drop she spilled, he did worse to her.

She has searched for a dropped needle in a room writhing with hungry rats. And for every minute longer than he thought it should take, he did worse to her.

There were always ways he could do so much worse to her. This was the lesson he taught her best.

His lessons have always been there in her mind. His face has always been there in the darkness behind her eyelids. Now, he stands before her. Now, he is held up to her as the architect of the fae's rebellion, and she knows immediately this is another breaking. It is not of her this time, and that is both better and worse. Because this, she is sure, is the breaking of the fae. Of Bee and the rest of the rebels. This kobold—this tutor—is teaching them all a lesson.

And she knows, as surely as she knows all these other things—purely and without the hesitation of doubt—that she has to warn them. She has to stop him.

"Imposter," she gasps. "Betrayer."

The others stare at her as she fights to make herself clear.

"He is Osmondo Red's fae!" she yells, and they keep on staring.

And there is no time. Only time to act. She draws her sword and—

"Mnemosyne."

And then there is no time left at all.

All the color in the world drains away. All the noise fades. Every voice screaming at her to act, to do something, to do what she wants to do, what she has always wanted to do. It all goes away.

"Osmondo's fae? What?"

A fae's voice. The fae called Bee. She takes stock of where he stands, the angle of his feet, how he holds his weight. *A blade to the throat,* she thinks. *Quick and fast.*

She mentally walks through each of their deaths then, plotting each blow, extrapolating scenarios for parrying their most predictable responses. She knows how she will cut off their attempts at retreat. She knows how many will be dead before Bee's body hits the floor.

And all the time, a voice is screaming inside of her, is screaming that she was free, that she was out, that they tried to fucking kill her.

Quietly, and without much thought, Sil kicks the knees out from beneath that voice, and grabs it by the hair, and drags it off to shut it behind the bars that suffuse her mind. It will not bother her much from there, she knows.

"Are you present and correct, asset Sil?" Skart says.

Sil bows her head.

"Asset Sil?" Bee echoes. "What the fuck?"

"I am exiting the building," Skart instructs her. "Minimize the witnesses."

Sil raises her sword, and as she does so, she thinks again that Skart has always had such dead eyes.

Knull

Knull sees it all come undone. He's looking right at Skart's eyes when the door opens, when Skart turns and sees the white-haired half-fae trying to pull her sword. He's looking right at those eyes when she calls Skart Osmondo's fae.

Knull has been caught in lies more than most. He is intimate with that moment when you must capitulate to the inevitable revelation. He knows what he's seeing, and he knows that he has heard the white-haired half-fae speak the truth. He knows he's finally starting to see Skart's angle.

The location of the Dust had been on the tip of his tongue. He'd been about to give it up. For a moment, the momentum of that decision nearly carries the words over the precipice of his lips so he almost blurts it into this pregnant moment, this harbinger of harm to come.

He bites down hard on his tongue.

"I am exiting the building," Skart says. "Minimize the witnesses." His voice holds no more emotion than if he were reciting a list of purchase orders. And Knull sees all the fear, and anger, and guilt flee from Skart's face, washed away by an expressionless mask.

Skart takes a step toward the office door. A sidhe with pale blue skin who is standing beside the white-haired half-fae raises a hand, says, "Wait," but the half-fae brings her sword down, and suddenly the sidhe has half the regular number of hands.

Knull shrieks. The sidhe screams. The amputated hand flops obscenely on the floor.

And Knull sees it all come undone.

The half-fae pivots and spirals. Her blade and her hair are twin flashes of white. The air is suddenly full of spraying blood.

Skart's arm jabs out. He seizes Knull by the collar and drags him almost off his feet. Knull struggles to be free, but the old kobold's arm seems to be made exclusively of muscle and steel beams.

The half-fae hacks and slashes, carving a path through the rebels. Bodies and blood spill across the floor. There is an awful smell of sweat and copper in the air. A gun goes off so close it feels as if it must have been pressed to Knull's head.

Then they're through the thicket of violence. More gunfire detonates behind them. Fae are screaming. Knull sees every eye in the basement fixed on them. He has his feet beneath him now. He starts to fight Skart's efforts full force.

Skart turns and buries his fist in Knull's throat. Knull's legs go out from under him. The world blurs and he sees it in gasping, tear-stained snatches: the half-fae running past them, her white hair spattered with red; a brownie running up to Skart, her mouth full of questions; Skart slashing a blade, and the brownie's mouth filling with blood.

Someone is driven into Skart in the tumult, and—twisting and writhing—Knull tears free. He stumbles a few steps, still gasping, then something snags his bad ankle and he sprawls forward, smashing his mouth against the basement's concrete floor.

More shots ring out. More screams. The floor trembles with the stampede of fleeing fae.

Knull twists, sees that Skart has him by his injured ankle. The kobold heaves and starts to drag him across the floor. Knull bellows, starts kicking at the kobold's hand with his free foot, half-blinded by pain. He strikes knuckles, and Skart howls. Another strike, and the kobold's hand springs open. Knull scrambles away across the floor. He glances back. Skart is snarling, advancing. His knife is out. Behind him, the white-haired half-fae is butchering rebels with savage abandon.

Then, with a massive howl, a huge dryad slams into Skart and the pair of them go flying. The dryad is yelling something into Skart's face, but Knull can't hear the words over the volume of his own panic. This is the only opening he is likely to get and it is narrow as a gnat's asshole.

He scrambles forward on all fours, finds his feet beneath him, and then he's up and running. He sees the stairs, the exit. He pounds toward them. He hears a gunshot, waits for pain, but then he's in the doorway, then he's on the stairs, taking them three at a time, his ankle screaming, not caring, not daring to slow, simply fleeing that basement, and its blood, and its murder, and all Skart's terrible, echoing lies.

Bee

What the fuck? What the actual ever-living—

Harretta is on the floor screaming. She is holding the spraying stump of her hand and screaming. Bee can see her hand on the floor. He wants to throw up.

Outside the small office room, Sil is still moving. She has her sword raised and through the throat of some staring half-pixie. Has her foot extended and is kicking a gnome in the temple. Is ripping the sword through flesh and muscle to bury it in the abdomen of an advancing sidhe.

His friends are on the floor. So many of them on the floor, dead, and dying, and screaming, and breathing out their last ragged breaths.

A shot rings out, someone firing in Sil's direction. The boom is massive and echoing. The shot goes wild. Wood explodes near Bee's head.

"Get down!" Someone grabs him around the waist, drives him to the floor. He grunts, eating concrete. He kicks and punches, realizes through the haze of terror he has Tharn by the throat.

"We've got to get out of here!" Tharn hisses.

More gunshots. They whine and scream overhead. Bee looks up, looks out at the factory basement. Sil has kicked the knees out from beneath a demi-dryad, is sawing his skull from his neck.

"We've got to try to—" Bee doesn't know the end of that sentence. *Save Sil?* But he needs to be saved from her. He doesn't know what's happened. Was it all a long con? Did she fool him? Was something done to her?

He doesn't know. He knows Tharn is right. They have to get out of here.

He grabs Harretta by her remaining hand, hauls her to her feet. She has her stump pressed to her stomach, is staining herself with blood.

Tharn pulls a pistol, opens fire. They run. The three of them. Maybe all that is left of the Fae Liberation Front. Bee doesn't know. He can't tell amid the chaos, among the fleeing, fighting bodies. In the debris of the whirlwind that is Sil hacking and slashing and gutting and executing her way through the room.

They had *laughed* together.

Tables are being overturned. Piles of crates collapsing as herd mentality swirls through the basement like a fever. Gunfire explodes around them, Sil dancing through the chaos with ballerina grace. Fae hit by stray shots go down, collapsing. Tharn fires off shots wildly, aiming too high. Bee drags Harretta left then right, trying to dodge obstacles, just trying to cross the hundred yards of space that will take them to the stairs.

Sil is ahead of them. Between them and the stairs. Their momentum falters.

"Give me the gun."

Bee turns. Tharn turns. Harretta wrenches her hand out of Bee's grip. She holds it out to Tharn. "I'm a better shot than you."

"But—"

She grabs it from him. Sets her sights. Her hand is shaking, Bee can tell, but he doesn't say anything.

"Payback, you—"

Harretta fires. And it is so close to being decisive. So close to putting a stop to this.

The shot spins off Sil's blade, nicks the edge. Sil turns. Sees them.

"Run!" Bee screams.

But she is between them and the door. And they run, but she is there to meet them.

Harretta is firing the pistol over and over and Sil is spinning, putting bodies between her and them. And Harretta is roaring. And then Sil leaps over a collapsing pixie, her sword still in its back, and she lands among them like a thunderbolt.

Bee throws a punch and it is like punching air. She just isn't there, pirouetting around him, driving the heel of her palm into Tharn's face.

And then Harretta is on Sil, driving her bloody stump into the half-fae's face, smearing gore into her eyes, howling. Bee falls back. Tharn gasps, but Harretta presses on, bearing Sil down to the floor with her weight, and her anger, and her pain.

The path to the stairs is open. Bee sees it.

"No!" Tharn flings himself at Sil and Harretta, and then Bee sees that Sil's collapse has not been a pratfall, or a mistake. She has thrown herself backward, has thrown herself within reach of her sword still protruding from the back of the fallen pixie, has grabbed it as she fell.

Tharn hits Sil's sword arm, pins it.

The gun. Bee can see Tharn's gun on the floor. His pistol. He scrambles toward it. Hears a cry, looks up. Sil has somehow jacknifed her body, has thrown Harretta up and off, piling her into Tharn. Sil's sword arm is still pinned, but she is slamming her free hand into the side of Harretta's skull over and over. Harretta moans.

The gun. Bee grabs the gun.

Tharn is between Bee and Sil. Has wrestled his way up, is trying to pull Harretta clear. Harretta reeling, blood spilling down her skull. And Bee screams at them, "No!" because Sil's sword arm is free—this is what she wanted. But it's too late, as Sil is on her feet fast as quicksilver, and her blade flashes forward.

Harretta convulses. Tharn stumbles back. Sil growls. Her blade protrudes from Harretta's back.

The path to the stairs is free.

Sil advances. Bee holds out his gun. Harretta's body is between him and Sil.

Tharn is staggering.

The path to the stairs is free.

He turns, he grabs Tharn's hand, and they run.

Skart

Brumble's phlegm is spraying into Skart's face. "You—" she brays. "You killed—"

"Yes." Skart doesn't see any more point in denying it. Sil is here. One way or another, his double life is over. It is only a question of how long he can drag things out, and the night is too far gone, and too far from all his carefully laid out plans to afford him any more delays.

"Why?" The pain in her face has nothing to do with his attempts to free himself. She has him fully pinned, splayed and immobile, her massive weight advantage rendering resistance an absurdity. So, why not tell her? Why not be done with it once and for all?

"Because this rebellion will fail," he says through gritted teeth. "They will all fail, and they will always fail, and the reprisals will always come. The cycle will repeat over and over, but I can finally end it. I can save the fae. From you. From all of you who just won't go quietly into the future. I can pull all of you out into the light to be crushed and forgotten. And finally, the rest of us will be left in peace. Because you will all be dead."

She gapes at him dumbly. "But," she manages. "But you…"

Skart doesn't feel much anymore. Scar tissue, tumors, and ruin aren't sensitive to any but the sharpest emotions. But now, the little of him that's left enjoys watching the shock roll through Brumble's broad, bovine face.

"Once," he says. Behind them, he can hear Sil still at work, the thudding meaty thwacks of her blade biting flesh. "Once, when I was still as stupid as you, before I was cured, that stupidity took the lives of my wife, and my children, and my friends. It tore through lives like a whirlwind of knives. And I almost died before I saw things true. That's what the rebellions cost me. What they cost all the fae. That is who your stupidity kills."

It was after the Red Rebellion that he saw things for how they truly are. It was the first of the major uprisings after the Iron War. And he had already lost so much. But he had also been so sure that they would win. He had been so sure that he could bring the goblins' rule to an end.

But he hadn't. He'd failed. And so many had died. And so much had been lost. And he'd lain in House Red's jail and learned about all the things that were so much worse than death. And finally, six months too late, what little was left of him had seen the truth of it: the fae's time was done. It was the goblins' time now. It was Osmondo Red's time.

He'd done many things for Osmondo Red since then. He'd done what he could to make things better for the fae along the way. Once he would have been ashamed of everything he's done. Now, he finds he doesn't really care.

He and Osmondo came up with the plan for tonight together. They decided they needed to do it. It was necessary because despite everything Skart had done to save the fae from pain they still insisted on bringing it down upon their own heads. The rebels and troublemakers still picked at the same old wounds. So, he and Osmondo had devised a way to gather them all up, to send them all out to where House Red Cap's troops were waiting, and finally remove them as a problem.

And Skart thinks he would be happy to explain all this to Brumble, to pick the scales of idiocy from her eyes, but abruptly there is no more time. Brumble's eyes go wide and wider still. She gasps. Blood joins the phlegm she has sprayed onto his chest.

Sil pulls her sword from Brumble's back. She kicks the heavy dryad aside and helps Skart to his feet.

"You took your time."

Around them, limbs and offal are spread like hay on a stable floor. Sil is soaked with red. She doesn't say anything. Skart doesn't expect her to. "Mnemosyne" was always a failsafe, a trigger buried deep in her psyche only to be pulled out as a last resort. It leaves her with only a little higher cognition.

He sighs. A lot of hard work wasted on all fronts. Still, the chance to put everything to rights remains within reach. The whole night can still be worthwhile. All he has to do is relocate Knull, and then beat the Dust's location from his bones.

Granny Spregg

Granny Spregg tries bribery. She tries flaunting her few remaining feminine charms. She even tries threats to life, limb, and offspring. But the guards Brethelda has posted at her door prove disappointingly, albeit predictably, resilient to all these approaches. She is most effectively imprisoned.

She stands in her bedroom. Her rugs smell of wet-vac chemicals and Thacker's blood stains have been erased. His body is missing. His presence annulled. She thinks about how she would have connived to evict him from her rooms, how he would have brought her own loyal forces to bear, and how she would have listened to the ensuing gunfight in the hall.

None of this is to be now. In the empty space of his absence.

She wipes irritatedly at one eye. When she examines the dampness on her finger, she finds it stained with red.

She doesn't have long now, she knows. The poison is clawing deeper and deeper into her system. The Dust has weakened her. Her only co-conspirator is dead. She has very few options left.

But she does still have some.

She reaches into her pocket and pulls out a small twist of plastic wrap. Brethelda really should have known better than to leave her alone in a room with the House's supply of Dust.

She hesitates before she takes it. She is not entirely sure she can survive it. It will make everything so much worse at the very least. But it is the only path left open to her, her only opportunity to stop the endless march of the future.

She buries her nose in the Dust. She grimaces. She inhales.

—a beast growling in a cave; blood splattered on rocks; a fire ravaging dead, dry wood; birds' bodies impaled on a thorn bush; red—

She grunts, comes back through the visions to her chambers. Magic and pain beat twin drums in her chest while her heart races to keep up. She sucks in an icy, scorching lungful of air and blood dribbles down her chin.

Her chambers are on the forty-eighth floor of House Spriggan, looking down on the Iron City. She goes to her window now. Fires are burning in the Fae Districts, creating a false dawn. She smiles and more blood leaks free. That is her work being done out there. Now she will finish it.

She reaches out a hand and twists the world. Where there was a window, there is now a ragged hole lined with black thorns. She steps though it, out into empty air.

She falls. Black wings bloom from her back, wing tips stained as red as the rain that falls from her body onto the streets below. She glides down and away from House Spriggan and Brethelda's clawing attempt to contain her. The wind rustles her newborn feathers, its cold pulsing against her crackling, cracking skin.

The magic leaves her five feet above street level. She gasps as reality crashes back, as she crashes down to cold blacktop. She lies there. When she breathes, her lungs are full of glass shards. When she moves, her bones are iron brands.

She cannot afford to be broken. She cannot stop. With raw palms, she slowly pushes herself up. Starbursts of pain radiate from her chest, claw down her arm. Her breath is quick and shallow.

She ignores it. She cannot afford to be broken. She takes a step forward. Her will is not broken. She takes a step forward. Her will is going to carry her on despite her failing flesh. She takes a step forward. Her will is carrying her now.

Step by step, she moves toward the Fae Districts, toward the Dust she needs to make all her dreams come true, and toward the end of any future but her own.

17

Life is Always Fatal

Knull

It is not so far, in the end, from the fae rebels' blood-spattered basement to the house Knull once called home. His screaming ankle makes it feel like miles, but in reality, it doesn't take him long to arrive back where this all started—this life, this obsessive need to escape his past.

Last time he was here, he was hesitant. Now, he crashes into the door full force, barreling through boxes, and flyers, and old take-out containers. He stomps down the filthy hallway, barking in pain with every step. At its far end—seeming distant as another planet—the living room is cast in the twitching glow of the TV's dead-channel static. Surely comatose, his parents offer him no welcome.

Before he gets to that scene, he's at the door to his old bedroom. He punches it open, reveals the same old scene beyond: rumpled bed, aging posters, stained desk. He feels the same old disgust at the sight of this abandoned prison. He thought he had escaped it years ago, shed its weight and fled to make what he could of his life. In the wake of tonight's events that ambition feels like the shallowest self-deception.

Now, he wants out utterly and totally. Tonight, he wants out of everything. Tonight, he is leaving the Fae Districts body and soul. The fact that he is penniless and prospectless are no longer relevant excuses. Anything is better than staying in this mire.

"Jag?"

The voice comes from behind him as he stomps deeper into the room. He spins around, grunts as he has to steady himself with his bad foot. Edwyll stands in the doorway, face pale, eyes red and raw. He looks, Knull thinks in that first fleeting moment, bereaved.

"Edwyll?" It's a question but he doesn't know exactly what he's asking. He doesn't know anything anymore.

"What are you doing?" Edwyll asks, and it's such a mundane question it seems out of place in the chaos of this night.

He's about to answer when a face appears over Edwyll's shoulder. It's dirt-stained, disheveled, and narrow, with an unmistakably slender nose and undeniably sharp teeth.

Goblin. The word screams through his brain. He jumps back, grabs for a weapon and ends up with an ancient poster tube in his hands. He brandishes the cardboard wildly.

"Get away from him!" he yells.

"No, Knull! No!" Edwyll steps forward, the goblin back. Edwyll reaches his hands out, the goblin spreads hers wide.

"She's with me," Edwyll says.

Knull stares from one to the other. "Why?"

"I—" the goblin says.

"She's my patron."

"What?" None of this makes any sense to Knull.

Edwyll hesitates. The goblin puts a hand on his shoulder. Knull can't tell if it's meant to be comforting or proprietary.

"The city *has* to change, Knull." It's almost a sob when Edwyll says it. His whole body seems racked by the sentiment. "*I* have to change it. But I can't do it on my own. So she's helping me. We're going to change the city. We're going to unite the fae. Because we have to. We have to bring them together—"

He's babbling, the words spilling out of him. The same old bullshit.

"—under a banner of the White Tree," Edwyll is saying. He's sketching something in midair. "Redefined. Reimagined. Freed from bullshit, and hypocrisy, and lies, and betrayal—"

"Shut up!" Knull yells the words. Hurls them into Edwyll's face. The goblin steps back, looks offended, looks appalled, but Knull's fists are balled and ready. He looks into Edwyll's eyes and sees the tears there, spilling down his face. He says more gently now, "Just shut up, Edwyll."

"I have to change it." A plea.

"You can't." Knull doesn't like saying it, but he needs Edwyll to hear it, finally this time, for it to get through. "You can't change it. It's too big. No one can. And art definitely can't. You can only pull yourself free of its sucking awfulness. And no picture of no fucking White Tree, no matter how you redesign it, is going to do that. You need money. And I can get money. I have the Dust. I just need a buyer. *Come with me*. Please." And somehow he has found his way to begging himself. "Please don't let this absurd dream drag you down. We can get out of the Fae Districts. I can get us out. I can."

He has to be able to.

Edwyll shakes his head. "That doesn't change anything, Knull. It can't."

"Neither can you."

All the distance they've gone, and they've travelled nowhere. They're still here at this impasse.

But then Edwyll steps forward and hugs him and says, "I do

wish you luck, Knull. I do. I wish you were right, even though I know you're not."

They break free after a moment, and Knull wants to say something to Edwyll, at the last, some final expression of brotherly affection, of how much hope he once had for Edwyll and his art, and how much that helped him on the nights when he felt utterly alone.

He can't, though. The words stick in his throat, and so he turns away from him and gets down on his knees. He starts to scrabble under his bed, desperately searching for the brick of Dust to which he has pinned all his hopes.

Skart

"Get me some Dust," Skart says. "One of the corpses will have some." He looks at Sil. "Then we shall run our quarry to ground."

Skart steps back then. He doesn't cajole Sil or offer her encouragement. She is little more than a machine now anyway, and he has set her mechanism.

If only, he thinks, all machines ran so smoothly. Out there in the Iron City, the clockwork of his plan is scattered in tatters about the burning streets.

And yet, he thinks, perhaps it is not too late. There are still bits and pieces of the plan that can be gathered up and made into something whole. Many of the rebels are already dead. Far more than after a usual uprising. He has achieved that much at least. And perhaps the revelation of his own betrayal will help break the fae more deeply than is typical.

Sil kneels beside a body. A sidhe. She can't be older than eighteen or nineteen. In the old days she wouldn't have been considered an adult. Sil eviscerated her neatly in the melee, and her intestines are spread out broadly. Sil kneels in them unflinching, rifling through pockets without a flicker of emotion on her face.

The real problem, Skart reflects, is hope. Has he killed hope? He doubts it. No matter how many times the rebellions are beaten down, no matter how often the weeds are torn up, the rebels grow back. And every set of reprisals just seeds fresh hatred, fresh rebellion, fresh hope. None of it ever truly salts the earth.

Empty-handed, Sil stands, goes to pick the pockets of an old gnome whose throat she had cut.

When Skart had first suggested the plan, Osmondo had balked at bringing so much Dust into the Iron City. The risk of exposure was monumental. Skart, though, had worked on him, had done his best to highlight the reward that balanced such risk. And Osmondo has always been ambitious. That, in the end, Skart believes, is why the future belongs to him: he will never sit upon his laurels the way the fae did.

It would have been easier if Osmondo had been willing to pay Cotter outright for the Dust. He could afford to. It was simple mean-spirited obstinateness that prevented it. Osmondo's unwillingness to see that much of his coin in the hands of a fae. Many of tonight's mishaps could have been avoided if Osmondo was just a little less miserly. But Skart had caved on that point, and in the end, only one objection remained—whoever created the future would never get to enjoy it. To use the volume of Dust Skart wanted was suicide.

If Skart was younger, or could be useful for longer, or if his loyalty was in any way in question then Osmondo would never have agreed. But Skart has had only his cause to live for for so long. Osmondo knows this. Osmondo caused this. He has heard

Skart thank him for it many times. And so, finally, Osmondo Red had agreed. This is how Skart would die: saving the fae.

Sil straightens. She comes toward him. In her hand she holds a small bag of Dust.

Skart smiles and offers out his open palm.

"How," Osmondo had asked him, "does one kill hope?"

Skart had leaned forward. He had shown his teeth. "With enough Dust you can kill anything. Mab used Dust to smash three cities and break the spirit of the fae. But where Mab used a hammer, I will use a scalpel.

"Another rebellion," he had said, and Osmondo had gone to interrupt, but Skart held up a hand to forestall him. "One different from the others. One that you and I and your best tacticians plan out. What would hurt us the most? What has the greatest chance to be successful? What would be our worst nightmare?"

Osmondo's eyes had narrowed.

"I will work with the fae," Skart had said. "I will bring the rebellion into being. I will cultivate their hope. I will make them believe that this time they have a chance."

"But they don't," Osmondo had hissed.

"No." Skart had twisted his face into a smile he didn't feel. "No, they never will. We will have orchestrated everything. We will know everything. And we will know how to shatter the rebellion at every turn, how to transform hope into despair."

Osmondo had leaned back, sneered. "That's it? Your grand plan is just an increase in the magnitude of our victory?" He waved a dismissive hand.

"No," Skart had said, and his smile had become truer, more honest. "It is different because it will never end. That is what I will use the Dust for. To trap their failure in time. To make it repeat over and over.

"I will use the Dust," he said, "to snip the rebels who gather in that warehouse that night from time. Twelve hours, from sundown to the sunrise they'll never see. Just them. Not the city. Not the whole of the fae. Just those who dared raise a hand against you.

"Every night the Dust will summon them from their graves, reconstitute their flesh and bones, just as they were in their homes, in the bars, in the factories. Every night they will be born as they were at the beginning of that one night. Full of ambition. Full of desperation. Full of dreams. Every night they will march through the streets of the Fae Districts, not seeing the world as it was, not listening to their loved ones who plead with them to do it differently this time, to not go, to stay, to live. Blind to the modern world. Trapped in that piece of the past I have crystallized and looped.

"They will march through the streets again, they will go to the warehouse again, they will leave and once more march off to their death. Again. Hundreds of fae. Doomed to be cut down. Doomed to have their dreams shattered. And their bodies will lie in the streets, and on the factory floors. And then the sun will come, and the magic will wash them away, will give a brief reprieve. And then when the next night comes, the Dust will summon them once more, will put them back once more, to do it all over again, and again, and again.

"It will be," he said, licking his lips, "a living monument. A testament in blood and shattered bone. A reminder to the fae of the futility of rebellion. Of the inevitable end of their dreams. It will force them to wake to the new reality of the world."

Osmondo had blinked. "New rebels every night?"

Skart had shaken his head. "The same ones. Reborn only to die. Imagine sitting in your dining room, and your dead son manifests out of dust and dirt. Imagine the pixie you have mourned nods at something you said three years ago, even as you scream at him not to do it, not to go this one time, even though you know he will. Imagine trailing him through the streets, grabbing at his arm, trying to haul him back. But you can't, because he moves with the inevitability of a clock's hand. He drags you along, unseeing, uncaring, unhearing. Imagine following him to a factory, and seeing bullets rip through him, tear him apart, spill his blood. Every night. Until the sun comes once more. And imagine in that light knowing that it's all going to happen all over again. Forever.

"That," he had said to Osmondo Red, "is how you kill hope."

Osmondo had thought about that for a long time. And then he'd started to laugh.

And now, Skart thinks, it's not all lost. There are enough pieces of the plan left. He can still pull it all back. He can still save the fae from this futile cycle. He can stop the reprisals. He can stop the endless repetitions of torture and death.

He just needs to find Knull.

So, he takes the Dust Sil has found him, and he feels the magic spring to life in him once more, this overture to the much greater magic to come. And he uses it to heighten his senses, to pick apart the hidden trails that lead up the stairs and up and away from the factory. He uses it to find the path of a fae with a half-broken ankle and a limp.

He follows the trail through the increasingly filthy streets, Sil beside him, faithful as a hound. He follows it past the burned-out buildings, and the bodies strung up from streetlamps. He follows without batting an eyelid. The birth of the future was always going to be painful.

Finally, he comes to one dirty, decaying, wedged-open door. He pauses there and checks his watch. There is not much of this night left, but there's still time for the dawn to usher in a new day. So, Skart heads into the moldering hallway, and toward the sound of voices, and he goes to end it all.

Sil

Skart enters the house. She follows. Skart marches forward down the hall. Sil smells the dank air, listens, and assesses the terrain, the inhabitants, and the threat. She can hear three distinct voices ahead of them. There is emotion in their words, but she can no longer be sure what it is. Not a threat is all she knows for certain.

She sees Skart reach the doorway. She sees him framed there. She hears silence fall abruptly. When she arrives beside him, she immediately glimpses the way one fae's weight moves—a brixie, the oldest of the three, a dirty street rat of a fae. He is about to fling himself forward despite the makeshift splint bound to his ankle. She brings her sword to rest upon his Adam's apple before he even has a chance to realize what he's decided to do.

"Hello, Knull," Skart says. He is smiling. He is happy.

There are two others in the room. Another brixie, younger, paler, more delicately boned and—

"How—" Knull's throat bounces against the sword blade.

Sil should be reading his body language now. She should be assessing the tone of his voice and the diameter of his pupils. But the third occupant of the room is Jag.

Slow ripples work their way across Sil's psyche. Jag. It is Jag. She was looking for Jag. She has to keep Jag safe. But… she has to keep *Skart* safe. She has to keep Jag safe. She has to keep Skart safe. She looks from one to the other, sees the resentment between them, the burgeoning antagonism.

Jag hasn't seen her yet, is focused on Skart. She moves slightly. She doesn't have to. It is not… required, but it is not forbidden either and so she does. Jag's eyes flick to her and go wide.

"Sil!"

The younger brixie looks at her too and blanches. "Oh shit. No. Not you."

Sil dismisses him. He offers no threat now.

"Ah," Skart says with his wide smile and his dead eyes. "Reunions. But, alas, I have no time for them." The smile drops away. "Give me the Dust," he tells Knull.

"Fuck you." Knull spits. Her blade nicks his skin as his throat works. And Skart doesn't even flinch as the phlegm hits him. There is so much worse, Sil knows, that has been done to him.

"Don't do this," Jag says, and it takes Sil a moment to realize from Jag's tone and intonation that she is talking to her. "Let us go."

Sil looks to Skart for confirmation. He doesn't look at her. She keeps her sword where it is, barring the way.

"Sil, ignore this kobold asshole and let us go!" Jag is half shouting.

She watches her own arm tremor. She should, she thinks, obey. This is Jag. She does what Jag says. But she must do what Skart says. But she always obeys Jag. She must look to Skart.

She looks at Skart. This time he glances at her. Infinitesimally, he shakes his head. Her arm grows steady once more.

"Sil!" Jag is pleading with her.

This time, she tries to not look at Skart. This time, she tries to keep her eyes only on Jag. She tries to move her arm. Somehow, she moves her head. She looks at Skart.

"No," Skart says in his calm dead voice. "I don't want to let them go. I want them—" He turns back to Knull. "—to give me—" His voice rises. "—the fucking Dust."

"Sil…"

Desperation, she thinks. That is the name of the emotion she hears in Jag's voice.

This time, though, she doesn't need to look at Skart. This time, despite all the warring voices in her head, she knows to shake her head herself.

"Give him," she hears herself say in a flat monotone, "the fucking Dust."

Knull

Knull won't do it. He won't give this asshole the fucking Dust. Finally, this deep in, he is discovering his own rebellion. He is embracing his own desire to disobey. Now, he wants to brandish his middle fingers in Skart's face. There's just the issue of the sword blade at his throat.

He opts for a more verbal attempt at defiance. "Why don't you go sit on that sword?" he says to the white-haired half-fae, the one the goblin called Sil.

He doesn't even get anger from her, though. She doesn't twitch.

"What did you do to her?" the goblin, Jag, demands from over Knull's shoulder, but quite frankly, Knull couldn't give two shits what she cares about right now.

Skart also seems disinterested. "Give me the Dust, you selfish child," he says to Knull, "so I can save the Iron City."

Knull laughs at that. There is something wrong with his laugh. It has gone as septic as the rest of the world. "Save the Iron City?" he says. "You? You're the thing it needs to be saved from. You're the thing it is. You're toxic. You're poison. You're murder. You're betrayal. You're… You're…" Words fail him. The image in his mind is of something malignant, something with a myriad grasping arms, groping, ensnaring.

"Give me the Dust," Skart says in the same calm tone, "or I will have Sil execute every living being in this house."

"You wouldn't dare," Jag says. "I am the heir to House Red, and my father—"

"Your father will be able to do nothing to me," Skart says. "Because I will have died in his service." A flicker of something—perhaps a smile, perhaps a grimace. "You have no ability to threaten me with his name. So be quiet before I have Sil drive that blade through your pretty throat."

"She'll do it," Edwyll says. The hatred in his voice is warring with the fear. "I've seen… She…" Edwyll looks like he's about to throw up.

"No." Jag's voice is as full of conviction as Edwyll's. "No, she won't." She looks Sil right in the eye. "Sil, you have to protect them."

Sil's arm is shaking again. Knull wishes she wouldn't do that. He can feel the sting of her blade as it nicks the tender flesh of his throat.

A look of irritation flashes across Skart's impassive face, the moment of animation almost startling. "Your sister is distracting you," he says to Sil. She doesn't respond. Her arm is still shaking. Skart reaches into his pocket and pulls out a switchblade. He takes his time opening it.

"Fine," Skart says. He turns to Sil. "I don't need you to see this through. Take Princess Jaggered back to House Red Cap." He looks at Knull. "I'll carve the answers I need out of this trash."

And that's it. All the preamble of the night is finally over. Perhaps, Knull thinks, this was always inevitable, ever since he and Skart first met in the street earlier that night.

Now, the end finally begins. And, in the alleyway, Knull saw Skart take on the goblin commandos. He finally understands what Skart is capable of. He knows how slim his chances are. But he sets his feet, and he readies himself for this fight.

Edwyll

Edwyll doesn't want to die. This hardly separates him from many fae, but it is still the spark that has driven so much of his life. It was Lila who helped him see it. That memory is tainted now, but it doesn't make her words less true: *Painting is way of staying alive, a way of lasting beyond death, of having an impact even when we're no longer here.*

Edwyll, in a city where the threat of death is ever-present for fae, has always fought against it. But now, as death bares its teeth at him, he doesn't know how to fight it.

He sees Knull make his move. Sil shifts her weight toward Jag, and Knull goes the other way, trying to get past her toward the kobold. But Sil seems to have anticipated this, and as she moves her sword whips back and forth, and the hilt hits Knull in the side of the head, driving his skull into the doorframe, and he just stands there dazed and blinking while the kobold smirks into his face.

Sil comes toward Edwyll. Death comes toward him. And he has still not done anything. He has still not changed anything. Whatever great work of art he has dreamed of creating is still unborn within him. Whatever type of immortality he dreamed of is out of reach. Because Edwyll is certain now that he will die. He has seen what the Iron City does to hope. He has seen what his brother has always known: that any softness it offers is just a thin veneer of wool pulled over fur, and claws, and teeth.

But Jag, he thinks, still offers hope. Because Jag isn't an artist. She isn't one voice. She is a chance for so many voices to ring out louder than they ever have in the Iron City. She is a patron, not just for him, but for all fae artists who dream of change. If only she has a chance. If only the city doesn't claim her now.

So he steps forward, into death, into Sil's path, to try and buy her that chance, that moment to escape.

He steps forward, and he is screaming something, some denial. He is getting in the way. He is preventing this last assault on all that he believed her life could one day be.

At first, he thinks that Sil has punched him. He feels the blow and staggers back. But he tries to collapse, and the pain is so blinding that he cries out. And then he looks down and the sword is inside him. He can see the silver of its blade ending abruptly where his shirt begins. He can feel its edge slicing deeper as he reels, tearing more of him apart.

He looks up. Sil's face is a grimace of horror. There is a tearing sensation in Edwyll's guts. Sil has stepped back. Edwyll can see all of her sword once more. Its white blade has turned to red.

Edwyll sits down very suddenly and very hard. He feels so overwhelmed by all this. There seems to be a lot of noise coming from all around him. Fae are shouting. Fae, he thinks, are screaming. He can't deal with that right now. It doesn't seem important anymore. Nothing seems very important anymore. He is very tired.

Slowly, Edwyll lies back, and closes his eyes.

Knull

Time stops. Hearts stop. Blood stops in veins. Arteries clog, clutching at their precious cargo. Outside, surely, fae stand static in the streets, their mouths open, their thoughts frozen. Vehicles must be motionless, the dirt kicked up by their tires hanging crystalline in the air.

Everything stops. Everything must stop. There can be no more progress from here. This must serve as the final period at the end of the history of the Iron City. Knull cannot permit it to continue any longer. He cannot. Edwyll is lying bleeding on the floor and if another second ticks past then he knows it will be his last. So, if time does not do this for Knull, if it maintains its relentless march toward the future, then Edwyll will be no more than an imprint in its footprint. He will never be here again to chastise Knull for leaving. He will never again ask Knull to abandon his dreams. And Knull will never again choose them over his brother. He will never let Edwyll down one more time. And all that will be left then will be the knowledge that he never turned it around. He never redeemed himself in Edwyll's eyes. Knull will always have failed his brother. Forever.

So, the Iron City must stop.

But it doesn't. The second hand ticks on. Traffic glides forward. Guns still fire. And hearts still beat, so blood still flows, and wounds still gush all over a bedroom's filthy floor.

The goblin loses it. She is screaming, howling, raging. She flings herself at Sil. The half-fae is staring at the body on the floor, and moves to block the goblin so slowly that several of her punches land before Sil finally turns and drives the butt of her sword hilt into the goblin's temple, and sends her to her knees.

The goblin stares dazedly at Sil. Knull stares at Edwyll on the floor.

"Get her out of here," Skart says from some other planet.

Sil picks up the half-conscious goblin and throws her over her shoulder. The goblin starts to kick and Sil rests her sword long enough to punch her captive hard in the kidneys. The goblin goes limp and Sil carries her away.

Knull just stares at Edwyll on the floor.

"Give me the Dust, Knull," Skart says. "It would be a shame if more fae had to die."

Knull tries to breathe. The world has not stopped. He is still living. He needs to perform the activities of the living. He needs to breathe.

"The Dust, Knull," Skart says from the cold empty world where he lives. "I am out of patience."

The Dust. Skart still cares about the Dust. It is such an absurd thing to want now, it seems. It is so preposterous that Skart still has ambitions, and goals, and schemes. That he still thinks it is important to rail against the world.

Not even Dust can bring back the dead. And there are only moments, Knull is sure, before Edwyll is dead. He could use the Dust himself, try to seal his wounds, twist the flesh together as if it were putty. But that wouldn't stop the skewered organs from gushing blood into the seal cavity. Wouldn't actually save a life, just make the end more painful. Knull is not a healer.

He wants the world to stop.

Although, Knull thinks, perhaps if there is one way to make sure the world stops, it is to give the Dust to Skart. Nothing, surely, can be more toxic to existence than that? Nothing can lead to a more rapid end.

Everything will stop hurting if he just gives Skart the Dust.

Won't it?

So, he gives in. He points. And Skart's laugh is disbelieving. "Under the bed?" he says, and Knull thinks perhaps he does see a little bit of it now—this truth that has just been revealed to him in all its horror and glory: how stupid, and pointless, and mad existence is.

"Everything almost fell apart," Skart says, "because you hid the

Dust under your fucking bed?" He shakes his head. "Get it for me."

Knull does it numbly, rooting around, heaving out the plastic-wrapped mass of it, shoving it at Skart.

Skart holds it like it's his child. Like a long-lost lover with whom he is finally reunited.

Knull barely pays attention. He doesn't care what Skart does or what he thinks. He is staring at Edwyll. At his brother. In his last moments, Edwyll is slowly opening and closing his eyes. He is looking back at Knull. If Knull stays here, he will be the last thing Edwyll sees.

Abruptly, Knull thinks he is going to throw up. Suddenly he is being crushed. The whole weight of the not-gone-away world is pressing down on him, and it is too much. It is all too much. He cannot breathe.

He stands up. He's not sure how. He can't feel his legs. He crashes against the doorframe on his way out. Maybe Skart looks up from what he's doing. Maybe he doesn't. Maybe he has the Dust. Perhaps not. Knull doesn't know. Knull doesn't care. It's all gone away. It's all stopped. It is all dead. Everything inside of him. Ambition. Hope. Dreams. Everything he thought he could be. It is all lying dead on the floor. It is all sprayed across the walls of a factory basement. It's all burning in the streets.

Everything falls down, but somehow Knull still stands, tottering his way down the hallway that leads away from what was never a home, and out into the empty annihilation of the burning night.

18

The View from Rock Bottom

Granny Spregg

"Where," Granny Spregg spits, "in the ever-living fuck is my Dust?"

The young Spriggan commando whose lapels she has just grabbed looks at her with something that hovers between shock and revulsion. He splutters, clearly unsure if he should be reaching for his weapon or not.

In all fairness to the young soldier, she has not really announced herself as much as she has lurched out of the Iron City's streets to assault him with requests for knowledge he doesn't have the clearance to possess. It would, she can see, be unsettling for anyone.

Granny Spregg, though, did not claw and gnaw her way to the top to be fair.

She slaps the young soldier as hard as her aching wrist will allow. "My Dust," she says, "you ass."

That seems to help him make his mind up about the gun. He unclips a pistol from his belt, points it at her with both hands. "Back off, you crazy old bitch."

Etiquette, Granny Spregg reflects, has never been House Spriggan's forte.

The soldier's compatriots are taking notice now. Some laugh. "Got yourself an admirer?" one asks. "You finally found the oldest whore in the Iron City?" calls another great wit.

"Need help taking down an old lady do you, rookie?" asks another. Several of his friends seem eager to assist.

Granny Spregg is bruised, battered, bereft, possibly mid-heart-attack, but she is not going to take shit like this.

She totters forward, putting up a protective hand while the soldier tries to defend himself, more from the taunts than from her. Which means he is not ready to fend her off when she grabs his gun barrel, and twists, and wrenches. He yelps, and then his gun is pressed hard against his mouth.

Around Granny Spregg a lot of curse words are suddenly yelled, and a lot of guns are suddenly brought to bear…

"The lesson," Granny Spregg tells the terrified young soldier, "shall begin with manners." Blood spills from her splitting lips as she talks.

"Oh shit. Oh shit. Oh fuck."

And then another voice. "What in the…?"

It is the voice she's been waiting for, the baritone that will carry across parade grounds. She turns and provides a blood-stained smile. "General Callart," she says.

"Madame Spregg," Callart says, and he's a good enough soldier to only sound mildly surprised. "To what do we owe the pleasure?"

There is a moment, and then a lot of guns are put away very quickly indeed, and the young soldier about to fellate a gun barrel moans softly.

"Has he caused offense?" Callart asks with mild curiosity.

"He called me a bitch."

Callart closes his eyes. When he opens them again, he looks tired. "Do you want to pull the trigger," he asks, "or shall I?"

After Granny Spregg has pistol-whipped the soldier to the extent she is able—although not at all to her satisfaction—she points her now throbbing hand at Callart. "Now," she says, "it's your turn. Tell me where my Dust is."

Callart cocks his head. "Dust, Madame Spregg?"

She sighs. "I do not have time for you to play the coy politician, Callart," she says. "But as I am too tired to beat sense into you, I am going to try to explain things.

"You know you are here at my design. You also know that I don't give a pig's wet fart what the fae think about their station in life. What I care about is *why* the fae felt that the bulge in their britches was big enough that they could rise up again. What I care about is *why* you keep running into House Red Cap patrols already in the Fae Districts."

Callart's face is carefully blank for a moment and then calculatedly shrewd.

"You're saying—" he starts.

"I am saying," she says, cutting him off because she truly does not have the time, "that you know something is happening tonight, but not what. That you know Brethelda is not in full control of it. And *I* know deep down what you care about most in the world is House Spriggan. That you want to watch the other Houses burn. And in that we are, and always have been, kindred spirits."

That might be laying it on a bit thick, but the time for subtlety is long gone. She leans in, manufactures a little intimacy, implies a conspiracy. "I'm telling you that if you trust me, I can make that dream come true. So, tell me—" She smiles again. "—what have you heard about my fucking Dust?"

Callart bites his lip, stares off down the smoke-choked streets for a moment. Then he nods. "I don't have it," he says.

"I know," she says. "If you had, you would have let these soldiers shoot me."

He smiles for a moment. "I always liked you more than Brethelda," he says. Then he puts the soldier façade back into place. "We haven't seen anything like what you've been talking about. If the fae have significant magical firepower, they're not deploying it. All I can say is that they've been unusually tenacious. Honestly, it's more like the bastards have a death wish." He pauses. "Or whoever is sending them out here does."

And Granny Spregg is bruised, battered, bereft, and possibly mid-heart-attack, but now she smiles.

"Yes. The one sending them out," she says. "That's the bastard I want."

Callart nods slowly. "Well, we only have a rough location." He rubs his chin. "There's talk of a factory."

"A name."

So, he tells her. And then he and Granny Spregg prepare to bring the whole might of the Spriggan armed forces down upon the head of a kobold called Skart.

Jag

Jag hits the back seat of the car hard. Her head rattles. Her kidneys ache. The car door slams and Sil heads to the driver's seat, jimmies the door open with her sword. In the back seat, Jag picks herself up dazedly. She tries the doors. They don't open. Sil fiddles with wires beneath the dash. When the engine coughs to life, she hits the gas.

"Sil," Jag says. "Sil. You have to listen to me."

Sil doesn't.

She tries the windows. Sil's de-activated the controls. She throws an elbow against the glass. She damages herself more than she damages it.

"Sil, please," she says. "I have to get back there." Edwyll is back there. Edwyll is bleeding on the floor. And she is not sure what he means to her, or why she needs to get back there, but with Edwyll there was the promise of a future she has never glimpsed before, and she felt as if finally she had a place in the world, and a direction, and that there might be something she could achieve one day that she could be proud of.

She cannot achieve anything in this car.

"Sil!" she yells. Sil doesn't turn around. Sil doesn't even flinch.

Jag launches herself at Sil, but Sil's elbow comes out of nowhere and collides with Jag's jaw, and suddenly she's faceplanting into a headrest, and bouncing off the floormat.

She doesn't give up. She can't. So, she grabs at Sil again, but Sil has seized her finger and there is so much pain that Jag screams.

When Sil releases her, Jag collapses back, nursing her hand.

"Sil, please." Jag tries again—desperately, urgently. "Just talk to me. Just tell me what's going on. We can't go back to House Red Cap. I can't. Not anymore. Please."

But she does. She can't stop Sil. Sil either can't or won't respond, and every attempt to grab at her, at the handbrake, at her seatbelt—it all ends in failure and pain.

Eventually, Sil steers them down into a parking lot beneath an apartment block. She leaves Jag there. Everything is locked. Jag fiddles with the wires Sil has eviscerated from beneath the dash. The engine doesn't even cough. She's still trying to dig her way out through the back seat when a blind, deaf, mute goblin leads a blindfolded Sil back down. He steps unerringly to the car, and uses a long-bladed knife to jimmy the car door. Jag lunges forward, desperate to get past, but he grabs her with his free hand, holds her without much strain. Then, with his fingers still wrapped around the knife hilt, he punches Jag, princess of the city, hard in the mouth. Sil stands by impassively as Jag's head bounces off the car's roof and stars explode before her eyes.

When Jag comes to, she is in the back seat of another car. She has been blindfolded just like Sil, and cotton has been stuffed in her ears. This is the way one returns to House Red Cap, the way she always returns, but she still panics. She gropes about blindly. Her fingers close on someone's hand.

"Sil?"

There's no response. Jag gropes at the door, the windows. She can find no escape. There is nothing she can do. She struggles anyway.

Eventually the car stops. Strong hands pull her out and down long corridors far beyond where the standard House Red Cap reception rooms lie. Normally she knows every twist and turn of this House—its hallways, and chambers, and hiding spots have been her home since she was born—but tonight it feels like foreign terrain. She is lost and hyperventilating, and then without any warning the blindfold is yanked from her head and light rushes in.

Details filter through the glare slowly. Sil's silhouette stands beside her. Light comes from above. Space echoes around her.

Someone, she sees, has taken Sil's sword from her. Sil is not permitted it in Osmondo's presence. Few weapons are. Her half-sister looks somehow diminished without it.

She is, she realizes, in the grand hall. It is her father's parody of some old fae king's castle. The tapestries on the walls depict war crimes and pornography. Where fairy tales might cause one to imagine paintings and delicate windows, her father has instead selected scrawled curse words and blood-stained weaponry. Osmondo Red loves to bring the nobility of other Houses here. It is a place for them to squirm. Jag is almost certain she's been brought here for the same reason.

Osmondo Red sits at the head of the room upon a cast-iron throne, its austerity undercut by the cushions his age demands. He is dressed in absurd urban camouflage, a beret perched on his craggy head, and medals he earned a lifetime ago stitched across his sunken chest. He peers at Jag with evident dissatisfaction.

"Hmm," he grunts. "You survived."

It is, Jag supposes, only a degree or two colder than most greetings from her father.

"I hope that's not too disappointing." Jag makes no attempt to hide her bile. This moment exists on a continuum of fights. The fact that this one feels more urgent doesn't incline her to pull her punches. "Now that you have so kindly checked in on my well-being," she says, "perhaps I could be excused?"

Osmondo seems oddly distracted, though. It takes him a while to rise to the bait, staring instead into the echoing space of the hall. Only a few soldiers line its walls today, and devoid of its typical squalls of nobles and hangers-on, the place feels more than a little desolate.

"Sil was not supposed to go into the Fae Districts with you tonight," Osmondo says. He doesn't look at Jag. "You were meant to go alone. You were meant to die."

Jag blinks at her father, approaches the absurd throne almost against her will. "I was what?"

Her father focuses finally. "You were in the thick of it—" He sneers. "—and you still understand nothing. It's shit like this that makes you disposable in the first place."

Such is the parental advice of Osmondo Red.

"Your existence as my seed," Osmondo says, "is a mistake. It shows a lack of faith in my own longevity. And you have continued to compound the error by not even having the fucking gumption to make yourself into a worthwhile rival. You're just a pampered dilettante without even the decency to have good taste. Of course you're disposable. You accepted the life of an empty symbol that was handed to you. Because the only thing you ever took from our history were the glasses of champagne it earned you. So, fuck you and your injured pride. You are a failed experiment, and I am tired of having that failure rubbed in my face every day.

"We are cleansing the city tonight, my daughter. My blind, dumb seed. We are getting rid of all the filth and washing it clean. And you were to be swept into the gutter along with it. A poor unfortunate casualty." He smiles at her.

And suddenly Jag realizes that the sabotaged car, the mercenary fae attacking her were not hired by usurping lordlings within House Red. They were hired by her own father. Fae mercenaries, because then fae could be blamed. Her father wouldn't even have to explain himself.

Except…

Except Sil saved her. Even when ordered away, she had come as soon as Jag asked her. She had been there by Jag's side. An act that could almost be called sisterly.

Osmondo has never liked that bond between them. Has never wanted Jag to see Sil that way. And thinking on that, Jag realizes that not everything Osmondo is saying reflects reality. No matter how much he might want it to.

"You say it's House Red cleansing the Fae Districts," she says. "But it's House Spriggan out there in the streets."

Osmondo nods, and his attention appears to be wandering again. His face sours as he speaks, and Jag has to step closer to catch everything. "Yes." He rubs his chin. "The bitch outplayed me. You are not the only part of this night to go awry." He looks up and almost through Jag. "Sil saved you."

Abruptly he snaps back to the present and squints at Sil, standing almost lifeless back at the entrance to the hall. "What's wrong with her?" he demands.

Jag stares. Because fuck her father's questions. Fuck the old goblin who just told her he wanted her dead. This mass-murdering, amoral, psychotic parody of a parent.

Except… perhaps in the answer to this question there is a clue to how she can salvage things. So, after a moment's hesitation, she bites down on her bile and says, "I don't know. She won't listen to me anymore. She would only do what some kobold was telling her."

Osmondo licks his teeth. "Ah. Mnemosyne," he says. "A shame."

"What does that even mean?"

"She's lost to you." Osmondo's voice has found its strength again. "Her mind is locked away. She's spent. Used up. You can keep her as a pet, or you can dispose of her. It doesn't matter to me."

"A pet?" Jag has rarely wanted a weapon more. "She's my *sister*. She's your *daughter*. What the fuck is wrong with you, you sick old—"

"What is wrong with *you*?" Osmondo suddenly roars. "You are a goblin! You are the child of warriors! You are the heir to all that this House represents. It is placed in your hands and you are incapable of taking it. What sort of empty fuck-up are you? How could you have spilled from my balls?"

He shakes his head with violence this time. "We are at war!" he shouts. "And even if you are an empty figurehead you are still my figurehead. *You* are going to war. You will march at the head of an army, not because you are deserving but because the plebs like a little pomp to die for. So, you will provide it whether you want to or not. And if you die out there, all the better. My days of pretending your will matters are done."

Osmondo slumps down into his throne. He is red-faced, almost deranged-looking.

"The bitch has not taken the city yet," he says. "So, if we go down we shall take it with us. We will leave her and the generations she spawns with nothing but a rotting corpse to rule."

Osmondo signals his guards. "Take her away. If you can't actually make her useful, at least make her look that way."

Jag doesn't resist. She doesn't want to be in this empty, echoing hall full of her father's rantings any longer. She will take any exit she can get. Sil follows after them, silent, affectless, staring off into nothing.

They reach a room, gray and windowless, some place dedicated to the utilitarian soullessness of daily House life. A uniform hangs there beside a bare porcelain sink.

"Clean yourself up," says the older of the guards. She thinks she recognizes him, but she has spent most of the past ten years trying to avoid her father, and the goblins he surrounds himself with. She can't be sure. Despite their lack of contact, however, the guard sounds as if he's almost as much a fan of Jag's as Osmondo Red. "Get dressed." He shoves Sil into the room after Jag. "We'll be back for you soon."

It is only for a moment, so fast it is possible she is mistaken, but Jag thinks she sees a look of purest hatred flash across Sil's slack features. Then it's gone, and the door swings shut behind them.

Jag, though, does not put on the uniform. She approaches Sil. She leans in, inches from her skin. "Sil," she says. "Sil, are you in there? Can you hear me?"

It is only the slightest convulsion around the eyes, but she rather thinks Sil can. And to Jag, for the first time since they were reunited, that feels like hope.

Knull

Knull is untethered. He is waiting and he is floating. An end is coming. He's sure of it. Until then, smoke bears him aloft down city streets, bouncing him off building walls. Until then, he is trying to endure. Until then, he is being mastered by currents he cannot understand.

It seems to him that he can see his whole life laid out below him. The whole pointless struggle of it all is mapped onto the asphalt beneath his feet. Here is where his mother shat him out into the world. Here is where she bought Dust to smother the pain of motherhood. Here is where he learned to hate her, and right here beside it, his father. And here is where Knull first tried Dust himself, in a moment of youthful experimentation, and despair, and self-immolation.

Here. Right here. He sees it clearly. Lying semi-conscious and aching on Cotter's couch, after the first hit he'd ever done. This is where the addiction really sunk its claws deep. Not to Dust. And the fact that it wasn't Dust made him feel so smart. But it was also the moment when he decided to believe the whole fucked-up promise of the Iron City. This is where he'd bought in to the idea that if he just hustled enough, just sacrificed enough, just screwed over enough fae, that he'd get out. That he'd be happy. Be rewarded. That happiness would become a sun burning inside of him. And once he'd swallowed that lie, then it had been so much easier to believe all the others he'd told himself.

But now all the lies are ending. Now, the whole system is exposed like guts to the sky, and the sun is coming to burn it all away. That distant unreachable star.

A noise brings him back to earth, crash-landing out of his own thoughts. He looks around bewildered. The present seems shockingly tangible compared to the mists of the past.

He doesn't know the street he's in. Not as it is now. Not with half the windows shattered, and a building front half-smashed. Not with a barricade of trashcans and sandbags blocking the road, and a fire burning in a pawnshop.

He tries to find it—the thing that pulled him out of his reverie. Then he freezes as part of the barricade gives way. Bricks grind against each other. There is someone there. And yet… if it is a goblin with a gun… that's an ending, isn't it? That's what he's waiting for. Isn't it?

He closes his eyes.

When he opens them again, a pair of eyes are looking right at him from over the edge of the barricade. "You," the mouth beneath them says. "You were in that office with Skart."

Knull blinks. And suddenly he realizes that he does know this street. He is barely a block from the factory that Skart brought him to—as if it is a lodestone and he is the world's most fucked-up magnet. And he does, he also realizes, recognize the fae staring at him. He has seen him in bars and on streets. He has a big mouth, and a bigger swagger. He has a group…

Had.

The word hits him hard. The scene from the factory basement flashes in front of his eyes—a kaleidoscopic flare of gore and horror. And Knull knows bone-deep that whoever this guy counted as a friend now exists very much in the past tense.

Like Edwyll.

As the thought hits, reality seems to shudder around him. His knees almost give out. He staggers to the barricade, leans on it, breathing hard.

"You okay?" the fae asks, which, given the sheet of blood covering half his own face is more than a little absurd.

A name comes to Knull. "Bee, right?" he asks.

"Yeah."

They look at each other in the flicker of the flaming pawnshop. And Knull doesn't know where to go from here. What does one say to someone else at the end of the world? And how do you walk away? After everything? After finally learning what that costs?

"You…" He falters, reaching for words. "You seen any goblins about?" It's easier, he thinks, to focus on the immediate *now* rather than on what has happened and where it will lead.

Bee shakes his head. "Just trying to take some shelter. Tharn couldn't get much further. He…" He can't quite finish. He gestures with his hand.

Confused, Knull peers over the barrier. He blanches. A krowbold he also slightly recognizes lies beside Bee, his usually ruddy skin pale as a ghost's, right up until it's not. At his midriff he becomes almost hallucinatory with color: bright reds, and vivid yellows, and septic, ghastly greens.

"Hey." Tharn raises a ghostly hand. Knull feels his gorge rising. He has no idea how the krowbold is still alive.

"Sorry," Tharn says weakly, "but this seems destined to be a pretty short get-to-know-you."

Bee

Bee isn't exactly certain how they got this far. He isn't exactly sure when he realized Tharn was trying to hold his guts in with his hand. He doesn't know exactly when he realized that Tharn was failing.

Somehow, they ended up here. Perhaps, he thinks, they're hiding. Perhaps they just collapsed at the most convenient spot. It all happened too fast for him to be sure. Pieces of the past are missing, and the present doesn't quite add up to something coherent.

He has seen so much death tonight. He has seen so many left behind and betrayed. It keeps playing out behind his eyes. The horrific past intruding relentlessly into the horrific present. So, now, he's not sure if he can quite believe that this fae standing in front of him is real. He wonders if perhaps he's losing his mind. Maybe, he thinks, it would be easier if he did.

In the end, though, all these questions about what happened, and how, and what is still happening—they can all only orbit the one central obsession that towers at the center of his mind.

Was it his fault?

Could he have predicted Sil's betrayal? Skart's? Should he have listened to Harretta or Tharn sooner? Could he have protected his friends better? If he'd just done something different? If he'd just been a little bit smarter?

Was it his fault?

Except he knows the answer. It's transparently clear. Because of course it wasn't. How could it be? And yet, of course it was.

He couldn't have known.

He should have.

There was no way to tell.

He wasn't looking hard enough.

He exists in the gap between both answers. They tear at him, fighting for what they can have of his psyche. And the idea that maybe his reason has fractured, and a hallucinatory world is slipping in through the edges, rather appeals.

But then Tharn waves to the brixie, and makes a joke, and introduces himself, and the brixie goes pale but manages, "I'm Knull."

Bee recognizes the name then. A low-level dealer. A neighborhood character. But their only real point of connection is the time they shared in the office with Skart as everything went to shit.

What does one say about that?

Apparently neither of them knows.

"So," Tharn says into the silence, "how's your night going?" He manages a smile. "Because, personally, I've had better." His teeth are red with flecks of blood. Bee thinks he's going to throw up. Knull grows paler.

"Tough crowd." Tharn coughs and they both watch his guts convulse.

Perhaps there is comfort for Tharn, Bee thinks, in the certainty of his fate. Perhaps the inevitability of his own ending has answered all his questions. Now, for him, there is just waiting left.

Quite suddenly, and with little warning, Knull starts to cry. He sobs loudly and messily, sagging against the barrier. Tears and snot stream from his face.

"Here." Bee stands awkwardly. "Come here." He tries to manhandle Knull around the barrier, but then doesn't know what to do with this brixie, only passingly familiar from a shared disaster.

They stand in silence. Slowly, Knull regains control of himself. He sits shakily, putting his back to the barrier. Firelight plays over his face. "I'm sorry..." he says. "It's just..." He wipes his face with the back of his hand. "It's all so fucking pointless." He stares into the flames for a minute. "I mean, we struggle, and we strive, and we try so fucking hard, and what does it achieve? What does it add up to? Where are we trying to get to?" His face scrunches up like a fist clenching. He seems on the edge of something. Bee feels on the edge of something too. Perhaps even the same thing as Knull. They're both reaching, he thinks, for a way to explain this place that exists between rage and despair. They're both trying to find a place where they can exist without being pulled apart.

Knull slowly lowers his head between his knees. "I thought I could be something in the Iron City," he says. "But it's something this place won't ever allow. I think it would rather burn to the ground than let me succeed."

And Bee hears another chord played in key with his own heart.

"I thought I could make the Iron City into something different," Bee says. "Somewhere that let the fae see the sun. Somewhere that isn't just a trap or a slaughterhouse." He looks around. He feels a lump growing in his throat. "I told fae I could win them sociopolitical equality. Such fucking hubris. As if it wasn't just me trying to chase away the dark."

They sit there, and around them, a restless city stirs and moans.

"Shit," Tharn grunts from the floor. "I might be missing some pretty important bits of my liver, but how come I'm the only one here who's still got his balls."

Bee wants to laugh. He wants to howl. How can he be about to lose this friend? This brother in the fight for liberation. He turns to Tharn, his jaw more than a little loose, tears dampening his eyes, and he doesn't know what to say.

"Look," Tharn grunts. "I get it. Everything I've done, and none of it has changed the Iron City. None of it has liberated the fae. But ask me right now if I think it was all for nothing. I dare you, Bee. Ask me right damn now."

He spits. It's pure red.

"I may not get to see the end of this fight, Bee, but I'm still so fucking glad I fought it. And you, you're still here, so you can't be crushed by this. You have to let it carry you to the next fight. And the next. And the next. And when *you're* the one bleeding out in some street somewhere, you have to know that your fight, your struggle…"

He lets out a sudden moan. His gut convulses and quivers obscenely. Bee holds his hand hard.

"…your struggle took others further," he says through gritted teeth. "Do you hear me, Bee? Because I need... I need..." He starts to cough again.

"I will," Bee tries to say the words but the lump has blocked his whole throat. He's wheezing words past it. And the more Tharn speaks, the weaker his hand feels in Bee's own. And Bee squeezes harder and harder. He holds on tighter and tighter.

"I need..." Tharn wheezes. "I need..." His guts shudder. "I..." He starts to convulse. Each spasm seems to wring more and more blood from him.

"I will," Bee manages. "I will. I will." He tries to pour the words into Tharn like blood. Like breath. Like life.

Finally, the shaking stops. And then after a moment more, Bee realizes that everything has stopped. Tharn has stopped. And he is sitting in the street holding his dead friend's hand.

Sil

Sil is trapped in a small gray room. She is standing in dull gray light. She is trying to pick out the line where the floor becomes a wall, and where a wall becomes the ceiling. But the more she looks, the more things seem to fade away, the more the firm delineation of space seems to disappear into mist. The more she looks, the less sure she is that she could ever find the door out of here again.

She is, she finds, quite calm about this transformation.

Sil, can you hear me?

The words come from a long way away. She looks around. She can't tell where the voice is coming from.

Sil, please.

There is something familiar about the voice. She tries to place it but has to give up. Memories are lost in the fog. She tries focusing instead on its words. What is it asking her to do?

She has, she finds, no idea. She looks around the room again. The walls are all gone now. Floor and ceiling are all one. She is inside a gray sphere. Everything is dissolving into… into… she's not sure.

Sil. Something has been done to you.

The words break in like a radio channel swarming out of static. She blinks and for a moment she can see shapes in the mist around her. She reaches toward them tentatively, but her fingers close on nothing but smoke.

Sil. It's me. It's Jag. You have to focus on my voice.

She tries. She really does. But there is nothing to focus on. There are just sounds echoing around her.

Sil, I don't know what they did to you. Flicked some switch they buried in your mind or… But, whatever they did, I need you to remember who you are. I need you to fight. I need you to remember how good you are at fighting.

Fighting… She looks down at her hands. The knuckles are bruised, the nails chipped. There are nicks and cuts all over her arms. A patina of bruises.

She blinks and it's gone. She thinks she does remember fighting, though. Something in that word triggers a desire to move. She gives in to it, watches herself move through forms she doesn't remember learning.

Yes, says the voice. *Yes, that's it.*

But she stops. She is not sure she wants to make the forms. She is not sure they make her happy.

Come on, Sil. Focus for me. Do you remember learning that? Do you remember the time we spent with the sparring master? You would destroy me every time.

She glimpses something through the mist. A small shadow. A child perhaps. She hears another voice. Another echo.

You must not strike the princess.

And then a small voice, tremulous. *You told me to.*

I did and you must always do as I tell you.

But…

The larger of the two shadows raises its hand. There is a sudden flash of pain across her cheek, sharp as a firebrand. Suddenly the mist clears, and the walls of the room are definite and clear. She sees a starched uniform hung from a hook, and—

The mist rushes back in, soft and comforting, washing everything away, leaving her calm again.

No, no, no! The first voice is back. *Fight it, Sil. I need you to fight it.*

But she doesn't want to fight it. She doesn't want to fight anything anymore. She shakes her head, mulish.

Remember tonight, the voice insists. *Remember the bar. After that. Fae mercenaries tried to kill us. Our father sent them. You fought them off.*

Again, shapes move in the fog around here. Threatening. Looming. She can hear screams. She can smell blood.

She does not like the voice. She does not think it has her best interests at heart.

Yes, the voice says. *I need you to remember that, Sil. I need you to come back to me.*

Why, Sil wonders, is she supposed to care what the voice wants?

What about what *she* wants?

Something in that thought changes things, though. Something in that thought echoes louder than the voice. The mist spasms. Images and ideas lurch out of it, into her head: a street full of flame and blood; a bottle raised to her lips, and fire in her throat; a smiling face; pain in her leg; anger; joy.

She shakes her head. She tries to clear it of the images, go back to the peace of the fog, but the more she shakes the more the mist seems to retreat, fleeing her and her thrashing.

Come on, Sil. Come on. It's me. It's Jag.

More images now. A child. Two children. They are being introduced. She is being introduced. She is being told, *This is Jag*. The goblin seems small, and pathetic, and absurd to her. They tell her the goblin wants her to be her friend. She says no. She says she has friends. The goblin cries. They break her arm. When they ask her to be the goblin's friend again, she says yes.

They are together. She is the goblin's shadow. She is taken away and beaten. She is returned to the goblin. The goblin laughs. She hates the goblin. She is told to love the goblin. She is beaten when she doesn't love the goblin. She pretends she loves the goblin. She is always pretending. She forgets what it's like to not be pretending. She's asked if she loves the goblin and she doesn't know if she does or not. They beat her.

Next, they tell her to protect the goblin. Next, they send fae to kill the goblin. She kills the fae instead. They tell her she killed them because she loves the goblin. They ask her if she loves the goblin. She says yes. They beat her and call her a liar. Then they tell her she loves the goblin.

They send her to the other, to the dead fae in live skin, to the kobold. They send her to him so she knows that a beating is a kindness. It is how they show her that they love her. The kobold shows her what hurt really is. He shows her what strength really is. He tells her it doesn't matter if she loves Jag or not. He tells her nothing she feels matters.

Nothing she wants matters.

When he is done, they ask her if she loves Jag. She says that is up to them. They do not beat her.

Sil. Sil. Sil. Sil. The voice says her name over and over. A desperate mantra weaving in and out of the images filling her head. The memories filling her. Her memories. Her memories that she does not want. That the voice is forcing upon her.

Jag's voice.

She recognizes it now. She recognizes a lot of things about it now. She recognizes that Jag was kind to her, and that she was the only one to show Sil love. And yet, it was because of Jag that all these things she remembers were forced upon her.

You can break free, Sil. You don't have to be what they made you.

She loves Jag. She hates Jag. It was always both.

I need you, Sil. I need you to set us free.

The voice only talks about what *it* needs. What *it* wants.

She was always told she wanted nothing. But now she sees, she understands, she has always wanted everything.

She's just never been able to choose what to do about it before.

She closes her eyes on the mist. On the gray. When she opens them again it is onto a small gray room, hard-edged and sharp-focused. A military uniform hangs from one peg on the wall. Jag stands in front of her.

"Sil," Jag says desperately.

"I'm here," she says.

Jag's eyes go wide. Her mouth opens. She flings her arms around Sil. "Thank Mab!"

She waits until it's over.

Jag releases her. "OK," she says. "OK." She starts to pace around the small room. "We need to get out of here. We need to steal a car. I think we've got to get Edwyll and then get out of the Iron City entirely. My father's lost it. I think there's going to be a House war. I think—"

"No," Sil says.

Jag stops and stares at her. "What?"

Sil smiles.

"No," she says again. "I have chosen to do something else."

With each word, she feels lighter. She feels fuller. She feels more and more like that child refusing to be Jag's friend.

"What?" Jag says again.

"You," she says, "can do what you like, but I have chosen to take revenge."

Knull

"We've got to carry on the fight."

Knull watches Bee sitting in the street holding his dead friend's hand and mumbling to himself.

"We've got to carry on the fight."

There is something obscene about the moment, Knull thinks. Something horribly broken.

Bee looks up at him. "We've got to carry on the fight."

"No." Knull shakes his head. "No, we don't. That's the city's game. That's engaging with these walls. These streets. I won't do that anymore. I won't be more meat for the grinder. I won't be another dumb cow marching into its blades."

He is having a hard time controlling the volume of his voice, a hard time stopping the images in his head from spilling out of his mouth. He shuts his lips tightly.

Bee sits and nods his head. He's still kneading his dead friend's hand. "Yeah," he says. "Yeah, that's what it wants you to think."

Bee wipes his mouth with the back of his free hand. "This whole city," he says. "It wants you upside down. It wants you back to front. It's had me fighting for freedom by helping a kobold working to oppress me. It's had you trying to escape poverty by selling the thing that keeps us all poor. And now, when we finally see the whole monumental horror of it all—of this city, this system—it wants us to see it as being so massive that we can't possibly imagine it failing. It wants us to think that it can't be *allowed* to fail. It wants us to find it easier to imagine our own annihilation than its destruction."

He leans in. "It's all a lie," he says. "It wants us to believe it's a city of iron, but it's a city of dust. It's lies and illusion, and paper-thin magic."

Knull closes his eyes. Let Bee have his private revelations. They're of no use to him.

"We have to fight," Bee says. "We have to fight *because* it doesn't want us to fight. We have to fight *because* it seems hopeless. We have to fight *because* we're overwhelmed. We've got to carry on the fight."

Knull puts his head back. He can feel the flames from the pawnshop fire on the side of his cheek. They're warm on a cool night.

"I have to find Skart," Bee says. "I have to keep up the fight. I have to stop him."

Knull opens his eyes. He doesn't want to, but fate is fucking with him again.

"What?"

"Skart." Bee is nodding to himself. He's still holding Tharn's cooling hand. "I don't know what he's doing, but I have to stop him. That's the only thing I know anymore."

Knull shakes his head. It feels almost like a tremor running through his whole body.

Edwyll's body lying dead and bleeding on the floor. Skart standing over him…

"You can't," Knull says.

Bee nods. "That's why I have to."

It doesn't make any sense. Bee doesn't make sense. Knull

closes his eyes. He tries to feel the warmth on his cheek. He tries to make everything else go away. He tries not to see Edwyll again.

It doesn't work. He hears Bee standing up. He opens his eyes against his better judgment.

"I don't blame you for giving up," Bee says, looking down. There is unbearable kindness in his eyes. "I see what's happening out in the city tonight. I get it. But… giving up is not the thing that will make the world better. Whatever was done to you tonight, the only thing that will make it better is getting its blood on your knuckles."

Knull wants him to shut up. Knull wants him to go away. Above all, Knull wants him to be wrong. But he can still see Edwyll on the floor. He can still see himself failing him. And he can still see his parents sitting on a couch, failing to get up, failing to care, failing to engage, failing again, and again, and again. And now, he can see himself sitting right beside them, hiding in Dust-fueled dreams while Edwyll and the rest of the world rot around them.

"I'm going to go and try to kill Skart," Bee says. "And I'm scared. And I'd rather not do it alone."

Knull wants to close his eyes. He wants to pretend the flames are warm and comforting. He wants to pretend that the world isn't on fire. He wants to pretend Edwyll is alive and well. He wants to pretend that revenge is petty. He wants to pretend he isn't responsible for whatever Skart does with that brick of Dust.

He wants to pretend he can thrive in the Iron City.

But he can't do that anymore.

"Fuck you," he says as he picks himself up.

Bee's gratitude is awful.

"Come on," Knull says. "I know where Skart is."

Edwyll

Edwyll has always thought that dying would be peaceful. He has always imagined himself lying on a bed covered with white linen sheets. He has always thought that his family would be there, that Knull would be standing beside him, head bent in contrition, reconciled.

He curls up tighter on the filth-crusted carpet and tries not to scream.

Someone is moving about the room. It's his parents' living room. He half remembers being dragged here. The kobold's face bent over his. A growled promise: "This magic will need blood before the end."

He opens his eyes, just for a moment. Just to try and grab hold of where he is. He's at the foot of the couch. His parents are still on it, unmoving. He can't tell if they're unconscious or dead. He's not in much of a state to work it out right now.

And the kobold. The kobold is here too. He must have pushed the couch to the edge of the room. He's pushed all the furniture, all the boxes, all the trash to the edge of the room. He's pacing in a circle. He's grunting to himself, bending down, doing something to the floor.

That's enough. No. No… that's too much. Edwyll closes his eyes tight. He can't hold in the scream.

"Ah." The kobold speaks. "You're still with me."

Edwyll doesn't respond. He can't. His guts are on fire and the rest of his body is cold.

"I thought perhaps you would slip away." Skart speaks softly, almost conversationally. "So many are weak now. This new generation. They forget that once we were warriors. They forget that sacrifice was nothing to us.

"Maybe that was why we fell," the kobold continues. "Maybe it wasn't Mab's Kiss coming down and blotting our cities from the world in mushroom clouds. Maybe it was just that we forgot how to sacrifice ourselves for a greater good. We forgot what it took to become who we were."

He pauses in his work, stands up and looks at Edwyll. "I'm sorry that you have to die," he says. "But please be reassured that I am saving everyone else."

Sil

"Revenge?" Jag looks at Sil, baffled. "But we need to—"

Sil doesn't bother listening to her. She turns and puts her foot through the door.

The two guards outside turn, startled. One reaches for his weapon a fraction before the other. He, she decides, will be the first to die.

Someone has taken her sword, and so she stabs her fingers into the guard's throat. She pivots. The other guard has freed his pistol. She chops his wrist with the blade of her hand. The gun clatters on the floor while the first guard hawks and gasps. She delivers an uppercut to the second with the heel of her palm. He sits down hard. She kicks him in the temple. He decides to lie down for a while.

She turns. The first guard is still gasping for air. She relieves him of his firearm and shoots him in the head. Then, she shoots his friend on the floor. Two to the temple just to be sure.

That's a good start.

Footsteps are coming now. That's to be expected from the noise she's been making. She stoops, takes the second guard's gun and stuffs it in her waistband. Jag is staring at her from inside the room. She turns to face down the corridor, kneels, steadies her arms against one knee, sights down the barrel.

She guns down the first guard, then the second. She discards the first gun, pulls the second from her waistband and takes out the third guard as he comes round the corner as well. Three little soldiers all lined up on the floor.

The fourth guard is wiser than his friends. He pauses at the corner, sends covering fire bouncing off the walls. That suits Sil just fine.

"What are you doing?" Jag manages.

She looks at Jag, just for a moment. "Exactly what I've always wanted to do." But that's all the breath worth wasting on her half-sister now, she thinks.

She takes off away from her and the nervous guard, running at a flat-out sprint as bullets hum in the air around her. She takes the second door she comes to. It's a narrow, functional corridor. It's lined with soldiers. They're pulling on jackets and boots, and strapping empty gun holsters to their chests in preparation for a visit to the armory. They're preparing for war, but they still think the war is out there, in the city. They think it's something they can approach at their own pace. They do not expect it to be here in their midst.

She smiles.

Her last four bullets take out the first four House Red Cap troops. After that, it gets bloody.

She chases after her shots, goes into the first soldier high and fast, jumping to put her full weight into the blow. She catches him on the nose, drives the cartilage back, sees his eyes go black as it punctures the thin shell of bone that protects his brain. That's five down.

Someone throws his boots at her. She blocks them but they are heavy and they bruise. They take the momentum out of her. She needs to have momentum. She cannot weather a slow, hard slog. There must be more than thirty soldiers in this corridor. There are doors from here into the barracks.

The next soldier comes at her low and hard, catches her around the midriff, drives her further back. She brings both elbows down, aiming for the neck. She hears vertebrae snap. The strength goes out of him.

That's six.

Others are coming now. A roaring wall of them charging down the corridor, intent on smothering her. They've been trained well.

She waits for them. One soldier is more eager than the others. He lunges forward heedless. She jumps. She puts her hands on his shoulders, either side of his shocked face. She flips fully over him, feet scraping the ceiling, driving him face first into the floor as his friends go sailing by. She lands just clear of his ankles. The others are already sliding to a halt, trying to figure out exactly what just happened. She doesn't hang around to explain it to them.

More soldiers are coming at her. The eager, dumber ones lead the charge. She ducks round one, puts her cupped hand to his ear with enough force to blow out the eardrum, but another one gets her around the legs and takes her to the floor.

Her head slams against tile. She kicks out blindly through ringing pain. *Always keep on kicking.* She hits something soft, keeps kicking until her vision clears.

Three goblins are closing fast. She rolls backwards, head over heels, ends up right under the feet of the ones she left back at the front of the hall. They kick and stamp. Her ribs start to complain fast and loud.

This is why she needed momentum.

She stabs a fist up, grabs a soldier by the balls. She hauls herself up as he goes down squealing. The others back up, square off, raise their fists.

She stamps down on the fallen soldier's face. There's a cracking sound. One of her opponents winces.

She keeps on stamping.

They don't take much of it. It's hard to watch your friend's face get pulped. When the first one breaks, she ducks to the side like a bullfighter, grabs him by his belt, and uses his weight and momentum to drive his face into another's midriff. Soldiers fall like ninepins and she darts through the gap.

But now one of these goblins has found a gun.

They're not supposed to have them here. Osmondo is fastidious about it. He has a fear of assassination attempts. And so guns are carefully controlled in House Red, only a handful of guards permitted them, and never those in Osmondo's direct presence. It's why she was taught with the sword and not the gun. Firearms are issued to troops like these only as they leave the House. That is what she was banking on. That was a critical part of the plan. But someone—and perhaps now she has more sympathy for them than ever before in her life—has disobeyed.

There's not much to take cover behind. There's not much room for adrenaline to shake his aim off course. She flattens herself against a wall, and the first shot whistles by her so close it trims her trailing hair. Behind her, a goblin screams.

The smart goblin takes a moment to wonder if he's all that smart after all.

She grabs a coat from a peg on the wall, flings it at the armed soldier. It's about as bulletproof as tissue paper but it's another thing for him to think about, it's something to obscure the steps she takes out of his line of fire.

She comes in low as he aims high with his second shot, trying to avoid shooting his friends in the face. She slides across the tiles, one leg held high, catches him in the crotch. He doubles over and she relieves him of his gun. Its third shot punches a hole in his forehead and redecorates the ceiling.

Around her goblins dive for cover.

She's only got three shots left. She makes them count.

She's already running when she fires the first shot over her shoulder. One to convince all the goblins back there that they don't want to be heroes after all, that trying to plug her in the back isn't worth the risk.

Two shots left.

She sends the next one forward, hits a big goblin in the gut. He won't die, but he's going to scream for a long time. Just one more thing for the goblins with hero complexes to think about.

One shot left. Ten yards to go. Most of the corridor behind her now. The door ahead of her like a beacon. She wants to save that shot.

The goblin comes at her through a doorway to her right. She's almost past it. If he'd waited a fraction of a second longer, he would have come at her from behind and she would have had no chance at all.

She flings herself sideways. He screams. He has a sword. He brings it down using both hands.

She catches the blow on her left forearm. It bites to the bone, but it stops there. She screams as she twists her arm. She smiles while she screams. She thinks it's the smile that makes him let go of the blade.

She's still smiling when she shoots him up through his chin and opens his head like a tin of soup.

She drops the gun. She yanks the blade free with her right

hand. She's down one arm, but now she has a sword. It's not a terrible trade.

There's five yards left of the corridor. She makes it, blood streaming down her arm.

She's through the door, she's in the antechamber before Osmondo's Great Hall. It's where she means to be. Where she chooses to be. Great, obscene murals are painted on the walls, framed by ornate plasterwork. Everything is red and gold.

Three ceremonial guards draped in regalia stand before a pair of double doors to the Great Hall. They are some of the few permitted to have rifles inside House Red. They have heard her coming. They open fire.

She's still moving fast. Two shots go wide. The third catches in the shoulder of her already ruined arm, spins her around and puts her on the floor. She can't believe she's been shot twice tonight.

The guard should end her then, of course. He should put his second shot in her head and his third in her chest. But he's cocky. He's good and he wants everyone else to know it.

Behind Sil, traumatized, raging goblins start to spill out of the door after her. They see her on the floor.

The guard walks toward her. He swaggers. He kicks her arm with his toe. She barks in pain.

He shoves his gun in her face.

He doesn't watch her hands. Because he thinks he's won. Because he thinks this is all it takes to beat the fight out of her.

She stabs upward with the sword. The others' shouts come too late. And Sil hopes this guard is happy with the number of children he's had because he won't be having any more.

He spasms. His shot hits the floor an inch from her ear. The barrel is still hot when she grabs it and wrenches the gun from him. Everyone is moving. She has to move faster.

It's hard to be accurate with the rifle when she only has one hand, so she doesn't try to be accurate. She braces it against her hip and holds down the trigger, lets it roar its throat hoarse.

She gets through the whole magazine in three seconds. Three seconds is long enough. Three seconds is plenty of time when you're fighting for your own life for the first time you can remember.

She drops the spent rifle among the fallen, screaming bodies. She picks up the sword. She's always liked the sword more than the gun. She pushes through the double doors.

Osmond Red is still there, waiting for her, perched on his iron throne, sneering as if it masks his fear.

"So," he says, "not even Mnemosyne could hold you." He curls his lip, works his hands. "Skart was not as clever as he believed. They all fail me at the last."

Sil doesn't say anything. She's tired. Her arm is numb and heavy. The blood loss is starting to make her dizzy.

"It is almost a shame this is as far as you'll come."

He has three guards. They advance. She holds up the sword, trying to forestall them.

"Trial—" she manages between panting breaths, "—by combat."

He almost laughs. "No."

She takes a breath. "You deny me because you're weak," she says. "Because you're afraid of your own daughter. Because you think a half-fae can best you and your finest soldiers." She goes directly for his masculinity. This is the way with goblins such as him. She knows this because the tutors he hired taught it to her. "You are nothing but a coward and a weakling."

If he agrees they will come at her one by one. It is the only chance she has even if it is as thin as a stiletto between the ribs.

Osmondo sneers. "You wish to goad me? By calling the flexing of might a weakness?"

"Is that what these guards will think," she says, "when they tell their friends about it in the guard rooms?" She is propping herself up on the blade now.

He looks at the guards. He has stayed in power for so long because he trusts no one, but she has been taught to transform anything into a weapon.

The only signal that he has conceded is a single flick of his finger. Then the first guard comes at her with a flurry of fists and blows. He catches her sword blade in his hands. He twists and she can't hold on. He throws the sword away. He kicks and sends her to the floor. He is very skilled. He is, in the end, better than her.

He keeps his distance for a long time, though, and he's broken two of her ribs before he'll get in a grapple with her. She can feel the broken ends of bone grating against each other as she latches an arm around his throat. He elbows her where he's done the damage. It should work, but she knows something he doesn't. She knows how much worse the pain can be. She knows how much worse it will be before the end. So, she holds on until his punches lose their strength. She holds on until he goes slack and limp. She keeps holding on.

Osmondo Red is leering. He is leaning forward in his seat.

The second guard comes at her at full charge. He is twice her size. He is young and eager. He wants to please his lord.

His size makes him slow, but not half as slow as most big heavy men. She ducks beneath the first two blows but the third catches her like a hammer to the side of the head. She flies through the air, crashes to the floor. The big guard is already chasing her down.

Her ribs are starting to scream. The floor is slick with the blood spilling from her arm. She sucks the wound in her forearm. She lets him come in close. She lets him get her up in a bear hug, her ribs screaming and screaming as a third one goes.

She spits a full mouthful of her own blood into his eyes

in a hard stream. He gasps, gags. She breaks his nose with her forehead. He drops her, shaking his big head. She is almost at her leisure as she retrieves her sword and guts him. She chokes him out with a loop of his own intestine.

Osmondo is up off his seat. His face is a rictus.

The third guard comes at her slow and measured. He has been watching. He has been waiting until he understands her. His first blow is slow and lazy. She parries it easily, but he dances around her riposte. She parries his second and third blows. He knows she will. She still can't hit him. He's testing her.

She's so fucking tired.

He accelerates slowly. He's careful. He keeps his guard close. He doesn't give her openings. She knows she needs to end this soon, but he won't let her.

He starts to smile.

She gets desperate. He knows she will. That's the point. She knows it is. But that doesn't stop her from being desperate. She lunges hard. He's been waiting for it the whole time. He's not like the first guard. He wants her close. He grabs her wrist as she comes in, fast as a viper. He wrenches her hand. Two of her fingers snap and the sword flies free.

He smiles.

His smile, she thinks, isn't like her smile. It's unconscious. It's true. He likes to hurt others.

It's the only opening she has.

She comes at him again. He breaks her wrist this time. Both arms are useless. She kicks at his head. He catches the foot, twists until her knee screams, until she screams.

He drops her foot. She just about stays up. She can see all his teeth. Osmondo Red is up in his chair. The head of House Red Cap is almost clapping.

The guard comes at her one more time. The last time. She puts up the best defense she can. He comes in under it, punches her in the gut, doubles her over, brings his knee into her nose. She can hardly see through the pain and the blood. He hits her in her busted ribs. She screams again.

He picks her up under her chin. He looks at her eye to eye. He's still smiling.

Because he doesn't understand. None of them do.

This can be survived. Whatever this man, or Osmondo Red, or this city thinks can be used to break her, she can survive it. She already has.

She lunges her head forward. She fixes her teeth in the guard's throat. She tears.

When she's done, she spits out a mouthful of flesh and blood. When she's done, the third guard drops.

Osmondo Red sits stock still in his chair.

It feels like it takes a long time for her to get her sword. It feels hard to hold. Blood loss has made her one good hand numb. She makes the effort, though. She makes the effort to walk across the hall and up the steps to the iron throne.

Osmondo Red waits for her the whole time. He's trembling.

"It was you who made me," she tells him. "It was you who brought me into this world. Everything I am is because of you." She looks at him, the blood falling off of her. "Everything that is happening now," she tells him, "is your legacy. This is what you leave behind."

He opens his mouth. She isn't interested in what he has to say. She puts the blade into it. It's hard to do with her busted arms, but she makes the effort.

19

And They All Lived Happily Ever After

Knull

Knull wants to punch someone. He wants to scream.

He's back here again. Every time he swears he'll never be back—he's back here again.

Bee looks at the house before them. He looks at Knull. "This place?"

"No." Knull hides behind a sneer. "I brought you here just because I like the ambiance so much."

Bee pinches his upper lip. With the other hand he fingers a pistol. "I wish I still had the machine gun," he says.

"Wish I had a gun," Knull says back.

Bee puts wide eyes on him. "Wait. You don't?"

Knull meets his gaze. "I'm an entrepreneur, not a thug."

Bee is still staring. "But… you're… you're a drug dealer."

"Notice how that's different from assassin?"

"But how are we…?"

Knull shrugs. "He's one kobold. One gun seems like enough."

Bee lets out a sound that is not exactly a laugh or a sob. "The half-sidhe with him, Sil. I've seen what she can do. And I don't know if he's done something to her, or if she just has no conscience at all, but I do not think that one gun is going to be enough."

Knull's sneer quivers. He tries to keep his breath steady. "You know," he manages, "back when you talked me into this it seemed like you had a spine."

Bee shakes his head. "We can't stop him if she's skewered us both."

Knull licks dry lips. The scream is just behind them. He almost can't get the words around the dry lump in his throat. "He sent her away," he says hoarsely.

"What? Why?"

"I don't know." Knull's voice is decidedly unsteady.

Bee hesitates over that, but he doesn't push it. It's the most Knull's liked him all night.

Instead, Bee looks down at his pistol. "You're sure you don't have a gun?"

"If I did, I would shoot you right now."

Bee chews his lip.

Knull can feel his control skipping. Everything is boiling inside him. He keeps seeing Edwyll lying on the floor. He keeps seeing the blood. He wants to run. He wants to scream. Instead he turns to Bee. "We can't just fucking stand here," he says. "We can't. We have to…" He rubs at his temples.

"I know," Bee says. "You're right. The only thing worse than doing this is not doing it."

And that's stupid, and nonsensical, and exactly how Knull feels too. So, they cross the street and approach the house. Knull feels exposed. He's waiting for a shout, a shot. He's waiting for the idiocy of all this to be laid bare.

There's an odd pressure in the air as they get closer. Knull's ears pop. His eyes water. He can taste something metallic in the back of his throat. Like iron. Like blood.

Bee wipes his nose, blinks hard. "What is that?"

"How should I know?"

But they both know it's Skart. They both know that it's his plan that they feel compelled to stop. They both know that somehow they have staked themselves and their survival on ending it, whatever it is. So, they keep moving toward the front door and no one shouts, and no one shoots them.

The door is open just a crack. Maybe Knull left it that way when he stormed out. Bee leans in, cocks an ear.

"I hear something," he says. "A voice."

Knull swallows. He lets Bee push the door open. It's stiff, still blocked by piles of useless crap, but he opens it enough for them to wedge themselves through. Just not wide enough for them to be confident of a quick exit.

All the lights in the hall of Knull's parents' house are out. Everything is shadows and black gaping doorways. The only light comes from the living room at the end of the hall. It is not, Knull notes, the blue-white flicker of the TV screen. It is not the failing glow of a single bare bulb strung from a mold-spattered ceiling. Rather, it is something otherworldly. It is something like daylight filtered through a scrim of blood.

He can hear birds as he approaches. Hawks screaming, shrill and savage. He can hear something roaring. A wind howling. He can smell something raw and feral. A scent of fur and meat.

They step forward. Bee has his gun held out in front of him. His hands are shaking. Knull's whole life feels like a funnel drawing him inexorably to this point. If he is ever going to be anything other than his father, he has to do this.

They stalk down the hallway. Past Edwyll's room. Past his own.

Past the kitchen. The living room is five yards away. Then three. Then two. Slowly they see more and more of what is happening. Of what they face.

It is as if two realities have been superimposed upon each other. One of them is a filthy, shit-strewn room. The collapsing furniture has been shoved up against walls covered by peeling wallpaper and spreading mold. There is a couch with a female brownie and male pixie collapsed on it. They may be sleeping. They may be dead. There is a curled-up figure at the foot of the couch…

The other image is something Knull can hardly place. It is something he has seen only in pictures and dreams. It is something he has seen dull reflections of when visiting his most addled customers. It is an image of a lost past.

Trees seem to rise all around him, towering high above the room's translucent ceiling. Their bark is black and twisted. Gnarls and knots writhe up their surface. Branches claw back down toward the dead brown leaves that blow across the floor. He can hear their desiccated rustling. The sky overhead is the color of drying blood. Birds wheel and scream. Bruised clouds twist in spiraling winds.

Skart is in a clearing at the center of the room. He is bent over, slowly tracing a circle on the ground, scratching at it with a tarry black branch. He marks symbols with sharp flicks of his wrist. He doesn't look up.

In the center of the clearing lies the brick of Dust. Knull's eyes linger on it only for a second, though. Then they go back to the body at the foot of the couch.

They go back to Edwyll.

The wind starts to howl.

Bee holds up the gun. His hand is shaking like one of the leaves caught in the winds above.

"Give me the gun."

Bee looks questioningly at Knull. Knull can feel resolve tightening in his gut like a fist.

"Give me the gun," he whispers.

Bee hesitates, but after a moment he gives Knull the gun. Maybe he knows that Knull needs to do this more than he does. Maybe he's just a coward. Knull doesn't really care.

The gun feels heavy and cold in his hands. He's never fired one before, but there is a certainty in him now as he raises it. As he closes one eye and looks down the barrel. This is right. This has to be. This is the one piece of magic the Iron City owes him.

He lines the sights up on the back of Skart's skull.

Skart

It's coming closer. It's approaching faster and faster. Skart can feel it, it's implacable inevitability. He can feel the weight of it, crushing every obstacle before it: the future.

He is the future's midwife. He is delivering a new golden age. Everything great again.

He takes the Dust pinch by pinch, letting its power build inside of him. He lets each high take him deeper in. He feels magic crackling on his breath, writhing beneath his fingernails.

He takes another pinch of Dust. When he pulls his fingers away, they're bloody. His sinuses feel raw and aching. His eyes are dry as stones.

He scratches more runes on the ground, more sigils. He breathes more words of power. He weaves the ritual, binds the magic tighter. Without it, he'd be dead already, lying on the floor choking on his own blood.

He takes another pinch of Dust.

As he works, he starts to feel a pressure in the back of his head. Dull at first, it sharpens, resolves, becomes something more definite. He focuses. He can feel two fae back there. He can sense a shared intent. Something red and malign clawing toward him…

He throws up a hand just as the gun goes off. A great screaming wind howls upward, a wall of air that the bullet cannot penetrate. The trees around him groan under the force of it. Leaves storm in hurricane-induced fury. He can hardly see through them. But he sees enough.

Knull. Bee. The pair of them staring, wide-eyed with alarm from around the barrel of a gun.

He sweeps an arm toward them. He barely even needs to focus his power to do it. He is so stuffed with magic it's almost indistinguishable from his own will. The wind screams towards them. A cyclone of torn leaves and snapped branches. The doorway they're using as cover detonates under its impact. Cheap plasterboard and rotting wood fly in ragged chunks as the pair are bowled away, head over ass.

The blow is more than the tottering house can stand. The whole ceiling starts to slump, bricks and timber crashing down. Dust billows. Skart barely pays it any attention. He is only half here now. He is lost in his vision, in his summoning, in what is about to be. Ghostly bricks tumble through him, roll away, become nothing more than clumps of sticks and moss.

He advances toward the devastation slowly. He forces another pinch of Dust into his nose. It feels like ramming a power cord into his face. His body jerks and his smile is a rictus. He is starting to have to concentrate on keeping himself whole. He is binding the magic to his body, to his cells. It stitches him together. When he releases it all, there will be nothing left of him. He will be atomized. He is looking forward to it. He is looking forward to being incorporated into everything the world becomes. An indelible stain.

He sweeps his arm again. The rubble rips aside. The wounded house moans. He sees the pair lying on the floor, bloody and bruised. Knull clutches at his ankle, face contorted.

Skart takes more Dust. His tongue feels like a wound.

"You," he says. His words feel like they have substance. Black-red mist gusts from his mouth. A blackbird flies out from between his teeth.

"You are the reason this is necessary."

The walls of the corridor are crawling with thorns and roaches. Black flowers bloom. "You refuse to learn," he says.

Mushrooms rise and fall as if the place is respiring.

"And so, I must teach you."

He raises an arm. His skin shimmers like a heat haze. Insects swarm off him. Bee makes some guttural noise.

And then, before he can bring the hand down, before the lesson can be learned, the wall to Skart's left disintegrates in a hail of .50 caliber shells.

Granny Spregg

Granny Spregg and her troops had been staring at a bloodbath in a factory basement when they'd felt it. She'd snapped her head around without fully understanding why she was doing it. She'd stared into nothing. There had been a pressure behind her eyes, a tingling in her sinuses. There had been the smell of rotting vegetation in the air, and the taste of soil on her tongue.

The last dregs of the Dust in her system had sung to her then.

They had sung a song of blood and wild growth. They had sung to her of hunger and glory.

She had cocked her head to one side, walked past the hacked-up bodies, and heaved herself back up the stairs to the factory entrance, the others following. The mystery of what had happened at Skart's last known whereabouts suddenly forgotten. What was happening out there had been much more urgent, much more pressing.

Bruised clouds had twisted overhead. Their epicenter was just half a mile away.

"Get in the trucks," she'd said. The soldiers were standing around her, also staring with a mix of horror and wonder. One had been weeping blood.

"What's happening?" Callart had asked her.

"He's using the Dust."

Now, the APCs scream through the streets. Their massive tires bounce and chew at the road. Heavy chassis shake and thunder. Goblin troops work at their weapons with worried hands. Sweat collects on Granny Spregg's upper lip.

Her chest hurts more than ever now. Her breath is short and ragged. There is a tremor in her left hand she can't stop. She's not totally sure she can see out of one eye.

But she's close, too. She's so close she can literally taste it. Flesh and dirt and sweet-sour berries at the back of her throat. It is so close to being hers: the future; the chance to be returned to what she once was, to reset the clock, to be glorious again.

The APC hurtles around a corner. She staggers, tries to catch herself, and then a soldier does it for her. It feels like her whole body almost snaps around his arm. She grunts and spits blood. The young soldier tries hard to mask his look of disgust.

Soon he will beg to have her.

The APC makes another lumbering charge down a street, then

its brakes scream. Granny Spregg feels nauseous as it slews to a stop. She takes unsteady steps toward the rear doors, almost falls into the street. Another soldier is supporting her. She doesn't even have the strength to shake him off. This is bullshit.

They are in front of a squalid house in a squalid street. So far, the night's violence hasn't spread here, but it's not as if things could get much worse. Roofs of corrugated iron hang askew. Windows are covered by plastic sheets and scraps of moldering cardboard. Some houses are even missing doors.

But it's the house in front of her that feels like it's trying to dig her eyeballs out of her skull. It's the house in front of her that throbs in her blood like a second heartbeat. It's the house in front of her that has clouds spiraling directly above its dilapidated roof.

She takes a step toward it. Then, from inside, there is a sound like an explosion. One wall slumps. The roof sags. There isn't time.

Her eyes fly back to the large machine gun mounted on the APC's back. She turns to the soldier holding her.

"Get me up there."

"Ma'am?"

She'd slap him if she wasn't worried it would break her wrist. "It's hardly a marriage proposal," she snaps at him. "You don't have to think it over."

He hoists her aloft. She grips the gun's controls.

"It's got a kick," he warns her. Other soldiers are moving to take cover. Callart looks nervous.

"Don't worry," she tells the soldier. "So do I."

She opens fire. The heavy machine gun bellows in joy, vomits flame and shells. The wall of the house tremors and crumbles as she hangs onto the bucking gun. It feels as if it is shaking her apart, as if she is on the edge of disintegrating. Her heart skips and jitters, but she hangs on. Glass shatters. Fist-sized holes smash through the wall. Architecture groans, gives way in a rush.

If only she had known lovers like this gun.

The troops are spreading out around her now, rifles pressed tight to shoulders. Callart is trying to roar louder than the gun. Everything is obscured by smoke.

Granny Spregg finally stops firing. It feels like everything in her body is broken. She hasn't felt this alive in years.

"Hold!" Callart is yelling. "Hold!"

She doesn't want to hold. It's in there. The Dust. Her Dust. She scrambles down the side of the APC, falls, lands hard. A soldier bends to pick her up.

A blast lifts him off his feet, sends him flying across the street. He hits a wall with enough force to dent it. Blood halos his slumping body.

Then, the kobold comes out of the smoke and dust, charging, his eyes wild. There is a ragged wound in his right arm, and everything below the bicep hangs by ragged threads. There is no blood, though. Instead, vines and creepers burst from the wound, something furry that ends with a ragged claw. She sees something with legs and teeth drop from it, scamper away.

The kobold comes on and with each step he takes, the asphalt cracks. Roots emerge, reach blindly. Insects and rodents crawl up from the depths.

The kobold sweeps his good left arm. Another soldier flies away, lands on a rooftop with a sickening crack.

"Fire!" Callart roars and the soldiers pull their triggers. Bullets pepper the kobold's body. Leaves and brambles burst from exit wounds. Birds and moths fly from him. He marches on. There is a roaring in Granny Spregg's ears. One of the soldiers disappears beneath a massive ball of rats that seems to come from nowhere.

Next to Granny Spregg, another soldier falls. Ugly white plants burst from his mouth and eyes. She seizes his gun, opens fire. Her mind is chattering as loudly as the weapon, screaming at her to run, but the Dust is so close. The future is so close.

All that stands in her way is this kobold. But the kobold comes on, and he brings rage and horror with him at every step.

Bee

Inside the house, Bee breathes through blood. He stares at a world-wheeling madcap. He thinks he's going to throw up.

There's a narrow beam of wood on his chest, pinning him to the floor. He pushes it off with one hand, grunts. He rolls over, heaves himself to all fours. As soon as he's up on his feet, though, his left knee buckles. He staggers, reaches for a wall that isn't there, goes down again.

Back on all fours, wheezing pain, he tries to get his bearings. He is in a half-collapsed corridor. He can hear thunder. *No.* He can hear gunfire.

He tries to put the moments back together. The story of then and now. Knull took the shot at Skart. Skart somehow deflected the bullet, attacked them. Then, the story loses joint. There is a blurry impression of falling over and over, of pain. It's not clear. Then Skart was standing over them. His mouth was full of hatred but Bee can't remember the words. And then… then…

Then gunfire. He looks through a haze of smoke and dust. He can see shapes moving, muzzle flashes flaring. He can hear screams.

He gets to his feet again, bends over, breathing hard. He spits nauseous streams of saliva onto the floor.

He starts to look for Knull. The drug dealer must be nearby. But then a bullet buzzes past his head and smacks dully into the wall behind him, and he looks up in time to see Skart advancing on a goblin with a gun. The kobold raises an arm that has somehow gone wrong at the elbow. Skart's arm spasms and something like a tree bursts from it. Its trunk spears the soldier; branches, still growing, burrow in then tear the goblin apart. He's screaming as he dies—a high-pitched, animal sound.

Bee staggers back, trips over something, sits down hard. He's on the floor for a third time. If this was a fairytale, he'd stay down now.

This is so much more than he has imagined. All the death he's seen tonight and none of it has prepared him for this. The air pulses with magic. It sloughs off Skart in waves, burning Bee's sinuses, pushing back the dull, eternal sting of the Iron Wall. The goblins can in no way cope with the fecundity of Skart's murderous power.

"We've got to carry on the fight."

Outside, Skart's arm has become a buzzing, boiling ball of insects. He plunges a goblin into its depths and the soldier dies shrieking.

"We've got to carry on the fight." Bee says it again, says it louder, so he can hear himself. He stands up once more, his lesson unlearned. His knee almost goes out but he braces himself. He doesn't have a gun anymore. He just has his will. He just has his refusal to stop in the face of all that is rational.

He stumbles out of the ruins of the building. The remaining goblins are still fighting, are still shooting at Skart. The kobold seems to grow under their assault. He seems to come undone a little, unspooling into snarls of brambles and knots of wood, unraveling into churning balls of fur and feet. He spawns antlers and horns, branches and vines. He towers and totters. He flickers in and out of focus. He exists both here and somewhere else, both now and in the future he is forcing into existence.

Bee bends down, picks up a stave of wood. He holds it out in front of himself like a sword. Like it's capable of achieving something.

"We've got to carry on the fight."

It's a good mantra, he thinks as he advances across the street, heading into the tiger's maw. It keeps his feet moving. It keeps him focused on things other than his pulse beating hard in his throat, other than the writhing mass that used to be a kobold, other than the bullets still ripping past his head, other than the only weapon in his hands being an overgrown twig.

Skart has his back to him for now. That's his only hope: that Skart is focused on the remaining goblins. They're falling back. One of them is scrambling up the side of their APC, trying to get to the machine gun mounted on top. The thing that is Skart or was Skart reaches out with a bramble hand. Creepers shred the soldier like razor wire.

One of the goblins made it to the APC, though, has found more significant artillery. He dives out of the back of the vehicle, holding something squat with a barrel as broad as an orange. He's older than the other troops. He lands heavily, takes aim. There's something determined and terrified on his lined face. The squat gun lets out a choked cough and something fat and sleek races through the air.

The RPG detonates against Skart's side. He reels away drunkenly. The street is suddenly full of swirling bats and butterflies. Flowers bloom in a great ragged burst. A fox breaks free of the kobold's form, flees. The goblin desperately breaks the breech of his gun, fumbles in another grenade.

The swollen mass of Skart rounds on him.

The goblin fires again. This time, the grenade hits Skart in the middle of his amorphous mass. He seems to balloon under the impact, reeling, swelling. Then something appears to rupture in him, and a great swarm of creatures burst forth, breaking through his branches, and leaves, and vines, and thorns. There is an impossible number of them—rats and stoats, pine martens and mice, ferrets and weasels. They bear down on the goblin as he cracks open his gun a third time. He disappears beneath the swarm before he gets a chance to reload.

The remaining goblins are running. Skart lumbers a few steps after them. Bee cannot imagine the look on his face. He cannot wholly imagine that Skart still has a face. So little of what Skart is now looks like a fae. He seems to have so many limbs, and so few of them seem to resemble anything like flesh.

And then Skart turns around, and Bee's one hope is stolen from him. He is just two yards behind the kobold now. He has the stave of wood raised above his head, but he can't tell exactly where to strike. He can't tell exactly what will hurt the swollen morass of foliage before him.

Then something leers out of the tangle. Eyes are visible behind bars of thorns. Teeth glisten from behind purple leaves. There is an impression of a bright red tongue.

"Why?" Skart asks in a voice raw and ragged. "Why do you persist?"

Bee opens his mouth to answer but only a scream comes out. Suddenly something is gripping him, piercing him, hauling him skyward. He feels stabbing pain, white hot in his arms, his legs, his chest.

A tree has burst forth, whether from the ground or from the mass of Skart himself Bee cannot tell. Its branches pin, and splay, and puncture him. They hold him aloft. He twitches. He gasps.

"You make this necessary," Skart says. His voice sounds guttural, wet, like something rising out of rot. "Fae like you are why I must do this."

A branch has pierced Bee's shoulder, bursts out just below his collarbone. Three more pin his left arm. There are two more jutting through the meat of his right thigh.

"I've got to carry on the fight." Something bubbles at the back of Bee's throat when he talks.

"No," Skart says, so quietly that Bee can hardly hear him above the pain shouting in his head. "No, you don't."

The tree holding Bee pulses. The branch in his right bicep rips up through the muscle. His arm sags. He fights to keep his grip on the wooden stave.

"What you have to do," Skart says, his voice rising like a tide, "is shut up and listen."

But Bee isn't listening. He's beyond that. Right now, all he's focused on is the fact that Skart is ignoring his right hand.

"You ignorant fucking—" Skart starts. And then Bee shouts to drown him out. And Skart roars. And then Bee drives the wooden stave hard into Skart's face. He screams as he does it. Blood bursts from the savage tear in his arm. His fingers spasm and his body shudders. But he holds on. He keeps up the fight. The only thing worse than attacking Skart is doing nothing at all.

The wooden pole enters into the mass of foliage. It plunges at the eyes, the mouth, the tongue. There is a moment of startled brightness in the pupils and then there is a moment of resistance, a moment when Bee thinks his strength has failed. Then something gives—in him, in Skart, in the world that was, and is, and will be, in the magic clogging the air between them. Something snaps and breaks. Bee screams. Skart screams. The wooden stave plunges in deeper and deeper, swallowing Bee's arm to the wrist, and Skart's bright eyes suddenly go dull.

Skart

Skart is barely there. He feels threadbare and insubstantial. The goblins have taken so much of him away, have spread so much of him across the streets. The meat and muscle of him is run through with holes.

He has stitched himself back together with magic as best he can. He has kept himself as whole as possible. But he is burning through the Dust so fast. It has required so much magic to end them all, to keep himself together. And every gunshot has accelerated his decay. If the magic gives out, he knows, so will he.

But he still has enough Dust left. He still has supplies aplenty back in the house. He still has time.

But then this. Then that bryad drives a wooden stave into his face. And there is so little of him left. There is so little skin and skull to resist the force of it. There is so little magic left to spare. And so, the stave spears through what remains of his skull.

It kills him. It is the final blow, the one he cannot take. So, here, he dies. Now, he dies. But Skart is no longer mostly here or mostly now. He is more than half in the future. He is less than half flesh and bone. The magic is still there, still burning, still carrying him forward.

Still, he is at least half dead. He has a thick pole of wood through his head and through his mind. It kills him.

Just not enough.

Skart drops Bee. He doesn't care about Bee anymore. The magic is a wildfire in his soul. It is burning and burning, desperately trying to hold him together. And there is so little Dust left for it to burn through. He needs to get back to the house, to his supplies. He needs to plunge himself into their depths, to inhale and ingest. If he can get back there, he has enough to sustain him, to keep him whole long enough to finish the ritual, to finish the creation of the future.

He is just no longer sure there is enough left in him to get back there.

He is on the ground. He reaches out with what appendages are left to him. Desperately, he hauls himself up and begins to stumble forward.

Granny Spregg

Not now. Not now.

Granny Spregg clutches at her chest.

Not now.

She has crawled through the dead and the dying. She has wormed face-first through the dirt. She has lain hidden and still in the blood of others as Death walked past her, flinging spells in a mindless march toward violent suicide. She has let rodents and vermin crawl over her. She has crept and crawled while her soldiers have sacrificed themselves at Skart's Dust-addled feet, and she has come so close to seizing victory, she can taste it.

She can see it before her. The sack of Dust sitting in the center of a filthy room. Sitting in the center of a forest clearing. Sitting in both. In two worlds colliding. But she can see it. She can get to it. She can make it her own. She can fix the future. She can amend all the missteps of the past.

And then her chest spasms like a grenade has detonated between her ribs, and she keels to the ground gasping. She claws at her chest, at her stutter-skipping heart.

Not now. Not now.

She is drenched in sweat. The pain is a lance impaling her from sternum to spine. Her left arm is paralyzed. Her chest is being crushed. The world seems hazed with purple light. She thinks she can hear her son's laughter in her ears.

But she refuses to give in. She has done so much. She has been born into a filthy hovel in the desolate North. She has loved and murdered a goblin who would block her path to power. She has marched into war at Mab's side. She has founded a city of iron. She has raised and been betrayed by three children. She has schemed and clawed and murdered. She has gotten all this way. She will not give in now just because her flesh is weak. Just because she is dying.

Not now. Not yet.

She puts one foot in front of the other. She takes a step. The world spins. And then she bites the dirt, as all around her the whole world comes crashing down.

Edwyll

Edwyll opens his eyes. He must have passed out. He wants to pass out again. His stomach is on fire. His fingers are numb. All his heat is being sucked into his guts and spilled out over the floor.

He lies there, eyes closed, just breathing. Breathing is all he can do. Even that hurts. Each inhalation. Every exhalation.

There is so much noise, he thinks. There is a sound like a war. The ground seems to shake. He thinks this might be worse than when Skart was talking.

He wonders if the kobold has done what he set out to do yet. Is that why he's quiet? Is the city already ruined?

Ruined. He turns that over in his head. *Already* ruined. Could Skart really ruin the Iron City any more than it already is?

He feels something rising within him as he lies there. He feels something unfurling into the space where his blood used to be.

He has always wanted so much better for this city. He has fought so hard for it. And he knows that his efforts were imperfect, but if just once—just one single time—this city had tried to meet him halfway. If it had just once looked at him with something like kindness. If it had looked at him like Jag looked at his art. But instead, it took the one spark of hope and kindness he found within its streets and it ripped her away.

He wants to see it one last time. This city. This place that betrayed his dreams. This place that has finally, totally, irrevocably broken his hope. He wants to see it in the grip of Skart's victory. He wants to laugh at them all. He wants to die laughing.

He opens his eyes. He's facing the couch, old and filthy. He is, inexplicably, lying on a bed of leaves. Wind is pulling at his clothes. He can see nothing, can understand even less about what he's feeling.

It is an act of will to roll over. The physical effort is almost negligible. But it is the pain he must prepare for, that he must decide he can take.

He does so. It is worse than he imagined it would be. His blood has soaked through the leaves and stuck him to the floor. When he's done, he lies there panting, eyes screwed shut tight against the pain of each breath.

Finally, he opens his eyes again. Finally, he sees.

He sees a clearing of tall dark trees surrounded by the fallen walls of his parents' home. He sees ruin and flame. He sees smoke drifting listlessly. A bruised, red sky churning overhead. Animals running, snarling and witless. Bodies strewn in a dirty street.

It makes no sense. It makes as much sense as the dry leaves beneath his cheek. It is as confused and terrible as this city has always been, has always insisted on being. It is just, he thinks, that now the horror of it all is right at the surface, boiling up for all to see.

This is what we created, he thinks. *Together, this is what we all achieved.*

And he knows it isn't his fault. He fought against this with every pencil line, and every brush stroke, and every sweep of his paint can. He tried to change the tide. It isn't even his fault that he failed.

He wants to scream now, at the last. He wants to yell at everyone standing by tonight that this is *their* fault. That all they had to do was listen, was engage, was do anything but silently accept the world as it was. But it's too late to scream. He's screamed a lot tonight and it hasn't achieved a thing.

He wishes Jag was here. He wishes he had someone to help him see it all a little better, a little clearer, someone to help him find some good in it all. He wishes she was here to help him feel just a little bit better about everything ending this way. Because this is an ending, he has no doubt about that.

And then, as he stares at the mess of it all, he sees something his eyes had missed at first. A package lying in the center of the clearing of trees, unguarded, untended. Just a few yards from him. A bundle of white plastic cut open. A package of Dust.

It is not, to him, a promise. It is not even an exit. It is not a solution or a weapon. He does not know the magic to heal himself. Rather, it is a paintbrush. To Edwyll, the source of all the night's chaos and heartbreak is a way to make a final statement, and to have one last go at changing the world.

And so, he decides to make it his.

Knull

Knull's whole world has been reduced to the size of his ankle. Its ragged drumbeat of pain is the only thing he can hear. The copper scent of its blood is the only thing he can smell. Its heat floods his senses. He lies on the floor, mouth open wide and eyes clenched tight as he squeezes at his own skin.

Finally, he has to look. He doesn't want to know, but he has to. He has to understand how bad it is, how fucked the shape of his life has become. He opens his eyes, and sees the unnatural angle, the white of the bone. Then everything is obscured by the rising tide of nausea.

He doesn't know how he's going to stand. He knows he has to stand. He knows he has to escape.

He knows too that he shouldn't want to escape. His parents are here somewhere. Edwyll. He should want to see if he can save them. Even if he is pretty certain that they're dead. He should want to make sure. He knows, too, what he promised to Bee, and all the things he said about having to do this, and about not doing it being the worst thing of all. Shit, he even meant it. He believed it. Skart *should* be stopped. He deserves to be stopped. He deserves to have his head snapped off and have someone piss on the stump. But there is a long distance, Knull sees now, between *should* and *shall*. Maybe with Bee beside him he had the spine to bridge that gap, but there is no sign of Bee now. There is only his traumatically snapped ankle. There is only the certainty of failure and pain. And he is not a fighter. He is not a rebel. He is just a brixie looking for a way out of a room with no doors.

His world expands by inches. He drags himself down the ruined front hallway of his parents' house. The external wall has collapsed. A lot of the ceiling is on the floor. He finds a column of pipes and wires and plaster that is still mostly standing. He hauls himself upward hand over hand. Every time his ankle bumps against the floor he lets out a grunt or squeal of pain. Tears leak down his face.

When he's upright he takes stock. Things have progressed since Skart deflected his bullet, and tore apart a doorway and

Knull's ankle. The ruins of an armored vehicle are on fire. Bushes like thorny fists, spawning great tuberous roots, have cracked the concrete. Bodies are caught in their branches, are scattered on the blacktop around them.

Knull looks back at where the living room used to be, back at the source of all this mess. He inhales sharply.

The brick of Dust is untended. It's just sitting there in the middle of the room. All its promise, all its potential, just a few yards away.

Knull recoils from the sight so hard he almost falls down. Balanced on one leg he clings to the column of pipes and plaster like a shipwrecked soul staring from a spar of wood at a circling shark.

Everything wrong with the Iron City, every lie it ever told him, every wrong decision he ever made, every fae he screwed over—it's all contained within that plastic wrapping. Everything that led him to this point is there. It wants him to take it now. He knows it. It wants him to keep trying to sell it, to work himself deeper and deeper into its tar pit of false promises and broken hope. It wants him to drag others in with him.

Like he already has.

Like Edwyll.

He looks away, almost afraid to take his eyes off it, almost convinced that when he looks back it will be closer to him, silently advancing. But he is looking for a path out, a way to navigate the wasteland beyond. There are things still moving out there. The wounded crawling. Vermin scattered and skittering over rubble and bodies. He looks for Bee but can't pick him out of the carnage that fills the torn-up street. Birds and bats wheel overhead. A mess of thorns and vines still sprawls and spreads, the last dregs of magic in it giving it the impression of intent, as if it is crawling toward the house. He shudders.

There's a broken bit of PVC pipe on the ground at his feet—a stained piece of plumbing that's just a little longer than his leg. Picking it up is precarious. He jars his shattered ankle over and over, barking with pain each time. Eventually he has it, tests it to see if it will take his weight. Its broken end bites against his palm but it's better than nothing.

You don't have to take all the Dust, a voice whispers in his head. *Just take a pinch of it to a healer and your ankle will never bother you again.*

He looks back at the brick almost against his will. Because if he gives in, just indulges for a moment, then everything would be easier…

He shudders again. The seduction of it is already working on him. He has to get away as fast as he can. He has to never look back.

But movement makes his eyes linger just a little longer. The suggestion of an arm reaching out. A slow, pained movement. He squints, tries to make out what he's seeing more clearly, because in the back of his head he knows he glimpsed a fae's body in there, he knows that it could be Edwyll, and even though he knows that in the Iron City hope is a lie, it is not quite dead in his heart.

The movement comes again—a jerking agonized spasm that sends an arm up into the air and then brings it down to the ground, the hand fixed in a claw.

A body hauls itself over the dirt and through the leaves, grunting and gasping as it comes.

"Edwyll." It's hardly a word. It's more a breath. A barely voiced wish.

Edwyll's other arm comes up, grabs at a root that breaks through the rotten old carpet.

"Edwyll!" He screams it. A flock of blackbirds perched around a body outside takes flight with a rush of wings. His brother doesn't look up.

Edwyll is, Knull realizes, making his way toward the Dust. The longer he watches, the clearer his brother's intent is. Edwyll's progress is brutally slow, but he is fixed on his goal. He can hear his grunts of pain now.

Knull goes to shout again but the words clog in his mouth. Because he needs to scream at his brother that no, this is not the way; that the only thing in that plastic wrapping is horror; that he has stayed clean this far; that he cannot succumb at the end. He cannot. But how can he say that to him? As he claws toward his only chance of survival, how can he tell his little brother to not do it? After all he has done himself? He should be there, hauling it toward Eddy, shoveling the shit into his nose, his mouth.

But Knull wants so badly to run. He wants so badly to not be here to see this, to see the inevitable end. He wants, desperately, to live.

He stands there, paralyzed, silent, a witness.

Then he sees Skart.

At first, he doesn't know what he's seeing. On the far side of the room the sprawling plant-thing rolls over the remains of an external wall, and tumbles toward the brick of Dust. Branches and leaves and pieces of thorn break from it as it falls, its bulk lessens, and Knull begins to make out the shape beneath. He realizes he is looking at the shape of a fae. Something awful has happened to him—transformative, traumatic—but despite it all he is somehow still alive, is still moving with purpose, is still moving toward the Dust. And that dreadful, implacable purpose lets him give that fae a name.

Skart and Edwyll. They are caught in the vortex, trapped by the inescapable currents of its influence. Both of them thinking the Dust will help them. Both of them thinking that it will let them escape.

Knull has seen a lot of fae take Dust. He knows the fae think

Dust is a lot of things: a path back to the past, bliss, part of their cultural heritage. They think it's the best way to hurt themselves they know. Knull has his own theory. Dust, to him, is nothing but an amplifier. It takes everything you are in a single moment and cranks it to eleven. Lust-filled fae become fecund fertility figures, rutting in golden leaves and bunny shit. The same fae snort Dust in a moment of hate and they become avatars of destruction. Those who look for escape find paths that burrow deep into their own navel. There's nothing very special about it to Knull. Dust just takes a fae, the best and worst of them, and makes it scream out loud.

Knull looks at Skart and Edwyll advancing on the Dust and he knows exactly who he wants to get there first. But the longer he looks, the longer he sees Edwyll make his slow, ragged movements, the clearer it is that he will get there last.

And still the easiest thing to do is leave. It always has been. He's done it before. He's done it again, and again. And he's got the crutch in his hand. He's got the path out of here all plotted out. Edwyll is already most of the way dead. If Knull is going to survive, he has to leave. He's got to escape the sucking mire of the Dust. He has to. There isn't a choice.

But of course, there isn't a choice. There hasn't been since he first saw Edwyll's arm move. Because he can't leave him to die again. As scared as he is. As foolish as it is. As futile as everything involving the Dust is. There is no choice. Because he's his brother. Because he has betrayed him as much as he can. Because this time he has to be there for him. He has to. There isn't a choice.

So, he lurches into motion, smashes his ankle against the floor, screams, staggers, almost falls, crashes through three more steps that feel more like falling than walking, and he keeps going, hobbling, hopping, careening from outcropping of rubble to trunk of half-present tree. He doesn't have a plan but he has a need. He has a goal and that's enough to keep propelling him forward.

He blunders through the remains of the doorway that marks the limits of his and Bee's previous intrusion into the house. He steps into the clearing of trees that Skart has half-summoned. The brick of Dust is close. He can feel it pulling with untapped power. Skart has done something to it, awakened it. Its siren song is a pulse inside his head.

They're all inside the room now. None of them are more than five yards from the Dust. Knull. Edwyll. What's left of Skart. They're all closing in on the prize, on the final moment between now and the future.

But Knull's still moving fastest. As damaged as he is, he is still more whole than Skart. He can still get there first. He can take it, can save Edwyll, can put the world to rights, can grind Skart beneath his heel. He can send the goblins tumbling from their glass towers and pull their opera houses down upon their ears. He can rip up the Iron Wall and scatter the pieces to the heavens. He can do whatever the fuck he wants. A life without limits. A life without fear.

He takes a step toward the Dust. Another.

Skart sees him. What's left of the kobold pauses in its lumbering progress for just a moment. Vines and creepers wave unsteadily in Knull's direction.

Knull takes another step toward the Dust.

Edwyll's crawl seems to have taken on a newfound urgency. He grunts and spits as he leaves a bloody trail behind him.

All three of them are steps away now; all three are just seconds away. The moment is closing down, all the possibilities in the world shrinking down to one.

Knull is close enough now. He could reach out. He could take the Dust.

He puts all his weight on his one good foot and takes his PVC pipe in both hands. He swings for the fences he's never been able to reach before.

The pipe crashes into Skart. PVC splinters with an audible snap. The kobold—despite his foliage bulk, reels, steps backward, is halted in his merciless progression. And then the torque of the blow catches up with Knull. The shock of the impact runs up his arms. It's all more than Knull's foot can take. He careens over, tumbles as Skart tumbles. The two of them sprawl, both howling, Knull in pain, Skart in impotent rage.

And Knull has pitched himself, has angled himself, so that he falls face first down into the Dust.

Because he can't walk away anymore.

Skart

He is so close. He is *so* close. Just feet away. All that is between him and the whole future of the fae, the goblins, the Iron City, are these two, these ignorant children.

And yet, for all their youth, for all their ineptitude, for all that they are—they are too much for him.

Knull

Knull breathes.

Dust in his nose, his lungs, his mouth. Dust clogging and cloying in his throat. Dust filling everything, burning, and scouring. Dust in his eyes, his ears. Euphoria and pain hand in hand inside him, reaching through him. Pain to rival the pain of a life wasted. Joy to rival that. Dust in every part of him. Dust in everything. Dust as everything. Dust as the world. His world. Making him into the world. Everything Dust. Everything him.

Knull breathes.

Knull rising. Knull on the wind. Knull as the wind. Knull above everything. Knull as everything he is above. Knull above himself. Looking down on himself. His body as the city. His body as iron. His body as Dust. Looking down on his body. Looking down on the ruin it has become.

He did not know it could be like this. His brief dalliances with the thrice-cut bullshit Cotter passed off to him—a Dust neophyte—in no way prepared him for this moment, for the doors of his perception being blown from their hinges, for the full breadth of experience charging through them without hesitation or caution.

Knull breathes.

Knull above. Knull below. Knull as a million fae. As a million fae refusing to look up. A million fae refusing to see the sun, or hope, or joy. As a million fae who have forgotten that life promised them something better if only they would fight for it.

Knull breathes. He sucks the Dust into himself. And he has not prepared the way Skart prepared. He does not know the ways to prolong this power. He is not building to an inferno. This is bright and hot. This is pure, flaming impulse.

Knull breathes. Dust burns.

Knull as the sun. Knull as the horizon, as the curtain about to be pulled back to reveal the light. Knull as the inevitable day that sweeps away the dark. Knull as warmth and hope. Knull as a promise of something better.

Knull breathes though his lungs are mostly gone now, dissolved away. His chest is full of Dust and blood.

Knull as the night. Knull as the long dark with no end. Knull as the blank cold. Knull as death. As reprisal. As condemnation for all that has been done, for all the opportunities wasted, for all the children betrayed. Knull as his own revenge.

Knull breathes.

Knull is full of Dust, is full of power. Knull is full of potential and full of rage and full of hope.

Knull as the future.

He can do anything, he realizes. He is magic, pure and simple. He is infinite potential and all he needs to be is shaped. All he needs is purpose, and here now, realizing that the only thing this magic will not let him do is survive, Knull realizes that he has never really had purpose. Has never really known what he would do when he escaped the Iron City. The dream has always been empty.

And yet, as he looks down, as he feels the lives all around him, the hearts and the minds, and all barriers peeled back, he knows that he has always been inches away from someone who has had a clear vision. Who has always been striving to recreate the future in a very specific image.

Knull as a voice in Edwyll's mind. Knull as a question.

Edwyll gasps, rolls back, flails. But Knull washes in and blots out the pain.

Knull as a promise. As a penitent. As a brother.

Knull breathes. Edwyll breathes. And they find a resonance. A synchronicity.

Knull as a question: What do you want?

And here, at the last, Knull finds, Edwyll can picture it so clearly.

Knull as a tool in his brother's hands. Knull as a paintbrush. Knull as a sculptor's clay.

Knull as a tree. Knull as the symbol of the fae. Knull as the thing they always look back at. Knull as the memory that has become a trap, a yoke. Knull as the heart of the fae, become sickly and weak.

Knull as a tree. Knull as a symbol transformed, renewed. Knull as something beautiful and blooming and full of life. Knull as something forcing the fae to look up.

Knull as a tree. Knull as a reminder, a reprimand, a rebuke. Knull as a refutation of nostalgia.

Knull as everything. In one moment. In one final defiant cry of creativity.

Knull breathes. Knull creates. Knull tries to say sorry to Edwyll for everything.

A tree grows in the Iron City. A tree spears up from the ground. A tree to dwarf all trees. A tree to dwarf a city. It rushes upward, towering over houses, over casinos, over high-rises. It rushes up to be a ceiling to the world. A tree with a trunk the size of a city block. A tree with a trunk that's growing larger. A tree that reaches out with vast branches the length of city districts.

It is a tree obsidian black. A tree the color of mourning. Because this is not a celebration. This is not the victory of the fae. This is so far from that. But neither is it a memorial. Neither is it a gravestone. Its curious, sharp-angled branches are alive. The buds on them hold the promise of life and beauty to come.

And still it grows. Every last dreg of Dust is pouring through Knull, is tearing him apart, is making him nothing but a conduit for this vision plucked from Edwyll's mind.

And still the tree reaches higher. It is impossible but real. It is absurd but undeniable. It is something for all to see. Something they cannot ignore. And across the Iron City heads start to turn. Heads start to look up. Eyes start to search for the sun.

Knull is not breathing anymore. There's not much of him left to breathe. But he has stopped hurting. And he can still see. He can see what he has created, what Edwyll has created through him, with him. He can see it towering over him, over the city, over everything. And it is, he sees, beautiful. And he realizes he never expected beauty from life. He never saw that possibility in himself, in the Iron City. And it seems now like a great failure on his part, but he is so very glad that he saw it before the end.

He can still feel the other lives around him. He feels impossibly connected to the city and its fae in this moment. He can feel Skart's impotence, and horror, and rage. He can feel the goblins' bile. And he still feels Edwyll too. His wonder at this creation. He can feel the blood pumping from Edwyll's wound.

And Knull finds that there is still a little magic left in this world for his brother.

He does not know how to repair wounds, how to knit flesh and sew back arteries and nerves. He knows no more of that than he did before. Perhaps if he had longer, he could pluck the knowledge from a healer's head. But he does not have longer. He only has this last final violent spasm of power. And yet he finds now that with this much Dust, knowledge can be superseded by intent alone, and he intends for Edwyll to live, to survive, to see this future that Knull is trying so desperately to create on his behalf.

He feels Edwyll gasp. Feels flesh knit.

He feels Bee close by. And he wants, he finds, to put him back together too. The bryad has earned that at least.

And he realizes at the last—the very last—he too would like to live. So he turns his will, his intent, his power upon himself.

But here he finds, like all do eventually, that his power fails him. The magic that heals is also the weapon that wounds. To try to heal himself is to tear himself apart. He cannot. His fate is sealed.

Knull as a fuse burning down to nothing. Knull as the last flicker of fire.

Knull as the future detonating. Knull as Edwyll's vision born. Knull undeniable. Knull as a brother. Knull as a fae not satisfied, but at peace with the little he has done, with the knowledge that others will still be able to carry on the fight.

Knull breathes no more. Knull finally escapes the Iron City.

20

Wasted Youth

Jag

Jag wanders through House Red in a daze, in a haze of gun smoke. Soldiers run past her, heavy boots clattering on delicate tile. Goblins shout but always one corridor away, always just around the corner. She cannot piece together what has happened. She hears Sil's name, she hears panic, but there are no details. There is just gun smoke drifting in empty halls.

Sil left her, Jag thinks, without a backward glance. And at first she was afraid, and aghast, but then she thought that perhaps that was actually everything she'd always been trying to help Sil achieve. That was the inevitable end goal.

She is, she finds, happy for her half-sister.

Her passage through the halls proceeds unimpeded. No one calls to her. No one bars her way. She is flotsam floating over chaos she doesn't quite understand. That she doesn't want to understand. She is leaving the Iron City. She is leaving all this behind. It is the only path for survival that she can still see.

She heads down the long broad corridor that is normally used to lead blindfolded guests in and out of House Red Cap. There is evidence that a great many soldiers were here recently. They're gone now. She finds a pistol lying on the floor, though, and slips it into the back of her waistband. She thinks perhaps she should be prepared to take care of herself now.

A single goblin waits at the end of the corridor, an anxious functionary with a starched collar and large, wild eyes.

"Passage," Jag demands.

"But..." the goblin stammers.

Jag is glad she picked up the gun. The functionary stares at it, breathing hard. Finally, he presses the button on his radio.

At the functionary's command, the wall dissolves into leaves and air. A robin flutters past Jag's head. She steps through into a room in which blindfolded fae kneel, bound hand and foot.

Her father never revealed the secret of her passage in and out of House Red's sealed walls. It is another secret he was too paranoid to let go. That the answer is horrifying does not shock her. It is just, she finds, sad. And disappointing that it has taken her this long to realize that the only way forward—for herself, for the House, for the Iron City as a whole—is for everything that her father has even striven for to be thrown away.

She shoots the handlers in quick succession. It's not hard. It takes a little longer to set the enslaved fae free. Some are so weak they cannot walk. She can't do much for them, but she shows them where the Dust is kept. She hopes that there is enough magic there to make their freedom last. She does stay long enough to see that they do not close the entrance to House Red Cap. That they leave the wound in its flank exposed.

That, she finds, makes her happy too.

From the fae it's a short walk to the House Red Cap garages. She finds a car—something broad, and black, and glistening, something built for comfort. She thinks she might be in it for a while.

It's rare that she drives herself, and it takes her a while to regain familiarity with the clutch and the accelerator, but she manages it, rolling out slowly onto an abandoned street. She glances at the clock on the dash. Dawn is almost here.

She doesn't know exactly where Edwyll's house is in the Fae Districts, but she knows the general direction. She can see the glow of the fires. She points the car in that direction and drives.

She doesn't know what she will do when she gets there. She just knows that she cannot leave without making sure that he's not still alive. So much of what has happened tonight, so many of her realizations about who she is and what she wants to achieve seem grounded in meeting him. She cannot save much in the city, but if she can save him, she will.

She is just entering the Fae Districts when it happens. The pulse passes through the whole city, through the entirety of its fabric. It is something seismic. It beats in her chest, and in her head. The car bucks beneath her. The street ripples. She slews to a stop, blinking, sucking on the air, trying to work out what just happened, trying to reconcile it all with the sudden ache in her chest.

It is a moment before she sees what is going on. Before her eyes are pulled upward. But then the movement catches her eye. Because the thing is still growing, is still jutting higher and higher into the heavens. This massive, impossible thing. This vast, towering black tree.

And she knows who made it as soon as she sees it. Edwyll's hands are in every sweep of every branch, in every line of its trunk. Seeing it, she can see Edwyll's intent, and his design. She can see the beauty of its truth, Edwyll's truth, the one that no one will be able to deny anymore.

He has brought hope to life once more in the Iron City.

She drives faster now, a desperation growing in her. A fear that this can only mean one thing. That she is too late.

But then she finds that she is not.

She is fighting through pedestrian traffic. Nosing the car through the throngs standing out on the streets, pointing, and staring, and talking. All the violence that has led to this moment seems forgotten, eclipsed by this sudden transformation of their home. And then, around a corner, the vast trunk is directly before her.

She jams on the brakes, comes to a halt only a yard from its broad black bark. She gets out of her car, shaking slightly. She looks up, and stares at its massive branches.

Between them, the sky is starting to lighten.

"Hey."

She looks round and there he is. Standing at the foot of his creation.

"Edwyll!" She runs to him, hugs him without thought. The full solidity of him. She steps back. And he is whole, the wound in his stomach gone.

"How?" She gestures at him, at the tree, at everything.

"My brother," Edwyll says. There's pain in his voice. "He… That kobold, he was after some Dust. A lot of Dust. My brother had it somehow. He took it. It killed him. But before he died he…" He gestures at the tree. "He took this out of my head." A smile suddenly touches Edwyll's lips. "I think, in the end, maybe he turned out to be my patron."

"He healed you?" Jag reaches out towards Edwyll's stomach, pauses, hands hesitating just above where the wound was.

"Yes. Bee too."

"Who?"

Edwyll points. There is a demi-dryad. Maybe a bryad or a prixad, she thinks. He has a spar of wood in one hand and is holding it as if ready to defend himself.

"Who's the goblin?" this new fae says.

She shrugs. She can't blame him for his fear. She can only prove it unjustified. "I'm Jag," she says. "I used to think I was important. That I could do something. But now, I think the best thing I can do for the Iron City, for myself, is to leave. To find something else, something better. I wanted to see if Edwyll could come with me." She smiles. "Who are you?"

Bee hesitates.

"He helped my brother," Edwyll says. "I think he lost a lot tonight."

Bee nods.

"You're welcome to come with us," Jag says. It seems the least she can offer.

Bee shakes his head. "No. No, I can't. I've got to carry on the fight."

Edwyll looks around. He sweeps an arm, not at their immediate surroundings but at the whole city. "What fight? What are you fighting for? What can be won here?"

Bee shrugs. "I don't know. Not for sure. But something better. Something that doesn't end here."

Jag takes Edwyll's arm. "I don't think you can build anything better on foundations this rotten. I think if there's anything better to be found, it's out there, out beyond the Iron Wall. Out in the world we've shut away."

Bee shrugs. "I've got to carry on the fight. I promised."

Jag opens her mouth to argue, but Edwyll turns away, heads to the car. Bee smiles at them, something sad and a little apologetic. And she lets it go. Who knows, maybe he's right. Wouldn't that be nice?

Edwyll's already sitting in the passenger seat as she climbs back behind the steering wheel. She fiddles with the radio until she finds something with a beat. They drive.

The Iron Wall comes at them like a dragon crouched low on

the horizon. It watches them approach, exuding malevolence.

Beside her, Edwyll starts to squirm. Jag thinks perhaps she should stop, should let them get out, but as soon as she touches the brakes, Edwyll says between gritted teeth, "Keep driving." So she does.

There are not many gates in and out of the Iron Wall. Ingress and egress are tightly controlled. The Iron City is a closed system. The world outside is big and bad. There are wolves at the doors, or so Jag was told. But so much of what she was told was a lie, she cannot believe that what is out there is any worse than what is in here. She can at least hope that it will be better.

As she approaches the Eastern Gate, a meat truck is just coming through. For a moment, the way is clear, but it is closing quickly. Jag starts to drive faster and faster. Around her, the city starts to blur. Before her, the Iron Wall comes closer and closer. Guards start to shout, to raise rifles. Jag desperately ekes the last dregs of power from the engine, hurls the car at the shrinking gap. And Jag can't tell if it's the wall roaring, or the engine, or herself. Edwyll starts to howl.

And then it's over. They're through. And a pressure like an anvil seems to lift from Jag's chest. She gasps with relief, and the car sails down the road, eating up the asphalt like it's been starving for it its whole life.

They keep driving. Beside her, Edwyll gasps, and sighs. She chuffs laughter in relief. And in the rearview, Jag can see the Iron City shrinking smaller and smaller, can see the black tree rising taller—a promise for the future and a reprimand for the past.

Before them, the sun starts to rise. Warmth and light spread through the cabin of the car. And as Jag takes one final look back, she sees that blossom has bloomed on the black tree's branches and is starting to fall in a soft white rain on the streets below.

EPILOGUE

A Cinderella Story

Brethelda

Dawn comes to the Iron City. A new day. And on the highest floor of the highest tower of House Spriggan, Brethelda Spregg surveys a city transformed.

There is still much she doesn't understand. The significance of the black tree. Its origin. The effect it will have. But things, she is sure, are going to be different.

As she stands there, one of her hands shakes slightly. She is holding a piece of paper, a report. It tells her that her mother is dead. Brethelda is, she is sure, going to be different too.

There are so many things to be uncertain about, but still Brethelda's next move is clear. She needs to make peace. She will not be able to keep House Spriggan safe during whatever comes next if House Red is spoiling for war.

And so, she descends. Servants scurry before and behind her, clearing her path and ensuring her passage leaves no trace, creating the illusion of perfect calm in a city still roiling from the night before. They have her car waiting. It slides away from the kerb the moment she leans back in her seat. Everything is clean and efficient. She wonders how much of that will last.

She is taken to the Opera House. She wants this to be formal. She wants to make sure it is done right.

She marches up the steps, and stalks down the richly decorated hallways. She enters the Hall of Horns. The seven severed hart heads regard her silently with their glass eyes. Her mother cut one of those heads free and mounted it there, she thinks. Her hand starts to quiver again.

On the opposite side of the room, a door opens. Brethelda straightens, stills herself. Osmondo will brook no weakness and will look for any opening he can find.

And yet, it is not Osmondo Red who enters the room. For a moment Brethelda is not even sure it is a goblin. She is slender and tall, delicately featured. Her hair falls in a white sheet, covering one eye.

"I apologize for making you wait," she says to Brethelda. "This morning finds House Red in a little bit of… disarray."

A half-goblin, Brethelda realizes. Half-fae. Perhaps pixie or sidhe. There is something regal about her, and so Brethelda would guess sidhe if she had to. But this is not the only thing the half-goblin's looks reveal. She has been on the receiving end of a brutal beating recently. Cuts and stitches crosshatch her arms, her hands, her face and neck. Everything exposed looks bruised or abraded. One arm is in a sling. The wrist of the other arm is wreathed in bandages.

"Who are you?" Brethelda snaps. "Why isn't Osmondo here himself?"

There are more diplomatic ways to deal with this, but Brethelda is caught flat-footed, is caught grieving and uncertain. She is closer to breaking than she would care to admit.

"Ah," the half-goblin smiles. It is broad and brims with

quite genuine joy. “I am afraid to say that Osmondo Red is… indisposed.”

“What?” Brethelda blinks. “How?”

The half-goblin’s smile widens. “*Permanently* indisposed?” she says. “*De*posed? I’m not sure the best way to say it.”

Brethelda’s eyebrows skyrocket. “He’s—?”

“Dead?” The half-goblin’s smile looks like it’s about to split her head apart. “Very.”

Which leads directly to Brethelda’s next question. “You?”

The half-goblin nods. “Yes. And with great pleasure.”

Brethelda takes her in again. This battered, beaten child of two worlds with her confident swagger, and her anarchic joy bursting out of the seams of her mouth. And she feels uncertain. And for the first time today she feels truly afraid.

“*Who* are you?” she asks again.

“Me?” The half-goblin gives a little curtsy, but there is nothing meek in her expression. No timidity in any line of her body. She straightens. She looks Brethelda in the eye.

“I am Sil. I am the new head of House Red. And I am the future.”

Acknowledgements

Every book takes a village, and I am exceptionally grateful to: my agent, Howard Morhaim, my editors, Cath Trechman and Joanna Harwood, my friends, Paul Jessup and Natania Barron, and above all others (sorry guys), my wife Tami. Without them—their support, their wisdom, and their encouragement—this book wouldn't exist. So, it's their fault. Blame them.

About the Author

J. P. Oakes is a writer and creative director living on Long Island, where he drinks too much tea, overthinks dumb action movies, and indulges in profound nerdery. Follow him on social media @jp_oakes for flash fiction and thoughts on the writing process, or if you want to engage someone for many long hours on the topic of Bioware Games.

ALSO AVAILABLE FROM TITAN BOOKS

The Lights of Prague

NICOLE JARVIS

In the quiet streets of Prague all manner of mysterious creatures lurk in the shadows. Unbeknownst to its citizens, their only hope against the tide of predators are the dauntless lamplighters—a secret elite of monster hunters whose light staves off the darkness each night. Domek Myska leads a life teeming with fraught encounters with the worst kind of evil: pijavice, bloodthirsty and soulless vampiric creatures. Despite this, Domek finds solace in his moments spent in the company of his friend, the clever and beautiful Lady Ora Fischerová—a widow with secrets of her own.

When Domek finds himself stalked by the spirit of the White Lady—a ghost who haunts the baroque halls of Prague castle—he stumbles across the sentient essence of a will-o'-the-wisp captured in a mysterious container. Now, as its bearer, Domek wields its power, but the wisp, known for leading travellers to their deaths, will not be so easily controlled.

After discovering a conspiracy amongst the pijavice that could see them unleash terror on the daylight world, Domek finds himself in a race against those who aim to twist alchemical science for their own dangerous gain.

"Fantasy fans will gobble up this moody, philosophical adventure"
Publishers Weekly

"Readers will fall hard for the humble, vampire-hunting Domek and the brazen, bloodthirsty Ora as they navigate their class differences—along with their mortal differences—while trying to save their city. A stunning debut"
Kristen Ciccarelli, author of *The Last Namsara*

TITANBOOKS.COM

ALSO AVAILABLE FROM TITAN BOOKS

The War of the Archons

A Demon in Silver
Hangman's Gate
Spear of Malice

R.S. FORD

In a world where magic has disappeared, rival nations vie for power in a continent devastated by war.

When a young farm girl, Livia, demonstrates magical powers for the first time in a century there are many across the land that will kill to obtain her power. The Duke of Gothelm's tallymen, the blood-soaked Qeltine Brotherhood, and cynical mercenary Josten Cade: all are searching for Livia and the power she wields.

But Livia finds that guardians can come from the most unlikely places… and that the old gods are returning to a world they abandoned.

Stunning epic fantasy for readers of Brandon Sanderson, Michael J. Sullivan and Brian Staveley.

PRAISE FOR THE SERIES

"Mixes the epic and the earthly, delivering gory battles and well-crafted banter" *SFX*

"A *Demon In Silver* is a brilliant book, and happily the first in a trilogy so there is more excitement to come" The Book Bag

"Exciting and fast-paced" *Booklist*

"Heroic fantasy at its bloodiest, muddiest, rudest and most entertaining" *Morning Star*

TITANBOOKS.COM

For more fantastic fiction, author events,
exclusive excerpts, competitions, limited editions and more

VISIT OUR WEBSITE
titanbooks.com

LIKE US ON FACEBOOK
facebook.com/titanbooks

FOLLOW US ON TWITTER AND INSTAGRAM
@TitanBooks

EMAIL US
readerfeedback@titanemail.com